five
unforgivable
things

Vivien Brown lives in Uxbridge, on the outskirts of London, with her husband and two cats. After a career in banking and accountancy and the birth of her twin daughters, she gave up working with numbers and moved into working with words and has never looked back.

In recent years, as a pre-school reading specialist and library storyteller, she has helped hundreds of young children to explore and enjoy books, has written extensively for pre-school and nursery magazines, and has had numerous short stories and children's poems published. Vivien loves reading romance novels and psychological thrillers (or better still, stories that combine the two), watching and taking part in TV quiz shows, and tackling really tricky cryptic crosswords, ideally in a sunny garden and with a bar of chocolate and an ice-cold Diet Pepsi close at hand.

Also by Vivien Brown

Lily Alone

five
unforgivable
things

Vivien Brown

A division of HarperCollins*Publishers*
www.harpercollins.co.uk

HarperImpulse
an imprint of HarperCollins*Publishers* Ltd
1 London Bridge Street
London SE1 9GF

www.harpercollins.co.uk

This paperback edition 2018

First published in Great Britain in ebook format by
HarperCollins*Publishers* 2018

A catalogue record for this book
is available from the British Library

ISBN: 978-0-00-825214-4

This novel is entirely a work of fiction.
The names, characters and incidents portrayed in it are
the work of the author's imagination. Any resemblance to
actual persons, living or dead, events or localities is
entirely coincidental.

Set in Birka by
Palimpsest Book Production Limited, Falkirk, Stirlingshire

Printed and bound by CPI Group (UK) Ltd, Croydon, CR0 4YY

MIX
Paper from
responsible sources
FSC
www.fsc.org   FSC® C007454

For all the babies we have longed for, loved or lost

Prologue

Kate

I don't know why I'm talking to you. It's not as if you can do anything to help, or undo what's already been done. You will listen, though. I know that much. You'll listen and you'll let me talk, let me work things out for myself, just as you always have. You don't tell me what to do, the way Dan does, or tries to, even now.

Dan and me. We were happy once. For a long time, we were happy, when it was just the two of us, loving and laughing, living in the moment, just enjoying being young. And being together. It seemed enough back then; more than enough. But it wasn't. Not in the end. Dan wanted more, and when it came down to the now-or-never moment, so did I. A baby, a family, a happy-ever-after.

But it wasn't what we got.

One last throw of the dice, that was what we were offered. A once-in-a-lifetime chance, with six numbers on it, and it could have landed on any one of them, or none of them at all. We both knew that. It all came down to luck, in the end. And to nature. Maybe even fate. Like most things in life, if you don't take control of them, if you take your eye off the ball...

I did all right for a while, dealt with all the bad stuff the best I could. There are ways, you see. Tricks I learned, disguises I plastered across my face, masks I hid behind. Ways to get from day to day, coping, managing, putting one foot in front of the other. Ways to go forward, when all you really want to do is go back. Not thinking too hard. Or trying not to think at all. Being grateful for what you have, instead of dwelling on what you've lost. Keeping busy. Well, that one was easy enough. Sleep, when you can get it, which wasn't so easy at all. Pills...

If there is one thing you've taught me, it's that pain fades, dampens into something less raw. And so do memories, if you let them. But I can't forget the mistakes. Everyone makes them, I suppose. But, for us, there were just too many. Things we did. Things we didn't do, but should have. Things we did wrong.

Oh, it wasn't just Dan. It was me too. I admit that. In fact, it was me who started it. Me who told the lie that set everything in motion, like a runaway train it's impossible to stop. Yes, we made mistakes. Big ones. Mistakes that can't be undone. Mistakes it's almost impossible to get back from, no matter how much you wish you could.

Moments in our lives, when the things one of us chose to do would alter everything for both of us, alter the course of our marriage. And they did. They altered it, almost irrevocably. And very nearly broke us.

Five unforgivable things.

NUMBER ONE

Chapter 1

Kate, 1976

The first time I set eyes on Dan Campbell, I didn't fancy him at all. He was younger than me, for a start. Only by a couple of years, as it turned out, but enough for it to show. And his hair was a strange kind of half-blonde, half-mouse colour. A bit streaky, like it was neither one thing nor the other. I wasn't sure if he'd made an attempt to colour it himself with some dubious home-dye kit or if it was what nature had dealt him, but in any case I had always preferred tall, dark handsome types, and Dan fell down on all three counts.

I was at a party in someone's flat, part of a tall Victorian terrace, indistinguishable from a hundred others, with a dirty brown front door and crumbling windowsills, somewhere in West London, with just a bit of gravel and a low wall and a badly- lit pavement lying between it and the main road. The flat was up three flights of stairs.

It was a bit grotty, with threadbare carpets and dodgy paintwork, and a dead spider plant on a shelf by the door with piles of bent fag ends squashed into what must once have passed as compost. Every time I went into the kitchen to look for another drink it felt like my shoes were sticking to the floor. Beer spurting in all directions when people pulled the tabs on shaken-up cans didn't help, not to mention the cheap wine dripping as it was poured, inexpertly, into plastic glasses, and the odd dropped sausage roll trodden greasily into the lino. Still, nobody seemed to notice, or care, except me.

To be honest, I wasn't really sure whose flat it was, or even whose party it was. Back then, once the pub closed, it didn't take much to get me to follow whoever I happened to be with to wherever they happened to be going. Anything was better than going back to my mum's, now that Trevor was there. That particular Saturday night, though, I wasn't really in the mood for partying. I'd only been there an hour or so, and the bloke I thought I was with had clearly had other ideas and moved on to a rather over-loud redhead with a low-cut top and eyelashes long enough to swat a fly. Not that I minded. He was hardly the love of my life. Still, his defection had left me worrying about how I was going to get home. Whether I'd missed the last bus, how far it was to walk, and how safe. Whether I could afford a taxi.

I was picking my way down the last of the narrow litter-strewn staircases, holding my bag in one hand and clutching the rickety banisters with the other, heading for the front door, when Dan Campbell walked in. Only, I didn't know who he was then. Just some random stranger, letting himself in, not even seeing I was there.

He had his head down, dripping rain from a long grey mac. He was fumbling a set of keys out of the lock and back into his pocket, and carrying a soggy carrier bag, bottles chinking together inside it as he stopped to stamp his shoes on the doormat. I peered out past him, through the open door, into the darkness, split only by the glow of passing traffic, still heavy despite the time of night, wipers thrashing, headlights on, hazy at the edges. Rain. Lots of it. It hadn't been raining when I'd arrived and it wasn't something I'd bargained for when I'd dressed to go out. Taxi it was, then, if I didn't want to ruin my new heels, or my hair. I'd just have to raid Mum's secret tin when I got home if it turned out I didn't have enough for the fare. Not that it was much of a secret when I knew exactly where she hid it. But Trevor didn't know, and that was what mattered.

I reached the bottom step and hesitated, waiting for this drenched man to finish wiping the water from his glasses and the mud from his shoes and notice me, move aside, leave my exit clear, but the door slammed behind him, shutting out the rumble of the traffic, enclosing us in that small space, with just the thump of the music above us, oozing its way through several layers of ceilings and floors.

And then he lifted his face and looked at me, a bit startled, and I looked right back at him, a lot less so, and you know how, sometimes, you just feel it? A connection, an understanding, something in the eyes that says, 'Stay. Stay and talk to me. It's much too early to leave. Come and re-join the party. You know you want to.' Actually, he may have said it for real, not just through his eyes. I can't be sure now. Whether he was already a bit drunk, or I was. It's a long time ago, and the combination of time and lager tends to tamper with the finer details, shroud them all in a woozy kind of fog that may or may not have been entirely unpleasant, or unwelcome.

But, for whatever reason, or possibly for no obvious reason at all, I picked up my bag from where I'd been resting it on the table in the communal hallway, the one with all the junk mail on it, and I followed him back up the stairs to the party. Even though he was clearly too young, too short, too streaky, not my type at all. Even though all those things ran instantly through my head and were just as instantly dismissed, I still followed him up those stairs. I still did as he asked, and stayed.

And it wasn't until the next morning, when I woke up in a different flat, with a pounding headache, wearing an unfamiliar man-sized t-shirt and no knickers, and watched him pull back the curtains and hand me a cup of tea and a broken custard cream, that I finally found out his name.

'Hi, Kate. Just in case you don't remember, I'm Dan,' he said, sitting down at the end of the bed. 'Dan Campbell. And if you want a couple of aspirin with that, just say. I'm sure I have some somewhere.'

I shook my head. A nip to the toilet and a quick escape into the fresh air were all I really needed right then. And answers to the sort of awkward questions I suddenly felt totally unable to ask. How exactly had I got here? In this bed? His bed? And did I ...? Did we ...?

I sat up, pulling the rumpled sheets and a mound of blankets up with me, careful not to let the t-shirt ride up and reveal anything it shouldn't, and drank my tea. It was way too milky and could have done with more sugar, and the biscuit was bordering on being stale, but I was feeling self-conscious enough just being there without complaining about the catering.

'I'll leave you to get up when you're ready.' He stood up and tossed a dressing gown onto the bed. 'Here, use this if you like. Bathroom's just through there. And I've got eggs, if you're interested.' He took the empty cup from my hands. 'And more tea. Plenty more tea. Anyway, I'll be in the kitchen. Pop in, please, even if it's only to say goodbye.'

He closed the door behind him and I lay back and just let myself breathe. Well, he was a gentleman, I'd give him that. Protecting my modesty, not trying to peek, or cop a feel or anything. I looked around the bedroom. It was small, quite dark and old-fashioned in décor, with a high ceiling and one of those big round paper light shades hanging right above my head. The walls were lined with shelves, piled high with records, paperbacks, magazines, all chucked in any old how. I was dying to see what they were, to work out what his taste was in music, what sort of stuff he read. I even had a strange urge to start tidying them for him, setting the books upright, shuffling things into some kind of order, but I didn't want him to come back in and catch me being nosey, interfering. It was none of my business what possessions he had, or how he chose to store them. It wasn't as if I had any plans to see him again, after all.

In the bathroom, I sat for a while, draining my bladder dry, waiting for the throbbing in my head to subside. I ran the taps in the sink for ages, but the water stayed alarmingly cold. I splashed it about as briefly as I could get away with, over my face and hands, under my armpits, then slipped back into the clothes I'd worn the night before. I'd found them all heaped up on a chair next to the bed, knickers on top, as if I'd removed them last. Or he had.

My mouth still tasted of alcohol, or the stale remains of it, at least. I picked up a rolled-up tube of toothpaste with the lid missing, squeezed a drop onto my finger and ran it backwards and forwards over my teeth, and did the best I could to sort out my tangled hair, short of actually washing it.

There was a waste bin under the sink. The most likely place to find evidence, if there was any. I bent down to pick it up. There wasn't a lot in it. A used razor, a cardboard tube from the middle of a toilet roll, a lump of dried-up chewing gum, but no sign of an empty Durex wrapper, which worried me. A lot. Either we hadn't, or we had done it without taking any precautions. Oh, my God. Doing it with a man I'd only just met would have been bad enough, but not being careful was unthinkable. I took a deep breath and opened the door. It was time I found my way to the kitchen.

'Before you ask ...' he said, as soon as I walked in, as if he was some kind of mind-reader. 'No, we didn't. Not that I wouldn't have liked to. But you were pretty drunk, and I'm not that sort of a bloke. Okay? It was late and you had no obvious way of getting home, and I couldn't let you even think of doing it alone anyway, in your state, so I offered you a bed. My bed. Apologies that I didn't change the sheets, but I'd had a few drinks myself, and the sofa was calling ...'

I nodded with relief and sat down at the small formica-covered table. 'Well, I'm glad we've cleared that one up. I don't usually ... you know ... with men I've only just met. But thanks, for the bed. And for putting my mind at rest. I did need to be sure.'

'Understood. Say no more about it.' He pulled at the fridge door and rummaged about inside. 'Now ... eggs. Scrambled or fried?'

I suddenly felt starving hungry, and Dan Campbell, it transpired, cooked exceedingly good eggs. Big and white with bright runny yolks, and bread cut into thick soldiers that we dipped and dripped with sheer abandon as we sat together and talked, starting slowly to feel a little less like strangers.

Dan was twenty-two, which surprised me as he looked younger, and a trainee accountant, which, taking one look at his dark-rimmed glasses and the pale, rather serious, face that peered out from behind them, somehow didn't surprise me at all. He lived three floors below last night's party, which was where we were now, in the flat to the left of the downstairs hallway. He told me that he shared it with someone called Rich, who, according to Dan, was probably still crashed out in a drunken post-party stupor on some grimy armchair upstairs and was unlikely to be back for a while yet.

Did I remember Rich? Tall, ginger hair, covered in freckles ... I tried to, but I couldn't. In fact, there was very little about the party after I re-joined it that I could remember with any clarity at all. I really should stop drinking so much. It didn't help with anything. With not having a proper job at the moment, or with still being stuck in my old room at Mum's, with the tape marks from my old pop posters still liberally splattered over the wallpaper, hideous flowery curtains and all. And it definitely didn't help with the Trevor problem. I wasn't sure that anything, except hiring a hit man, was going to shift Trevor, so it was probably time I just accepted he was there to stay. Mum's house, Mum's rules, Mum's choice. A bad one, but she'd have to find that out for herself. It wasn't as if I hadn't made a few bad choices myself recently.

'Would you like to meet up again? Go for a drink or something?' Dan was clearing away the plates and had his back to me so I couldn't see his face, whether he really meant it, or was just being polite.

'I don't know.'

'Why not?' He turned back towards me and there it was again, that look, that connection, as his gaze locked on to mine. 'I think you might actually enjoy it. If you let yourself. Go on, Kate, take a chance. What's the worst that can happen? We sit in some pub all evening with nothing to say to each other? Find we have nothing in common? You discover I'm the world's worst kisser, or I bore the pants off you, or you can't stand my after-shave? At least you get a free half of shandy and a ride home. Let's be honest. You have nothing to lose!'

And he was right, of course. I had nothing to lose but my heart, and by the time I walked out of that flat just thirty minutes later, into a bright cloudless Sunday morning that suddenly sparkled with possibilities, I was fairly sure a big chunk of it was already gone.

Chapter 2

Natalie, 2017

Natalie hesitated outside the bridal shop. The lights were on inside, so it was still open, even though it was almost five-thirty. The dress in the window was absolutely stunning, in sleek sculptured ivory satin with just a hint of lace in all the right places, and tiny buttons that glinted like pearls. It was exactly the kind of dress she had longed for ever since she and Phil had finally set the date, but going inside a shop like that by herself would just feel way too strange. Even if she tried the dress on, which she so wanted to do, how would she know it was right with nobody there to *oooh* and *aaah* and spin her around in all directions and take sneaky pictures on their phones?

Natalie wasn't used to doing things alone. In fact, these last few days had probably – no, definitely – been the first she had ever spent entirely by herself. Phil was away at a work conference so boring she didn't even want to hear about it when he called, let alone be there with him, and Mum was off on one of her regular retreats, her mobile deliberately switched off. Jenny and Beth were visiting some seaside spa place together on a cheap mid-week deal for two. Natalie hadn't been able to get the time off work to join them, even if squeezing an extra bed into their room had been a possibility, but the truth was she hadn't been asked. Despite their distance, the bridesmaid question still hung in the air between them, unspoken but so obviously there, and she knew that by the time they came back, it needed to be answered.

Natalie shook her thoughts away, tentatively leaned into the glass door of the shop and eased it open. Although the best of the summer was over and the days were already starting to get noticeably shorter again, the sun was bright today and she could feel her spirits lift along with it. The path through the park was bordered by bouncing rows of tiny-headed purple pansies, newly planted in neat rows, and, after a week of relentless drizzle, her raincoat and boots were at last stuffed back in the hall cupboard in favour of a lighter jacket and her favourite sandals. There was something about the change in the weather that seemed to promise better things to come, making her feel suddenly bold. It was her wedding, after all. Not theirs. And she would do things the way she wanted to, whatever any of them said.

The shop's interior was an oasis of beauty and calm. There was a deep cream carpet and floor-to-ceiling mirrors without so much as a smudge on their shiny gilt-edged glass. The sweet scent of jasmine drifted in the air but, in the absence of any real flowers, it seemed to be coming from a huge fat candle that floated in the centre of a bowl of water on a shelf, well out of harm's way, behind a small desk in the corner. Little red velvet-covered chairs were dotted about around the edges of the room, between tall slim glass cases with the most wonderful satin shoes, beaded bags and glittering tiaras displayed on their shelves. One wall, the longest one, off to her right, was swamped by an unbroken row of big billowing floor-length dresses that brought the phrase 'as far as the eye can see' instantly to her mind. There was nobody else about and, for a moment, she just came to a standstill right in the centre of it all, feeling completely overwhelmed.

'Can I help you?' A small bird-like woman, with a slight foreign accent Natalie couldn't quite place, and a tape measure looped loosely around her neck, emerged from behind a curtain at the back of the shop, revealing a brief glimpse of a hidden workroom beyond, with a sewing machine and scraps of satin and lace strewn across a cluttered table in the centre, and yet more dresses, draped on hangers from an over-full coat stand and all encased in see-through plastic bags.

Natalie saw the look of surprise that flickered across the woman's heavily made-up face before it was swallowed up in what was clearly a well-practised customer-friendly smile. It was a look she was used to, one that told her she was not quite who, or what, had been expected to come rolling in.

'Sorry ... about the carpet.' Natalie turned her head to indicate the small trail of dirt and soggy leaves her wheels had brought in with them.

'That's all right. Can't be helped.' The woman's face flushed as she came forward, fiddling nervously with the tape around her neck.

'I'd like to look at a dress, please,' Natalie said. 'The ivory one in the window. And, I'm sorry, but I might need a bit of help to try it on.'

***

The house felt cold and empty when she got back, echoing with an unfamiliar silence as she eased her chair into the hall. The one thing you could say about a house normally full of women was that it was rarely quiet, and Natalie was surprised just how much she was missing the hustle and bustle of her family in full swing. Only two nights and the girls, at least, would be back. Mum was a different prospect altogether. If she wasn't standing on her head or wrapping her legs around her own neck at some yoga class, she'd be trying out a new aromatherapy course or letting herself be hypnotised into thinking she was once Cleopatra, or sitting in a circle in the woods with a group of protesters, waving 'Save our copse' placards while communing with the lesser-spotted tree frog. This time it was something involving immersing herself in healing water, though quite what it was that needed healing, Natalie wasn't at all sure. She'd said she'd be back on Sunday but, with Mum, it was best to take all plans with a pinch of salt and just wait and see what happened.

She knew she should go and check on Ollie but the thought unsettled her. She never knew what mood he might be in, and if it was a bad one she didn't want to have to cope with it alone. If he'd just lay off the booze for a while, it might help. Laura had been gone almost five months now, and his way of grieving, which involved nothing more than bemoaning his life and the world in general through the bottom of a bottle, was never going to work. Oblivion, yes, but bringing her back, no. And as for even the slightest movement towards acceptance or recovery, definitely not.

Natalie had liked Laura. Loved her, even. She and Ollie had lived together for almost two years and they'd all thought of her as family. Natalie had been thrilled at the prospect of the little niece or nephew they'd announced was on the way, and Mum had been so excited she'd got an old pair of knitting needles out, not that anyone had ever actually seen her use them. In the end, she didn't get the chance.

The miscarriage had been devastating, for Laura, for Mum, for all of them, but on the face of it, Ollie had seemed to cope remarkably well. He'd done all the right things, assuring Laura they could try again, that it was just one of those things, and that everything would be fine next time. But, as things turned out, it wasn't. And Natalie knew it was hard for him, being the man, trying to be the rock that Laura needed, when it was so obvious that all he wanted, every time, was to curl up in a ball and just sob his heart out.

Laura left after they lost the third. Just after Easter. Said she couldn't take any more, that Ollie deserved someone better, someone whole, someone who could do this one simple thing that her body was refusing to do, and no amount of pleading would change her mind.

Natalie had always expected Laura to come back. Ollie probably had too. At the start, anyway. Her giant Easter egg was still sitting on the dining table, unopened, unmoved, untouched, since the day she went, its huge yellow ribbon like one of those 'Come home' messages tied around a tree that you hear about in songs. But she didn't come back. She just went off, not even leaving

an address behind, asking them all to respect her decision and not come after her, and poor Ollie still hadn't
got over it. Losing her, or the babies.

There were three tiny crosses on the wall over the
bed at his flat, each one carefully carved out of wood.
He'd put his heart and soul into making those crosses.
Not bad for a man who said he didn't believe in God,
and who spent far too much time with a glass of whisky
in his hand, even more so in recent weeks, when there
had been no work to think about. Natalie used to envy
him those long school holidays, with nothing but a bit
of lesson planning to think about, but now she was
grateful that September had come around and he'd
finally had to go back. He wouldn't risk his career, would
he?

Ah, but it was Wednesday, she realised, with a sudden
sigh of relief. Ollie's chess club night. He'd be out for
most of the evening, and with other people, so she
wouldn't have to do her Good Samaritan act after all.
He'd probably be drinking, between games at least, but
there was little she could do about that. She wasn't his
keeper. None of them were, even though Mum seemed
to think it was their mission to help him. To save him,
even. But then, Mum knew, better than any of them,
how it felt, struggling to have babies, and losing them.
No matter how many survived, it was still the ones lost
along the way that left their special mark.

She poured some baked beans into a pan and toasted a couple of slices of bread. She'd have a quiet evening in, with an easy meal and a good book, and make the most of this rare time by herself. It might give her the chance to think clearly about the wedding arrangements too, without the constant input of the world and his wife telling her what to do, who to invite, what was expected, how much they all wanted to play their part.

Why was it so wrong to want to keep things small? Phil wouldn't care one way or the other. He was happy to leave the decisions to her. Whatever made her feel most comfortable. All the fuss of parading up the aisle, with everyone watching, and bridesmaids and ushers … none of that mattered in the grand scheme of things, did it? It wasn't as if she could link her arm through Dad's and walk beside him. She'd have enough trouble managing her dress and making sure her hem didn't get caught in her wheels. That was the bridesmaids' job, really, if she relented and decided to have any, but short of crouching down next to her or edging along on their knees, she couldn't picture how it could be made to work. In fact, beautiful though that dress was earlier, the impracticalities of wearing something like that, something meant to flow and sway and skim along the floor, probably made it a no-go. Dresses like that just weren't meant for the likes of her.

After a lifetime of trying to be as unobtrusive and

normal as she could, so people wouldn't stare at her or ask all those embarrassingly awkward questions, it wasn't easy to find herself thrust forward, forced to take centre stage. Wasn't it possible to just be the bride, to slip into the church and marry the love of her life without having to lead an attention-grabbing cavalcade of followers up the aisle? And in a dress bunched up around her lap too? It was a shame, but wedding dresses – proper wedding dresses – were expensive. It was a lot of money to spend, money they were going to be quite short of once they'd paid for the honeymoon and all the adaptations Phil's small house needed just so she could get comfortably through the front door and up the stairs. No, it would have to be something simpler, shorter, cheaper ...

When the phone rang it made her jump. She'd been staring ahead at the wall, imagining the worst, as usual. The beans had gone cold on the plate and she was surprised to find she had tears in her eyes.

'Hey, Nat. How are you, sweetheart? I miss you.'

Phil. Wonderful, kind and caring Phil. Not for the first time, she couldn't help wondering what on earth he saw in her, Natalie Campbell, a girl who couldn't walk or run or even give him a playful kick when he deserved one. Why her, when he could have had anyone? She didn't know the answer, never had, but she did know she was so very, very lucky to have him.

Chapter 3

Kate, 1977

Dan was so bloody annoying sometimes. He knew I couldn't get away from the bank much before five – I hadn't worked there long enough to feel I could ask for favours – and he'd booked us onto a six o'clock train. How was I meant to get home, changed, packed, back out again and onto a train in less than an hour? I hadn't even decided what to wear yet. What sort of thing was expected in the wilds of rural Somerset in mid-September, at a farm I had never seen but had always imagined as a mixture of elegant low-beamed interiors and squelching knee-deep mud imbued with the smell of cows the moment you stepped outside? And what did he expect us to do about food? I was sure it wouldn't be the sort of train that served meals, not on our limited budget, and I'd only had a cheese sandwich and the edible half of a windfall apple at lunch.

I hadn't met his family before and wasn't totally sure I was ready to now, but there were only so many excuses I could come up with and, after almost a year of going out together, I'd pretty much exhausted the list. No, this was it. The packed Friday-evening train, the awkward introductions when they came to pick us up at the station, assorted aunts and uncles and cousins all coming to get a look at me at the party on Saturday evening, and the spare bedroom that had once been his sister Jane's set aside especially for me, no doubt with a vase of freshly picked flowers awaiting me beside the bed. It was all arranged, set in stone and there was no getting out of it now.

Of course they would all be lovely. Well, they were Dan's family, and Dan was lovely, so they were bound to be. But I was nervous, if not actually downright scared, and had no idea how to admit it. It felt so important that they liked me, and accepted me, because Dan was without doubt the best thing ever to happen to me, and I badly wanted these people, their home, their way of life, to accept me, wrap themselves around me and let me in. But what if they didn't? What if I wasn't what they had in mind for Dan at all? After all, what did I know about farming or about living in the country? I was strictly a town girl and always had been. I had never even owned a pair of wellies!

'My mum will love you,' Dan had assured me when

I'd tried to voice my concerns the night before. 'Almost as much as I do. And Dad ... well, you'll probably hardly see him. But right now, Rich is out and I have the flat, and you, all to myself, so ...' And he'd nuzzled my neck and run his fingers through my hair, and steered me gently towards his bedroom, and after that I'd got so caught up in other things I'd forgotten to worry about it any more.

Trevor was slumped in front of the telly when I got in from work. It was only a quarter past five but he was already asleep, his head lolled to one side, his big grunting breaths lifting the edge of the newspaper that lay open across his chest and dropping it down again, as regular as the clock ticking away behind me in the hall.

I kicked off my shoes and padded past the open door of the living room, trying not to wake him up, and went into the kitchen, flicking the kettle on and grabbing a digestive biscuit from a packet which someone, probably Trevor, had left open, with a trail of careless crumbs scattered not only on the table but across a good part of the floor as well. Still, there wasn't time to start making any sort of meal, so I took another couple and ran up the stairs with them, hurriedly peering in through each of the open doors at the top, but there was no sign of Mum. Just when I could have used her help, too.

I threw my small case open on the bed and piled in all the essentials I didn't have to think about. Toothbrush and paste, shampoo, hairbrush, pyjamas, a spare bra and tights, three pairs of knickers – not the slinky ones, just the everyday kind, as there seemed little chance of Dan getting anywhere near them. I'd travel in jeans and a jumper, with a coat in case of chilly country weather and the high probability that someone would expect me to walk somewhere, involving fresh air and fields, so all I really had to do now was sling in another pair of trousers, a t-shirt or two and choose a dress for the party. Oh, and shoes. What on earth should I do about shoes?

***

We made it to the station with moments to spare, the case heavier than I'd expected it to be, bumping hard against my knees as we ran, hand in hand, along the platform and clambered in to the waiting train just before the guard started slamming the doors shut behind us.

'Okay?' Dan said, shoving our bags up into the rack above our heads and plonking down into the seat beside me. 'All set for the big welcome?'

'As I'll ever be, I suppose.'

'They're not ogres, you know. A bit rough round the

edges, maybe, but that's just how it is, being farmers. You won't even notice after a while. All the crumpled corduroys and big boots and mucky fingernails ...'

'And that's just your Mum!'

'Ha, ha. No, seriously though, Kate, they're probably just as nervous as you are. A city girl in her posh clothes turning up in their little village, seeing things through city girl's eyes.'

'Posh clothes? You must be joking. Look at me!'

'I am looking at you, and you look great. Okay, not posh, then, but smart. Different. Smart clothes don't usually figure all that highly where I come from. Not every day, anyway, but they know how important you are to me. They'll make an effort to make a good impression, I'm sure. You won't be looking at overalls or mucky boots this evening. Dad will have been ordered to have a shave. And probably a bath too! Believe me, Kate, they'll want you to feel comfortable while you're staying, and to have a good time. Just take them as you find them, and they'll do the same. They're family. *My* family ...'

'Yes, I know.' I gazed out of the window as the train started to chug its way out of the station. 'It's just me being silly.'

'Well, don't be.'

'So, how about the party tomorrow? I didn't know what to bring. Long dress, short dress, jewellery, high heels?'

'Whatever you've brought will be fine. It's not a fashion show, and nobody's judging you. Although Mum will have got her pearls out specially, I bet. And bought her first new dress in yonks. It's not every day a couple get to celebrate twenty-five years of marriage, is it? I wonder if we'll be that lucky?'

I was still staring out of the window into the darkness, the buildings rushing past unseen, so I could only see him as a shaky shape reflected in the glass. Us? Lucky? Could he possibly mean ...? No, now I really was being silly. If Dan was talking about marriage, about us getting married, he wouldn't do it like this, would he? Dropping hints on a packed train. He'd do it properly, romantically, privately, and when we were both ready. But maybe he was ready. Maybe we both were? Oh, my God! Was this why he was taking me home to meet his parents? Was he going to propose?

I didn't look at him. Whether it had been a deliberate 'looking for a reaction' moment or just an unguarded slip of the tongue, I'd let it go. Say nothing. Do nothing. Pretend I hadn't noticed. I closed my eyes and leant my head against the cold glass, visions of rings and flowers and me in a stunning white dress floating through my mind. I waited, hardly daring to breathe, but he didn't say any more.

When I did finally turn my face back towards him, he was reading a newspaper, his legs crossed, his body turned away from me, and whatever the moment had been, it was clear that it had well and truly passed.

As it turned out there was no reception committee. Dan's dad was waiting outside the station, by himself in the dark, sitting sideways in the front of an old Mini that seemed too small to accommodate his long legs, and parked a bit haphazardly beneath a tree. I got the impression he'd been there some time, no doubt ushered out early to make sure he wasn't late, because when I first saw him he was almost certainly asleep, his mouth open and his forehead marked with a big wide crease where it had been pressed for too long against the glass.

Dan laughed as he tapped on the window and his dad's head flew up in surprise.

'Oh, there you are, lad.' He opened his door and slowly unravelled himself out onto the pavement. 'And this must be Kate ...' He took my hand in his large weathered one and unexpectedly lifted it briefly to his lips before lifting my bag up as if it was light as a feather and chucking it onto the back seat. 'Now, you sit up front with me, and our Dan can rough it in the back with the luggage. I'm Dan's dad, by the way, as you've probably guessed. Samuel Campbell, at your service. But you can call me Sam. Everybody does. Now let's get you home in the warm and see what Mother's rustled up for supper, shall we?'

I liked Sam straight away. He had one of those crumpled brown faces that comes from spending a lot more time out of doors than in, and the car smelled of warm straw and a gentle hint of unidentifiable animal that I soon came to realise hovered about him most of the time, whether he was in the car or not.

We drove at breakneck speed through unlit country lanes so narrow I could hear the bushes brush and scratch against the side of the car on every bend. More than once I felt myself flinch, convinced we were about to find ourselves upside down in a ditch, but Sam obviously knew the area like the back of his own hand and we arrived, promptly and safely, at the farmhouse in less than ten minutes.

An old black and white collie came rushing out into the yard as soon as we opened the car doors and immediately leapt upon Dan, frantically nudging him with his nose and licking his hands, as if they were long-separated brothers. Which, in a way, I suppose they were. 'Hello, boy.' Dan knelt down in the gravel and let the dog lick his face. 'Kate, this is Micky. He's twelve, but it feels like he's been here much longer than that. For ever, in fact. He's half blind these days, but a more loving and loyal dog you couldn't wish to find. Come over and say hello. Give him a hand and let him get your scent.'

I wasn't used to dogs, let alone being slobbered over by one, but I did as Dan asked, which was why, when his mum appeared in the doorway, the hand I slipped into hers to be shaken was decidedly damp and smelly. She didn't seem to mind, moving swiftly into a hug, one of her soft plump arms still draped around my shoulders as we went inside. 'Dan's never been great at introductions,' she said, not in all honesty having given him much chance to try. 'But I'm Molly. And I am so glad to meet you at last.'

There were just the four of us that first night, sitting around the huge kitchen table eating the most delicious beef with mounds of potatoes, which Molly proudly told me she grew herself in the vegetable garden right outside the window, adding that I was more than welcome to take some home with me as I'd clearly enjoyed them so much. I tried to say that they might be a bit heavy, what with us travelling by train, but somehow I already knew I'd have to take some just to keep her happy.

The bedroom Molly had prepared for me was just as I had expected it to be. A big metal-framed bed was piled high with layers of blankets and feather pillows, topped with a home-made patchwork quilt, and next to it, on a small pine cabinet, was a lamp with a frilly edged, slightly faded shade and the vase of flowers I would have bet money was going to be there. Deep-red dahlias, a couple of their spiky petals already detached and lying alongside.

Across the room, facing the window, was a small dressing table with one of those old-fashioned three-sided jointed mirrors that let you see yourself from all angles at once. The top two drawers had been cleared to make space for my things, and the lower ones, which I shouldn't have looked in but did, were crammed full of all sorts of old stuff left behind by the previous occupant, Dan's now-married sister, Jane. No wardrobe, which worried me a bit, having brought the kind of dress that would definitely benefit from being hung up for a few hours to de-crease itself. I later discovered that Jane had taken the wardrobe with her when she'd left, her new home having a greater need for it than her abandoned and now little-used bedroom here. Still, when I closed the door to get changed in private, I did find a plastic hook glued to the back of it. That would just have to do.

The small window looked out over fields; not that I could see them until the next morning as it was so utterly, scarily, pitch dark outside on the night we arrived. Not a streetlight or a passing set of headlights to shed even a glimmer across the all-enveloping blackness. And the quiet! I couldn't get to sleep, and in the end, I had to open my door just enough to pick up the distant comforting sound of Dan's familiar snoring seeping out from his room across the hall.

***

Dan's family was nothing like mine. Different places, different values, different lives. If it wasn't for that chance meeting with Dan at the party our paths would never have crossed. But that's probably what happens to all of us, isn't it? How friends, colleagues, couples come together. Sheer chance. A meeting of place and time, and circumstance. If he'd arrived a few minutes later at the door I would have been long gone, out into the rain. Earlier, and I would have been still upstairs, just another blurry face, merging into all the others in the dark of the party.

They say opposites attract, don't they? Farm boy, city girl. Him so careful, always planning and worrying, while I just took my chances, took life as it came. Together, and happy, nevertheless. But sometimes I think we just wanted different things. Expected different things. And, even though it was Dan who broke us, I know I played my part. Maybe we were doomed to fail, or is that just the sad me, the defeated me, talking? Star-crossed lovers. Isn't that what Shakespeare said? Not that Dan and I were anything like Romeo and Juliet, but we did love each other. Shared something passionate and caring, and special. For a long time, we did.

The girls think I'm off communing with nature somewhere. I never elaborate, never try to explain, how much I need these talks we have, how much I need to get away sometimes, just to be alone. How much I need you. I sometimes think you're the only one who understands, the only one who never judges, who sees me exactly for what I am. I don't think of you as my guilty secret. Never that. I don't want anyone to think I'm mad. Or desperate. But you are my secret, just the same.

***

Twenty-five years! I watched Dan's parents taking an inexpert but exceedingly happy turn around the dance floor, and wondered how different things might have been if my dad had lived long enough for my own parents to celebrate such a momentous anniversary. As it was, there was just Trevor, like a big balding cuckoo in the nest, trying to fill my dad's shoes and failing miserably.

It was hard to imagine being with the same man for so long. Day in and day out, living, breathing, eating, side by side. Sharing the same bed, going on holidays together, making babies. None of my boyfriends had lasted more than a month or two before Dan, and most of them I would be perfectly happy never to set eyes on again. It made me wonder what I'd seen in them in the first place, how I could have been dragged in by some phoney chat-up line or the lure of muscly arms or twinkly eyes, but I suppose you have to work your way past the initial attraction to find out if there's anything solid enough underneath to make a man worth keeping. With Dan, I knew I had finally found it, and this weekend, with me being included in the celebrations and so thoroughly embraced by his family, I was getting the impression that Dan felt the same way, that this really could be some kind of trial run for something more permanent. Our future together was starting to feel more secure, more certain, more wonderful, every moment we were here.

I had never been to a party quite like it before. It was in a big open-fronted barn tucked away behind the house, on their own land, with a couple of spotlights attached to electric cables draped high over the beams and managing to provide enough light to dance by, while fat white candles flickered more intimately on the tables. I did worry the flames might be a little too close to the bales of hay, or straw, or whatever it was, stacked around the edges, but that was just the townie in me talking. These were country people who lived with barns and straw every day of their lives, and I had to suppose they knew what they were doing. They certainly knew how to have a good time.

There was a long table stretching right across the back wall, heaped with so much food I couldn't help thinking that the local pigs would have a field day with all the leftovers in the morning, but everyone who arrived seemed to squeeze on yet another plate of food they'd brought from home, until it was just about impossible to see the tablecloth any more. Some had even brought their dogs along, so nothing dropped on the floor stayed there for long.

A couple called Dolly and Frank were providing the music, perched on stools with two battered old guitars and a tambourine, switching over to an enormous ghetto-blaster that pumped out disco hits whenever they needed a break or the dancing needed livening up. It was very amateur but strangely hypnotic, and enormous fun too, with nobody too embarrassed to let themselves go a bit, all whooping like kids, kicking their legs up and swinging each other around the floor.

Dan was like a different person that night. He had stopped being the quiet, smart, suited accountant I had grown to know and love and transformed into Dan Campbell, farm boy. He wore an open-necked checked shirt I was sure I had never seen before, and moved around the room, kicking his heels and swaying his shoulders to the music and greeting every newcomer as if he'd known them all his life, which he probably had. Every now and then, when he could tell from my face that I was struggling, he would come and rescue me from a baffling conversation about milk quotas or silage and pull me back into his arms to dance.

'Well? What do you think? Is country life what you expected?' he said, sitting me down in front of a plate of bread and cheese and spooning a dollop of his mum's home-made pickle out onto the side.

'Not at all. But I'm sure it's not like this all the time, is it?' I gazed at his face as his warm fingers brushed against mine and the candlelight sent tiny flecks of colour bouncing and sparkling in his eyes, and just for a moment I wondered what it would be like to give in to what I was feeling, to forget the world outside, Mum and Trevor, my job at the bank, and just stay here in this magical place for ever.

'Of course not. Dad will be up milking at the crack of dawn as usual, and Mum will be out here with a broom in one hand and probably feeding the hens with the other! It's who they are. Creatures of habit. Hard workers. At one with the land and all that. But it's not everyone's cup of tea, and probably not mine, to be honest ... Now, come over and meet Helen. She was the first girl I ever kissed! A long time ago, in the playground when we were five, but I've never forgotten it, even though she probably has!'

The floorboards creaked later, on the landing between Dan's room and mine, as he crept across and closed the door behind him, like a naughty schoolboy sneaking about after lights out, but suddenly I couldn't bear the thought of us sleeping separately, and if anybody heard us they were probably too tipsy to care. I couldn't bear the thought of him kissing anyone but me either, even if it had been years ago when this Helen friend of his was just a little girl with pigtails. I'd met her tonight and she wasn't so little nowadays, particularly in the breasts department. And Dan was mine now. Whoever he had chatted to, danced with, even flirted with in a mild kind of way, during the party, it was my bed he was curled up in that night, and my breasts that were squashed, snugly and sweatily, against his skin.

I think that was the night I decided I would marry him. Not that he'd asked me yet, despite his mumblings on the train, but it was coming. I knew it was. I could feel it. And big happy dreams of our future life together filled my head as I slept, my head resting on his bare chest as it rose and fell, and the gentle contented sounds of his snoring filled the room.

Chapter 4

Ollie, 2017

Ollie put his glass down and reached for another handful of crisps. He really mustn't drink too much tonight. He needed to keep his wits about him and create a good impression if he could.

He took a deep breath, feeling the familiar tightness that he often felt in stressful situations, wished he had thought to bring his inhaler, and turned his attention back to the girl sitting in front of him. She was small and pretty, with a rather chubby but cheeky face surrounded by an unruly mane of dark curly hair. In the brief silence that fell while they were both thinking of something to talk about next, she was toying nervously with the stem of her wine glass. Her fingernails were painted in a shiny shade of pale pink with a strange darker pink band sweeping across the tip of each, and he wondered how long it must have taken her to do that, and why she would even want to.

The bell rang and she stood up. 'Well, it's been nice meeting you, Ollie.'

He took her hand and half rose from his chair to lean forward and kiss her on the cheek. Were you allowed to do that? Probably not. Still, she didn't seem to object. 'You too ...' Oh, no. His mind had gone blank and he had no idea of her name. 'Yeah, you too!'

Within seconds another girl arrived to take her place across the table. 'Hi, I'm Caroline.'

'Ollie.'

He could already tell that this one was not his type at all. Too tall, too loud, too heavily made up. Still, he only had to be polite to her for three minutes. How hard could that be? He reached for his drink, took a swig and started counting the seconds off, one by one, in his head.

He hadn't told anyone he was coming here tonight. He wasn't really sure why he had come, except that there had to be more to life than sitting alone most evenings and feeling sorry for himself. He missed female company, someone to have a laugh with, to chat to, someone to share a bottle of wine with, to stop him drinking it all himself. And, yes, he missed the sex. Of course he did. He was a young man, a man on his own, and it had been a while.

He should have been at the chess club tonight, silently gazing at a wooden board, the clock counting down beside him as he pondered his next move. He hadn't played much chess since he was a child but he'd come back to it recently, finding it somehow therapeutic, something to focus the mind.

He smiled to himself. The chess club wasn't actually all that dissimilar to where he'd ended up, was it? In the back room of the Crown and Treaty, a very plain and ordinary West London pub, facing a series of strangers over a small table, with only minutes to decide when and if to make his move. Winners and losers, and not hard to guess which he was likely to be.

There were a lot more girls here than guys, which struck him as odd but, in theory, should work in his favour. Not bad looking most of them, which made him wonder why they were here at all, why they were finding it hard – perhaps as hard as he was – to meet someone in a more conventional way, or pluck up the courage to do something about their lives. It was probably all just a bit of fun for most of them, though, groups of girls giggling together at the bar afterwards as they compared notes and decided whether to put ticks or crosses against the names on their little slips of paper.

Nobody would choose him, of course. He'd not taken the trouble even to try to impress, either in what he was wearing (old jeans, frayed at the hem, and his favourite comfy grey jumper that hadn't seen a washing machine in weeks) or in what he'd said. In fact, he'd sat back and let each of them do most of the talking and just added the occasional nod or grunt when it seemed expected. Was that because he couldn't be bothered, or had he lost the art of conversation? Forgotten how to chat up women? It all seemed like such a lot of effort for so little reward. He was hardly going to find the love of his life tonight, was he? Not when he already knew exactly who she was, and where. Not here, that was where. Hundreds of miles away, probably, and not coming back.

The last girl stood up and moved away. He didn't kiss this one. Didn't feel the urge to. Looking down at the slip in front of him, he realised he'd stopped making any sort of mark on it three girls ago, when he'd rather rashly put a tick against the busty one. Julie. Not that he could remember much about her face, but he did like a good pair of tits, and you never knew, she just might let him have a feel later, if he bought her a few drinks and offered to share a taxi home. The drivers didn't usually care what went on in the back, so long as you tipped well and kept bare flesh and bodily fluids off the seats.

Oh, God! He was starting to think like some kind of perv. Perhaps it was time to slip away before having to face the embarrassment of finding himself without a single match. He glanced at his watch. The chess would still be on down at the Scout hut. A bit late to get a game, maybe, but he could sit and watch, and have a quiet drink or two while he did. He pulled his coat off the back of his chair and put it on, crumpled up his voting slip (and with it any chance of becoming better acquainted with Julie's cleavage) and dropped it onto the table, then went out into the street before anyone could call him back. The sounds of laughter dimmed as the heavy wooden door swung shut behind him. The offie should still be open on the high street, and it was a lot cheaper option than buying drinks here in the pub, that was for sure. He pulled his collar up against the rain and quickly walked away.

Chapter 5

Kate, 1978

I'll never know for sure why Dan proposed when he did. Perhaps he'd been thinking about it for a while, just as I had. Perhaps he had already chosen the ring, and the place, and the date. Love and marriage, going together like the inevitable horse and carriage. The traditional route through life. Our life. Perhaps it would always have been our next step. Or perhaps it was simply because of the baby.

We hadn't planned on me getting pregnant. In fact, like most couples our age, still building our careers, still enjoying a life that revolved around pubs and music and each other, we were pretty active in trying to prevent it at all costs. And the pill was almost fool proof, wasn't it? All you had to do was remember to swallow it and the rest just took care of itself. So, when my period failed to arrive on time, I didn't worry. In fact, I didn't even notice at first, and when I did, about a week later, I was quick to put its absence down to just about everything but the obvious. I must have marked the wrong date on the calendar. It must be some kind of hormone thing. I must be stressed or overdoing things at work or coming down with a cold.

I put off buying a test for as long as I could, wearing a sanitary towel in bed every night, expecting every morning to find it soaked, or at least trickled, in blood. Waiting for the inevitable crippling cramps, that would probably be worse than usual, what with being so late in coming, so I might even need a day off work, curled up with a hot water bottle on the sofa. I couldn't see my boss being too pleased, could already imagine the muttered tut-tuts that signalled his utter inability to comprehend the inner workings of the female reproductive system but, if the bloody (ha, ha!) thing would just hurry up and come, then putting up with all that would be worth it in reassurance levels alone.

It didn't come. I re-checked the calendar and decided to wait. Just one more day. And then another. I was in denial, pushing the thought of what it might mean out of my head, telling no one. Burying my head in the sand doesn't even come close to covering it. Of course I was pregnant, as the little blue line told me in no uncertain terms within a minute or two of dipping the stick into my traitorous wee. Still, it could be a mistake, couldn't it? A false reading, or something contaminating the stick, or me not understanding the instructions properly. So I bought another pack, a different make this time, read the leaflet from beginning to end, waited another twenty-four hours to make sure my wee was extra early-morning strong, washed my hands and the sink and every little nook and cranny in the space between my legs ... and the second test told me exactly the same thing. I was definitely, absolutely, one hundred per cent pregnant.

It all felt so unlikely, so unexpected, so unreal. I was twenty-six, with no husband, no savings, no home of my own. I wasn't ready. And I was pretty sure Dan wasn't ready either.

***

We were in his room when I told him. We'd not long been home from work and Dan was still wearing his suit, and a blue and grey striped tie that made him look like some sort of public schoolboy. Somehow the formality made it easier. Like it wasn't the real Dan. Like I was telling it to someone else.

'No! Oh, Kate, you can't be.'

I watched his face turn white right in front of my eyes.

'Yes, I can. And I am.'

'Well, how the hell did that happen?'

'The usual way, I imagine. As far as I remember it, you took my clothes off, we kissed for a while, and then you put your penis inside my ...'

'Yes, okay. I know that part, so you can cut the sarcasm. I mean, how did it not work? The pill? I thought you said ...'

'That it was safe? I know I did, and I believed it, honestly, but it looks like I was wrong.'

We both sat there, side by side, on the edge of his bed, and stared at everything but each other. The alarm clock ticked rhythmically beside us. We didn't speak for what felt like ages. Well, what was there to say? The enormity of the situation was only just starting to sink in for me, and I'd had a few days to get used to it, so what must it be like for Dan?

I could hear his flatmate Rich moving about in the kitchen down the hall, banging a spoon against a pan as he cooked something that was bound to be red and spicy – it always was – for our dinner, singing along tunelessly to the music on the radio. The Bee Gees, 'Night Fever', turned up way too loud. Even without being able to see him, I knew the moves he would be making as he danced like Travolta's poor ginger-headed relation, jabbing his long spiky arms into the air, whatever was on the spoon flicking off and landing in little splatters across the tiles. Thank God he didn't have a white suit!

'So, what do you want to do?'

'Do?'

'About the pregnancy. About the baby?'

'I don't know, Dan. At the moment I'm trying not to think about it as a baby at all. I'm only a couple of weeks overdue, so it's very early days. I don't suppose it even has arms or legs or anything yet.'

'Like some sort of amoeba thing, you mean? Just a shapeless blob?'

'Maybe.'

'We still have to do something though, don't we? Make decisions, I mean. It may just be cells or jelly or whatever, and nothing like a proper baby yet, but it isn't going to stay that way for long.'

'No.'

'So?'

I closed my eyes and screwed my fists into balls, feeling my jagged nails dig in to my palms. I'd been nibbling them a lot these last few days, and not very expertly either. 'I don't know. All right? I just don't know. I need more time to think about it.'

'Okay. I guess I do too.'

We both jumped as Rich thumped hard on the door. 'Dinner's up, you two! Come and get it!'

'Shall we?' Dan reached for my hand and pulled me to my feet.

'Well, I don't suppose putting it off for a few hours

is going to make much difference, is it? And I'm starving.'

'Eating for two already?' He forced a smile and ran his hands in little cautious circles over my tummy.

'It's not funny, Dan.'

'I know.' He sat down again and untied his laces, slipping his feet out of his shoes, then pulled off his tie and flicked the top button of his shirt open. I caught a glimpse of a few lone hairs curling high on his chest, and there was a big hole in the toe of his sock. Dan. This was Dan. Ordinary, down to earth, and suddenly vulnerable, Dan. Not some stranger in a suit, but my Dan. This was the man I loved, the man I had accidentally made a baby with, and nothing could change that. It was done, and whatever happened now, we were in it together.

'Not a word to Rich, all right?' I slipped my hand into Dan's and squeezed it. 'Not so much as a hint.'

'Of course not. And if we decide to ... you know ... then there'll be nothing to tell anyway, will there?'

'Decide to what, Dan?'

'Come on, Kate.' He shook his head but he wouldn't look at me. 'That's enough for now. No more talk. We need time, like we said, okay? Time to think, before we do or say anything else. Before we decide. Together. Now, let's go out there, just act as normally as we can, and eat, shall we?'

But I knew what he meant. It was as near as either of us had come to saying the dreaded word out loud. Abortion. The word that had been banging around in my head, almost from the moment I'd known. But it wasn't the only option, was it? And Dan obviously didn't think so either, because three days later, kneeling amongst the damp autumn leaves rotting to mush on the path as I sat shivering on a bench in the park, he pulled out a ring in a red velvet box and asked me to marry him.

***

There didn't seem much point in waiting. Hanging on until we'd saved enough for a big glitzy wedding or the deposit on a house was pretty pointless in our situation, because it would have taken years, and we didn't have years. We were getting married for two reasons only: because we loved each other and because I was pregnant. And it made sense to do it as soon as possible, before the baby was born.

I hadn't been inside a church, except for the usual hatches, matches and despatches, for years, so the local register office would have suited me just fine, but Dan had other ideas. 'We Campbells are a very traditional family,' he said, clasping my newly ringed hand in his and wearing his serious face. 'So, if you don't have any particular leanings towards a church around here, then I'd quite like us to do it back at home, in the church in the village. It's a lovely old building, ivy on the walls and all that, and it's where my parents got married, and Jane, and where we were both christened. Mum will take care of the flowers, and the food. It's what she's good at. And we can use the barn again, for the party afterwards. It'll be easy to arrange – and quick – and it will hardly cost us anything. What do you think?'

'I suppose we could. But how about my family? My friends? My mum?'

'They can all come down. It's not far on the train. Your mum will be very welcome to come and stay at the farm, of course, for a few days. Or for as long as she likes. And Trevor.'

'Trevor?'

'Well, she'll want him there, won't she? And you'll need him there to give you away ...'

'Oh, no, I won't.'

'Sorry. I just thought that, without a dad, he would be the next best thing, and you might ...'

'No way!'

'Well, who then?'

'I don't know. Can't your dad do it?'

'I don't think it works like that. It's meant to be someone from your family, someone handing you over to me. You know, body and soul, to be my chattel for ever, in exchange for a few camels, that kind of thing. And so I can have my wicked way with you whenever I want to!'

'Well, it will be pretty obvious to everyone that you already have if we don't get a move on. I would like to be able to squeeze into an at least half-decent dress on the day. Not some great baggy tent thing that the guests are likely to mistake for a marquee! Maybe I can have Mum do the giving-away bit?'

'Okay. It's a bit unconventional, but we can ask. The vicar's a family friend – well, a sort of second cousin, actually – so I don't think he'll say no. So that's it? We can do it? Get married in Somerset? Set a date?'

Oh, he could be persuasive when he wanted to be, but I didn't have an alternative plan, or the energy to argue. In fact, sitting down with my feet up and letting Molly Campbell sort it all out for me was actually quite an attractive prospect. 'Yes, we can. But soon, all right? Before I'm the biggest balloon in the barn, and definitely before I'm anywhere near ready to pop!'

'We'll tell them at Christmas, when everyone's in a good mood and feeling festive. We can go down there together, or do it on the phone. Whichever you prefer. And talk to the vicar, to book a date. There's nothing like news of a new baby to make Christmas complete!'

'I'm not the bloody Virgin Mary, Dan. And this,' I lay

my hand on my tummy and patted it, 'is not the baby Jesus.'

He laughed. 'I know. And there will be no mangers, I promise, even if we do have the wedding in the barn.'

Chapter 6

Beth, 2017

'It's a very long way to come just for a spa! Surely there was somewhere nearer to home?' Beth dragged her case up the hotel steps and banged her way through the revolving doors. 'All the time we were stuck on that stupid train we could have been lying back luxuriating in a whirlpool bath or whacking down a cocktail or three in the bar.'

'Oh, stop your moaning. We're here now, aren't we?' Jenny followed in her wake, stopping in the foyer to admire the giant floral displays and gaze up at the glittering chandeliers. 'And, you have to admit, it looks great!'

'Wait until we've seen our room, dumped this lot and found our way to the pool, and then I'll tell you if it's great.'

'Oh, you are such a spoilsport sometimes. We got it

half price, remember? And there's a complimentary head massage thrown in later on, so let's just get on and enjoy it all, shall we? And the first drink is on me, by the way.'

'Well, now you're talking. And, while you're doing that, you can tell me why we're really here.'

'I don't know what you mean.'

'Oh, yes, you do! We didn't come all the way up here just to eat three calorie-controlled meals a day and get our heads rubbed, and you know it.'

'Campbell. Room for two. We have booked.' Jenny had turned away and was sorting out the room keys with the woman behind the reception desk, but not before Beth had seen the red flush that was flooding her face and making its way up the back of her neck. She knew damn well there was more to this trip than her sneaky so-called sister was letting on.

The lift came quickly and transported them just as quickly up to Room 316.

'Ooh, look, there's a mini-bar!' Beth was working her way around the room, opening cupboards and exploring light switches before Jenny had so much as found somewhere to put her case down. 'Little dinky bottles of wine. Coke. Lager. They've even got peanuts!'

'And they'll all cost a fortune. We don't need them, Beth. Just wait until we get to the bar. Or, better still, find a shop and stock up with our own supplies. No point throwing money away.'

'Oh, okay.' Reluctantly, Beth closed the fridge door and started pulling clothes out of her case and chucking them all over the bed by the window. 'You always were the voice of reason, weren't you? Dad's daughter, that's for sure! He'll make an accountant out of you yet!'

'I don't think so. All those boring spreadsheets and columns of numbers you have to balance. There's nothing I'd like less.'

'Except dipping your hands into vats of smelly perming lotion and confronting other people's nits, like me, I bet!'

'Believe me, wiping old men's bums comes pretty close!'

'Ugh! Rather you than me.' Beth sat down among the piles of clothes on the bed. 'I didn't always want to be a hairdresser, you know. If Mum and Dad had been a bit better off, I'd have liked to have ballet lessons or learned the piano or gone off to some posh stage school and learned to act and sing, and then I might even be famous by now. Musicals, maybe. I can just see myself as Dorothy, tripping down the yellow brick road in a pair of ruby slippers, or swishing my skirts about being Nancy in *Oliver*, or having a bash at *Evita* … Making a living with a microphone in my hand, not scissors and a soggy towel.'

'I remember! You dancing about all the time when we were kids, like some demented prima donna. But I have to admit, you can sing pretty well. A lot better than me, anyway. And it's never too late, you know.'

'Oh, I think it is.' Beth stood up, bounced onto her toes and did an exaggerated twirl. 'It's just me, hankering after what I can't have and dreaming about what might have been, just like everybody else. Hairdressing's okay, really, and I am pretty good at it, though I say so myself, but the best bit about coming away like this is the not having to stand up all day, listening to people's boring holiday stories. It wouldn't be so bad if I had a proper holiday of my own to look forward to. Still, this will do for now. Pool first, is it? I still feel all hot and sticky from the journey. Then I'll take you up on the offer of that drink you promised me.'

'I'm not so sure about that. Not now you've nabbed the best bed. Just look at that view. And what have I got over on my side of the room? A kettle, a pile of tourist leaflets and three steps nearer to the toilet! Whatever happened to democracy?' Jenny stood with her hands on her hips, trying to look stern, but there was a twinkle in her eyes that made it clear it didn't really matter. 'We could have tossed for it.'

'Now who's moaning?' Beth laughed, burst into a rousing chorus of 'Don't Cry for me, Argentina', and disappeared into the bathroom with a swimsuit in one hand and a bottle of screw-top wine she'd just grabbed from the mini-bar in the other.

***

'We need to go into dinner early tonight.' They'd spent most of Thursday, barring a break for lunch, having their backs pummelled by a rather over-zealous and over-talkative woman with green fingernails and a white coat, and then lazing about in the water to giggle about it and get over it. Now Jenny was drying her still-tangled hair under a particularly noisy dryer in the ladies' changing room. It didn't seem to occur to her just how loudly she was speaking.

'Ssshh!' Beth put her index finger up to her lips, noticed how horribly wrinkled it was from being too long under water, and put it down again. 'We don't want the whole hotel to know.'

'Sorry!' Jenny mouthed, now so quietly Beth could hardly hear her at all. She flicked the switch off to silence the dryer and put it back into its holder on the wall.

'So, why do we have to eat early? I thought eight o'clock worked really well last night. Just right for a few drinks before and a bit of TV after. What's your hurry? Or, more to the point, what's your game? I know you're up to something.'

Jenny didn't answer straight away, choosing to fiddle a bit more with her hair before throwing her damp towel into the wicker laundry bin provided and turning back towards her. Beth was sure she was looking especially shifty, the way she used to when she'd broken a plate and didn't want Mum to know, or when she'd sneakily borrowed a top from her or Nat and tried to put it back without owning up to the streaks of make-up down the front.

'And, while we're at it ... You told Natalie this place was somewhere at the seaside, and it's not, is it? We're miles from the sea. Now, why would you do that? What if she expects a postcard or a stick of rock or something? We won't even be going back with sand in our shoes!'

'Oh, Beth, you are always so suspicious.'

'With every reason, it seems to me. Now, come on, spill!'

'Well ...'

'Yes?'

'Well, there's someone I've arranged for us to meet. This evening, at half-past seven.'

'Now we're getting somewhere. The truth at last. So, what sort of someone? And why's it so secret that you couldn't tell me before now? Or Nat? What are you up to, Jen? It's not some internet date or something like that, is it? Someone you were too scared to meet in the flesh without a chaperone? Because I'm not playing along unless you tell me. And I don't fancy playing gooseberry either. I'll get a table for one at eight and then have an early night, and you can go and meet your mystery person by yourself!'

Jenny was squirming now. 'Nat's got enough on her plate, with the wedding to sort out. I didn't want to add to that. And if I'd told you any sooner you might have blabbed. Or refused to come with me. And I needed you to come with me ...'

'So, one: this is going to worry Nat, and two: I can't be trusted to keep my mouth shut. Charming, I'm sure! So, who the hell are we meeting, Jen?'

'Well ... look, it might all come to nothing. I didn't want to get anyone's hopes up, that's all. It was hard enough to track her down at all, and even harder to talk her into meeting up.'

'Her?'

'Yes. It's Laura.'

'Ollie's Laura?' Beth's eyes had widened almost as much as her mouth, which was now gaping open in shock.

'Well, not Ollie's any more, obviously, seeing as she left him months ago. But I kind of hoped that now the dust has settled, I might be able to talk her into coming back. Ollie misses her so much. I miss her. But there's something you need to know, Beth. Because you'll realise anyway, as soon as you see her.'

'She's not married someone else, has she? Or got engaged? Not so soon. Ollie will be heartbroken if she has. Not that he isn't already, poor bugger.'

'No. Not married.' Jenny picked up her bag and started back towards their room. 'But she is six months pregnant.'

Chapter 7

Kate, 1979

We opted for a January wedding. It was long enough after Christmas for the shops to be open again and decoration-free, so we could at least hope that any presents would be wrapped in something other than silver foil with robins on it. And for the trains to be running at half empty again, with the fare prices back to normal. But soon enough to beat the bulge. The last thing I wanted was for my tummy to dominate not only the photos, but the gossip too, on what was supposed to be the most wonderful day of my life.

Mum had taken the news well. Naturally she would have preferred her only daughter to be a shining example of purity, gliding down the aisle in a dress like a meringue, but the thought of an imminent grandchild soon overrode all that. And she liked the fact that I'd told her first, before Dan's mum, who she had still to meet.

'You must let Trevor and me help pay for the wedding,' she insisted. 'I know you say it won't be a grand affair, but maybe we could cover the cost of the car or your dress or something. And buy the pram. Grandmas always buy the pram, you know. It gives us the right to first push round the park!'

I liked seeing Mum so happy. I had wondered if the inevitable reminders of her own wedding day might have been a bit much for her, but she didn't say anything. Only that Dad would have been so proud, and would have loved to be there, taking me down the aisle. And that being asked to do it in his place was absolutely the next best thing.

She drove down with Trevor. They offered us a lift too, but I knew I'd rather go on the train. That way, Dan and I, and my friend Linda from work, could all travel together. Linda had agreed to be my chief brides-maid – my *only* bridesmaid – and the Campbells had offered us rooms at the farm the night before the cere-mony, and for a few days afterwards too, if we wanted to stay on. We let Mum take all the bags in the car, though. My dress and Linda's, our posh handbags and new satin shoes, Dan's suit, and a big vanity case stuffed with toiletries and lipstick and lemon-scented shampoo. All we had to carry with us was a packed lunch that Linda and the other girls at work had insisted on putting together, made up of all the posh things we would never normally have eaten but that felt somehow appropriate for a bride and groom on their way to seal their fate. Smoked salmon sandwich triangles with the crusts cut off, strawberries (God knows where they got them from in January!), fancy chocolates in an even fancier box. There were a couple of quail's eggs too, still in their shells, and wrapped up tightly in foil, although none of was quite sure what to do with them, or if we actually fancied trying them at all.

But it was the thought that counted and, by the time we arrived, a good hour ahead of Mum and Trevor, and with Dan and Linda already a bit tipsy on the wine I had righteously, as a woman in a certain condition, refused to drink, it dawned on me at last that we were really going to do this. In less than forty-eight hours I was going to be the new, and ever expanding, Mrs Dan Campbell.

The dress. What can I say about the dress? We did try a few bridal shops, Mum and me, and a couple of local dressmakers who worked from their front rooms, but apparently it takes time to make one, a proper posh one anyway, and time was something I didn't have a lot of. With all the detailed measuring involved, I also knew damn well that, weeks later, the thing would never fit the way it should, unless I came clean about being up the duff. And why should I? To some total stranger.

So, we trawled around the ordinary shops, the department stores and boutiques, looking for something at least partially white, and long, and a teensy bit loose. What we found was pretty, in its own hippy kind of way. It was made of thin creamy-coloured cheesecloth, with several layers of lining to give it a bit of shape and stop the sun shining right through and revealing my knickers, a wide lace-edged neckline, and a big bow that tied at the back. I twirled about in front of the full-length mirror in a changing room no bigger than an under-stairs cupboard, and tried to imagine myself wearing it in the church. Was it just a touch too ordinary? A touch too flimsy? Would I be too cold? What would it look like from behind? That was the view everyone was going to get throughout the ceremony, after all, except for the groom and the vicar. I bought it, though. Or Mum did, insisting on paying for the shoes too.

I held it again now, staring out at the fields, the steeple of the small village church poking its old head above the lines of leaf-stripped trees. I was in the same bedroom I'd had that first time I'd visited the farm, but sharing with Linda this time. A vase of holly, packed with fat red berries, had replaced the flowers, but every-thing else was just the same. I had hoped we might have snow to make things just a little more magical, but despite a harsh grey sky and a chilly draught that seeped in through the gaps around the ancient windows, it had not obliged.

Linda and I had unpacked the bags all over the bed, declaring the room a girls-only zone and banning Dan, and in fact anyone of the male persuasion, from crossing the threshold at any time from now until the wedding was over, and were now giggling like tipsy teenagers as we moved an old towelling dressing gown, trying to guess who it belonged to, and hung our dresses in its place on the hook on the back of the door.

'You sure you want to do this, Kate?' Linda said, shoving the messy heap of toiletries and underwear aside and flopping down flat on her back on the eiderdown.

'It's a bit late to ask me that now, isn't it?'

'Of course not. It's never too late, right up to the bit where you say 'I do.' A cousin of mine did a runner the moment she stood in the church doorway and saw all those people inside in their fancy hats, all standing up and turning to look at her when the organ started knocking out the music. She said that was when it all became real. What she was doing, and committing to, for ever. All that expectation on their faces. Up until then it had just been a fantasy thing, the chance to dress up and be the centre of attention. She ended up being that, all right, legging it down the road in her wedding dress and hopping on the first bus that came along!'

'Linda! I'm not going to do anything like that, all right? I am getting married because I want to.'

'And because you have to.'

'Oh, don't say it like that. I didn't have to do it at all. There are always other options, but we chose not to take them. So, no, I am not backing out. And neither is Dan.'

'Fine. Just felt I had to ask. A bridesmaid's duty and all that. Especially as you haven't got a dad to do it.'

'Is that what dads do? Is that why you see them whispering a few last words to the bride before they come arm in arm down the aisle? It's the 'last chance to stop it all' speech, is it?'

'Do you know, Kate, I think it quite often is. Really. Even when dads have spent all that money they will still abandon the whole thing if they think for a moment that their precious little girl might be making a mistake.'

'Oh, stop it. You're making me cry now.' Thinking about my dad did that, a lot. Would he have approved of Dan, considered him the right choice, or urged me not to be hurried into something I might regret? I'd never know, would I?

'Sorry. Had to be done. But now I am going to be the perfect bridesmaid and make sure you are extra specially cosseted and super-happy, like a beautiful blushing bride should be.' Linda bounced back upright, swung her legs over onto the faded rag rug beside the bed, and made for the door.

'Blushing?'

'Well, I could have said blooming, but we don't want the guests to put two and two together, do we? Now, where's the toilet? I'm bursting after all that drink I put away on the train.'

***

'Ready?' Linda put the hairbrush down, tweaked a few loose strands around my face, and gazed into the mirror.

'I think so.'

'You look lovely.'

'Thank you.'

'And Dan will think so too. He'll be bowled over, I just know it.' Linda looked at her watch. 'In around ... forty eight minutes. Assuming he turns up!'

'Well, if he doesn't, he won't be hard to track down and drag back, will he? Not in a village this size, where most of the locals have shotguns! And he's not likely to get lost or stuck in traffic, either, when the church is only five minutes down the lane.'

'I guess the wedding's going ahead, then! How are you feeling? Nervous?'

'A bit sick, actually. And I've got butterflies in my tummy, bumping around so much they must think they're having a party!'

'Want a tablet? '

I put a hand on my tummy and shook my head. 'Better not.'

'Brandy?'

I laughed. 'I'd love one, but ...'

'Better not?'

'It's no joke being pregnant, is it? So many things I can't have, can't do ...'

'Is sex allowed?'

'Linda!'

'Well, it is your wedding night tonight. It's expected. And it'd be a shame not to, wouldn't it? Grounds for annulment if the deed doesn't get done, so I hear.'

'Probably not in our case, with a baby on the way. It's pretty clear the deed's already been done! And who says either of us would want an annulment anyway? This marriage is for keeps.'

It took me a while to realise that the pains might be more than just nerves. The sick feeling was getting worse, and my back was hurting. It reminded me of the worst kind of periods, the ones that creep up on you and strike right out of the blue and take your whole body over. From okay to agony in minutes, so all you want is a bed and a hot water bottle, and to be left alone to curl up and cry. But this couldn't be a period, could it? I hadn't had one of those in a while. And the chances of being left alone, today of all days, were absolutely zero.

'I think I need to have a bit of a lie down, Lin.' I turned away from the dressing table and stood up, clutching the edge to stop me from wobbling. 'Just for a moment or two. I don't feel quite right all of a sudden. How long have we got?'

She checked her watch again. 'Twenty-two minutes and ...' She giggled. 'Fifteen seconds!'

'You know, I might have to risk a couple of tablets after all, just to sort me out before we set off.'

'Oh, my God!'

'What? What's the matter?'

Linda's hands had flown up to cover her mouth and she was staring at me as if she'd seen a ghost. Suddenly she wasn't laughing any more.

'I don't want to panic you, Kate, but I think you should just take a look over your shoulder. In the mirror. Your dress ...'

So I looked, thinking maybe there was a spider on my back, or my zip had burst open at the seams, but no. It was much, much worse than that. There, seeping through my lovely cream dress, right on the bit I'd been sitting on just seconds before, was a small red stain.

'No! No, it can't be. Not blood.' I wanted to collapse in a heap, to sit right back down again and tell myself I was wrong, but I knew I wasn't. 'Can it?'

'I'm pretty sure it is. What are you thinking, Kate? Is

it normal to bleed this far into a pregnancy? Like a show or something?'

'I don't think so. And it hurts, Lin. It bloody hurts. This can only be a miscarriage, can't it? I must be losing it. Oh, hell, what do we do? What do I do?'

'I don't know.' She was looking as pale and helpless as I felt. 'Call a doctor? Ambulance? For now, at least lie down flat and cross your legs or something, try to keep it in ...'

'But my dress?'

'Come on, pull it off quickly ... Okay. It's not too bad. We can sponge it off, and stick it under a hair-dryer or something. But I don't think the dress should be our main worry here, do you? Here ...' She grabbed the old dressing gown we'd found behind the door. 'Put this towelling thing on the bed and lie down on it, and keep still. Don't move, okay? Shall I try to find Dan?'

'No. Not Dan. He'll be at the church by now. Let's not worry him yet. Not until we know ...'

'Okay, you're right. But we need help. Stay here, and don't panic, all right? I'm going to get your mum ... or Molly.'

'Mum. Get Mum. Everybody else will have already left the house.'

I listened to her feet thundering away down the stairs, leaving just an eerie silence into which thumped my own heartbeat, faster, louder than I had ever heard it before.

And then, from across the fields, the church bells started to ring. Ding-dong-ding-dong. Ding-dong-ding-dong. A happy tune that just kept repeating itself, over and over, as if it was waiting for something to happen and wouldn't stop until it did. My wedding. Mine and Dan's.

I lay still and waited for Linda to come back. Maybe she'd have a sanitary towel in her luggage. If not, I'd wrap myself layers deep in every pair of knickers I could find, pad them out with toilet paper or cotton wool, anything to hold things at bay. For an hour. Just an hour, that's all I needed, or maybe two. For me to get to that church, and for Mum to walk me down the aisle, and for me to stand there just long enough to say the words that would turn me into the new Mrs Dan Campbell, and to get our photos done outside.

Then they could cart me off to hospital, or confine me to bed, or hang me upside down with my legs in the air, or whatever it was they had to do. But for now, it was going to take more than a drop of blood to stop me. The bells were calling and I was going to that wedding, *my* wedding, come hell or high water. Or quite possibly both.

Chapter 8

Jenny, 2017

When Jenny spotted Laura coming towards them along the street, she looked different somehow. It wasn't just the obvious pregnancy bump emerging from the front of her open coat. It was her thin, pale face, and the way she walked, slowly, with her head down, as if she was finding something vaguely fascinating about her own feet. She wasn't looking radiant or blooming or any of that stuff. Not like a woman who had finally achieved her life's dream. In fact, she just looked small and lost, and defeated.

Jenny rushed forward and flung her arms around her. 'Oh, Laura. It's so good to see you.'

'You too.'

'Are you okay? We've all been so worried about you.' Laura looked past Jenny at Beth and gave a little wave. 'Hi, Beth. I didn't know you'd be here as well.'

'Sorry about that.' Jenny linked her arm through Laura's and started to lead her towards the door of the pub where they had agreed to meet. 'I just thought ...'

'Safety in numbers? Or that it would be easier for two of you to grab me if I tried to run away again?'

'No. No, not at all. But you're family, aren't you? Or as good as. And I thought, hoped, that if we both came, you'd feel more ... well, loved, I suppose. And missed.'

'Right.'

They found a table in a corner and took off their coats.

'Wow! It's real, isn't it?' Jenny gazed at Laura's unfamiliar shape in awe. 'You really are having a baby!'

'Of course I am! Did you think I was lying? Or that it was just wishful thinking?'

'Sorry. Course not. It's just so lovely to see, after all the previous ... Oh, you know what I mean. Let me get everyone a drink. White wine, Beth? And ...'

'No alcohol for me, obviously. Just an orange juice, please.'

Jenny went to the bar. There was a queue, but leaving the others alone together for a while might not be a bad idea. Beth could be very persuasive when she wanted to be. And someone had to persuade Laura to come home, for Ollie's sake, before he drank himself into a hospital bed, or worse. If only Laura's new no-alcohol rule applied to him!

When she returned to their table, they were talking about something totally different. A book they had both read, and the TV adaptation of it that had got them both swooning over the leading man. Jenny put the drinks down in front of them and waited for a lull in the conversation.

'Oh, it's so nice to be back together,' she said, taking a sip. 'It's just like old times.'

'No Nat? Kate? I'm surprised you didn't hire a minibus and bring the whole family.'

'Don't be daft. Mum's gone off somewhere herself for a few days anyway, so she doesn't even know we're away from home. And Nat's up to her eyes in wedding planning. Oh, I do wish you'd come, Laura. We'd all love you to be there. You do know where it is, don't you? And the date?'

'Of course I do. Unless she's done a massive u-turn, the details of this wedding have been set in stone for what seems like years! But ... oh, you know. It's still weeks away. A long way off. Anything could happen. You didn't tell her, though, did you? Nat? About finding me?'

'No. Poor girl's got enough to worry about.'

'Is that what I am?' Laura cut in. 'Just another thing to worry about?'

Jenny put her hand on Laura's. It was surprisingly cold. 'Well, we have been worried. All of us. You've no idea how hard I had to work to track you down. Finding your aunt, and then twisting her arm to get even a hint of where you might be.'

'So, why did you?'

'To start with, it was just curiosity. To find out where you'd gone and to make sure you were okay. But then, when I dragged it out of you about the baby ... that changed things. And the truth is that I brought Beth with me because ... well, if I couldn't get you to come back home, then I hoped maybe Beth could.'

'I haven't said anything about coming back home.'

'No, I know. But now you're having a baby – Ollie's baby – I thought maybe you would. Or at least think about it. Babies need two parents; parents who stick together whatever life throws at them ...'

'Of course they do. And you know about that more than most. But this is different.'

'Is it?'

'You haven't told him, have you?'

'Ollie? No. It's been hard not to, though. I haven't told anyone at all, not even Beth until this afternoon. I promised I wouldn't, so I won't.'

'So, why haven't you told him yourself?' Beth had been saying very little up until now, but she'd finally asked out loud what Jenny had been dying to ask ever since she'd first found out, although she wouldn't have chosen to come out with it quite so bluntly. 'Only, I do think he has a right to know, don't you? Unless he's not the father, of course.'

There was a stunned silence, broken only by a strangled sob coming from somewhere deep down in Laura's throat. 'Is that what you think of me, Beth? Really?'

'I don't know what to think, actually. I thought you left because you couldn't give him a baby, and now here you are, clearly several months gone – which is what you both said you wanted so much – and you're cutting him out of the equation altogether. It doesn't make any sense to me.'

'Beth!' Jenny turned towards her sister and tried to stop her from saying anything else, but it was too late. Laura was already up and shoving her arms down the sleeves of her coat.

'I shouldn't have come,' she said, pushing through the gap between them as best she could, one hand protectively covering her bump. 'I knew you wouldn't understand. Any of you.'

Jenny followed her out into the street. Pregnant women not being the fastest of movers, she wasn't too difficult to catch up with.

'Laura. Wait!'

'What for? I came because I thought it might be good to see you, and maybe to try to explain. I didn't expect you to start ganging up on me.'

'That's not what we're trying to do. Honestly. Come

back inside, Laura. Please. We'll go easy on you, I promise. And I do keep my promises, as you well know. If I didn't, it would be Ollie standing here right now, pleading with you. Not me.'

Laura hesitated for a moment, but Jenny could tell she had given in. In fact, there seemed very little fight left in her at all.

'All right. I'll come in, but that doesn't mean I'm coming back home, or telling Ollie. Not right now, anyway. Just because you make all these rash promises doesn't mean that I have to, okay?'

Jenny slid her arm through Laura's. 'Of course you don't. Whatever you want is fine by me. But I do want to hear all about junior here. Boy or girl? Due date? Possible names? Everything. Wow, Laura, I'm going to be an auntie, aren't I?' She laughed. 'That sounds really funny, doesn't it? Auntie, aren't I! But I am. Going to be an auntie. Auntie Jen, the practical one, that'll be me, opening it a savings account and buying it sensible shoes. And Auntie Beth can take it partying and do its hair, and Nat can ... oh, I don't know, take it for wheelie spins in her chair! It's going to be just great.'

'Slow down, Jen. This baby isn't even born yet, and on my past record it still might not be.'

'But you're six months gone. You won't miscarry this one. Not now. You're home and dry!'

'If only I could believe that, but there's still a long

way to go. Anything could happen. Anything could still go wrong. And not a day goes by, Jen, not an hour or a minute when I don't worry that it will.'

Jenny didn't know what to say. The sheer misery etched on Laura's face brought tears stinging into her own eyes.

'It will be all right, Laura.'

'Will it? You can't possibly know that. And it's what I thought the first time, isn't it? And the second. And this is the fourth, remember. Four! I hardly sleep, and when I do I just dream these horrible dreams. I can't settle, or relax, or plan. Ever. It's like I'm in a living nightmare, Jen, and it's one I'm not going to wake up from until this baby is born safely, all in one piece, and lying in my arms. Do you think I could put Ollie through all this too? No! Never. It's best he doesn't know, doesn't have to feel what I'm feeling, fret and stress and tie himself up in knots. Best he doesn't have to go on blaming himself – or me.'

'Blaming? For what?'

'Oh, God, Jen, you really don't understand, do you? Please, let's go back in to Beth and find something else to talk about for once. Books, clothes, the sodding weather if we have to. But any more baby talk and I think I just might explode!'

Chapter 9

Kate, 1979

Ipacked my pants with a double layer of padding, swallowed three aspirins, and wore the dress back to front. Nobody would know. The neckline was a bit higher at the front than it would have been and the shaping, such as it was, was all wrong (thank God for small breasts), but the giant ribbons attached at the sides had been as easy to tie one way around as they had the other, and I was now eternally grateful I hadn't gone for something with a train that would have made such improvising pretty much impossible. The small stain, still damp and not quite invisible, despite Linda's frantic scrubbing, was now at the front of the dress, disguised, along with my bump, by the long trailing bouquet I was clutching so tightly that my knuckles had gone white.

Mum gripped my hand on the step. 'Sure you're okay

to do this, love?' she said, looking anxious. 'Maybe you should have stayed lying down. It might make a difference.'

'I doubt it. I don't think babies fall out just because the mother is upright, do you? If I'm going to lose it, there's not a lot I can do to stop it now. And I will see a doctor as soon as I can, I promise. But I think we all know it might already be too late.'

I took a pace forward to the door and tried not to think about what was happening inside my own body. If I'd thought too hard about it I would probably have crumpled, gone in there crying my eyes out, tripped over my own feet or something. Somehow it was easier to ignore it, pretend it wasn't happening, tell myself that none of it was true. This baby had not been planned but over the last few weeks I had grown to love it, to want it. And now all I wanted was for it to hang on and live, to become a part of our brand-new family. Baby Blob, that was what Dan had taken to calling her, his hand stroking over my belly, his ear pushed against my skin as if he could hear her breathe. Her? Why did we just both assume it was a she? Little Baby Blob. No, don't think about it. Concentrate on what's happening right now. The wedding. Dan. Us ...

Peering into the church, I could just see him standing at the front. Dan, with his back to me, hopping from foot to foot and straightening his tie, and Rich standing beside him, fiddling with something in his pocket. Probably the rings. And between them and me, a small rolling sea of heads and hats, a general murmuring of whispered conversation, and an unmistakable air of anticipation.

I was late. Only by ten minutes, which we'd needed to try to sort out the dress, but that was probably enough to get tongues wagging. Where is she? Is something wrong? Is she going to turn up? The flash of an image popped into my head, of that woman Linda knew, seeing it all ahead of her, turning away and running scared, all the way to the bus. But not me. For better or worse, that's what this was all about. And things didn't come much worse than this.

'Do you want me to slip in there and have a word with Dan? In private? Tell him what's happening?' Mum asked, her forehead creased into a frown, as she pulled a mirror from her handbag and had a last check of her lipstick. She looked, like me, as if all she really wanted was to get on with it, get it over with, as quickly as possible.

'No, Mum. It's not as if there's anything he can do. And you whispering in his ear in front of that lot in there could hardly be less private, could it? Let him enjoy his own wedding, eh? No point all of us worrying ourselves sick, is there? Ready, Lin?'

Linda nodded as she pulled my hem into line and

did a final tweak of my hair. 'Then, let's get in there, shall we? There'll be time enough to tell Dan afterwards. When it's too late for him to change his mind!'

They both laughed in a muted, nervous kind of way, but a little piece of me wondered if it was true. If he was only marrying me because of the baby, and now there was no baby ...

The bells stopped ringing then and, having spotted us waiting in the open doorway, the organist started up and everyone suddenly stood and turned and stared. It was too late to do anything but go through with it. I grabbed Mum's arm and pulled my flowers hard against me. Then, taking a big collective breath, all three of us stepped over the threshold and into the church, and made our way, very slowly, up the aisle.

***

Was that it? The moment I sealed my fate. Our fate? Walking down the aisle without telling him? Without saying a word? I knew it was the baby – the accidental baby – that had brought us there, to that day, that church, that rushed decision we might never otherwise have made. And now there might not be a baby, I could have stopped it all, the whole charade. Not that he ever complained, but it must have crossed his mind from time to time, later on, mustn't it? That I'd tricked him somehow, not given him the choice. I was wrong. I know that now. I could have – should have – just told him, stopped the wedding, set him free. Or at least given him the option. But I didn't.

It wasn't easy to think straight. Everything was happening too quickly. I was bleeding, I was in pain, I wasn't in control. Yes, I know they just sound like excuses now, but it would have taken more courage than I could muster to stop it. All those people, all that expectation, and no convenient bus waiting to whisk me away, blood-stained dress flapping wildly in the wind.

I loved Dan. Reliable, responsible, oh-so-conventional Dan, wearing a new suit and a carnation, and already there, waiting for me at the front of the church. Not only for me, but for our little blob of a baby too, because we came as a package now, didn't we? One hidden away inside the other, like Russian dolls.

I should have told him the package had come undone, that our plans were already unravelling like an unruly ball of string. I should have given him the choice, to tie the knot or let it go, but I didn't say a word, until it was too late.

It was the first big lie in our relationship, the first truly unforgivable thing I had ever done. And no way to embark on a life, a marriage …

I think I may have been paying for it ever since.

***

According to Rich, who'd travelled down by train early that morning with three more of Dan's friends, and with the sole intention, best-man duties aside, of having a bloody good time, the reception was a hoot. Knowing how much booze that lot were able to put down their gullets, and Rich in particular, I was surprised he was able to remember it at all.

'These country folk sure know how to party, don't they?' he said, perched by the side of my hospital bed, with one elbow on the blankets, and working his way through the grapes he'd brought with him, spitting the pips into his hand. 'Drinking cider and chomping through mounds of food – delicious, by the way – and dancing the night away like there was no tomorrow. How your dad manages to get up and milk cows after a night like that I'll never know. I take my hat off to him. My head's still pounding like a sledgehammer, and I left before any of them. And the price of a taxi at that time of night, you wouldn't believe! It was only five miles to our hotel too. Should have walked.'

Dan chuckled. 'Walked? Staggered, more like, knowing you lot. And down those little dark lanes? You'd have ended up in a ditch.'

'Bit rough though, wasn't it? You two missing your own reception.'

'At least we made it to the wedding. That's the most important thing.' Dan squeezed my hand and I felt my new ring push its way gently into my flesh. His eyes were looking watery again and he quickly rubbed a sleeve over them. He'd been with me all night, dozing beside me in a chair, and had held my hand this morning, just as he was doing now, when the scan had shown us what we already knew. The baby was gone.

Rich looked uncomfortable, and I knew it wasn't just because of his hangover or the hard plastic chair he was sitting on. He wasn't good with emotional stuff, and the sight of his best mate on the verge of tears was not something he knew how to deal with. 'Well, I just wanted to look in before I left,' he said, bundling the last of the bunch of grapes, which by now wasn't much more than a collection of stalks, back into their paper bag and dropping them on the bedside cabinet. He held out a hand to shake, but Dan walked around the bed and pulled him into an awkward bear hug.

'Thanks for coming, mate. And, you know ... for not losing the rings and everything.'

'My pleasure. And I'm sorry about the baby.'

'Yeah, I know.'

We watched in silence as Rich walked away down the ward, turning to wave before heading out towards the lifts.

Dan idly lifted up the paper bag, opened it and peered inside. 'Grape?' he said, plonking himself down on the bed and holding it out to me.

'I don't really fancy them now. Not having seen him spitting all those pips.'

'Cup of tea, then?'

'I'd love one. Although, now I'm not pregnant any more, I suppose we should push the boat out and have a proper drink. Of course, we may have to improvise a bit until we get out of here.'

'Champagne, to celebrate?'

'Well, maybe not celebrate exactly, in the circumstances. But at least to toast our future together, as we didn't get to do it at the reception. Which reminds me, I never got to hear your speech, did I? Or the best man's.'

'Good job. They were rubbish anyway.'

And that was how our married life began. Just the two of us, where there should have been three, trying desperately hard not to cry, and sipping weak hospital tea with our eyes shut, pretending it was bursting with bubbles.

NUMBER TWO

Chapter 10

Natalie, 2017

'Welcome home, you two.' Natalie watched her sisters drop their coats and bags in the hall and went back to stirring a bowl of pasta sauce on the hob. She lifted the wooden spoon, licked it carefully – they were family so nobody would mind – then put it back into the pan. 'So, what did you get up to on this spa break of yours?'

'Oh, you know, just chilling out really,' Beth said, bounding into the kitchen and sniffing the air appreciatively. 'Lettuce leaves for lunch, a bit of swimming, some woman bashing away at our backs and rubbing our heads too hard. That kind of thing.'

'Did you get to the beach?'

'Not really the weather for it.'

'And we didn't get a lot of time,' Jenny cut in, slipping into a chair and fiddling with the cutlery Natalie had already laid on the table. 'So, sorry we didn't bring you anything back.'

'I didn't expect you to.'

'When's Mum home?'

Natalie tilted the steaming pan and started spooning the sauce over plates piled high with too much spaghetti. 'Sunday, I think. I've not heard from her. She didn't take her phone. I found it on the hall table.'

'Typical!' Beth carried two of the plates to the table and went back for the third.

'Got any Parmesan, Nat?' Jenny was already twirling the pasta inexpertly around her fork and dropping most of it back onto the plate.

'Anyone would think I'm the only one who lives here! You know where the fridge is.'

'Don't bother yourselves, either of you,' Beth said, using her best put-upon voice. 'I'm still standing. I'll get it.' She rummaged around in the fridge, tore open a bag of ready-grated cheese, poured it into a bowl and sat down with it still in her hand. 'And thanks for cooking, Nat. It's been a very long journey and I'm famished.'

'Not *that* long,' Jenny said. 'But I think all that sea air must have made us hungry.'

Natalie wheeled her chair over to the table and slid it into her usual place. 'I've missed this,' she said when they were all settled and eating. 'I know you were only gone two nights, but ...'

'Better get used to it, girl. You won't have us two around all the time once you're married, you know.'

'I know. It's like the end of an era, though, isn't it?'

'You didn't say that when Ollie left home.'

'That was different somehow. This is … well, I don't know, I love Ollie, of course I do, but maybe it's just because we're the girls. It feels like the break-up of the Three Musketeers or something. You know, all for one and one for all.'

If only it was really like that, she thought. The three of them doing everything together. Because, although she knew they meant nothing by it and the last thing they would want would be to hurt her, they did make her feel a bit left out sometimes. Sharing a room for so long had brought the two of them closer, along with all the whispering and giggling together after lights out that had inevitably come with it. And hadn't they just been away together and left her at home? Still, she shouldn't blame them. Her wheelchair made it harder to do things together. Normal things, that didn't need loads of planning and thinking about stairs and ramps and space. It even put her at a different level, a good couple of feet below everyone else, so even hugs were hard sometimes.

But she was being too harsh. She knew she was. Just look at how Beth had carried the plates and gone to the fridge for the cheese. They were always making allowances for the things Natalie couldn't do as easily, or as quickly, as the others, anyway. Both of them, always being extra kind, extra helpful. And they were her sisters, for God's sake. They knew her inside out, but for weeks now the elephant had been stomping about in the room. The wedding they seemed to find it so hard to talk about. The wedding that Natalie wanted, and the one – the very different one – they were trying to push upon her. If they still didn't understand that all she needed was to feel normal and relaxed and comfortable, especially when it came to her own wedding, what hope was there that anyone else would?

'Is Phil back at the weekend too?' Beth said.

Natalie nodded, her mouth too full of food to talk.

'More wedding stuff to sort out, I suppose. You really should get out more and have some fun, you know.'

'Yes, you're like an old married couple already,' Jenny added. 'Still, not long to go now, eh?'

Natalie swallowed the pasta and wiped her mouth. Ah, here we go, she thought. They've brought the conversation back round to their favourite topic. She wondered what had taken them so long. 'Eleven weeks. As you well know!'

'Chosen the dress yet?' Jenny asked. 'Only, you do seem to be cutting it a bit fine.'

'Well ... I did try something on, but I've decided I'm going for simple. I can't be doing with all the flounces and trains and stuff. Probably straight from a shop rail, so I've still got plenty of time. For now, it's getting invitations out and making sure you all get something to eat at the reception that's taking priority.'

'Oh, so we are invited, then?' Beth said, sounding very much like she was only half-joking.

'Of course you're invited! You've already had the 'save the date' card. In fact, I can see it from here, stuck on the fridge door. Oh, I get it. This is about the bridesmaid thing again, isn't it? Look, I want you there as guests. Very important guests, but I've already told you I don't want bridesmaids.'

'And we don't believe you. Everyone has bridesmaids! And if you leave it much longer to change your mind, we won't have time to get our dresses sorted out.'

'Oh, for heaven's sake! I haven't even got a dress myself, and you're already worrying about yours. Whose wedding is it anyway?'

'Yours, Nat. And that is why, as your loving and loyal sisters, we don't want to see you make a mistake you will come to regret, like not having a big white dress and us right there behind you. As your bridesmaids. In pink.'

'Pink? You've already chosen the colour?'

'Well, it's up to you, obviously, but we've talked about it, just in a what-if kind of a way, and we do think pink would look best. The bright-fuchsia kind of pink, obviously, not the wishy-washy baby kind. Or maybe some kind of purple. Blue or green don't really work for bridesmaids, do they? Too cold. Although Mum's planning on wearing blue, so she says. And I know it'll be nearly Christmas, but red would just be way too much like we were trying to look like robins, or Mrs Santa Claus! And, besides, I've seen the most gorgeous shocking- pink satin shoes. Not too high. I know you won't want us to look too tall ...'

'Beth!' Natalie had to raise her voice to be heard. 'Beth!'

'What?'

'Okay.'

'Okay what?'

'Okay, I give in.' Natalie couldn't help but laugh. Beth was nothing if not persistent. 'You can be my bridesmaids. Both of you. But we do it by my rules, okay? And no fuchsia pink. Absolutely, definitely no fuchsia pink.'

Chapter 11

Kate, 1983

Four years had been a long time to wait. Mum had offered, had said that Dan could move into my room at home, that the two of us could treat her house as our own home for as long as we needed, but living with Mum would have meant living with Trevor and I felt I'd done that for more than long enough already. No, living at Dan's place hadn't been too terrible in the end, and Rich wasn't too bad as flatmates go (he tidied up, cooked well and smelled okay), so things could have been a lot worse.

In fact, those first four years of married life were fantastic. Like they say about schooldays, they were probably the best days of our lives. And nights. Being one half of a couple was like nothing I had ever experienced before. Living together, taking the good with the bad, sharing the chores and the worries and the joys, and learning to become the invincible team we had always suspected we were meant to be. And being squashed into that small room wasn't so bad either, or into that not-big-enough bed, as we curled up under the covers at night, moulded sweatily together like two smoothly curved spoons that fitted inside each other as if they had been made to do nothing else. Whispering so Rich couldn't hear us, and giggling when he banged on the wall, making it clear that he had.

But it was good to finally have saved enough for the deposit to buy a place of our own, where we could spread out, make noise, run around naked if we felt like it, and start buying the furniture and curtains and sets of matching plates we needed to make a proper home together.

Working at the bank had turned out to be a godsend when it came to getting an affordable mortgage, and now we'd painted the small lounge and smartened up the kitchen, it was time to turn our attention to the bedrooms. There were three, although the smallest was little more than a box room, with just about enough space for a single bed and a wardrobe.

'This will make a great nursery,' Dan said, standing in the middle of the empty room with a paintbrush in his hand. 'Are you sure you want it this neutral magnolia colour? Not covered in Disney characters or Winnie the

Pooh or something? It would save having to change it again later.'

'Nursery?' It was the first time either of us had mentioned the possibility of another baby and just hearing the word stopped me in my tracks.

'Well, not right away, obviously, but one day soon ...'

'Really? But, Dan, we haven't even talked about it.'

'Then maybe it's time we did. I'll be hitting thirty soon, and you're ...'

'Yeah, I know. There already, and beyond. Don't rub it in. But a baby? I didn't think you were that keen. I mean, last time was an accident, so it's not as if it was something you'd ever said you wanted. Or me, for that matter. Much as we'd got used to the idea ...'

'Baby Blob. Remember?' He grabbed my hand and gave it a squeeze.

'Of course I remember.'

'I do wonder about her sometimes, you know. What she would have looked like. A little bit of me and a little bit of you. Can you imagine it, Kate? She'd be four now, wouldn't she? Probably starting school.'

'She!' I smiled at him, my hand automatically moving to draw little circles over my tummy. 'Why did we always think of it as a girl? It could have been a boy, you know.'

'Maybe the next one will be.'

'Oh, Dan, really? Are we ready to try again, do you think? What if something goes wrong again? I don't think I could face it ... And shouldn't we get the house the way we want it first?'

'How long can that take? We're halfway there already. Another couple of months, maybe, to decorate up here and buy a few more bits and pieces? And babies do take nine months to cook, don't they? Plenty of time, even if you fell straight away. And there's no reason to fear the worst, is there? The doctor said there was no reason we couldn't have more, didn't she? When the time was right.'

I sat down on the bare floor and rested my back against the wall. 'You've really thought about this, haven't you? Where was I when you were plotting away with a calendar in your hand?'

'Don't be daft. But I do think it's something we should be thinking about now, and talking about. Maybe even doing something about ...' He lay the paintbrush down on top of the tin and sat down next to me, throwing an arm around my shoulders and planting a kiss on my forehead before moving his lips down to cover mine.

'What? *Now?*' I laughed, pushing him away.

'Why not? Don't you think it's time we added a little heir to the Campbell empire? What's the point of having three bedrooms if we don't fill them up? Come on, Kate, at least think about it. We're not getting any younger, are we?'

'But, what about my job?'

'Women do it every day, and so can you. Work, bring up babies, find help ...'

'Women give up work too. Look after their own babies, and stay at home getting fat.'

'Well, if that's what you want, I'm sure it's a possibility. We'll manage somehow, money-wise. For a while, anyway. But don't get fat. Please don't get fat.' He grinned. 'I don't think I could cope with that!'

We sat for a few minutes, saying nothing, his fingers playing with my hair, a jumble of images suddenly flashing through my mind. The blood on my dress, the pain, the awful empty feeling when it was over. Did I really want to risk all that again? But there really was no reason to think anything would go wrong again. Just one of those things, the doctor had said. Everything in working order, ready to try again. And this time we could do things properly, couldn't we? Actually try. Not just let it happen. We could plan things. Get excited instead of scared. We had a nice home now. We'd be good parents. And I'd know for sure this time that Dan wasn't just saying he wanted it. That he really did. As much as, or maybe even more than, I did.

'Hold back on the magnolia, then.' I looked around the room, slowly, the morning light flooding in through the window and throwing a long bright beam across the floor at our feet, tiny dust motes dancing in the air, a thin strand of lacy cobweb dangling high up in the corner. 'Maybe lemon, so it will work for a boy or a girl. And, actually, I do quite like Pooh Bear ...'

'You mean it?' Dan turned my face to his and gazed into my eyes, a look of sheer joy on his face as I nodded.

And that's how we did it, just like that, made a momentous life-changing decision in minutes, over a big tin of emulsion that never did get opened.

***

I knew getting pregnant could take time. There was nothing unusual in having to wait a few months, maybe a year, before things clicked. I'd read enough magazine articles and agony aunt problem pages to know that. Not many couples get lucky in the first month they try. But I'd been there before, managed it without even trying at all, and while taking the pill as well. What did that say about my fertility levels? And Dan's? So, I half expected a quick result.

'What are you grinning at?' Linda said at work one morning. 'You look like the cat that got the cream. The whole jug, in fact!'

I was a day late. Only one, but I was normally pretty regular, so I had already convinced myself this was it.

'You'll know soon enough,' I said, refusing to explain.

'Ooh, now I'm intrigued.'

We were opening up our adjacent tills, ready for the

onslaught of customers that always greeted us first thing on a Monday, so there was no more time to talk, or for her to start guessing. If she did, I knew it wouldn't take her long. There are only so many happy secrets it's possible for a woman to have.

By the time we stopped for lunch, it was too late. There was no secret, and no baby. I was bleeding.

'Never mind,' said Dan, when I got home and told him the news. 'It's early days. Put your feet up and I'll cook tonight. And if you're really good I might even make you a hot water bottle.'

'If I'm good?'

'Well, you know what I mean. No crying, or worrying about it. We've got plenty of time, and having a few more practice goes at it could actually be quite fun. Practice makes perfect, after all! Now, what do you fancy to eat? Fish fingers or chicken pie? I think there's one in the freezer somewhere.'

'Fish please. It's good for baby-making. I'm sure I read that somewhere.'

'Really? Maybe it's time we read up on all this stuff, eh? Get our facts straight. You know, loose underpants and cold showers, and timing things with a thermometer and all that. Give ourselves the best chance. We'll get a book out of the library.'

Typical Dan. Methodical, organised, a planner through and through. I suppose that was the accountant in him. Left to me, we'd be taking things as they came, letting nature take its unpredictable course, leaping into an early bed a bit more often and just enjoying the ride.

'Okay. No harm in that, I suppose. And can I have carrots with my fish fingers?'

'Carrots? I thought they were for helping you to see in the dark.'

'Well, I'm going to need to do that too, aren't I? If we're planning on doing a lot of under- the-covers baby-factory stuff, I would like to see what it is I'm getting hold of!'

'How about we just leave the light on?'

'Or get a torch? I used to have one to read in bed when I was a kid. You know, all sneaky, under the blankets when I was meant to be asleep. Dad used to do his nut when he caught me. 'You've got school in the morning,' he'd say. He even took the batteries away once!'

'Ah, but we don't have to be sneaky, do we? We're in our own home now and we can leave the lights on all night if we want to. In fact, we can do whatever we like. Even things that involve batteries, if you fancy it! And, besides, I don't want to be the one holding the torch. I rather like having both hands free for ...' I giggled as he grabbed me, one jumper-covered breast neatly cupped in each of his open palms.

'Not tonight, Josephine! I'm bleeding, remember?' I

pushed him off, pulling his face down towards me for a kiss. 'Now, go on, get out in that kitchen and make me that hot water bottle you promised me. Oh, and chips. Got to have chips with fish fingers.'

'Yes, your Majesty. Whatever you say, your Majesty.' He backed away, bowing and laughing at the same time. 'Your wish is my command.'

***

Dan looked funny in boxer shorts, his legs pale and spindly. I'd bought him some plain white ones, a pack of six, and deliberately a size too big, to be on the safe side, and he'd come home with a bright-red pair with little Mickey Mouse faces all over them, which he was now modelling in front of the bedroom mirror. I marvelled at how our tastes could be so different at times.

'How can I take this whole thing seriously if I have to look at those monstrosities every time you take your trousers off?' I said, bundling up all his old bottom-hugging clingy y-fronts and chucking them in the bin.

'I won't be wearing them every time, will I? In fact, if you don't like them, I'll keep them for my day off.'

'Day off?'

'You've bought six pairs. Monday to Saturday, right? I'll wear the Mickeys on Sundays. So, no sex on Sundays, okay? My day of rest.'

'Dan, that's not how it's done. We're not supposed to make love every night. Not even six out of seven. We're not machines. It still needs to be fun, not some sort of chore. And sperm has to build up its strength a bit, over a few days, if you want it at its best.'

'I know how it feels!'

'Dan, we've hardly started. Anyway, it's quality that counts, not quantity.'

'You've been reading the book.'

'Of course I have.'

'You'd better draw up a timetable, then. Make sure I don't accidentally get an erection on the wrong day!'

'Now you're just being stupid. But I am going to start taking my temperature every day, and when that tells us the time's right, you'd better be ready. All guns blazing.'

'I've only got one gun, sweetheart.'

'One's all we need. So long as the bullets you're firing aren't blanks.'

'Not likely, is it? We've made a baby once, so things must be in working order.'

'True. So, do you fancy a trial run?'

'Now, you mean?'

'Well, not if you have something better to do. Like mow the lawn or clean the oven, or something.'

'Well, come to think of it, there was that silver tankard I've been promising myself I'd polish ...'

'Dan!'

'Oh, all right then. Seeing as you've asked so nicely. I dare say the silverware can wait.'

'But you're still wearing the Mickeys. Didn't you say no sex when you're ...'

'Oh, don't you worry. That's easily solved. I'll take them off. Let's be honest, it's a lot easier naked, isn't it?' And, with that, he pushed me down onto the bed and wriggled me out of my jeans, and we tried really, really hard to make a baby.

Chapter 12

Ollie, 2017

A teacher who drinks. Is that what he was turning into? Was that the kind of example he was setting the kids he worked with? Not that they knew. But *he* knew. And, if he carried on this way, it would only be a matter of time before someone smelt it on his breath or he got caught swigging from a hip flask in the games cupboard, and then what? Career over. Reputation in tatters.

Ollie peered at his face in the mirror above the bathroom sink. He looked tired. When he bared his teeth they had taken on a dull yellowish tinge, and his tongue was coated in a layer of white gunk that tasted like old socks, or the way he imagined old socks to taste, having never actually tried any. He spent longer than usual scrubbing away with his toothbrush, until he tasted blood and knew it was time to stop. Not only to stop brushing, but to stop drinking too, and feeling sorry for himself, and moping over a woman who was very clearly never coming back.

His first class of the day was athletics. The field stuff, not the track. Okay, so it was September, but there were only so many more chances to enjoy being outside before the kids were confined to using the shoddy gym equipment in the hall or out battling the elements with their hands and faces turning blue with cold on the hockey field come winter. And it could be fun. Ten and eleven year olds, having their first go at holding the javelin (the school only owned one), learning to carry it, launch it safely, aim it in a graceful arc (some hope of that happening!) through the air with only a small chance of it landing where it was supposed to. Like Cupid's arrow, he thought, flying wildly about and finding its own spot, no matter how hard you tried to tell it where you wanted it to go. But now he was being fanciful. They were no cherubs, they were just kids, kitted out in baggy shorts and school polo shirts, half of them out for a lark and enjoying the freedom of escaping their desks, and the rest – mainly the girls – wishing they could be somewhere else entirely. And, amongst the lot of them, maybe one, just one if he was lucky, who might have some shred of athletic talent and ambition. He couldn't help wondering sometimes why he bothered wasting his time, why he hadn't opted to teach secondary school kids, where he might have at least run into a spark or two of enthusiasm.

He pulled on his jacket, checked the pockets for stray cans, and threw his finished cereal bowl into the sink to join all the plates and cutlery and pans that had been accumulating there over the weekend. He'd wash up later. But then, that's what he always said, and later there was usually something else more pressing or enticing, or more than likely liquid, vying for his attention, and that meant he never quite got around to it.

He closed the door behind him and stood for a few seconds, breathing in big gulps of cool, clean morning air. The school was only a twenty-minute walk away. That's why they'd chosen this flat, to save on fares and petrol, and if a games teacher wasn't fit and healthy enough, barring the asthma that had hung around since childhood and still reared its ugly head from time to time, to manage a brisk walk to and from work every day, then, as he'd jokingly said many times, there was something wrong with the world.

The trouble now was that he was living in the flat all alone, so something very definitely was wrong with the world, or his small part of it at least. Whatever the advantages of its location, Ollie wasn't good at being alone. From as far back as he could remember, he had never had to be alone. They say that twins have a special bond, having started out side by side from day one, their tiny growing bodies curled together in the cramped space of their mother's womb, being pushed out into the world within minutes of each other, sharing all of childhood's little milestones and miracles. But this, this connection he felt with his sisters, was something else. Something bigger, greater and even more infuriating. It was something so few people had, or understood.

He quickened his pace, glancing at his watch. He was going to be late again, and it was starting to rain. Little rivulets ran over his collar and trickled down his neck. Year six, taking on the javelin in the rain. Was that the only highlight his day had to offer? Oh, what joy!

For a moment he thought about turning back, going home and hiding under the crumpled duvet cover he hadn't washed in a while. Or even going back to Mum's for a few days and letting her look after him, the way she had when he was small and feeling under the weather, smothering him in blankets and sympathy and soup. But it was only the third week of term. Time off mid-term was frowned upon, unless he said he was sick. Lied. The thought of it was certainly appealing, going back to bed, or the sofa, losing himself in sleep, waiting for the rain to stop. Waiting for something, anything, to happen that would shake him out of this hole he'd been sliding into ever since Laura had left. The hole with such slippery sides that escape just got harder and harder to envisage. But they'd find him and pull him back, however deep he fell. His mum and his sisters. They always did. Because they knew. When he was in trouble, when he was in pain, they just knew. And that was exactly why he was avoiding them.

***

'I know it seems early to be thinking about Christmas ...'

Ollie stood in front of the head teacher's vast and surprisingly empty desk. He had half expected his summons might have something to do with his drinking, that he'd been rumbled somehow and was about to be given his marching orders. During the short walk from the staff room, he had been bricking it, his mind whirling about, trying to come up with answers before he even knew what the questions might be. But Christmas?

'Yes, I suppose it is,' he said, lamely, with no idea what was coming next. It was only the end of September, for heaven's sake, and they'd hardly seen the back of summer yet. The kids' holiday memories, in all their poetic and artistic glory, were still pinned to the walls in the library. Christmas remained a distant nightmare he was nowhere near ready to contemplate.

'But if we want to do something well, I do think it's important to give ourselves plenty of time to plan, don't you, Oliver?'

'Yes, of course.'

'And now you're wondering why I've asked you here this morning? To be honest, it's to ask a favour. I would normally have felt able to count on Mrs Carter as usual, but, as you know, she'll be on maternity leave over the Christmas period, so I need someone else to step in. I was hoping that someone might be you. It's a job that calls for great enthusiasm, organisational skills, and a certain amount of ... well, stamina, for want of a better word.'

'Now I'm intrigued.'

'The nativity play, Oliver. Staff, children, a few willing parents, all working together, you know? We've done nativity plays for as long as I can remember. Tea-towel head dresses, the girls squabbling over who's going to be Mary, the boys desperate to avoid being in it at all, not to mention the plastic baby Jesus. Let's just say I have visions of something a little different this year. More lively. Costumes, music, perhaps bringing a more modern twist to it. Mrs Carter will be missed, of course, but her absence does give us an opportunity for change, do you see?'

Ollie nodded, not entirely sure that he did see at all, but it usually paid to agree with the boss. 'And, er, how do I fit into this exactly?'

'I want you to lead, Oliver. Plan, produce, put a team together, casting, rehearsals, all of that. Organise the whole thing. You know, from a different perspective, the whole thing seen through fresh eyes ...'

'Me?' Ollie pulled a chair over from a corner, deciding this was as good a time as any to sit down. He could be here for some time. 'But I have absolutely no experience of anything like that. I don't go to church, so the religious side of a nativity is ... well, not really my thing. I can't act, I can't sing, and I haven't been inside a theatre since I was at school myself. Hamlet, I think it was. I can still see him holding that mouldy old skull. Gave me nightmares for weeks afterwards.'

'Hardly the same thing. And I said organise it, Oliver. I'm not asking you to lead a church service, or to get up on stage and perform. Unless you want to, of course. Sometimes you don't know where your talents lie until you try. Now, take your class earlier this morning, for instance. I was watching through the window, and little Victoria Bennett threw an almost perfect javelin, didn't she? Never touched one before, I bet. We could even have a future champion on our hands.'

'Lucky fluke, more like.'

'That may be so, but she tried something new, and look what happened. So, my request stands. Go away and think about it if you like, but I would like to get the ball rolling sooner rather than later. Perhaps I could have your answer after lunch?'

***

He left it until the bell rang for the end of the school day. Well, half-past three still counted as after lunch, didn't it? The Head was busy with a mound of paperwork, a cup of coffee gone cold beside him, and Ollie knew better than to linger too long. They both knew he didn't want to do it, but neither of them seemed surprised when he said he would.

As he left he ran into Victoria Bennett and her mother, dithering about at the school gates, two younger kids clutching not quite dry paintings and clinging to the handle of a pram, which was occupied by presumably yet another Bennett, one that Ollie hadn't even known had been expected, let alone born. The mother was fishing about in an enormous shopping bag, pulling out various bits and pieces, including a brown mushy banana and a roll of nappy sacks, until she managed to locate and extricate a bright-green plastic purse. 'Now, only get the cheap stuff, you hear me?' she said, pushing a pound coin into her daughter's hand. 'And no dawdling on the way home.'

'Bread ...' she said, by way of explanation, standing aside to make room for Ollie to pass as Victoria ran off in the direction of the corner shop. 'She's a good girl, really. Just a bit scatty sometimes.' She laughed. 'But then, you'd know that, wouldn't you, sir?'

'Mrs Bennett, I've told you before, you don't have to call me sir. Mr Campbell, please ...'

'Right, sir, er, Mr Campbell. She doing all right is she, my Vicky? At her lessons and that?'

'Well, I can't speak for her work in class as I don't teach her, but she proved herself surprisingly good with the javelin this morning. Hidden talents there!'

'Really? I didn't know you were doing gardening with them now. Javelins, eh? They're those pretty little white ones, aren't they? That smell so nice. Well, fancy that, my Vicky with green fingers, eh? Who'd have thought it? Anyway, mustn't keep you sir. I've got the kids' tea to be getting on with as soon as I get back. If our Vicky remembers the bread and doesn't come back with a packet of seeds instead, that is. Ha, ha!'

Ollie stood for a moment gazing after her. He had absolutely no idea what she was talking about. But she had inadvertently reminded him that he needed to get some bread too. The last lot was going as mouldy as that old skull he remembered from Hamlet, and he'd need some for toasting if he was going to have beans again.

Chapter 13

Kate, 1986

I'd seen all the stuff in the papers about Louise Brown, the baby born through the miracle of IVF. I can't say I'd paid a lot of attention to the finer details of it at the time, but if I was going to have eggs taken out of me and messed about with in some test tube, there was a lot I needed to know.

'It's a complex process, and still a relatively new one, but it will all be fully explained at the clinic, if things get that far. But, of course, there is a waiting list,' Doctor Meredith said, slipping his specs off his nose and rubbing at the lenses with a tissue from the box on his desk. I couldn't help wondering if he was doing it just so he wouldn't have to look me in the eye. 'And I'm afraid,' he went on, 'that the NHS is unlikely to offer more than one or two attempts, even if you're deemed suitable for treatment. It's a very costly procedure with far from guaranteed results. And then, there's your age to consider ...'

'What do you mean, my age? I'm thirty-four. That's surely not too old, is it? I know lots of people who've had babies at my age. Or older. My aunt Nora was nearly forty.'

'Ah, but these other mothers, they may simply have delayed starting a family, Mrs Campbell. Or had a happy accident, shall we say? But things are different, in your case, where we know there is a problem ...'

'But we don't actually know what the problem is, do we?'

'Your infertility remains unexplained, certainly. But after this long without contraception and without a pregnancy, it's safe to say that there is a problem. Not with your husband's sperm, we know that much, but ...'

'Me. You mean that the problem is me.'

'I wouldn't have put it quite like that, no.' He put his glasses back on and picked up the thick wad of papers that made up my medical notes, skimming through the top couple of sheets and reminding himself of the facts. 'You appear to be ovulating, and your periods are reasonably regular, but our tests have shown a blockage in one of your tubes, so ...'

'Yes, I know that. But I still have the other one, don't I? It only needs one tube to make a baby.'

'It does indeed. But making a baby is not happening, is it? We have come to the point where you are in need of more specialist help. IVF may indeed be the best option left to you, other than waiting and hoping, which, as your doctor, is not a course of action I'd recommend. At your age ...'

'There you go again. My age.'

'What I'm trying to say is that IVF may well be our preferred choice but the NHS is very unlikely to offer treatment to a woman over the age of thirty-five. In fact, to be blunt ...'

'But I'm not thirty-five. Not yet.' This couldn't be right. What was he saying? That the sorry-we-can't-help-you signs would come down like steel shutters the moment some calendar said I was past my prime? No, I was still young. We both were. And we had a good marriage, Dan and me, a home of our own, a nursery all painted and waiting, things so many younger would-be parents didn't have to offer a child. 'I still have a year ...'

'That's true, but ...'

'But what?'

'The NHS waiting time is currently standing at two years, Mrs Campbell. I'm sorry, but by the time you reach the top of the list you will already be too old.'

***

'I suppose we could adopt.'

'Dan! I can't believe you just said that.'

'Lots of people do. And there are babies out there needing good homes, aren't there?'

'Maybe so, but why would we want to do that, when we can have one of our own?'

'But we can't, can we? Be realistic, sweetheart. It's not happening, and it might not ever happen. The one we lost just might be the only one we were ever meant to have.'

'*Meant* to have? You make it sound like the whole thing is pre-ordained somehow. Written in the stars, or something. Fate.'

'Maybe it is. But it's been a long time now and we have to face facts. So, I think we should start looking at alternatives, don't you? Before we really *are* too old.'

'How can you be so defeatist?' I knew I was starting to shout, but why on earth couldn't Dan see things the way I did? What did he expect us to do, exactly? Just because some doctor thought we were wasting our time, we should nod our heads like obedient sheep, lie down and take it, just give up? 'Don't you want a baby that looks like you? Or me? One that's really ours, one they can make from our own genes and stuff?'

'Make from our own genes and stuff?' He was laughing at me now. 'Very scientific, I'm sure ...'

'So I may not be Einstein, and I freely admit I don't know enough about how IVF works, but I do know I'm not ready to give up just yet. Maybe not ever. Having babies is a natural thing, isn't it? It's sort of what we're here for, to keep the species going. And if Auntie Nora could do it at forty, why the hell shouldn't I?'

'But IVF, Kate? Really? It's still quite experimental, you know. Needles and scans, and getting pumped full of dodgy drugs with who knows what kind of side-effects, and all the fertilising bit done in some lab somewhere without either of us even being there. It's so clinical, I don't think actually having sex comes into it at all. And you call that natural? Nobody even really knows why it works, or why it doesn't. And, let's be honest, it usually doesn't.'

'How do you know? What makes you such an expert all of a sudden?'

'Okay, so I've been reading up a bit about it. Researching things. It's what I always do, before I go into anything new. You know that.'

'Like reading *Which?* magazine, you mean? Customer reviews and checking out value for money? For God's sake, Dan, this isn't quite the same as buying a new washing machine or a fancy lawn mower, is it?'

'Why not? Look, if the NHS is a no-go, and you're so dead set against adoption, then there's only one way left, isn't there? And that's to go private. If we're going to invest a fortune in trying for this baby of yours ...'

'*Ours.*'

'Yes, ours. I meant ours. But, if we do, then I want to

make sure we choose the best clinic. Look at what's involved. Where they are. What they cost. The ones with the best results ...'

'You mean it?' I hadn't seen that coming. 'No adoption? We can really do this? IVF? And find a way to pay for it?'

'If it means that much to you, yes. But it's not cheap, Kate. We could try it once, twice, God knows how many times, totally bankrupt ourselves, and still end up with nothing.'

'Or with a baby.'

'Yes. If we're lucky, with a baby.'

I slung my arms around his neck and hugged him so tightly he had to push me away before I stopped the air getting to his lungs. 'Thank you, Dan,' I said, the tears flooding into my eyes. 'And it will work. Whatever the stars have to say about it, luck will be on our side. I just know it will.'

Chapter 14

Beth, 2017

Beth slathered a big dollop of rose-scented hand cream onto her palms and rubbed her hands together, fingers slipping between each other and up and down over her thumbs, trying to smooth the roughness of her skin and remove the lingering smell of perming lotion. She always wore gloves when chemicals were involved, but somehow the smells still got through. Her nails were looking ragged too. Time for a bit of a pampering session with a giant emery board, a little bottle of shiny varnish and a much bigger bottle of Pinot in front of a mushy DVD.

She rolled over on the bed and let her face sink into the softness of the pillow. It had been a long and tiring day and she felt inordinately glad that she didn't have to go out tonight. Jake calling to cancel had come as a welcome relief, her comfy pyjamas holding a lot more appeal than the tight jeans and t-shirt and painful push-up bra she'd lined up for their planned evening at the pub.

There had been a time when not seeing Jake would have hurt. When missing out on his company would have left her feeling abandoned and wondering what he was up to instead. Now she hadn't even thought to ask. Out of sight, out of mind? A vision of Ollie popped into her head. Ollie without Laura, still hurting, but gradually learning to live without her. What if he finally gave up on Laura altogether and started looking for someone else? What a disaster that would be, just as things were finally looking like they could actually work out for them.

A baby, at last. She could hardly believe it, and the urge to rush straight over and tell her brother had been nagging at her ever since they'd got back from the spa. It was only Laura's very real threat to disappear if she did that held her back.

As for Jake, well, he was a very different kettle of fish, as her gran would no doubt say. There wasn't much chance of him pining for her if they split up, not the way Ollie had for Laura. Oh, he'd probably knock back a drink or two, but he did a lot of that anyway. And as for babies ... she really couldn't imagine him as any kind of a father, let alone a willing or doting one.

Jake had been a part of her life for a long time, ever

since school, when they'd found themselves unexpectedly kissing in someone's kitchen at an end-of-term party. Neither of them could quite recall how that had happened, but they'd liked it, or what they could remember of it through the inevitable hangovers that followed, and had both been up for a repeat performance as soon as possible. She hadn't really looked at anyone else since then, or, she was rather ashamed to say, kissed anyone else either, let alone slept with anyone. She wasn't absolutely sure that Jake could say the same, but sometimes it was easier not to know.

Did she love Jake? It was a question she tried to avoid thinking about. What they had fell much more into the friends-with-benefits camp than the true-love, everlasting-passion category. She'd watched enough romantic films and read enough Mills and Boon to know that something was missing. No shiver of anticipation ran through her, no spark lit up in her eyes, or in his, for that matter, when he came into a room. But being with Jake was easy. She knew what he was thinking, most of the time anyway. Knew his opinions, his likes and dislikes. She was even able to finish his sentences, the way old married couples do. She was all too familiar with the state of his underwear and the holes in his socks too, and with the little wrinkly bits between his legs where there wasn't much hair, and with the rather smelly workings of his digestive system after they'd eaten a curry. Maybe this was what marriages were built on, the inside-out knowledge of another person, the everyday mundanity of bodily functions and boxers left on the bathroom floor when they should be in a laundry basket, and not on that elusive heart-stopping desire she would so badly love to feel, even if only the once, just to know what it was really like.

But, at the moment anyway, there was no question of marriage. Well, if there was, it was a question he had never asked. Just the thought of it happening and maybe taking her by surprise one day, Jake on one knee brandishing a ring she'd had no part in choosing, was a worrying one. What would she say if he did? What would everyone else say if he didn't? These things were expected after a while, weren't they?

She was so glad she'd resisted moving in with Jake when his flatmate Tony had left. There was something about the timing of it all that had made it pretty obvious that him asking her was a lot more about helping to pay the rent without the hassle of advertising for a replacement than it was about two lovers who couldn't bear to be apart. Here she had her own space, especially since Ollie had moved out and into the flat when he'd hooked up with Laura. Jenny, who'd shared a room with her for years, had dragged all her belongings across the landing within hours of Ollie leaving and decamped to his old room, which, in the absolute certainty that he had found the love of his life and was never likely to come back, she'd immediately painted pink.

'Beth?' Jenny flung the door open now and barged in uninvited. The fact that this was no longer her room seemed not to matter a jot. So much for Beth having her own space. 'Oh, there you are. Mum wants to know if you want any dinner, seeing as you're not going out?'

'What is it?'

'Some kind of lentil stew, by the look of it. And sweet potatoes.'

Beth wrinkled her nose. The smell of it was already finding its way up the stairs. 'No, make some excuse for me, will you? Say I've got a headache or I'm asleep or something. Not sure I can face all that veggie stuff tonight. I might just slip out for some chips later.'

'Oooh, really? Can you get me some too? Not too much vinegar. Thanks.'

'Jenny, can we talk about ...'

But before Beth could even finish her sentence her sister was gone again, leaving the bedroom door wide open and the cooking smells drawing closer and closer by the second.

Beth pulled out her mobile and scrolled down to Ollie's number. She hadn't spoken to her brother in several days, which she knew was not a good idea. Left too long to his own devices, he was likely to go a bit off the rails again, drinkwise, and knowing what she now did, she couldn't let that happen. And she needed to make sure he kept away from women too. Laura was the only girl for Ollie. Everyone knew that, and she needed to make it her mission now to keep him on the straight and narrow until Laura was ready to confess all. A father! Okay, so Ollie didn't know that, and was apparently not allowed to know, but he was going to have to start acting more responsibly, like a good father should. And, while Jenny seemed to have appointed herself Laura's best friend and guardian of her secret at all costs, it was going to be up to Beth to take Ollie under her wing and make absolutely sure that he did just that. Her nails would have to wait for another night. Mission Ollie came first.

'Hey, Ollie,' she said when he picked up. 'How's things? Yeah, fine. I'm just sitting here twiddling my thumbs, with nothing but one of Mum's weird rabbit-food concoctions on offer, so I thought I'd see what you're up to. I don't suppose you fancy fish and chips, do you? My treat.'

'Fine. I don't have any other plans. Twenty minutes?' He sounded a bit down. She'd have to fix that.

She pulled on some jogging bottoms and a sweatshirt and checked her purse to make sure she actually had enough cash to pay for the food. The customers had been generous today with the tips but they tended to come mostly in fifty pence pieces. Would the chip shop take that many? She laughed to herself. Money's money. They'd be unlikely to turn her away, especially once two fat pieces of cod were wrapped and starting to go cold on the counter.

She took a last longing look at the bottle of nail varnish and the pile of DVDs that could have made up her evening and crept down the stairs, slipping into her trainers and grabbing her coat before closing the front door as quietly as she could behind her. She knew what her mum could be like when there was a huge vat of something yellow and close to inedible bubbling on the cooker and not enough people to eat it, and she was definitely not going to get caught.

***

It was a bit chilly to sit eating on a wall outside, but the warmth seeping through the greasy paper onto her hands and the steam rising from the freshly cooked fish soon worked their magic.

'How's work?' Beth found the whole idea of teaching as boring as hell, and knew nothing about sport whatsoever, but she had to at least pretend to be interested.

'Well, they haven't found me out yet, if that's what you mean.' Ollie blew on a chip and pushed it into his mouth in one piece.

'That's not what I meant at all.'

'Look, Beth ...' He swallowed. 'I know what you're asking. Yes, I still like a drink from time to time. No, I do not have a secret stash in the games cupboard. Well, not any more. And no, I do not drink in working hours. Okay? It's not as if you don't like a drop or two yourself. Jenny's told me about you and the mini-bar. So, what was that all about anyway? Your little trip away.'

Thank God it was dark or he might have seen her blush, and blushing was not something Beth did often. Still, she couldn't think about the spa break without remembering Laura, all pregnant and pale, and so scared that history was going to repeat itself and another miscarriage was going to happen at any moment. Laura begging them to keep quiet, and threatening all sorts if they didn't.

She did feel guilty about not telling him. They didn't have secrets, never had, and just thinking about it was eating her up, but she couldn't take the risk that Laura meant what she'd said about disappearing and that none of them would ever see her again. At least, this way, there was some chance that everything would work out all right once the baby was born.

'Earth to Beth! You were miles away there. The spa? I asked what that was all about?'

'Oh, you know Jenny. It was just a last-minute deal, and she can't resist a bargain. We did a bit of swimming, lay around a lot, ate way too much salad! And, okay, so I might have enjoyed a bottle or three of wine, but we were on holiday so it doesn't count.'

'One rule for you, and another for me, eh? Maybe I should go on a little holiday of my own, pack my case with whisky and get away from you lot nagging me.'

'We both know you can't. School rules. You're trapped until half term, mate, whether you like it or not.'

'I do like it, actually. Work gives me something to do, something to focus on. I'm not all that fond of my own company. No, I was only joking about a holiday. It's the last thing I need. That long summer break was not good for me.'

'We noticed.'

They ate in silence for a while, the breath floating out from their mouths and noses like smoky wisps into the chilly evening air.

'Anyway,' Ollie said at last, 'the Head must think I'm responsible enough. He's given me a job to do.'

'You've *got* a job!'

'I mean a special job, like an extra-curricular task. Not that I had much choice about it, but I intend to take it seriously and give it my best shot. You are now looking at the director of the next school nativity play.'

'*You?*' Beth almost choked on a chip. 'Directing a play? You've never even been to watch one.'

'Oh, yes, I have, Miss Smartypants. It was *Hamlet*. Or was it *Macbeth*?'

'You can't even remember which one it was! And it's hardly the same thing. And, besides, that was years ago, when we were kids. I got out of going. Do you remember? I said I had toothache.'

'Oh, yeah. Hang on, you *said* you had toothache? You mean you didn't really?'

'Course I didn't. Shakespeare and me – we don't get on. Never have. Now, give me *The Sound of Music* and I'd have been there like a shot.'

Ollie laughed. 'Since when did you get to be such a good liar?'

If only you knew, Beth thought, turning her head just in case he could see it in her eyes. 'Only when I really have to be,' she said, and pushed the last of her fish into her mouth to make sure she wasn't tempted to say anything else.

Chapter 15

Kate, 1986

I was sitting on an underground train with my thighs squeezed tightly together and my knees shaking, trying so hard not to wet myself that I almost missed my stop. Buildings and trees shot past the grimy windows in a blur, and the man opposite was chewing gum with his mouth slightly open and one foot tapping in time to the rattling noises of the train as it whizzed along the track.

It was one of those days when every detail counts. A day when progress would be checked and decisions would be made. I remember that it was cloudy, that the walk from tube to clinic took exactly seven minutes, that one shoe was rubbing and I was in danger of getting a blister. I even remember what knickers I was wearing. Blue, with lacy edges, and a tiny bow at the waist. I just hoped I could keep them dry long enough to get there.

The clinic was as quiet and calming as ever, all pale walls and deep, plush carpets, hoovered to within an inch of their lives. Nothing like the NHS hospital, with its long corridors and plastic chairs, and that odd smell that seemed to hang around every inch of the place. No, this was how the other half lived. I could so easily get used to private medicine and all the hotel-like luxury that came with it, but I really hoped I wouldn't have to.

When I emerged from the lift, a few women were sitting silently in a circle around the water dispenser, swigging from throwaway cups like there was no tomorrow. Some had their partners with them, but I wasn't sure what good they were doing. Nobody spoke. I couldn't join them. Another twenty seconds and my bladder would be bursting open like Niagara Falls, gallons of water tumbling out and flooding everything in sight. I made it to the pristine white loo just in time to tug my trousers down before it was too late.

'Just start again, Mrs Campbell,' the girl at reception said when I reported in. 'It happens. Rather a lot, believe me! There's plenty of water. Just drink as much as you can and give me a nod when you're full up again. You won't lose your slot, it'll just be put back a while.' She pointed me towards the circle of women, and one or two looked up and smiled, but I could tell they were all intent on the same task. Like drivers at a petrol station, all trying to cram just one more drop into the tank before the gauge told them there wasn't room for more.

I don't know how long it took me, but I read three magazines from cover to cover while I was waiting. Without so much as a poster on the wall to distract me, and no TV, there was nothing else to do. Women came and went, names were called, doors opened and closed. Who knew a bladder could hold so much?

'Joanne will see you now, Mrs Campbell. Just through there ...'

The scan, when I finally made it through to the inner sanctum, showed a cluster of ripening follicles. I couldn't pretend to know what a ripe follicle was, but according to Joanne, the sonographer, it was good news. The drugs I'd been sniffing up my nose for the last couple of weeks, and the needles they'd been shoving into my bottom, had done their job. I had eggs! Enough to feed an army, by the look of things. We were almost ready for the next stage now. Collecting them. Visions of farmyard chickens and wicker baskets came to mind, but when Joanne slid the scanner through the jelly on my stomach and pushed just a bit too hard, all thoughts, except where the nearest toilet was, flew out of my head. Niagara was back, with a vengeance.

I was booked in for Tuesday. An early start, with an empty stomach, an anaesthetic, a couple of incisions, and wham! My eggs would be out and raring to go. This felt exciting. Scary as hell, but exciting.

Dan moaned when I told him. Tuesdays were team-meeting mornings, he said, and missing one would not be favourably looked upon. Missing taking me to the clinic and being there when I woke up could look a lot worse, I reminded him. Especially with the marks from my heels embedded, and likely to be stinging like mad for some considerable time, in the middle of his bollocks. And how exactly was he going to supply the necessary sperm if he was ensconced in the boardroom at work?

He wisely decided to call in sick and come with me.

***

It didn't work, but, of course, you know that. First attempts rarely did, so they told us, but that didn't make things feel any better. I wonder now if fate was trying to tell us something, to guide our hands. Was that when we should have accepted things as they were and given up? All that 'playing at God' stuff was too technical, too scientific, too clinical. I felt uneasy about it. Test tubes were cold glass receptacles. Hard. As hard as having to use them. Not warm flesh, a myriad of cells pulsating, burrowing, nurturing. Test tubes weren't wombs.

Where was the love, the action of body against body, the tried and trusted method that had seen millions of women create babies since time began? Sex for us – oh, I know you probably don't want to hear about that – but sex was becoming an act carried out solely with a purpose in mind, something we only did because there might be an end in sight. But that end was slipping further and further away from us. So, what was the point?

The truth was staring me in the face. We were never going to make a baby on our own. Never.

It was already costing us a fortune, our peace of mind, our sanity. It was straining at the bonds of our marriage, pulling us as tight as an elastic band that could snap at any moment, but I couldn't let it go. Not now we had come so far. Bang, bang, bang, it kept thumping away at me, like a tiny insistent heartbeat, pounding in my head, in my heart. And, for the first time, I realised just how badly I wanted it. To beat the system, beat the odds, stick two fingers up at my stupid useless body and let science make us a family.

I think I wanted it then much more than Dan did. More than anything in the world. But how much of that was real, and how much simply because it was something I couldn't have? Because some unseen hand was denying me, pushing me down, and I didn't want to be pushed?

Was that when I got stubborn, dug my heels in, started throwing my toys out of the pram? I can be such a spoilt brat sometimes.

***

Dan sat at the table with a notepad and a calculator, working out what it had all cost and how on earth we were going to pay the electricity bill, let alone think about trying again. I just sat on the sofa with a hot water bottle and cried.

I'd done my best to make it happen. Lay down for hours, willing the three tiny little embryos they'd picked out as the most likely to succeed to hang on in there and not fall out. Taken leave from work to avoid the stress and the questions and being vertical for any longer than necessary. Had no alcohol, no spicy food and no sex, for almost a fortnight. Prayed to a God I wasn't sure I believed in, but what was there to lose in doing it anyway? But there was no mistaking the end result. It had failed. I had failed. I was bleeding. A lot.

I can't pretend that any of it had been painless or easy, but there had been a feeling of hope lingering behind it all, through every step of the treatment, and in knowing that we were doing something positive at last, not just sitting and waiting for it to happen all by itself. Now even that was gone.

'We'll have to give it a year,' Dan said, putting his pen down. 'There's no chance of saving enough before that. And, before you even say it, no, we can't borrow it either. The mortgage is manageable, but taking on any more debt just wouldn't make sense.'

'Can't we just forget about being sensible for once?'

'Oh, Kate. This is all still so recent. So raw. It's like being kicked in the teeth, isn't it? Neither of us is going to be thinking straight for a while. Can't we leave it a while before we start thinking about another try?'

'But the longer we leave it, the older we'll be. And the older we are – the older *I* am – the less chance of it working at all. You must see that?'

'Yes, of course I do, but ...'

'So we have to try again, Dan. Not in a year, but now. Before it's too late. There has to be a way of finding the money, surely?'

'I don't know, Kate. I really don't know.'

'But you'll think about it? You won't give up? Because I can't give up. Not while there's still a chance. I don't want us to look back at all this in ten years' time, or twenty, and say 'If only we'd found a way'...'

Dan got up and walked over to the sofa, flopped down beside me and gave me a hug. 'I know. I do. Honestly. But let's sleep on it, shall we? Wait for this period to pass and your body to recover a bit before we do anything. Take a month or two off from it, at least. I'd kind of like to see your bum without pinholes in it, for a change. In fact, I'd quite like to see your bum, full stop. It's been a while ...'

'Is that all you can think about? Sex? For God's sake, Dan. Now, of all days. It's not as if sex is going to make a baby, so what's the bloody point in doing it at all?'

I wasn't looking at him, but I could feel him pull away from me, even before his angry words started to spit their way out of his mouth just inches from my ear.

'I can't believe you just said that. Is that all I am to you nowadays? A sperm machine? No baby, no sex? How about doing it for love? To feel close to each other again, to give some comfort? Have fun, even? Do you think having to do it into a sample bottle was my idea of fun? Because, believe me, it wasn't. It was bloody humiliating, to tell you the truth. That nasty little room, the pile of mucky magazines, and knowing there were people right outside the door who knew exactly what I was doing in there? No, I did it because I had to, because the clinic needed it, then and there, made to order, but as far as I'm concerned, there's still a lot to be said for good old-fashioned penetration. If I can still remember how, it's been so fucking long ...'

'There's no need to swear.' I turned round and stared at him, my husband, suddenly ragingly angry, and why? Because I wasn't jumping straight into bed with my legs in the air? Or because he too was struggling and lashing out, looking for someone to blame?

'No need? There's every need. This whole IVF business is taking away any kind of normality. We don't talk about anything but scans and embryos. We don't go out any more because you can't, or won't, drink, and we don't have the spare cash anyway. If I so much as try to cuddle up to you in bed I get pushed away. This isn't what I signed up for, Kate. I want a baby, of course I do, but I want you more. *Us*. I want us. The way we were before.'

'But we can't be like that now.' I was trying really hard not to raise my voice, not to give our neighbours on the other side of the wall any more gossip to dine out on than they'd already had. 'We're not those same people any more, are we? The carefree couple, with all the time in the world and nothing to think about but ourselves. We're ... we're ...'

'We're what? Go on, tell me, because I'd like to know.'

I tried to grab for his hand, to calm him down a bit, to stop him shouting and just make him talk and listen, and be reasonable, but he wouldn't have it. 'We're patients, I suppose. Infertility patients, or clients, or whatever they like to call us. Things are out of our hands. We're dependent on other people now, to give us what we want. To provide the miracle.'

'Patients? We're not sick, Kate. We're just ...'

'Yes? Just what? Doing it for the sheer hell of it? On a whim? No, Dan. We are patients, because we need help. Medical help. We're not on some stupid joyride, able to hop off when we've had enough. This is real and it's important, and I'm not getting off until we've seen it through to the end.'

'Whatever the end is.'

'A baby, of course. What did you think I meant?'

'You tell me. You're the one with all the answers. But as for patience ... I don't have a lot of that left.' And then he walked out, slamming the door so hard behind him it dislodged a picture on the wall. I sat for a long time, staring at it, wanting to get up and straighten it but not having the energy. And, all the while, my embryos were swimming away, tiny dots of matter, lost in the blood that was leaking out of me, never to be seen again. Didn't he understand that? Didn't he care?

I clutched the hot water bottle in its knitted cover and cried. It smelled of rubber and soggy wool, and it had gone almost cold, so there wasn't much hope of it helping, but right then I couldn't think of anything that would. The future opened up in front of me like a big black, gaping hole. There was no knowing how many more attempts it might take. There was one woman I'd met at the clinic who was on her seventh and somehow she kept on smiling, kept on wishing and hoping. How did she do that? We'd only just begun, but already I didn't know how much more pain and disappointment I would be able to take.

Chapter 16

Jenny, 2017

Laura was still staying with her Aunt Clara. Jenny had wheedled her new mobile number out of her so she didn't have to keep calling the house and trying to get past what must be the most protective aunt in all of Christendom.

'Are you sure you don't want me to do anything?' she said now, whispering into her phone in the kitchen so Natalie wouldn't hear her through the wall. 'If you won't let me tell Ollie, then at least let me help you. I hate to think of you all alone and coping with everything by yourself. And we're family, or as good as. Money? How about money?'

Laura laughed. 'Jen, you don't have any money. You've never had any money, as long as I've known you. But I'm fine, honestly. And I'm not on my own. Clara's been great. She's like a mum to me. Always has been, ever since my own mum died. And she's given me a roof over my head, a safe haven, a comfy room. You of all people know how important that is ...'

'I do. Of course I do, but ...'

'Look, Clara doesn't charge me any rent, and I have enough put by to pay my way in food and clothes. Once the baby's born and I know everything is all right, then, and only then, I will tell Ollie he's a dad, I promise. And we'll see what happens next. Okay? Let's be honest, he may not even want me back after I walked out on him, but we'll see ... Now, stop fussing and let me get some sleep. It's tiring, you know, having a big lump like this to contend with all day long!'

'Talking about Ollie again?'

'Not *that* big lump.' Laura giggled. 'How's he doing, anyway? I do miss him. And I worry about him, you know, but there are only so many worries I can deal with at once, and keeping this baby alive and well has to come first. You do get that, don't you?'

'Of course. Go on, you get off to bed. Ollie will be fine. We all take it in turns to babysit him. And you give my little niece or nephew a big kiss from me.'

'How exactly am I supposed to manage that?'

'Kiss your hand and rub it on your tummy. That'll have to do until it's born. Here ... Catch this!' Jenny blew a loud kiss down the phone and rang off.

Laura had sounded okay, but it could all be just a

front. Still, there wasn't much she could do about it from this distance, and you can't help someone who doesn't want to be helped. She knew that only too well, from some of the cantankerous old buggers she had to deal with at work.

'Who were you talking to so furtively?' Natalie had come in behind her and was getting milk from the fridge.

'Nobody.'

'Do you always blow goodnight kisses to nobody?' Natalie teased. 'I think you just might be hiding something, missy. A secret boyfriend, maybe? Go on, cough up. What's his name?'

'Never you mind.' Jenny couldn't resist teasing her, leading her on. One whiff of a bit of gossip and her sisters would be hanging around her like moths around a flame. James. That's what she'd say if they forced it out of her. She'd always fancied having a boyfriend called James. Six feet tall, dark wavy hair, big brown smouldering eyes. Ha! If only!

***

Old Mr Jenkins was refusing his porridge again. He was sitting at the small table in the corner, still wearing his pyjamas, and the TV across the other side of the room was on way too loud. Jenny only had twenty minutes here and then she'd have to leave to get to her next client.

'Come on, Mr J. Eat a little bit, just for me? I've put honey on it, just the way you like it. We still have to get you washed and dressed, and the bed made before I go. And you haven't told me what you fancy for lunch yet. Shall I make you up a nice sandwich and leave it in the fridge? Cheese and pickle, or ham? You like a nice bit of ham, don't you?'

The old man didn't answer. He was trying to peer round her to get a better view of the TV screen. She suspected he'd taken a liking to that Susannah Reid. His face always seemed to perk up when she was on.

'I'll turn it off if you don't co-operate.' She grabbed for the remote control and waved it in front of him.

'You wouldn't dare!'

'Oh, so you do speak, then? I was beginning to wonder if you'd lost your voice. Or your hearing! That volume really is turned up much too high, you know.'

'Stops me having to listen to you.' He was teasing her now, the twinkle back in his eyes, but he didn't object when she turned it down.

'Bathroom. Now!'

'Oh, all right. Have you got my clothes out ready? I thought I might wear the navy pinstripe today, and my best dress shirt with the ruffles ... and my Eton tie of course.'

'Oh, get away with you, you old devil.'

'You sound just like my Vera. She used to nag me too.'

'You miss her, don't you?'

'Of course I miss her. Every day. Lovely blonde hair she had, just like yours, when she was young. So pretty, she was too. And she used to tell me what to wear, just like you do. Not that I minded. Not really one for fashion, me.'

'Right! So, it's up to me, is it? It'll be your corduroy trousers and the green jumper, then, okay? Or I'll leave you in your PJs all day.'

'Suits me. Not as if I'm going anywhere, so nobody's going to see what I wear anyway. Except you. And you don't count.'

'You won't be saying that if I leave you with no lunch, now, will you? Come on, let's get you scrubbed behind the ears and settled in your armchair, or you'll be getting me the sack.'

'Right you are.' He heaved himself slowly out of the chair, spooning a last dollop of cold porridge into his mouth and spilling half of it down the front of his pyjama top. 'And I'll have cheese please. Getting a bit sick of ham all the time. Make a nice change, it will. Variety's the spice of life, so they say. Not that there's much of it going on around here.'

A quarter of an hour later Jenny was back outside

and waiting for the bus. Getting about without a car was a real hassle, but she was lucky most of her clients lived within walking distance of each other, a couple even in the same sheltered block. It was only Mrs Crabbe who was far enough out to warrant the bus ride.

Laura had certainly been right about one thing last night. She didn't have any money, and probably never would while she carried on like this. Most of her friends were either forging proper careers for themselves or had already settled down with children, but she wasn't ready for that. Not at her age. The trouble was that she still couldn't decide what she really wanted to do with her life. Having watched her dad juggling piles of paper and fretting over a calculator year in and year out, and Natalie coming home drained from another day stuck at a desk with a phone in her hand, she knew she couldn't face an office job. At least the others were doing something ... improving, for want of a better word. Beth cutting women's hair, making them look and feel better about themselves, Ollie running kids around a chilly field, keeping them fit and healthy and secretly hoping he'd one day discover a future Olympic champion.

It was certainly the jobs that would bring her into contact with people, real people she could help in some way, which held the greatest pull. Becoming a carer wasn't something she'd planned, but in many ways it

suited her. Coming out of school with a set of average qualifications and a need to earn some cash, she'd dabbled with shop work before seeing an ad asking for carers, thought it looked easy enough and had fallen into the job more as a stopgap than a long-term career. Still, it had its rewards. Some of the people she visited were difficult, resentful of her presence, convinced they could still manage alone when it was clear to everyone else that they couldn't. But the majority were okay. Usually quite frail, often lonely and glad of a friendly face every morning and evening, a helping hand when they needed it, someone to talk to.

The bus pulled up with a squeak of brakes and she climbed on. It was only four stops to get to Mrs Crabbe's, but after visiting three elderly clients and a hip replacement already this morning, she lacked the energy to walk. She settled in a seat near the front, yawning as she gazed out of the window and already looking forward to getting away from Mrs Crabbe's and back home, putting her feet up for a while before the evening shift.

Hang on! Wasn't that Jake over there? Beth's Jake? She turned her head as the bus eased past. It wasn't the best of angles and the window was grimy, but it was definitely him, leaning against a wall by the green, sort of half sitting on it, his legs stretched out ahead of him across the pavement, his arms locked tight around the

waist of some girl whose face she couldn't see. Partly because the girl had her back towards her, but mainly because she was bent forwards and pressed against Jake, nose to nose, her lips locked onto his.

The bus had gone right past them now and was speeding away, and Jenny was twisting around in her seat, trying to get a final glimpse before they disappeared from sight. Jake wasn't looking up at all. Too busy sucking the girl's face off to notice a bus or who was on it, let alone realise he'd been rumbled.

My God! How on earth was she going to tell Beth? Or should she say nothing, pretend she hadn't seen a thing, let her sister find out for herself what a slime ball her so-called boyfriend really was? Don't shoot the messenger, that's what they said in situations like this. She knew there'd be hell to pay when Beth heard about it, especially if she figured out that Jenny had known all along and not told her, so she'd have to say something. But Beth could be very fiery when she wanted to be, and getting caught in the firing line, innocent bringer of bad news or not, didn't seem to Jenny like the ideal place to be.

She was still trying to work out what to do when she looked up to see Mrs Crabbe's house outside the window and she had to jump up and dash for the doors to get out before they slid shut behind her and the bus moved off again.

Chapter 17

Kate, 1987

Dan had gone down to visit his parents. I could have gone too, but there was no knowing when I might need to ask for more time off work, either for treatment or just to rest afterwards. Our IVF attempt had taken its toll, and I was still feeling drained, listless, trying to find someone to blame, yet constantly blaming myself. It seemed a waste to use up precious leave on family visits, something we could do at any time. But I didn't try to stop Dan from going alone.

I wondered how much he'd told them. Our infertility problems weren't something Dan found easy to talk about, not even with those closest to him, and certainly not down the phone. Perhaps that was part of the reason he'd gone, to tell them all about it face to face. Maybe even to ask for money, a loan, a gift, a donation, whatever, so we could get started on our next attempt. Either

that, or he'd gone to get away from me. Things hadn't been easy for a while, I had to admit. A few days apart could be just what we both needed.

After he left, I watched TV and went to bed early. I slept badly, turning over and over in the bed with nobody to bump into, my dreams a swirling mess of jumbled images that reminded me of the insides of my own abdomen as seen on the ultrasound screen, and left me feeling more exhausted when I woke up than when I'd gone to bed. I sat in the kitchen the next morning, hugging a cup of strong coffee, wondering if I should have gone with him, and thinking about my own parents.

Dad had been gone so long now I was having trouble picturing his face. Remembering the coffin lying at the front of the crematorium, covered in flowers, was easy. The muted music playing, the mourners filing past after the service, just me and Mum waiting behind to say a silent goodbye before it slid away for the final time. I didn't think I'd ever forget that moment, yet I was struggling with the good stuff. The bike rides, the Christmases, the holidays in caravans, building sandcastles on the beach. I knew they were all there, at the back of my mind, but sometimes they just wouldn't come to the front, not with any clarity. They were all just days that blurred into one another, as if they had happened to someone else.

I hadn't seen Mum for a few weeks, hadn't told her much about the treatment, except that it had happened and hadn't worked. She and Trevor had announced at Christmas that they'd decided to get married, which hadn't come as that much of a surprise, I suppose, after they'd lived together for so long, but I still felt uneasy about it. This man who was living in Dad's house, sleeping in his bed, taking over his life, wasn't Dad and never would be.

Mum wanted me to get involved with the wedding, help her plan things, choose flowers, be her bridesmaid, and I was putting it off. Waiting. Making a baby was my first priority, and once I had that in the bag, I could have coped with just about anything, Mum's wedding included. Now it hadn't happened, I knew I couldn't put things off any longer. I had run out of excuses.

I'd have to go over there. She'd be thinking something was wrong, that she'd upset me in some way. Just as she'd announced her big news, I'd done a disappearing act.

It was a Sunday, late in January, cold but bright outside. I decided to walk, pulling on boots and wrapping a scarf around my neck, eager to take in some fresh air and clear my head. It was about three miles to Mum's, which was just about manageable, one way at least. I could always get the bus back if I didn't feel up to a repeat performance, and depending on how long I stayed. I didn't much fancy walking home alone once it got dark.

As I turned the corner into Rose Walk – I loved that name, even though there was hardly a rose in sight – I could see Trevor's car on Mum's drive, and the little rivulets of soapy water that had run away from it and were already semi-frozen on the pavement outside. He'd obviously been giving it a wash, and the house windows too, by the look of things.

'Kate!' Mum was wearing an apron and peeling off a mucky rubber glove so she could open the door without covering it in grease. 'Why didn't you tell us you were coming? I'm cleaning the oven – horrible job – but come on in.' She stood back to allow me room to squeeze past her. 'No Dan?'

'No, he's gone down to his parents'. So, it's just me. You sure it's okay? If you're busy, I can always come another day.'

'Of course it's okay, you daft thing. It's lovely to see you. Go straight into the kitchen, but mind the bowl on the floor. It started out full of hot soapy water but it's all gone a horrible greasy brown now, and you wouldn't believe how many sponges I've got through already. It's only been a few weeks since I did it the last time. With just the two of us, you'd think the damn thing would stay clean a bit longer, wouldn't you? It's not as if we cook roast dinners every day of the week.'

'Not cooking one today then, obviously!'

'Oh, dear. Did you want to stay for lunch? You can, of course, but I was only going to have a bowl of soup.'

'It's all right, Mum. I wasn't hinting. Soup will be great, if you've got enough to go round.'

She lifted the big plastic washing-up bowl and carried it over to the sink, carefully tipping its contents away, then went back to close the oven door. 'That'll have to do, I think. It's looking better than it was anyway. Now, tea? Coffee? Or I've got some of that nice lemonade you like. The old-fashioned kind.'

'Tea's fine, Mum. Where's Trevor? I saw the sparkly car, so I guess he's in cleaning mode today too, is he?'

'Oh, he took a stroll down to the pub as soon as his chores were done. I don't suppose he'll be back for a good while yet.'

'Didn't you want to go with him? You always used to go with Dad, didn't you?'

'No, love. Not always, though I sometimes wish I had.'

'You'd get Mrs Blackwell in to babysit me. I remember that. Saturday nights. And you used to leave me a Mars bar to eat while I watched TV, but she was only allowed to give it to me if I was good.'

'Which you usually were. Or so she'd tell us when we got home.' Mum shook her head, as if to clear her thoughts. 'But I've never been one for lunchtime drinking, you know that, and Trevor's got a chess match planned, I think. With George from next door. They often do that, find a quiet table near the fire, get the pints lined up, and then they can be there for hours. Not my idea of fun! No, I'm much happier here, at home. Besides, it's so much easier to clean without him under my feet.'

You enjoy getting rid of him for a while, more like, I thought, a bit uncharitably. She used to stick to Dad like glue, from what I could remember. Couldn't bear to let him out of her sight. That was love, the real thing, like being two halves of the same person. It was what Dan and I had been like for so long, and hopefully would be again, as soon as this IVF nightmare was out of the way. It was such a shame Mum was having to settle for second best this time around. For lanky Trevor, with his baggy jumpers, and his boring chess games. Still, they weren't married yet, were they? Anything could happen.

She placed two cups of tea on the table and sat down next to me. 'So?'

'So, what?'

'Oh, you know what I mean. Don't make me have to drag it out of you. I've hardly seen you lately. How's the treatment going?'

'Not much to say, really. You already know it didn't work the first time, and I can't say I'm looking forward to doing it all again. It's not all that pleasant. Lots of drugs and injections, all designed to help me make eggs, which I did, thankfully, so that bodes well. And they fertilised them okay, in their little dish. It's not actually a test tube, despite what the papers like to call it. But when they were back inside me – three of them – they didn't take. I'm starting to think it's not meant to be. That something inside me must have rejected them, killed them off.'

'Don't be silly. Of course it's meant to be. It's early days yet. It will happen, in its own good time. And blaming yourself isn't going to help at all.'

I sipped at my tea and gazed out of the window at the garden, which still had a surprising amount of greenery for the time of year, even though the lawn was looking a bit sorry for itself in places. A lone crocus had pushed its way through the hard earth and was flashing its tiny yellow petals at the foot of the one and only tree.

Mum followed my gaze. 'See?' she said, laying a hand over mine. 'New life popping up where and when you least expect it. I don't even remember planting that one. Your time will come ...'

'I hope so. But it's all so difficult, so stressful, so bloody expensive.'

'How much is it all costing? If you don't mind me asking. Can I help out in any way?'

'It's been thousands already, Mum. And it will be even more thousands if we want to carry on. Whether it works or not, it costs just the same. And we don't have it.'

I saw her shake her head, a blast of air blow out through pursed lips.

'We can't even book another try until we've saved up again. Just the drugs on their own run into hundreds every time. I don't suppose you have a hidden fortune in old fivers stashed under the mattress, do you?'

'I'm afraid not.' She stirred her tea, slowly, her head lowered. 'But, believe me, love, if I did, you'd be more than welcome to it.'

'The price of becoming a granny, eh? I bet you didn't have all this trouble, did you? Getting pregnant with me?'

'No, I can't say that I did. If anything, you came a bit too easily. A little accident, let's say. Right out of the blue. Not exactly planned! And we were still so young, only married a couple of months.'

'You didn't consider having an abortion, though?'

'Kate! What a thing to say. Of course not. How could you even think such a thing? You were the best thing that ever happened to us, your dad and me. After we got over the initial shock, that is.'

'But you didn't have any more, did you?'

'You know we didn't.'

'Was I that bad a child?' I sort of half smiled, not even sure myself whether I meant it. 'Did I put you off having another one?'

'I don't know what's going on in that head of yours today, I really don't! You were never a bad child, and we couldn't have loved you more. But the time was never right to have another. Lack of money ... your dad losing his job ... lots of things. We concentrated what we had into looking after you, giving you the best we possibly could, and, in the end, having just one child was enough. More than enough.'

'Right now, I'd settle for just the one.'

'I know you would, love. But two would be nice, wouldn't it? One of each. And I've heard that a lot of IVF ladies end up with twins.' She laughed and pulled me towards her in a hug. 'Two for the price of one, Kate. Imagine that!'

I tried to, but right then I could no more summon up that image than I could my own dad's face.

Chapter 18

Natalie, 2017

The wedding was getting nearer and nearer, but at last she had a dress. They'd found a shop with one of those huge communal changing rooms, so there was room for all of them, and the wheelchair. Jenny had guarded the door, or curtain to be more accurate, turning customers away with some made-up tale about her sister feeling ill and likely to be sick any minute, while Natalie waited in her underwear and Beth ran backwards and forwards, bringing dress after dress, and Mum just stood back and watched, with a silly proud sort of a grin on her face. Luckily, it was a Monday lunchtime and it was raining, so there were very few shoppers about and the staff who had offered help had been only too pleased to find it wasn't needed and skulk back to the stockroom for a sneaky sit-down or to slip outside for a fag.

'Are you all right, Jen?' Natalie asked, when Beth had

disappeared yet again, two cast-offs slung over her shoulder and on a mission to track down the cream silk dress they all liked but in a bigger size, and Mum had popped out in search of a loo.

'Yeah. Why?'

'You're acting a bit funny, that's all. Around Beth. You two haven't fallen out, have you?'

'No, of course not.'

'Well, tell me to mind my own business if you like, but I can tell something's up.'

'Leave it, Nat. This is your day. We're here for you, and to find you the dress of your dreams, come what may. Let's concentrate on that, shall we?'

'There is something, then? Look, Jen, I'll only worry about it now, or spend all my energy trying to wheedle it out of you when I should be heaving myself in and out of dresses. So, spill!'

'Got it!' Beth came bounding back in then, the cream silk dress draped over her arm, and putting a hasty end to any revelations that might have been about to be made. 'The last one too. God, this one had better fit or I'll be writing a letter of complaint.'

'Who to?' Natalie laughed.

'Oh, I don't know. Whoever sticks these silly size labels in without actually measuring any real people. If that last one was a twelve, then I'm a doughnut.'

'It's me eating too many doughnuts that's probably

stopping it from fitting in the first place.' Natalie edged forward and raised her bottom up from the chair as her sisters lowered the dress over her head and eased it down, Beth sliding the zip up at the back as Jenny re-arranged the folds of material at the front.

'Oh, wow. It's beautiful,' Mum said, arriving back just in time and placing her hand gently on Natalie's shoulder as if to steady herself. Were those tears in her eyes? 'The first of my girls to get married. It's all feeling very real all of a sudden.'

'It's real all right.' Jenny lifted Mum's hand and kissed it, then swivelled Natalie's chair round slowly so it faced the big mirror on the wall. 'Oh, Nat, you look like a princess.'

'Which one? Princess Anne?' Natalie giggled.

'No! I meant a Disney princess. What with all the silvery bits and the way it nips in at the waist, all you need now is a tiara and some silver shoes and you could pass for Cinderella!'

'Better make sure I'm home by midnight then, or God knows what might happen. I don't want Phil turning into a pumpkin or something.'

'Isn't that the coach? Not the groom ...' Beth smiled. 'It does look great, though, Nat.'

'So, this is it?' Jenny was gazing into the mirror over Natalie's shoulder, playing with the back of her hair. 'This is the dress you're going to get married in?'

Natalie turned and lifted her arms above her head, lowered them to run her hands over the slinky material as she adjusted the neckline, and rode her chair round in a big circle, until she'd seen herself from every possible angle except upside down. Then she laughed out loud.

'Yes!' she said, excitedly. 'I do believe it is.'

***

When Beth had reluctantly headed back to the salon, already late for her two o'clock perm, and Mum had gone rushing off to Gran's to show her the sneaky phot of the dress she'd taken on her phone, Natalie finally got the chance to question Jenny again. They were in the small coffee shop at the foot of the escalators in the shopping precinct, the one where there were no doors to navigate, and each hugging a much-needed hot choc-olate and a Danish.

'Okay, now you can tell me what it is you don't want to say in front of Beth.'

'Do I have to?'

'It's what sisters are for, Jen. So, what's she done?'

'She hasn't done anything. That's the trouble. She's completely innocent in all this. It's that ... that ...'

Natalie waited.

'That nasty little rat Jake, that's who. He's a dirty two-timing cheat and Beth deserves so much better.'

'Oh, dear. What's he been up to, exactly?'

'Exactly ... I don't know, but I can guess. I saw him yesterday, snogging some girl's face off in the street, where anyone could see, so who knows what they get up to in private? And now I wish I hadn't seen because it leaves me feeling like I have to tell her. But I don't want to, Nat. Why should I have to be the one to break her heart when it's that swine who's doing it? And behind her back too?'

'Don't, then. Don't tell her. Let her find out for herself.'

'But what if she doesn't? He could have been at it for months, for all we know. And could go on doing it for many more, without her ever finding out. Two girls on the go at once, having his cake and eating it ...' She bit into her Danish, viciously, as if she was biting Jake's scrawny head off.

'Your choice, Jen. Tell her and upset her, or don't tell her, wait for the shit to hit the fan and hope to God she never finds out that you knew all along.'

'Some choice! And why is it always me stuck in this position, worrying about all the grown-up stuff, trying to keep everyone happy? I'm meant to be the baby of the family ... '

Natalie looked quizzically at her sister, wondering what on earth she was talking about. Was there something else? But she had turned away and clearly had no intention of elaborating.

They sat without speaking for a while, chewing on the last morsels of their pastries, the hubbub of chatter and hissing coffee machines and hurrying feet going on all around them, and occasional announcements about opening hours and lost children, and free knives for the first twenty customers to get to the third-floor kitchen department in Debenhams. 'Shall we?' Natalie said, half-heartedly. 'Maybe I could do with a new knife, for when I'm married.'

'There'll be some long boring demonstration to put up with first,' Jenny said. 'And you can bet the knife's just some cheap thing anyway. They're hardly going to be parting with the good stuff, are they?'

'True. Did I have any knives on my wedding gift list, by the way? I can't remember.'

'There's so much on that list, I'm not surprised you can't remember. Now, come on, let's hit a few more shops, shall we? Find you some shoes.'

'Fine by me. And Jake? What are we going to do about him?'

'*We?*'

'Well, you've told me now, haven't you? A secret told can never be untold, as they say. So, I guess it's my problem too now, isn't it?'

'And?'

'And maybe we should go and get hold of one of those free knives after all. Stick it where the sun don't shine!'

'Nat!'

'Only joking. No, we'll tell her. I think we have to, don't you? And if she wants to slice bits off him, that's up to her. I'll happily hold him down.' Natalie drained her cup and wiped away the ring of chocolatey froth that she knew, without looking in a mirror, was bound to be stuck around her mouth, then released the brake on her wheelchair. 'Yes, we'll tell her tonight. But, for now ...'

'Shoes?'

'Shoes!'

Chapter 19

Kate, 1987

That summer felt different somehow, as if a weight had been lifted, at least for a while. And it was a good summer, wonderfully warm and leafy green, and surprisingly carefree. Scraping together every penny we could find, we'd had a second attempt at IVF in the spring, another failure, but were not about to rush into a third. We were exhausted by it all, and in need of a break, and the truth was that there was no point in considering it or planning it or pining for it anyway, not until we'd saved up enough money, and enough resilience, to put ourselves through it all again

But we were happy. As happy as we could be. For the first time in a long while, we had pushed away that lurking grey shadow that had been hanging over us, and we were just a couple again, in our mid-thirties, still in love, maybe not in quite the same way as when we'd started out, but having a go at leading a normal uncomplicated life again, making love for the fun and the feel of it, because we wanted to, not because we had to, and not even trying to get pregnant. And it felt surprisingly good.

Dan wanted us to go away on holiday. I remember protesting that we couldn't afford it, that the money should be kept for treatment, not frittered away on luxuries, but Dan insisted it was what we both needed. Time to relax and regroup, to enjoy the calm before the storm. And I knew, when he said that, that he was still with me, that we were still in this thing together, and that he was right. We would try again, as soon as we were ready, and we would weather the storm, whatever it brought with it, and be stronger than before.

We went to Italy.

Venice in June, and the sun was out, glinting on the water, highlighting the old buildings as the tourists queued to go inside, the pigeons flapping overhead and pecking hungrily at whatever scraps they could find on the ground around our feet. We strolled about, hand in hand, through narrow alleys and over tiny bridges, discovering hidden churches and cafés, and each other. We ate cheaply, filling up on pizza, and slept cheaply in a small hotel a water bus away, and resisted the romantic urge to climb into a gondola and pay the earth for the privilege, still mindful of the budget we'd set ourselves, the things we knew to be important and the things we knew were not. Dan's nose reddened and peeled, and my arms and legs, free of their usual bank clerk clothes, took on a warm lightly bronzed glow that just about passed as a tan.

On the plane home, late at night, leaning snugly against each other, both tired but feeling closer than we'd been for ages, Dan told me we had the money. He'd known for a while but he'd wanted this time together first. He gripped my hand and squeezed it tightly. I asked where the money had come from, but he wouldn't say, raising his free hand and touching his sore pink nose in a 'you don't need to know' way. Had he borrowed it? Won it? Stolen it? Unlikely. His parents. It had to be, but I didn't really care. Let them keep their secrets.

Now Round Three could begin.

***

Eleven! I had made eleven eggs. I lifted my head from the pillow, still groggy from the anaesthetic, and smiled into my husband's eyes. 'It's going to work,' I said. 'I just know it. We only had two last time, didn't we? But eleven. Wow!'

'The holiday must have done you good. You look like a happy little hen,' Dan said, laughing. 'Snuggled down in your straw, laying away, churning them out to order.'

'Let's hope they're good ones. The free range kind!' I closed my eyes again, trying not to let the nausea get the better of me. 'Have you ... you know, done your bit?'

'Yes.' He put his hand over mine and whispered in my ear. I still found it amusing how embarrassing he found the whole sperm production thing. 'Package safely delivered, and on its way to meet the eggs as we speak. And a fine sample it was, though I say so myself.'

'Ugh!' I pulled my hand back and giggled. 'I hope you've washed that hand. I know where it's been!'

'Are you complaining? Really? Cos I can always go and ask for it back, you know. My little bottle of baby juice ...'

'Don't you dare!'

I must have nodded off for a while, but I woke up to find a nurse standing over me, wrapping the blood pressure cuff around my arm and waiting to check my temperature. The clock on the wall on the far side of the small ward told me it was two-thirty, so I'd been out of it for about three hours. Dan was nowhere to be seen. Probably out grabbing some lunch somewhere.

'How do you feel?'

'Okay, I think. A bit sore.'

'Not sick?'

'No. No, I don't think so. That sleep's helped a lot. But, tell me, I didn't dream it, did I? Eleven eggs?'

'That's right, Kate. Well done. Hardest bit's out of the way now.'

She nodded and patted my hand, like I was a schoolgirl who'd just passed a spelling test, and soon had me sitting up with a cup of tea and two slices of lukewarm toast.

'Okay.' She took another look at my charts and took my plate away. 'You can go home now, as soon as you're ready, and when your husband comes back to escort you, of course. And, if all goes well, we'll see you back in a couple of days for the embryo transfer.'

'I look forward to it.'

'Fingers crossed, eh?'

'And legs! They're staying in this time, if I have to use super glue to seal myself up.'

'Not a good idea. In nine months' time, they just might need a way out again!'

'Thank you.' I could feel the tears welling up and brushed them away.

'What for?'

'For saying exactly the right thing. In nine months' time, I really could have a baby, couldn't I?'

'Let's hope so. But not eleven of them, eh? Just imagine it. Your very own football team!'

***

Infertility hurts. Believe me, it hurts like hell. Oops, sorry! Mustn't swear. So when a chance comes along, you grab it, don't you? With both hands. You trust the doctors, the scientists, God, to do what your own body can't. To take the pain away, and give you what you've always wanted. A baby – or, if you're lucky, maybe two. But, more? Nowadays it couldn't happen, wouldn't be allowed to happen. But things were different then ...

Should I have worried more, about the risks? Probably, but who wants to hear about those? I know I didn't. After all that trying and hoping and trying again, living in dread of every tell-tale drop of blood, behaving like performing seals whenever the temperature charts said we must, being pricked with needles and pumped full of drugs, who wouldn't feel bad enough already, pretty much all the time, without needing to know, or think, or care, about the risks? Sometimes it's easier to just stop listening. It's like reading the small print, or ticking a box to say you've understood all the terms and conditions. Well, you don't, do you? Read them, let alone understand.

And Dan? The truth is that I didn't even stop to check if he was still there beside me, wanting it, willing it to happen as much as I was. Oh, he was there in body all right, sitting up straight, almost rigid, his hand just slightly shaking on top of mine, but in spirit? Well, you try asking a man a shall-we, shan't-we question like that, even a man who really wants a child, and you'll see that flicker of hesitation, that almost imperceptible moment of uncertainty. But only if you choose to look.

***

'Well, Mrs Campbell, you'll be pleased to know that nine of your eggs have successfully fertilised.' The doctor beamed at us across his desk.

'Nine! But that's fantastic. So, what happens now?'

'We can't use them all, obviously, and the embryologist has been assessing their quality this morning. There are three that we can safely say aren't dividing as well as we'd like, so we'll be discarding those, I'm afraid. But the other six are all looking viable.'

'Viable?' Dan was doing that jaw-clenching thing he always did when he was feeling tense. 'You mean we could actually use all six?'

'I know you've not had this decision to make before, but this time it's a possibility, yes. I wouldn't normally recommend transferring more than three, but ...'

'But what?' Dan's elbows were on the desk now, his knuckles supporting his head as he leaned forward, lines of concentration etched across his forehead.

'But because of Mrs Campbell's age, and the fact that you've tried unsuccessfully ...' He glanced at his notes. 'Twice before ...'

'We can have all six?' That was me, not Dan, my

voice rising in that shrill, over-excited way I sometimes can't hold back.

'Hang on a minute, Kate.' Dan again. The voice of reason. 'Six is too big a risk. What if all of them ...?'

'That won't happen. Look at the first time. Three. And last time. Just two. But they didn't make it, did they? None of them, even though we did everything right. Six are hardly going to all survive, are they? One, or even two, if we're lucky. But at least with six ...'

'Think carefully, Mrs Campbell.' The doctor's voice was suddenly grave. 'Yes, I know what you're thinking, and with six, yes, you would have a significantly higher chance of achieving a pregnancy, but also, I have to remind you, a significantly higher chance that it could be a multiple pregnancy.'

'Not all of them, though?' Dan had his accountant's head on again. 'Not all six? I mean, twins might actually be quite nice. It would save us having to come back here again in a couple of years' time to try for baby number two, wouldn't it? But we're not going to end up with sextuplets here, are we?'

I expected the doctor to laugh, but he didn't. 'There are no guarantees, Mr Campbell. I've always tried to make that clear to you, to all my patients. As outcomes go, it's highly unlikely, but it is still a risk. A small one, in my view. But, if you want to take it, then yes, I am prepared to transfer all of them.'

'Today?' I could feel my heart pounding hard, my pulse rate rising, with the sort of adrenalin rush that comes with wanting to dive straight into something exciting and exhilarating and dangerous, or to run away from it. Which was it now? I wish I knew.

'Yes, of course. But, it's a big decision. Take your time. I will get someone to sit with you, to talk it all through. We're ready to go ahead, as soon as you are. But I do recommend caution. We could replace two or three embryos, as we have before, and freeze any you decide not to use today. That would give you a much easier – and safer – attempt next time. No stimulation drugs, no anaesthetic, no egg recovery. Quite a bit cheaper too, in those circumstances.'

'Go through it all again, just to use embryos we already have? And money we don't? When the embryos are here now, ready and waiting? They could die in the freezer before we even get that far.'

'Die is an emotive word. Mrs Campbell. These are not babies we're talking about. Embryos, or pre-embryos, as I prefer to call them at this early stage, are nothing more than a few cells, quite incapable of independent life.'

'They're babies to me. Or they could be, couldn't they, once they're back inside me, growing, where they're supposed to be? I don't want to put any of them into the freezer, or come back later. I want to give them their chance of an independent life. Any kind of life. All of them. And I want to do it now.' I looked at Dan, not at all sure what was going through his mind, not really wanting to know. 'Please.'

They *were* babies. *My* babies. And, yes, I would go through the motions, listen to the advice, consider the risks, to me and to them, talk it through for as long as they made me. But I already knew what I was going to do. Cross my fingers, close my eyes, hope and pray and wish and wonder. I was going to take my chances, throw an invisible dice in the air. The dice with exactly the right numbers on it, the numbers one to six.

God only knew on which number it might fall, how many babies I might have, but there isn't a zero on a dice, is there? It was a sign. It had to be. A reassurance, in a world that had had so little of it lately. The end was in sight, and this time I really believed we couldn't fail.

***

They don't feel it like we do. Men. Not in the same way. The emptiness, the longing, the guilt. Well, they can't, can they? It's not their womb waiting to be filled. No, men worry about different things. Dan did, anyway. Still does, thirty years later. It's not the will-its or won't-its that bother him, but the what-happens-when? Best-case scenario. Or worst, depending on how you look at it. Because it could have happened, couldn't it? All of them hanging on, developing, surviving. It was thousands-to-one improbable, but …

Think of the cost, said Dan. Mister Accountant. Mister Careful. The cost of prams and cots, and toys and clothes, and mounds of nappies as high as the ceiling. Think of a lifetime of school uniforms, and massive food bills, and teaching them all to drive. The weddings we'd have to save for, if they're girls. Or boys, for that matter. Think of the lack of sleep and the drop in income, and saying goodbye to any kind of freedom for years and years to come. Think about the house, and whether it will be big enough. And the same for the car. The price there is to pay. A price that isn't only measured in cash.

He was right, of course, but I didn't listen. Not then. I didn't care. I didn't even want to consider what that price might be. I was thirty-five, my biological clock was ticking, time trickling away like sand through an hourglass. My egg supply wasn't going to last for ever, and neither was our bank balance. It couldn't go on. We both knew that, although neither of us said it out loud. If we didn't do it then, take that giant leap of faith, take that chance, then that could be it. You do understand that, don't you? Why I had to do it? It was the end of the road. Or, with just a sprinkling of luck on our side, maybe the beginning …

Chapter 20

Ollie, 2017

A queue had started forming outside the door to the school hall and was snaking its way down the corridor almost as far as the library when Ollie arrived to start auditioning for the nativity play. Word had got out that this year was going to be different, some kind of cross between *Jesus Christ Superstar* and *The X Factor*, and it was soon evident that a good eighty per cent of the kids waiting in line were not only girls but that just about all of them were desperate to play the part of Mary. What was wrong with just being a shepherd or even a sheep, Ollie wondered? Everybody wanted to be a star these days.

There were so many candidates, he only gave them a couple of quick lines to say: 'Oh, Joseph, I am so weary. When can we find a place to sleep?' It was amazing how hearing those words spoken over and

over again, in voices ranging from the timid and virtually inaudible to the kind of strident yelling they'd
probably be able to hear as far away as Bethlehem, had
the power to send him to the very brink of sleep. Feet
stomping across the dusty boards, they came and went,
lugging baby dolls and draping scraps of cloth over
their heads, repeating their lines like parrots. Yawning
into his hand, Ollie was finding it harder and harder
to remember who was who, let alone pick one out from
among the rest. And then Victoria Bennett stepped onto
the stage.

She wore her light-brown hair in uneven bunches
and the hem of her second-hand uniform was starting
to come undone, but she had a presence about her.
From the moment she stood there in front of him,
utterly still, with no props but a hand held protectively
across her tummy, and gazed out unblinkingly into the
hall, he knew he had found his Mary. Even without a
javelin in her hand, Victoria, it would seem, had more
hidden talents than he'd given her credit for.

The other roles were easy enough to cast, and soon
he had a whole list of willing and excited volunteers.
The hardest part was breaking it to those who were
left, and dealing with the inevitable tantrums and tears
of the would-be stars who had failed to make their
mark. They could always help with some of the other
important jobs, he told them, like being ushers or

managing the props backstage, but very few seemed convinced.

'I won't have to ... kiss anybody, will I, sir?' Victoria said, coming to find him at the end, lugging her school bag up and over her shoulder, ready to leave. 'Like Joseph, I mean?'

'No, Victoria. You definitely won't have to kiss anybody.'

'Not even the baby?'

'The baby?' His mind had gone blank for a moment and he couldn't for the life of him think what she meant.

'The baby Jesus, sir.'

'Oh, yes, I see. Yes, I suppose it would be all right to kiss the baby. It's only a doll, after all.'

'My brother Benny could be it, if you want.'

Ollie laughed. 'That's a lovely idea, but I think we'll use a doll. That's what usually happens.'

'But it's different this year, isn't it, sir? Not like the plays we've had before.'

'What makes you say that?'

'Everybody says that, sir. That you're going to make it like a real show this year. With lights and fireworks, and dancers and everything. I think that'll be really good. Can I be a dancer too?'

'I'm not sure about the fireworks, Victoria! A bit too dangerous in a school hall, I think. And I'm not sure

Mary actually gets to dance, either. Remember she's having a baby.'

'My mum still danced when she had Benny in her tummy. All round the kitchen, waving a tea towel in the air, and singing too. And she danced with Dad sometimes, in our living room, when they were watching *Strictly*, although she did bump into things a lot. Having babies doesn't have to stop you doing the things you love to do, sir. I think Mary might have wanted to dance, don't you? Because she was so happy she was having a baby. God's baby.'

'You may be right there! Now, go on, off home with you.' Ollie waved his hand towards the door, surprised to realise that everybody else had already gone. 'And I'll think about the dancing. I promise.'

He sat for a while after she'd gone, turning the cast list over and over in his hand. She was right, of course. He had been asked to make this show different, and here he was still lining up all the usual characters, ready to act out the same old story. Where was the creativity, the energy, the imagination the head teacher had expected from him?

He'd let so many children down, those who'd taken the time and trouble to come along after school and line up in the hope of being picked and had no doubt gone off now, feeling unwanted and not good enough. How had he let that happen? That wasn't the sort of teacher he wanted to be. No, if he was going to do something exciting with this show, then he should start with including everyone who wanted to be in it. So, they couldn't all deliver a line clearly enough to be heard. Some would probably have trouble remembering their lines at all, but everyone was good at something, weren't they? Even if they didn't know it yet. Like little Victoria with that first throw of the javelin.

What was it she'd said? That *having* babies didn't have to stop you doing what you loved doing? And doesn't everyone dance when they're happy? Such wisdom from one so young. She could certainly teach him a thing or two. All of those children wanted to be in his show. They'd set their hearts on it. Who was he to dash their hopes and tell them they couldn't? It was time to take down the barriers and find out just what these kids were capable of when they were allowed to do the things they loved doing, and when they were happy.

He took a last look at the list in his hand, then carefully ripped it into tiny pieces. It was time to start all over again and he knew just the person to help him.

***

'Me? What can I possibly do?' Beth stopped fiddling with the stem of her wine glass and gave her brother a look that said she was still finding it hard to believe they were sitting in a pub and he was drinking nothing stronger than a pint of orange squash.

Ollie chose to ignore her disdainful expression, took a huge gulp of squash to prove a point and carried on regardless. 'Be my right-hand woman, that's what. Help me give these kids a show to remember. Make a few dreams come true.'

'What do I know about that sort of thing?'

'A hairbrush microphone, remember? Dancing in front of your bedroom mirror? Don't try telling me you haven't always had a secret desire to get into show business.'

'You leave my secret desires out of this! And I'm not sure a primary school nativity is really what I would call show business. Not by any stretch of the imagination.'

'Maybe not, but you still know a lot more about this singing and dancing stuff than I do. And you're a hairdresser. You can do the hair and make-up too.'

'Would you like me to make the scenery and do the refreshments and sell the tickets as well?'

'Well, if you're offering ...' Ollie ducked as his sister took a swing at his head. 'No, no, okay, I'm sure I can find some kids, and maybe even a few parents, to do all that. But where I really need help is with the ... what's the word? The vision, that's it. Someone who can see the overall picture, help me come up with something different, exciting, spectacular even, but still have that essence of the Christmas story about it.'

'Like big musical numbers and fantastic costumes, and rockets going off, you mean?'

'You can forget the rockets, thanks very much, although you're not the first person to suggest something like that! As for the rest of it ... yes, please. So far all I've got for definite is a Mary. The rest is a blank canvas, just waiting to be filled. We need ideas, and lots of them. But we haven't got all that long. Only seven weeks, actually. So when can we get started?'

'We? What's with the *we*? I haven't said I'll do it yet!'

'Ah, but you will, though, won't you?' He leant his head on her shoulder and snuggled into her, then reached across the table for her empty glass. 'Please. Pretty please. There's another drink in it for you if you do.'

'A drink? God, Ollie, it'll have to be a whole bottle at least.'

'Done! Cheap at half the price.'

'Is that how you get round all the girls? Ply them with booze to get your wicked way? Good job I'm only your sister.'

'And thank God you are. And a great one too.' He stood and rummaged in his pocket for his wallet. 'Thanks, Beth. You're a star. House red, is it?'

'And a bag of crisps.'

'God, you strike a hard bargain.' He shook his head and pretended to count the coins from his pocket. 'You'll bankrupt me at this rate, but go on then. I suppose you're worth it!'

The bar was busy but he finally made it to the front and ordered. The barmaid rammed the corkscrew into the bottle, twisted it and removed the cork, then handed the bottle over. 'How many glasses with that?' she asked, turning to pull a bag of cheese and onion out of a large cardboard box behind her.

'Best make it two.' He couldn't have Beth downing a whole bottle by herself.

'Ollie?' Beth said, as he settled back down and poured them both a drink. 'Can I ask you something?'

'Sounds serious, but yes, of course you can. So long as it's not about my drinking again. I'm only having one glass to keep you company.'

'No, not the drink. Not this time. It's about Jake. Did you know ... well, that he might be cheating on me?'

Ollie thumped his glass down on the table. 'What? No, I didn't. Bloody hell, Beth. How long has this been going on? I'll kill the little shit.'

'No, you won't.' She put a restraining hand on his arm. 'The truth is, I don't really seem to mind all that much. I thought I would, but I don't. That says a lot, doesn't it?'

'You don't mind? Are you mad? You two have been together for bloody ever! But you only said that he might be. Aren't you sure?'

'As sure as I can be. It was something Jen said last night. Oh, she was cagey about it. Said she could be mistaken but she thought she'd seen him, in the street, kissing some random girl she didn't recognise. Of course, that meant she definitely had seen him, but she was trying to let me know gently, you know? Not wanting to hit me with it all in one go. Drop in a few seeds of doubt and see how the land lies. But the land didn't even rock, Ollie. I didn't feel a stab to the heart or anything like that. Didn't feel much at all, really. What sort of a girlfriend does that make me?'

'Oh, come on now. Surely what you should be asking yourself is what sort of boyfriend it makes him?'

'Yeah, I know. But, in a way, if it's true, then I'm sort of glad. It lets me ...'

'What?'

'Well, it lets me take action, I suppose. Have a bit of a rant at him, then tell him it's all over. I'm actually quite looking forward to that. Having the upper hand, and getting out without any of it being my fault.'

'Wow. Getting out? Is that how you see it? And I thought you loved the guy.'

'Funnily enough, so did I. But obviously not. I've seen how you've been since you lost Laura, and I know it's not quite the same, but that's just not the way I feel. I think maybe it's been over for a while but neither of us wanted to face up to it. But now I can.'

He leant over and gave her a hug. 'That's my girl. You make sure you give him what for, though, before you dump him. Make the bugger squirm.'

'Oh, I intend to. And then I'm going to throw myself into something that really is important.'

'Like?'

'Your school show.'

'You'll do it, then?'

'If it keeps you out of trouble, and out of the pub, of course I'll bloody do it.' She ripped open her bag of crisps and stuffed two into her mouth at once, spluttering through the crumbs. 'Just you try and stop me!'

Chapter 21

Kate, 1987

Such a sense of responsibility! Walking around carrying six almost-babies inside me, trying desperately to make them stay exactly where they were. In fact, I hardly walked at all. I took a fortnight off work, which didn't go down too well so soon after the Venice break, but there are some things far more important than a job and this was one of them. Let them sack me if they wanted to, I didn't care. I'd be leaving soon anyway, if things went according to plan.

I was meant to wait two weeks, then go back for a blood test to see if I really was pregnant – properly 'yes they've made it' pregnant – but it was so hard having to wait that I was tempted to buy a home test from Boots. I picked up a packet and read the instructions, but it looked like it wouldn't be able to give me a reliable result quite so soon. I'd done pregnancy tests before, of course, but I'd hoped technology might have moved on since then, that by some miracle a test would already know the fate of my embryos within days of their arrival, but you needed to wait a good week or so after a missed period for it to work, and I hadn't even reached that stage yet, so I put it back on the shelf.

It had been stupid of me to go out to the shops anyway. Why on earth wasn't I at home with my feet up? Just carry on as normal, everyone had said, but I didn't want to, didn't feel I should. Walk, work, move about, even have sex if you want to, they said. Forget they're in there. As if I could!

I was doing everything I could to keep these babies, and myself, healthy and strong. No alcohol, no hot baths, no dashing about. I read a book about eating well too, and made a bit of a snap decision to eat more healthily. Lots of fresh vegetables, more fruit, only the leanest of meat, plenty of iron, and far fewer chips. Not that I'd ever been much of a cook, but making up big vats of vegetable soup was easy, and it did me good to feel I was looking after myself properly.

When the usual day of my period came and went and I was still blood-free, I couldn't help getting my hopes up. On the Saturday, when our appointment for the test came around, I had woken up feeling decidedly sick and had heaved over the toilet for a while, although

I hadn't managed to expel anything other than a bit of spit.

'It's probably just nerves,' Dan said, as we climbed into the car and set off for the clinic. 'You can't possibly be showing any pregnancy signs already. Not this early. They're still the size of full stops. If they're even still in there ...'

'Oh, thanks for the positive words of encouragement!' I turned and gazed out of the window at the early morning traffic, not wanting him to see how much his words had stung me. Didn't he realise just how important today was for me? For us? I was four days late now, and we hadn't got this far on the two previous attempts, the blood arriving promptly and painfully on both occasions, before I'd had the chance to have any tests to confirm what I already knew.

'Sorry,' he mumbled, looking at me instead of at the road, a horn blaring out at us as he pulled out in front of another car at a junction and had to swerve to avoid hitting it. 'Jesus! That was close.'

'See! You're just as distracted as I am. Your mind's not on what you're doing. Please just be careful, Dan. You could have got us all killed.'

'*All?*'

'You know ... me, you and the babies.'

'Well, tell them all to put their little seatbelts on then. The road's a dangerous place for defenceless embryos!'

Dan laughed then, and reluctantly I found myself smiling too.

'It will be all right this time, won't it?'

He took his left hand off the wheel and touched my tummy. 'Hope so, sweetheart. I really do.'

The rest of that day passed in a blur, as if I was watching events happening through a permanent cloud of tears. Which, I suppose, I was. The test was positive, and I can remember hugging everyone in sight. The nurse, the doctor, at least three other patients in the waiting room, Dan ...

'There's still a long road ahead, Mrs Campbell.'

I was nodding but I was still too busy crying to listen.

'We won't be able to count the embryos for a while. They're still too small to show up accurately on an ultrasound ...'

'Yes.' I nodded again, but I still wasn't listening.

'We'll see you again at about seven weeks.'

'Yes.'

'The receptionist will make you an appointment.'

'Yes, okay.'

We must have walked down the corridor, travelled down in the lift, passed the shop, but I don't remember any of it. Without even knowing how we'd got there, we were suddenly back out in the street. A light rain had started to fall, and we walked back to the car, arm in arm, without an umbrella, splashing through the shallow puddles on the pavement, turning corners, crossing roads, neither of us saying a word.

Dan fumbled for his keys, opened the car door for me and helped me in, holding on to my arm until I was safely seated, as if I was made of glass, as if I might break. He'd never done that before.

'We've done it,' he said, once he'd climbed in the other side and closed the door. The rain was heavier now, pounding on the roof and sliding down the windscreen. 'We've really done it this time. We're actually pregnant.'

'Yes, we are. We really are.' And then we were in each other's arms, the car full of the sound of the rain and our own heartbeats drumming away in tandem, and our eyes closed, and both sobbing like it was the end of the world.

***

Of course, it wasn't the end of the world. Only of the world as we knew it. That day was just the beginning, and just a few worrying weeks later we were back, part excited, part terrified. 'If all six are alive in there, we'll be famous,' Dan said just before we went in. 'With cameras following us everywhere. Like the Waltons.'

'Goodnight Johnboy.' I laughed at my own pathetic attempt at an American accent. 'Goodnight Jimbob!'

'Not those Waltons, you dope! I meant the sextuplets. You know, all of them girls. That poor father! What he must have to suffer ...'

'Don't you count your chickens, Dan. That could be you in a few minutes, looking at your future brood. If you'll excuse the pun.'

'Ha, ha. Well, they did start out as eggs, didn't they? And you've been acting like some protective mother hen ever since. But, I tell you what. If they're all girls – not that we'll know that today, of course – then I'm leaving home. Running away to sea or somewhere. I'll be condemned to a life surrounded by pink frilly stuff and mountains of sanitary towels! And I'll have nobody to play football with.'

'Girls can play football ...'

'Ready, Kate? And you must be Dan? Come on in. How have you been?' It was Joanne, the same girl who'd scanned me before, and as she ushered us in all the banter just dried in our throats. This was serious stuff.

The jelly was thick and cold as Joanne ran it over my exposed tummy, pushing down with the flat end of her scanner. I squeezed my eyes up tight and tried hard not to wee on the table. 'Don't worry. I won't push too hard,' she joked. 'I know it can be a bit uncomfortable.'

Dan was gripping my hand. I could feel the tension in his fingers, running right through him and into me.

Or maybe it was the other way round. 'Well?' he said, impatient to know. 'Can you tell how many?'

'Give me a few moments, Dan. Let's just have a look around first and get our bearings, shall we?'

I turned my head to the side, away from Dan, so I could look at the screen. Not that any of what I saw made a lot of sense. Black areas, grey areas, all swirling about and into each other as the girl moved her scanner around. No arms and legs and heads, no tiny heartbeats thumping in and out, the way I'd imagined. But then, this was a very early scan. Way earlier than in a normal pregnancy, and we weren't looking for size or checking for health problems or working out whether we were having a boy or a girl. We were looking for numbers. Nothing but numbers. Trying to find out if Dan was going to get his footballers. A whole five-a-side team, maybe, with a substitute thrown in for good measure.

'There's one ...'

Joanne was pointing at something on the screen. Something small and shapeless that didn't look anything like a baby, but if she said it was one then I believed her. I needed to believe her. This was all starting to feel incredibly and magically real.

'And another.'

Dan's hand clenched over mine, so tightly I could feel his nails break into my skin.

'And ... wait a moment ... let's just take a peek over here. Yes, there's number three.'

'Three? You mean we're going to have triplets.' Dan's voice sounded wobbly, like he wasn't sure what to say, or how to say it. 'Oh, wow! I can't believe it!'

'Sorry, Dan. No, it's not triplets.'

'Not ...?'

'There, if I'm not mistaken, is our number four.'

'*What? Four?* Are you sure?'

'Well, unless anyone's playing hide and seek and there's a sneaky one or two I haven't spotted, then yes, I would say you definitely have four. We'll let you run straight to the loo now, Kate, then get you both in to see the doctor, to talk about what happens next, but in the meantime ...' She held out her hand and shook Dan's before grabbing for mine and breaking into a huge grin. 'Well done, both of you. It's not often we achieve a result like this. Congratulations!'

Chapter 22

Beth, 2017

It was odd, seeing as they were born just minutes apart, but Beth had always felt older than the others. Yes, she'd been first into the world, so technically she was the oldest, but minutes hardly counted, really, did they? Yet she was big sister Beth, and always had been, there to sort out the others' problems, wade in and fight their battles for them and, when necessary, stop them from fighting each other. Always the one with bucketloads of advice and handfuls of tissues when things got tough. But now, after all these years, it was her turn to need a shoulder to cry on. Except there wasn't one available. The house was empty and she was on her own.

She sat on her bed in the dark and listened to the sound of Jake's car retreating down the road. The brakes squealed as he took the corner way too quickly, then there was nothing but silence. He had gone and she knew it was for the last time.

At least he hadn't denied it; she'd give him that. He may have been messing around behind her back for God knows how long but when confronted he hadn't tried to lie about it. Hadn't begged for forgiveness or promised to make it up to her either, so it had been fairly obvious this was the end. She wasn't sure which of them had been more relieved to have it all out in the open and the decision made. It still felt odd, though, knowing it was over, and that she was, for the first time in her entire adult life, actually single.

She lay down and stared up at the ceiling for a while. Beams of light moved across it in waves each time a car passed, highlighting the cracks in the plaster and the odd cobweb. She cast her mind back to the first time she had brought Jake here, sneaking in when everyone else was out for the evening, giggling in the dark as they pounced on each other, peeling their clothes off and a condom on, rolling about inexpertly and over-excitedly under the bedcovers. She'd looked up then, at the same ceiling, peering past Jake's spotty shoulders, and known that her life had changed, that with her virginity gone she'd passed through a barrier and could never go back. In some strange way, that was how she felt again now. A new phase of her life was beginning, and scary though it was, she was not going to regret what she'd done this evening, any more than she had that previous time.

Beth wiped a few stray tears away from her eyes, pulled herself to her feet and went over to close the curtains, taking a last look along the road to make sure he really had gone and wasn't right now camped outside and staring up, like some love-struck Romeo, at her window. He wasn't.

Flicking on the light, she walked to the mirror and took a good close look at herself. She was a tad overweight, no denying that, and her hair was looking a bit wild, which wasn't surprising after she'd spent the last couple of days running her hands through it like a mad woman trying to decide what to do, and the last half an hour squashing the back of it flat on the bed, but what sort of a hairdresser would she be if she couldn't fix that?

No, all in all, she wasn't bad looking. Just because Jake had chosen to look elsewhere, didn't mean she was necessarily lacking in any way. His loss, someone else's gain! Now she'd hauled herself out of the rut that for too long had been known as Beth-and-Jake, a whole host of possibilities could open up for her. It could be Beth-and-Brad Pitt next. Unlikely, as he lived in America and already had six kids, but you never know! Or Beth-and-the-bloke-in-the-chip-shop. She'd always thought he had a soft spot for her, piling a few extra chips onto her portion and keeping his hand over hers for just a little longer than needed when handing her the change. Or, better still, Beth-and-Mister-Mystery. A man she hadn't even met yet, who could be waiting just around the corner, ready and willing to sweep her off her feet. Not that she was in any hurry. A bit of time on her own, to get used to her Jakelessness, and to adjust to being young, free and single wouldn't be a bad thing. But one day ...

She switched on the straighteners and went to work on her hair. If there was one thing she was good at, it was hair. And for now, she needed to feel good at something. Needed to feel special. Then, remembering something Ollie had said the other night, she picked up a brush and held it up in front of her face, smiled to herself and pretending it was a microphone, she started to sing, tentatively at first, but remembering there was nobody else in the house to hear her, she was soon belting out the words of 'I will survive' like Gloria Gaynor on speed.

And I will survive, she thought, when she'd sung her heart out and reached the final chorus. Too damned right I will. In fact, I'll do better than that. I'll thrive. Who needs Jake? Jake who? In fact, sod Jake, that's what I say. She was quite surprised to see her own face looking back at her from the mirror, strong, defiant and laughing. Not a sorry-for-herself tear in sight.

Once upon a time, she'd have screamed blue murder, cried, probably tried to scratch the other girl's eyes out. But not now. Now, the older and wiser Beth Campbell hadn't even bothered to ask the girl's name. And, why? Because she didn't want to know. That was why. Didn't need to know. What difference would it make to anything? It wouldn't bring Jake back, the old Jake she had once loved and trusted, and had finally outgrown. Once a cheat, always a cheat. What he'd done to Beth he'd probably do to this new girl in time. And to the one after that. Let the poor cow have him. From now on, Beth thought, putting her impromptu mike down and reaching for the straighteners, it's all going to be about me.

Chapter 23

Kate, 1987

I'd never heard the term 'selective reduction' until that moment, but the doctor was dropping it into the conversation as if it was the most natural thing in the world. 'Carrying four babies will be hard,' he was saying, looking down at my notes rather than into my eyes. 'On you, and on them. And dangerous. Your uterus would be stretched to well beyond its normal capacity, you'd probably have to spend a considerable time on bed rest in hospital and you'd be unlikely to go anywhere near full term, with all the risks of prematurity. Poor birth weight, underdeveloped lungs, disability, even death ... In short, four is too many. We knew there were risks when we agreed to try with so many embryos but, with your age and your previous history, having this many survive the implantation process was always extremely unlikely. It's come as something of a surprise, to us and to you. It's not an ideal situation, but it is one we can try to correct.'

'Correct? You're talking about abortion, right?'

'Not a word I would choose to use in these circumstances, but yes, if we were to reduce things to a twin pregnancy, say, it would certainly be safer for all of you. And much easier to manage, and to maintain.'

'Twins? So you want to just get rid of two of them? Is that what you're suggesting?' I clutched hard at Dan's hand, aware that he was sitting very still and hadn't yet said a word. 'Two have already slipped away of their own accord, and now you want me to abort two more? Of my own babies. After everything we went through to get this far ...'

'They're still very small. Not really babies yet. Try not to think of them as babies. What would happen is that we'd inject a chemical into two of the foetuses and they would simply cease to develop.'

'They'd die, you mean?'

'What I mean is that they would no longer have the potential to grow, develop, form a living baby. It's not quite the same thing. Please don't upset yourself so much. In the long run, it would be the best and safest option. And the nervous system isn't fully in place at this stage, so they wouldn't feel a thing, I can assure you of that. No pain.'

'But I would, wouldn't I? Let me tell you what I'd

feel. Like a bloody murderer, that's what. After all this time, waiting and hoping for a baby ...'

'A baby. *One* baby. I'm sure you didn't actually hope for four at once?'

'But that's what I've got, isn't it?' I tried to get him to look at me. Properly look at me. But he had his doctor face on, the one that talks science and not emotion. 'And you expect me to just discard them as if they're nothing? How would you even select which ones live and which ones die, anyway? Because that's what you're talking about, isn't it? Selecting. Playing God.'

'Just as we did when selecting embryos, we would try to hang on to the biggest, the strongest, the ones that appear to be most likely to succeed.'

'Well, God help the little people, then, eh? Condemned for being small. Not given a chance ...'

'Kate!' Dan flung an arm across my shoulders, I think more to hold me down and stop me from hitting someone than to offer any comfort. 'I think maybe we need to go away and calm down a bit and talk about this.'

'There's nothing to talk about. I'm not doing it. It's my body and they're my babies. And I'm having them. All four of them.'

'But, the risks? Please, Kate, let's look at the risks. Weigh up the pros and cons.' Oh, God, sometimes I wished Dan wasn't an accountant.

'This isn't about some balance sheet, Dan. Life's a

risk. Stepping out into the road is a risk. Sometimes you just have to take risks, don't you? If you want to get to the other side.'

***

Four babies. I just kept telling myself that at least it was better than six. Easier to carry, a better chance of survival. Not as expensive. I never thought I would, but I realised I had started to sound horribly like Dan.

But then I felt guilty about the two that had started out inside me but had already gone and I was worried sick the rest would follow. What was done was done now. We had more than expected, probably more than we knew how to cope with, but I believed we would learn. Like all parents do. No going back. You do realise that, don't you? You do believe me? That I would have done anything – anything – to keep all four alive.

There would be no selective reduction. No choosing which to keep and which to dispose of. We would stick together like glue – all of us – and everything would be all right in the end. But I couldn't promise that, could I? Couldn't promise anything. It was all down to hope and luck. All bravado. Deep inside, with five heartbeats now inextricably linked and playing in tune, believe me, I was absolutely terrified.

***

'Quads are pretty unusual, you know.' Dan was sitting at the other end of the sofa, tapping at a calculator with one hand and rubbing my feet under the blanket with the other. It had been a tough day, one that had started with the kind of overwhelming sickness that had prevented me eating anything all morning and ended with me having to leave work early because I was just too tired to stand up.

'Yes, I expect they are. I've never met any, have you?'

'Nope. And I was thinking about the Waltons again. How they would have managed, you know, practically, financially, with so many kids, if they hadn't become front page news, such a media sensation ...'

'They had six, Dan. And all girls, which made them even more special. No wonder the TV people snapped them up. But I don't see what they have to do with us. Our situation is totally different. We're only having four and we've no idea about their sex.'

'Still unusual, though, isn't it? Having four. Not something you see every day, walking down the high street. Enough to draw attention. Lots of attention.'

'And?'

'Well, let's face it, if we get through this and end up with all four, there's no way you'll be able to keep going to work. It's all you can do to stagger in there every day now and you're hardly even showing yet. The cost of childcare would outweigh anything you can earn, and my salary isn't going to be enough, is it? I've been trying to tot it all up. Clothes, milk, nappies, prams and the car will need replacing, let alone where they're all going to sleep, especially when they get older. We'll probably have to move, or build an extension, just to get all the beds in. Yes, I can work some extra hours, maybe even push for a pay rise or a promotion, but then I'll be working so much I'll hardly ever be here, hardly see my own kids. It's not ideal, when you're going to need all the help you can get.'

'There's always Mum.'

'Of course, and I'm sure she'll want to help out as much as she can, but she's getting older. She may not have the energy. And she does have a life of her own, what with her wedding coming up soon. And, besides, she doesn't live here with us, so she can't be here all the time, can't help with all the night feeds and stuff. No, what we need is something to take the financial pressure off a bit, maybe even allow me to cut my working hours back instead of upping them, and I think that's some kind of sponsorship deal.'

'What do you mean? Have their little faces on nappy packets or something?'

'Yes. Why not? Although nappy packets are more likely to show bottoms than faces, I should think. But there's talcum powder, milk, maybe those wipe things, or they could model for baby clothes catalogues ...'

'I don't know. I hadn't thought about it. But it's a possibility, I suppose. Do you think there's much money in it?'

'I have no idea, but I intend to find out. So, you just get on with lying there and keeping them warm, and I'll do what I do best, eh? Finding us a way to afford it.'

'And while I'm lying here keeping them warm, do you think you might be able to rustle up some dinner tonight?'

'Dinner? I thought you were too sick to eat?'

'That was earlier. Now I'm so ravenous I could eat a horse!'

'I can check in the freezer, but I don't think we have any horse. But, okay then. You rest, I'll cook. Just don't make a habit of it and expect me to be at your beck and call every night for the next six months or more. There'll be enough of that *after* they're born. Will lasagne do?'

'Lovely. Make it a big one. I am eating for five, remember?'

'As if I could forget.' He dropped the calculator down on the carpet and eased his hand out from under the blanket. 'And, if it's going to be that big a lasagne, how about I invite your mum and Trev round to share it? It's time we told them what's going on, don't you think? Now that it's all definite.'

'I want to tell her. Of course I do. I want to tell the whole world! But what if something goes wrong? It's still very early days. I can hardly believe any of it myself yet, and I feel like I might jinx the whole thing if I even say it out loud.'

'That's silly, and you know it. Now shall I call them, or will you?'

'But, Trevor? Do we have to? Can't we just ask Mum to come round on her own?'

'No, we can't. This silly feud has to stop now, Kate. It's gone on long enough and I've never understood why. So, he's not your dad. He can hardly help that, can he? And, as far as I can see, he's done nothing wrong. He's not an axe murderer or a drug addict. And your mum loves him. Enough to marry him. And as you're supposed to be her bridesmaid, I think it's probably time you explained why you just might need a considerably bigger dress.'

'And what if she's making a mistake?'

'What if *we* are?'

'Dan! You can't think that.'

'But, if it turns out that way, then at least it was our mistake to make. Just like marrying Trevor is hers. And he's not so bad, you know.'

'Really?'

'Really. Now make the call and I'll make a start on chopping the onions. Get the crying started early, because I'm sure there's going to be plenty of it once you tell your mum she's going to be a granny four times over!'

Chapter 24

Jenny, 2017

Jenny had never had a client die before. It was bound to happen sooner or later, she supposed, when you worked with the elderly, but still a shock when it happened for real. Mr Jenkins may have been a stubborn old devil sometimes, but she'd had a soft spot for him, and the phone call from the agency this morning, telling her that he'd passed away over the weekend and that there was no need to call there any more had hit her hard.

'I feel like there's something I should have done,' she wailed, dabbing at her eyes with a torn lump of soggy tissue.

Beth was sitting close to her on the bed, still in her pyjamas. 'Like what, Jen? He was an old man. If it was his time ...'

'But he was okay. He was eating his porridge and

watching TV, just like anybody else. He didn't know he only had a few days left, did he?'

'None of us know when though, do we? Imagine if we did. If we knew exactly when we were going to die, then I don't think we'd ever be able to enjoy living. It would be like some horrible countdown ticking relentlessly away over our heads and nothing we could do to stop it. Better to just go, surely?'

'But he was on his own, Beth. His daughter found him in bed, just gone in his sleep. It's so sad. I don't like to think of him dying all by himself.'

'But, if he was asleep, he won't have known anything about it. It's not like he was found on the floor, clutching his chest, or he'd lain there for hours in agony with a broken hip or something. Best way to go, I think, in your own bed. Who knows? He might have been having a lovely dream and just drifted away ...'

'Yeah, maybe.' Jenny took a last loud sniff and threw the tissue at the bin in the corner. 'And I know it's silly but it's made me think of Dad, living all by himself, when he should have his family around him.'

'Hardly the same thing, Jen. And Dad's not old. Well, not *that* old.'

'I know. It's just sad though, isn't it? People splitting up, losing loved ones, trying to get by on memories ...'

'Dad's okay. He's still got us. It's not as if we're going

anywhere, is it? And don't forget he's had – what? – three girlfriends since he left!'

'That we know of.' Jenny tried to laugh but it still came out as a sob. 'But what's happened, with old Mr J, well, it's made me realise something. I don't want to do this job any more. Caring. It's not really for me, not long term.'

'Jenny, you do know you're the most caring person I know, don't you? But, okay, what do you want to do instead?'

'I'm not sure, but seeing Laura, and listening to her, it's made me realise there must be so many women out there battling with pregnancy problems, losing babies, maybe struggling to get pregnant in the first place. Feeling anxious and guilty, and lots of them coping with their feelings all on their own. I mean, it's not just Laura. It happened to Mum too, didn't it? Miscarriage. Infertility. IVF. Post-natal depression. All those awful things women have to deal with. I just wish I could do something.'

'Like?'

'Well, I was wondering if I could train to be a midwife or a health visitor or even some kind of specialist counsellor. I'd love to be involved in helping mums to bring new babies into the world, not watching old people leave it.'

'But those jobs will need a lot of training, Jen. College, exams, probably years of it. You sure you're up for that?'

'Well, I won't know unless I make the effort to find out, will I?'

'True. But right now ...' Beth looked at her watch. 'We're both going to be late for work. I have a full head of foils and two cut and blows awaiting me this morning.'

'And I've got five breakfasts to make, a pair of compression stockings to peel off and rinse through, and Mrs Crabbe's toenails in need of a good cutting. Not that I'm supposed to do it, but there's nobody else and she can't reach! Best get to it, eh?'

'That's the spirit. Life goes on, Jen.' Beth turned at the door. 'Warts and all!'

***

Jenny sat on the bus later, staring out of the grimy rain-splashed window and thought about James. Okay, so he wasn't real, but that didn't seem to matter much. Ever since Natalie had caught her whispering down the phone to Laura and assumed she was seeing someone, she'd been giving James a lot more thought. He'd always been tall, dark and handsome. Well, that went without saying, didn't it? What self-respecting hero wasn't? But lately he'd started to develop much more clearly defined features. He had the sort of hair, for instance, that roughed up in the wind (she imagined him out in the wind quite often, for some strange reason) and needed to be flattened down again, with the aid of a strong hand displaying long tanned fingers and short neatly trimmed nails. A vision of the thick yellowed nails she'd just left at the end of Mrs Crabbe's toes tried to creep into her mind but was swiftly pushed aside.

James had a thin scar too, just a small one, almost faded, to the left of his mouth, one that she liked to touch whenever his face came close enough to kiss. She didn't know where the scar had come from, but she was sure it was the result of some selfless heroic act. Rescuing a child who'd fallen into the river, or a frightened cat from a tree, perhaps. Yes, she liked the idea of the cat. A man should be kind to animals. It said a lot. The mental image of James that sprang up, his long legs scaling the tree, his strong arms encircling the poor animal as the branches scratched and dug into the skin of his handsome face, etched itself indelibly into her memory as if she'd seen it all happening right in front of her eyes. Ah, James! If only ...

She hopped off the bus, pulled her scarf around her ears and walked the last quarter of a mile home, wishing she'd worn a more sensible pair of shoes as she stepped into yet another puddle she hadn't noticed was there. The house would be empty and, after a quick shower, she would have plenty of time to grab her laptop and start researching training courses and job possibilities before her teatime shift. It would have to be something that paid as she trained, though. She couldn't expect her dad to fund her studies. Not that he could afford to anyway, with the money he still contributed towards the household bills and the rent on his own flat to pay. She wished, not for the first time, that he hadn't left. Okay, so it was obvious that things weren't right between him and Mum, and hadn't been for a long time. Hardly surprising, considering what had happened, but that was years ago and they'd got by, hadn't they? For a long time, they'd chugged along, been a family, albeit an unconventional one.

The house felt chilly. October had arrived with a vengeance, violent winds and sheets of driving rain pounding at the windows overnight and wiping out the last of the flowers in the garden. It was calmer now, just the odd fallen branch lying on the lawn and a fence panel swaying precariously between its posts as if it might come flopping down at any minute, but winter was definitely on its way.

At least there was Natalie's wedding to look forward to. On a whim she ran up the stairs and pulled her bridesmaid's dress out of the wardrobe. It was pink, but not quite the bold fuchsia pink Beth had been after to match her favourite shoes. Natalie had put her foot down there, although that was probably not quite the right phrase to use in Natalie's case. But it was her wedding, after all, and with Beth and Jenny finally being asked to be bridesmaids, fighting over colours would probably have been a step too far and could well have made Natalie change her mind again, and neither of them had wanted to take that risk. So, a paler, softer pink it was and, to placate Beth, new shoes to match, courtesy of the lovely Phil and his ever-open wallet.

Jenny stepped out of her work clothes and into the dress, reaching behind her and sliding the zip up to the top. It was not a traditional bridesmaid style, more of a party dress, with its simple lines, knee-length hem and off-the-shoulder neckline, but that was good. It meant it was a dress she could wear again. To have fun in, go clubbing, dancing ...

She pulled the shoebox out from under her bed, parted the tissue paper to reveal her new shoes, slipped them on and stepped across the hall, going into Beth's room so she could look at herself in the full-length mirror. Turning from one side to the other, she was pleased with what she saw. Lifting her arms, she did a little self-conscious twirl, turning full circle, and then did it again, more boldly, laughing to herself, knowing there was nobody there to see. Yes, the dress would be great for dancing. She swayed into the faltering not-quite-right steps of a waltz and closed her eyes, listening to the music only she could hear, her feet moving to the rhythm of a hundred violins, wondering if somewhere in heaven Mr Jenkins might, at this very moment, be dancing with his beloved Vera. Now, if only James were here ...

She was so wrapped up in her fantasy world that she didn't hear the front door opening at first, and wasn't aware that anyone had come in until the heavy thump of wheels as they rebounded off the hall walls brought her back to reality. Then the front door slammed shut so loudly it sounded like the glass might break.

'Nat?' She ran out onto the landing, her heart racing and looked down. 'Is that you? What's going on?'

When there was no answer, she kicked her shoes off and ran down the stairs. 'Nat? Nat, where are you?'

The kitchen door was open and her sister was there, with her back to her, her wheelchair rammed up against the table. She was slumped forward with her arms outstretched on the table and her head down on top of them, great sobs making her shoulders heave up and down.

'Nat? Oh, my God, whatever's happened? Are you all right?'

Chapter 25

Kate, 1987–1988

I was still working at the bank, still serving customers at the counter. I'd long since passed up the opportunity to move up the career ladder. It would have meant moving around between different branches, taking exams, taking charge, and it just wasn't me. I liked the face-to-face stuff, talking to customers, handling the money, getting to go home at regular hours without the worries that a pile of outstanding paperwork or a last-minute staffing crisis can cause. I'd seen the way Dan was and I didn't want that for me.

Linda was long gone. She'd married, given up work, had a couple of kids in quick succession, as easy as shelling peas, got a big house and a dog. It wouldn't be totally accurate to say I was jealous, but it had put a strain on our friendship, her having babies so easily while I was struggling, and I didn't see her often.

Mum and Trevor had married without fuss, just a handful of people gathered together at the register office and a meal at a posh hotel. Of course, Dan and I had been there, but any idea of me standing behind her in a bridesmaid dress had been quietly pushed aside, and I was glad of the chance to sit throughout the ceremony, feeling strangely weepy, without even being allowed a drop of alcohol to put me in the party mood.

'It's time to let old grudges go,' Dan whispered as we waited in line to hug the new Mrs Brookfield and shake the groom's hand, so I plastered on a smile and tried to do just that. Mum looked happy enough, in a new cream-coloured suit and clutching her bouquet of small pink roses, hanging on to Trevor's hand in all the photographs, and I wanted things to work out well for her. I really did.

'I never told you before,' Dan said later, when we'd slipped away after the dessert and were back at home, my feet up on the sofa and Dan still picking bits of confetti out of my hair. 'But it's time you knew. Where the money came from, for the treatment ...'

'But that was your parents, wasn't it? I assumed ...'

'No, Kate. It wasn't. He didn't want me to say, didn't want you to think he was trying to bribe you or something, or worse still for you to throw it back in his face, but now he's family, I think you should know. It was Trevor.'

'*Trevor?* Trevor loaned us the money for the IVF?'

'Not loaned, Kate. Gave. He's a good bloke. Really, he is.'

'Oh.' I didn't know what to say. Trevor? I'd never even tried to hide how I felt about him, always keeping him at arm's length, hoping he might go away again, the man who had tried and failed to take Dad's place. Not that anyone could.

'He sold his own flat when he moved in with your mum. See, he wasn't just after a roof over his head at all. He already had one but chose to give it up to be with her. Not that you ever asked, or cared, you were so quick to judge. So, not quite the leech you've made him out to be.'

'Oh,' I said again, feeling confused, and more than a little ashamed.

'So he's had the money from the flat sale tucked away for a while. He told me he wanted to put it to good use, and that he knew helping your mum to become a granny would make her happy. And that would make him happy.'

'But, how ...? Dan, I'm amazed you even asked him.'

'I didn't have to. He came to me. Wanted it to be our secret. Even your mum doesn't know. So there's no need to say anything. This stays between us, okay? But ... well, go easy on him, eh? He desperately wants to be accepted as part of the family, and I think he's earned that right, don't you?'

'I suppose so.'

'There's no suppose about it, Kate. He's married to your mum now. He's family, whether you like it or not.'

'She did look lovely, didn't she?'

'She did. But then, maybe that's what love does for a person, eh?'

'And do you love me, Dan Campbell?'

'Of course I do, you daft thing.' He reached across and pulled my face towards him for a kiss. 'Come here and let me show you how much. And, by the way, you look lovely too.'

'But I'm all fat and bloated.'

'No, Kate. That's not fat.' He undid the tiny buttons down the front of my dress and lay his hand on the warm skin of my belly. 'That's babies. Our babies. And believe me, you've never looked lovelier ...'

***

We spent that Christmas down in Somerset, with me being fussed over by Dan's mum as if I was the most precious, fragile thing. It quite surprised me, with them being farming people and dealing with animal births all the time. I had expected Molly Campbell to be all practical and gung-ho and wreathed in calm, but I guess it's different when the impending birth is that of your own grandchildren, and being back there, in that house, was probably making all of us remember the way I'd lost the last one.

'I wonder what we would have called her?' Dan said, whispering into my hair as we lay spooned as usual in the old lumpy bed. How had he known what I had been thinking about, lying there in the dark?

'Apart from Baby Blob, you mean? I don't know. We did have a sort of list, didn't we? I remember that Amanda was on it.'

'And I remember how much I hated that name! It's probably time we started making a list again, isn't it? And this time we have to choose four names we both like. It won't be easy!'

'I still like Amanda ...'

'I'd better hope for boys then. It might be the only way to dissuade you.'

'God, no! Not all boys, please. I'll give up the name if you promise me at least one girl.'

'I can't promise you anything, sweetheart. I only wish I could.' He nuzzled his face into the back of my neck, and if it hadn't been for my feelings of utter exhaustion I would have turned around right then and asked for a whole lot more.

'But I do quite like Elizabeth,' he said, clearly oblivious to the tingling feeling running straight down to the places only he knew how to reach. 'You know, like the Queen.'

'Oh, Dan, you are so ... what's the word? Traditional? But it's an okay name, I suppose. Although I'd probably prefer to shorten it. Maybe Beth?'

'Beth ... Yes, I like it. Okay, that's one down and three to go.'

He ran his hand over my bump and back up to my breast, where it cupped me gently for a while before falling still, his gentle snores drifting into the silence of the room. I think he was as shattered as I was.

We stayed a few days. Kind though Dan's family were, it didn't feel like home and I was glad to leave, to get back to my own routine, my own bed, and a kind of normality I knew couldn't last. My growing girth was making that abundantly clear.

I enjoyed work but, as the weeks passed, I knew I couldn't keep it up for much longer. It was mainly the tiredness, dragging me down into the depths of the sofa as soon as I got home, and usually into bed before nine. And the winter weather wasn't helping, with me so afraid I'd slip on an icy pavement at any minute and do myself, or the babies, damage, that I was getting more and more scared to step outside on my own. Yet Dan seemed to have found a new lease of life, a sort of frantic energy that had him painting both spare rooms, scouring second-hand shops for some of the baby things we could never afford new, juggling with columns of figures and making phone calls like there was no tomorrow.

'Have you ever heard of a company called Goo Goo?' he asked, rushing in from work one evening with his excited face on.

I hadn't been long home myself, and was still trying to decide whether to make some dinner or just flop for a while first. 'Sounds like something a baby would say. Goo goo, ga ga ...'

'Exactly! A contented baby. That's probably why they chose the name. They're a baby food company. The one with those TV adverts where a big ginger cat jumps up and steals the food, remember?'

'Oh, yeah, I know. I always thought that was a stupid ad. What's a cat got to do with baby food? We don't have ads with babies helping themselves to a bowl of Whiskas, do we?'

'No, we don't. And it's obvious others must feel the same, because they're thinking of changing their image. Looking for a new advertising angle. Concentrating on actual babies this time.'

'And?'

'And they quite like the idea of using four babies. *Our* babies ...'

'Really? But they haven't even been born yet, Dan. And babies don't start eating baby food for months, do they?'

'They're happy to wait. It takes a while to get a campaign together, apparently, and the cat thing still has a while to run. And they say we're just what they're looking for. First-time parents, expecting a lot more than we bargained for, everything new and worrying, needing a reliable brand we can feel confident about, to show us how to feed our babies ... They want *us*, Kate. Or they've as good as said they do, all bar signing on the dotted line.'

'Oh. Wow! You really did mean it when you talked about our own little mini set of Waltons and getting them on the telly, didn't you?'

'Of course. We have to find ways of financing this whole thing. So we can give them the best life we can. And you haven't heard the best bit yet.'

'Which is?'

'How much they're willing to pay. And, guess what? If they're all the same sex, we get a bonus!'

'I don't want them all to be the same sex. Especially if it's boys ...'

'Well, it's too late to do much about that now, isn't it? They are what they are. But, Kate, listen, we're talking thousands here. Thousands! Our family could become the new faces of Goo Goo. You know, on TV, in magazines, maybe even have our picture on the jars. Or the kids' pictures, anyway. And Goo Goo food is just part of a much bigger company. They've got interests in sterilising equipment, feeding bottles, highchairs – you name it. Just think, Kate, if this works out we could get free stuff, all the jars of baby food we'll ever need. *And get paid!*'

I gave up on the idea of cooking and opted for the sofa, pulling up my jumper, folding my hands over my balloon-like belly and waiting for the tiny flickers I'd started to feel lately, that meant, despite their limited space, that they were beginning to kick.

'Hello in there,' I said, my voice dropping down to a whisper as I rubbed gently over the bump. 'Did you hear that? You're going to be famous.' I looked back up at Dan. 'That's not what's really important, though, is it? All I really want is for them to be healthy. And to be happy.'

'Of course.' Dan knelt down on the carpet beside me and placed his hands over mine. 'But having money helps.'

***

I spent three weeks in bed, in the end. The doctors had warned me it was likely, and as soon as my blood pressure went sky-high, my skin as taut as the surface of a drum, and my ankles couldn't take the strain any more, they whisked me into hospital and kept me there.

'It's really too early, but the ways things are, you could go into labour any day, and you will unless we try to prevent that from happening. The important thing now is that you hang onto them as long as possible,' I was told. 'Quads rarely go beyond thirty-one weeks, and that's if you're lucky. It could be sooner, but they don't have a lot of room in there, and their growth is going to start slowing down now. They will be small, we can't avoid that, but every day inside is another day for them to grow just a little bit bigger and stronger.'

I liked the sound of that, having bigger, stronger babies, so I did as I was told. No unnecessary strain, no stress, no moving about overdoing things. I ate my meals in bed, read books, slept a lot, made friends with the other patients as they came and went, got up only to go to the toilet or to lie in a warm bath, and just waited.

I felt like a fraud. Not ill. Not incapable. Just lying there, doing nothing, counting off the days, enjoying the calm before the storm. Mum came in, of course. Fussing around me, bringing fruit and magazines, and little knitted bootees, all matching, all white. Sometimes Trevor was there too, hovering behind her, going off to fetch cups of tea, clearly feeling a bit awkward, like a spare part only invited along because he was the one with the car she needed to transport her there and back. I didn't say it but I was glad he was there, not just for Mum but so he could see the results of his generosity, the day coming ever nearer when he would get to see the children he had helped to create. I felt I should thank him, but Dan had told me to say nothing, so I didn't. It might take a while for me to change the way I had felt about Trevor for so long, but I was getting there, slowly.

***

We made it to twenty-nine weeks and six days. The babies couldn't wait any longer. They were ready, but I wasn't. I'd never been so scared as I was that day, being wheeled along a long white corridor, seeing Dan all gowned up, with just his eyes, big and terrified, showing above his mask.

I'd known all along that it would have to be a Caesarean birth. The easiest, quickest, safest way of getting them out into the world. A team of doctors and nurses and all kinds of specialists gathered around me, waiting to grab each one as soon as it emerged, check it, treat it, whisk it away. I'd looked at the books, seen just how tiny a foetus was at that stage, how underdeveloped it was, knew just how many things could go wrong. And I had four to worry about.

I didn't feel a thing as they sliced me open. Not in the womb area, anyway. Just sick. Sick with nerves and a chilling, almost paralysing, fear.

Beth came first. Through my groggy half-there state, I managed a watery smile as they pulled her out and held her up, very briefly, all small and slimy, above the barrier built to keep me away from watching the gorier end of the action. I'd wanted at least one girl, and here she was. 'Three pounds exactly,' someone said, before she was taken away, before I'd even heard her cry.

I hadn't really thought before, about how quickly they would come. The next baby, a boy, was out and screaming before I'd even lowered my head and taken another breath. 'Oliver,' I said, plucking the top boy's name from the list we had finally agreed upon. This was it. It was really happening. The names were coming off the list and attaching themselves to babies. Real babies. And I was a mother at last!

'Smaller,' said the voice from somewhere out of sight. 'Two pounds, twelve, but in good shape. Wriggling like a fish. He's a little fighter, this one!'

There was a longer gap this time, and I was aware of a lot of hurried movement that I couldn't feel and couldn't properly see, footsteps retreating away from me, whispers, then too much silence, and no pronouncement at all. 'What's happening? Is it a boy or a girl?' I tried to lift my head. Nobody spoke. Not even Dan.

And then, 'Another girl,' the doctor said, handing the last baby back to some unseen body behind him, his face impassive, professional, leaning over me, doing his job, getting ready to sew me up. But I couldn't name this one. I couldn't. My head, and my heart, were still back there, just moments earlier, with baby number three. There was an order to be followed here. one, two, three ... Where was baby number three? What was it? Why had nobody told me? Its sex, weight ...

'Two pounds, ten ounces.'

No. Wait! They were talking about baby number four, weren't they? Something was wrong here. There had to be something badly wrong with my third baby. But why weren't they doing something about it? Rushing about, shouting, slapping it like they do on TV, making it cry ...

I looked up into Dan's face and suddenly I knew. I had delivered four babies, but one of them was already dead.

***

It was my fault, of course. Pushing Dan into this thing. Trying to make so many babies, all at once. Expecting them to survive, against all the advice, all the odds. Thinking I was some kind of superwoman, superwomb, supermum. I didn't listen; not properly. Didn't want to. Not to the doctor, to Dan, to reason. I was reckless, blinkered, obstinate.

I forgot we were supposed to be a couple, supposed to decide things together.

It was the second spur of the moment decision I had made, the second truly unforgivable thing I had done, to

232

our marriage, to our life. And, again, just like on our wedding day, when I had stood at the church door and decided to walk, babyless, up the aisle, I did it without talking to him, without even trying to hear what he thought, what he felt, without thinking beyond the here and now. And look where it took us. All of us.

This was the worst, most unimaginably, hopelessly sad day of my life. And it was all my own fault. On the unforgivable scale it was two – nil to me. If only I'd known then that Dan would soon be evening the score.

NUMBER THREE

Chapter 26

Natalie, 2017

Natalie couldn't believe it. Her dad, the precious dad, who she saw so little of these days but who still meant so much to her, was letting her down. How could he do this? And why? He must have known how hurtful it would be, telling her he couldn't give her away, and that he might not even be able to make it to the wedding at all. And he hadn't even had the courage to come and see her in person. Just a phone call at work, as she was about to eat her lunchtime sandwich. A call full of apologies and awkward silences, but lacking in any real explanations.

She felt Jenny's arms encircling her and turned around, burying her face in the soft front of what, even at this close range, looked suspiciously like her sister's bridesmaid dress, sobbing hard and spilling out the whole sorry story.

'How could he, Jen? There are only a few weeks to go, and now he tells me. *Now!*'

'He must have his reasons, Nat. He loves you. He'd want to be there, more than anything. Any father would.'

'You think so?' Natalie lifted her head, sniffed hard and wiped her sleeve across her eyes. 'Then why won't he do it, then? Make the effort, for my wedding. For me. It has to be some woman, I bet. Some jealous new girlfriend, who doesn't want him being too close to his family.'

'Is that what he said?'

Natalie sniffed, rubbing her sleeve over her blotchy face. 'No.'

'Then you're just being silly. Dad would never let some woman keep him away from you. From any of us. Especially on such an important day. No, there has to be more to it.'

'So, why not just tell me? I'd rather know his reasons than be left trying to guess them. It's me. I just know it is. He doesn't want me to get married at all. He thinks I'm still a child, that because of my disability I can't cope with everyday things that normal people do, like moving out, making a home, going on a plane. Let alone having sex ...'

'Too much information for any dad to have to think about!'

'Okay, that's true, but it still bothers him that I even

go out to work without someone driving me from door to door and holding an umbrella over my head when it rains. He still wants me all wrapped up in cotton wool. Doesn't he know how hard I've battled to be normal, Jen?'

'You *are* normal, you daft thing!'

'Well he obviously doesn't think so. So, it's either that, or he feels too embarrassed, having to escort a chair down the aisle. I bet it will be different when it's Beth's turn. Or yours. All long dresses with trains, striding down the aisle side by side in time to some march or other, him dancing with the bride at the reception ...'

'Nat! Don't be ridiculous. You are not a chair. You are a person who just happens to need a chair to get along. And who says he can't dance with you? He looks past the chair, at the real you. Just like Phil does. Like we all do. It's not important. Sometimes, do you know, I forget you even have a chair ...'

'Ah, but he can't. He can never forget, can he? Because it was him who put me in it.'

'It was an accident, though, wasn't it, Nat?' Jenny sounded shocked. 'Surely you've forgiven him by now?'

'I hardly remember it, Jen. It's so long ago and I was so young. Forgiveness doesn't really come into it. It is what it is. Was what it was. In the past. Done. Unchangeable. But Mum hasn't forgiven him, has she? Ever.'

'She's never forgiven herself, Nat. There's a difference.'

'But *she's* coming to my wedding, isn't she? You all are. And he isn't. I think you'll find that's the difference that actually matters. And why are you wearing that dress anyway?'

'Because I love it and I wanted to see myself in it again, that's all. Look, I will take care of it, honest I will.' Jenny pulled out a kitchen chair and sat on it, carefully smoothing down the front of the dress. 'So, what now? Are you just going to leave things like this? Or would you like me to go round and talk to Dad? Find out what's really going on?'

'Who says he'll tell you any more than he's told me?'

'Because face to face is very different to down a phone line, Nat. And I can tell when he's hiding something, or when he's lying. Always could.'

'I don't know if I even want him to come now. If he can't be bothered, then neither can I. Maybe I'll just ask someone else to give me away.'

'Like Mum asked Gran, you mean?'

'Yes, but that was because she didn't have a dad. He was already dead by then, so she didn't have a lot of choice. And the truth is that our dad might as well be dead too, for all the use he is to us ...'

'You don't mean that, Nat. You know you don't. It's just the shock talking. He's always been a great dad, to all of us. Always done his best. And I'll sort this out

– whatever it is. I promise I will. Now, come on, wipe your eyes. Have you eaten yet?'

Natalie shook her head. 'There's a soggy tear-stained cheese-and-pickle sarnie still sat on my desk at work. Someone's probably nicked it by now. Or thrown it out for the birds.'

'Okay, forget that, then. I'll make you some lunch before you go back. If you think you're skiving off for the afternoon when the rest of us have to work, and just because of a few tears, then you're very much mistaken. And, by the way, you do have another choice, don't you? You could ask Ollie to give you away. But first, let me have a try with Dad, eh? And if he hasn't got something utterly compelling to say in his own defence, then ...'

'Then what?'

'I haven't quite decided yet, but he won't like it, I know that much. I'm on your side here, Nat. Now, do you want mustard on this ham or not?'

'Yes, please. But take the dress off first. I don't want you getting food all over it. Not until after the ceremony, anyway!'

***

Phil was waiting for Natalie on the pavement outside her office when she came out at five o'clock.

'I wasn't expecting you!' She smiled up into his eyes as he leant down to kiss her, one cold hand flat against each of her cheeks. 'God, you're freezing. What have you been doing? Juggling bags of frozen peas?'

'Not exactly. But I hear you've had a bit of an upset, so I thought I might treat you to a little something. Now, hold your hands out and close your eyes ...'

'Aaah!' Something cold landed in her hands and she quickly opened her eyes. It was a choc ice. 'Phil?'

'Well, I know you like ice cream, and it makes a change from flowers! Go on, open it and get it down you before it melts.'

'I think it already has.'

'Nonsense. It's just gone a bit soft, that's all. But make any more fuss and I won't be buying you any more. Ever!'

She laughed. 'No, no. I'm not complaining. I love ice cream. I just wasn't expecting any today, that's all.' She peeled back the corner of the wrapper and sucked at the gooey chocolate. 'Yum, it's lovely. Thank you.'

'Here, let me push ...'

'Phil, you don't have to do that. I'm not incapable. I can push myself.'

'With your hands full of choc ice? I think not. And, besides, I like to push. You can be too independent for your own good, you know. You have to let me take care of you sometimes. It's what husbands do.'

'Most husbands just take their turn at the washing up or the supermarket run. They don't have wheelchairs to push.'

'Maybe not, but then I'm not most husbands, am I? And there are advantages. A chair comes in really handy to hang the shopping bags on, doesn't it? And when you've had a few too many to drink, at least you're already safely sitting down and I won't have to be grabbing at your arm to stop you wobbling off your high heels into the gutter!'

'I never have too many to drink!'

'Then maybe it's time you did. Come on, when you've guzzled that choc ice I'm taking you straight to the White Lion.'

'Jenny's put you up to this, hasn't she? Always the peacemaker.'

'She may have mentioned a little problem with your dad, yes. Which you may, or may not, want to talk about. Up to you. But don't make it sound like Jenny's forced me into something I didn't want to do. An early dinner, a bottle of vino, and the company of my beautiful fiancée. What more could a man want?'

'Football on the telly?'

'Well, there is that, of course. But that's where eating early comes in, you see. Still plenty of time to get home for the match.'

She would have taken a swipe at him if he hadn't

been right behind her and annoyingly out of reach. 'How's it going, at the house? Have they finished the stair lift yet?'

'Don't you worry about any of that. It's all in hand, and by the time we get back from honeymoon, it will be done. I promise.'

'About that ...'

'Nat, you can ask as many times as you like and I'm still not going to tell you. I want to surprise you.' He swivelled the chair around and backed into the pub, nudging the door with his hip like a seasoned professional.

'But what do I pack? And how about getting currency and checking the passports? I'm assuming we need them, and we're not just going to Skegness!'

'All taken care of. Now, stop worrying and park yourself somewhere over there near the fire while I get us a drink. And that's another plus point for your faithful old chair. You never have to wait for a seat, do you? No matter how busy the place is. Not when you've got your own with you!'

'You make me sound like a snail, carrying my own little shell house with me everywhere I go!'

'Exactly! But I bet even the best snail residences don't have their own stair lifts. So, never forget how lucky you are. White wine okay?'

Natalie wiped her chocolatey hands on a tissue and

pulled her chair up to a small table in the corner, nicely tucked away, but from which she could still watch the world go by. Or watch Phil at the bar, anyway, shoving his wallet back into his trousers pocket and juggling a bottle and two glasses as he weaved his way back between the tables to find her. He was so handsome, so special, just so damned nice. She was indeed lucky, and she had no intention of forgetting it.

'Here. Nicely chilled, and I thought I'd get sparkling, for a change. Time we started to celebrate.'

'Celebrate what?'

'Being almost married. Our last days of freedom, and still smiling, despite all the planning, and the stress of it all.'

'I suppose. If it wasn't for Dad putting a dampener on things.'

'He must have his reasons.'

'Yes, he can't be bothered.'

'I think that's very harsh of you, Nat. And it's unlikely to be true. No, Jenny says she'll have a word with him, so let's not jump the gun, eh? It'll all work out in the end. And there's always Ollie, if your dad doesn't come good. Nothing to panic about. Now, let's forget all that for this evening.' He picked up the menu. 'So, what do you fancy?'

'You.' She picked up his hand and kissed it. 'Of course!'

Chapter 27

Kate, 1988

The first days slipped by as if I was in a dream. The babies were slow to feed, and they cried a lot, but the nurses helped with all of that. All three of them were doing well. Small and surprisingly healthy, with their perfect little faces, and their soft wiggly little hands hardly any bigger than Dan's thumb, and the very beginnings of dark brown hair, just like mine, already starting to appear like a faint shadow on the top of their wrinkly pink heads. But they were not yet ready to go home. I was sore and exhausted and still in shock, and I would have preferred not to go home either.

It hurt where they'd cut me, even to sit up, and I was given a long list of things I wasn't supposed to do, at least until the stitches came out, but some of them for weeks afterwards. Like pushing a hoover about. As if that was high on my agenda.

I was encouraged to pump my milk out, to keep it flowing, for when they were able to come off the tubes. And when they did, it was a nightmare. Day and night, seemingly non-stop, like a production line. Small stomachs only able to hold small amounts. Me trying and failing, always failing. And with two breasts and three babies, the maths didn't quite add up anyway, so there seemed always to be one who was yelling for food I wasn't able to give. And it hurt too, having tiny mouths latched on to me, one after the other, almost permanently, sucking away until I was so sore I bled.

Despite a lot of cajoling from the staff, I quickly realised I couldn't keep it up. Bottles meant the load could be shared. Bottles worked. For me, they did, anyway. And for the babies, who didn't seem to care who gave them their milk so long as they got it, and fast.

We settled into a kind of haphazard routine in those early days, finding a way of managing this strange new existence the best we could, with Dan rushing backwards and forwards between home and work and hospital, Mum popping in at least once a day, and me in desperate need of sleep but thrown in at the deep end and battling rapidly through a crash course in how to be a mum.

None of us said very much about the baby we had lost, although Dan and I had both held her, wrapped up tightly in a blanket, and kissed her, and cried over her, and named her. Rosie Jane Campbell. Someone took photos and made an imprint of her feet, and put it all into a memory box, to be kept, put away somewhere, looked at later, when we were ready.

'At least she won't be alone,' I said to Dan, reluctantly handing her back to a nurse who looked almost as upset as we were. 'She'll be with Baby Bump now, won't she? On a cloud somewhere, watching over us. Our two lost children, looking after each other ...'

'Maybe.' He swallowed back a sob and turned his face away, and that was it. It was just too hard to say anything else, to speak about her, to each other, to anyone.

Although I knew she was gone, somehow she stayed with me. A part of me I could never let go. She stayed in my head, in my thoughts, her sweet little face white and still, haunting my dreams, and I couldn't believe she would ever go away.

I couldn't stay in hospital indefinitely, so they sent me home, to a house with four Moses baskets and two twin prams and a horrible deathly silence that should have given me the chance to sleep at last but only served to remind me that my babies weren't with me, and that one never would be.

We went together to the register office, coming away with four birth certificates and one death certificate, all dated the same day. Dan clutched at my hand as a couple, just married, burst out through the doors and into the sunshine, cameras clicking and confetti flying in the wind, and we scurried away with our heads down. I don't think I had ever felt so utterly numb.

***

Post-natal depression they'd call it now. Probably would have called it that back then too, if I'd ever been to a doctor and confessed to it. But what would have been the point? I had lost a child, but I still had the others to look after. There was nothing anyone could do. To me, it was just grief. And, as far as I know, there's no cure for that.

***

I couldn't face giving Rosie a proper funeral. I'd seen those tiny white coffins before, being carried into churches, the parents insisting everyone wore bright colours, nothing black and gloomy. But how could it not be black and gloomy? My baby was dead. And who would we invite? It wasn't as if anyone had known her. Not even us. So she was cremated, privately, and we scattered her ashes in our own garden, and Dan planted a rose, a beautiful pure-white rose, one that would grow up the fence and entwine itself into the very fabric of the garden, as she had entwined herself in our hearts. I didn't know then if it would be enough, if later I might regret not making more of a ceremony of it, but it felt right at the time.

I visited the others in the hospital all the time, feeding, changing, holding them, waiting for the doctors to decide they were ready to go home, then heading back to eat, have a bath and fall into bed and my restless Rosie-filled dreams, ready for it all to start again the next morning. Dan joined me whenever he could, but he had to get back to work, earning the money we so badly needed to survive, and that only helped me to feel more alone, as if the weight of it all was falling on me, and from some great invisible, unstoppable height.

Ollie caught a chest infection and for a few days we had to watch him struggling to breathe, Dan screwing his fists into tight white balls and walking about, restlessly, and me silently worrying myself sick that this baby would die too. But he fought it off. My only son; my Ollie. A real little fighter they had said, when he had been born, and they were right. The doctors said it was normal among premature babies to have problems with their lungs, but nothing felt very normal to me. It was all so hugely terrifying, so bafflingly new.

The babies took over my life. Their needs, their demands were all that really mattered now, and making sure they stayed healthy, avoided any more infection and kept on growing. Big and strong enough to fill the hole their sister had left behind.

They came home when they were eight weeks old, still so small, so frighteningly fragile, in three little car seats, all lined up in the people carrier Dan had found for us, second hand, and which was already piled full of baby stuff before our new life as a family had even begun. He drove carefully, taking corners like a cautious old-age pensioner out driving on a Sunday afternoon. And then the house wasn't silent any more.

***

'Kate, I've got some bad news.' Dan had just come in from work and I was up to my eyes in washing, a trail of baby sick down my shoulder that had been there since lunchtime, but I hadn't yet found the time or the inclination to wipe it away.

'Then I don't want to hear it. I don't think I can cope with any more bad news. Not ever.'

'Come on. Stop all that and sit down for a minute. You look done in.'

'That's because I am. Look, they're asleep. All three of them, at the same time. Do you have any idea how rarely that happens? If I don't sort out these bits now, I may not get the chance again for hours ...'

'Kate. Please. Remember what the health visitor said.

When they rest, you rest. You have to look after yourself. Housework comes way down the list.'

'They have to have clothes to wear, Dan. And so do you. You can't go to work in a dirty shirt, can you?'

'Then, ask your mum to help. She's offered enough times.'

'She does help. With the babies, anyway. Cuddling and feeding and changing nappies. And at least that gives me time to do all the other stuff.'

'Seems the wrong way round to me, Kate. You should be spending time with the babies and getting to know them, while she does all the other stuff.'

'Yeah, maybe. But at least she's here. Which is more than can be said for you.'

'Oh, come on. That's unfair. Someone has to go out and earn the money, and I do what I can when I get home. You know I do.'

I could see the hurt in his eyes and I knew he was right. I was being unfair and I was worrying too much about keeping the house clean and ironing shirts, which would probably look perfectly acceptable if I just hung them up and let the creases fall out by themselves. 'I'm sorry, Dan.' I sank into a chair and dropped the little pile of damp baby vests onto the kitchen table. 'It's just all ... well, so overwhelming. I had no idea I'd be so tired, that there'd be so much to do, that I wouldn't get a moment to myself. Ever. I can't remember when I last read a magazine or watched a TV programme from beginning to end or even properly blow-dried my hair.'

He ran his fingers up and down the back of my hand and along my arm. I waited for the tingles to run through me, but nothing happened. When had I last felt even a flicker of sexual desire? That night in Somerset, probably, and even then I had been too shattered to do anything about it. But perhaps sex was something we just had to put on the back burner for a while too, along with the ironing and the hoovering. The babies had to come first.

'Kate, listen. I had a call from Goo Goo. The ad campaign ... it isn't going to happen, I'm afraid. Or, if it does, it won't be with us in it.'

'What? Why? I thought we were the perfect family, exactly what they were looking for?'

'We were. But we're not any more. It seems triplets aren't quite as unusual as quads. Not as newsworthy.'

'But we don't have triplets!'

'As far as they're concerned, we do. Three babies is not the image they're after. It seems it was four or nothing.'

'But, Rosie ...?'

'They don't give a shit about Rosie. According to them, we've broken the contract. If we can't supply four babies, then the deal's off.'

'And the money? The thousands they promised us?'

'There won't be any money. We're on our own again.'

I just stared at him, aware that my mouth had fallen open. 'So, how will we manage?'

'I'm not sure. Overtime. Or I could try for a promotion. But both options mean I'd be out of the house even more, leaving you on your own.'

'Oh, Dan. No.'

'You might have to rely even more on your mum. And Trevor ...'

'Trevor? Ask him for more money, you mean? We can't do that, can we?'

'No, of course not. I just meant that maybe he'd like to be a bit more involved. You know, be a proper granddad. Walk them to the park, that sort of thing. It doesn't seem right to keep shutting him out, especially with your mum spending so much time here. And we do owe him, you know. Big time.'

'But, Dan, these are *our* babies. Yours and mine. I don't want to raise them on my own. Or with Mum and Trevor. I want to do it with you.'

'I'm sorry, Kate. Really. But things will work out somehow. They usually do. And it will be okay. In the end.'

I lay my head on his shoulder and said nothing, just felt his body moving as he breathed, as an image of the old us floated through my head. The old carefree us, with nothing and no one to think about but ourselves.

Had that really been only a year or so ago? And then one of the babies woke up and started howling. I wasn't sure which one. I still hadn't learned to tell them apart by their cries. What sort of a mother did that make me? Not that it mattered because, within seconds, they were all at it. All yelling together, like the Three Degrees on a bad day.

'My turn,' Dan said, slipping out of his work jacket and heading for the stairs. 'I might as well do something useful for once. While I'm here.'

Chapter 28

Ollie, 2017

Ollie rolled up his sleeves and slapped another coat of paint onto the stable door, being careful not to breathe in any of the fumes and risk one of his annoying asthma attacks. Rehearsals were going well and Beth was clearly enjoying the whole process as much as he was, dipping into her annual leave allowance and taking a couple of afternoons off from the salon every week to take the kids through their paces, and dashing straight here after work on most of the other days to help out with all the behind-the-scenes stuff. Perhaps, for both of them, it had come at just the right time, to take the focus off their failed love lives and let them concentrate their time and energy on something new.

He hadn't touched a drop of alcohol in over a week and had even stopped his regular visits to the chess club. Since Granddad Trev had died, he'd played sporad-ically, never really enjoying it the way he felt he should. Chess was something they had always done together, sitting on either side of a fancy marble board, sometimes for hours at a time, and it had been Trev who'd taught him all the moves. He had to admit it was a bit too solitary and serious these days, not good for his frame of mind. It was time he did something with a bit more sociability about it. And a lot more fun. Thankfully, the school show seemed to have filled the void and was now taking up every minute of his spare time. Perhaps all those years of tactics and concentration, and having to plan several moves ahead, was actually coming in handy, because he was already feeling immensely proud of how it was all going, what they were managing to achieve. It was a good feeling.

'How are you getting on with the costumes?' he asked, hearing someone coming into the empty hall behind him and assuming it was Beth.

'Ha! You won't catch me with a needle and thread, mate.'

Ollie turned round and laughed. It was Sean Harper, the supply teacher over from Australia, who was standing in for the absent Mrs Carter until she'd had her baby. 'Sorry, Sean, I thought you were someone else. My sister ...'

'Ah. Is that the pretty brunette with the very big hair?

I've seen her around but I thought maybe she was your ... er ...'

'What? Girlfriend? No, that position is currently vacant. Long story ... No, Beth's just here helping me out with the show. Much more her sort of thing than mine, although I have to admit I'm quite into it all now.'

'You taking to the stage yourself, then?'

'No! I'm not going that far. Other than just to welcome the audience, then I'm off back behind that curtain, where I belong. Let's just say acting and me are not natural bedfellows!'

'Right! Can't say I blame you, mate. I just popped by to see if you needed help with anything, scenery-wise. The Head said you might need a hand, and I'm quite good with a hammer and nails! Happy to leave the sewing side of things to your sister, though, obviously!'

'Thanks, Sean. It's the manger, you know, the crib thing I was going to tackle next. Do you think you could do anything with that lot over there?' He pointed to a pile of wood and a large bag of straw, donated by one of the parents. 'I don't have any kind of instructions, so it's just make it up as you go along, really. Or you can take over the painting if you prefer.'

'No, the manger's fine. Not worth two of us getting covered in the green stuff!' He pointed to the large smear of green paint that Ollie hadn't noticed was running right down his sleeve, walked over to the wood and picked up a few pieces. 'I like a bit of a challenge. Got any tools?'

'In my bag, over by the door.' Ollie rubbed uselessly at his sleeve with the palm of his hand. 'Oh, and Sean ...?'

'Yeah?'

'My sister. She's single, if you're interested. Only you did happen to mention you thought she was pretty.'

'Oh, right. Okay.' He'd turned his back so Ollie couldn't judge his reaction. 'I'll bear that in mind!'

When Beth arrived five minutes later, she was puffing like a train. 'Sorry, sorry,' she said, banging the door back hard against the wall, dropping a huge carrier bag on the floor and sinking into a chair. 'Didn't mean to be so late, but I just couldn't get rid of my last lady. A bit more trimmed off here, a reshaping of the fringe there, and was the colour quite right, did I think? God, I don't why I do it sometimes. Oh!' She stopped talking when she spotted Sean. 'Sorry, Ollie. I thought you were on your own.'

Ollie smiled. Oh, he did like to see Beth thrown off balance sometimes, her cheeks reddening like a pair of cherries.

'Don't mind me.' Sean put his saw down, plucked a strand of straw from his hair and came over to introduce himself. 'Sean Harper. I work with your brother. And I'm having a go at making a manger, if you hadn't already guessed.'

'Hi, Sean. I'm Beth. Sorry about that. It's sometimes hard to switch off after work. Hairdressing. Not all that exciting, I know, but it's a living. Still, I'm here to help get this show sorted out, not just to moan about my clients. Honest!'

'Oh, I don't mind a bit of a moan. You should try working with some of the little horrors in my class! But I don't suppose I should say that, should I?'

'Probably not.' Beth reached into her bag and hauled out a fluffy white bundle. 'So, anyway, what do you think of this?' She held the fabric up and gave it a shake. It was clearly meant to be a sheep, legs and all.

'That's fantastic! Did you make it?' Sean seemed to have forgotten to return to his saw and seemed suddenly much more interested in the subject of nativity costumes than he had been earlier.

'No, not me. One of the mums. Aren't they great?' She pulled another two identical costumes out of her bag. 'There's a lot of hidden talent out there when you go looking for it. So many parents have offered to help since we put up that notice on the board. I've even got someone having a go at putting a donkey together. You know, like a pantomime horse, which two kids can get inside. And Ollie says he's got just the right boys to take on the role.'

'Let me guess,' Sean said. 'The Higgins twins!'

'Ha! Great minds think alike.' Ollie laughed.

'They'll be perfect for it. Can't think of anyone better!'

'Now I am curious.' Beth laughed. 'I can't wait to meet them.'

'Just as soon as the costume's ready, you will. I'm not sure we can actually risk sitting our Mary on top, though. It'll only need one of them to start giggling and she'll fall off.'

'And we can't have that, can we? Health and safety and all that ...' Sean said, putting on a serious voice.

'Especially in her condition,' Ollie chipped in, sticking out his belly as if he was nine months gone, and all three of them started giggling.

'This show is going to be so much fun,' Beth said. Ollie noticed that her hand was resting on Sean's arm, as if to steady herself as she laughed, which was a bit odd, seeing as she was still sitting down.

'Right, come on, you two. Things to be done. Let's give it an hour or so, then I suggest we adjourn to the pub. My treat, to say thank you for your help and to welcome you on board, Sean. I don't know how I'd manage this thing without people like you two.'

'Okay, boss, that sounds great.' Sean went back to his wood and started sawing again. He certainly seemed to know what he was doing. Already the bones of a crib were in evidence.

'*Pub?*' Beth whispered.

'I'm not drinking, Beth, don't worry. I just fancy a

night out and something to eat. No booze, I promise. Unless you count the steak and ale pie, of course, but I don't suppose there's an awful lot of ale in that.'

'Sorry. I don't mean to be bossy.'

'It's fine. It's probably just what I need. Someone keeping an eye on me, making sure I stay on the straight and narrow.'

'My thoughts exactly! And Sean? Where did he come from?'

'Australia!'

'Yeah, the accent's a bit of a giveaway, but you know what I meant.'

'Course I did. He's our new supply teacher. Came and asked if he could help, so I could hardly say no. And he seems like a good bloke. Don't you agree?'

From the way her eyes were following the guy, he had a pretty good idea that she did. It was time Beth met someone new, after what that scumbag Jake had done, and he could definitely detect a few tentative sparks. Shame Sean was only in the country for a year, so any long-term matchmaking was out of the question, but at least she hadn't jumped down his throat and said no to a trip to the pub.

He'd have to eat with them, of course, as the whole thing had been his idea. The chicken leg he had left thawing in his fridge for tea would just have to wait for another night. But he was sure he could come up with some excuse to leave early. After that, it would be up to them.

***

Ollie lay on his bed and gazed up at the three little wooden crosses on the wall. For some strange reason a vision of Granddad Trev came into his head, holding a saw in one hand and a screwdriver in the other. Sometimes he found it hard to remember the old man's face, but he would always remember the things he'd taught him. His love of chess and having a go at making things. And what it meant to feel that close to another human being that you could just enjoy being together and sharing things, without even having to talk. He'd had that with Laura too ...

Watching Beth and Sean so easy in each other's company seemed to have brought Laura back into his thoughts. Not that she had ever really left them. He still missed that feeling of being half of a couple, having someone there for him, but as time dragged on her loss no longer felt quite so achingly raw. He hoped that she was okay, wherever she was. And that she was happy.

Being apart probably made some sort of sense, especially as being together just hadn't worked. Not after baby number three, with the grief so huge and overpowering they could almost touch it. For him, at least, those feelings had subsided a bit now, or maybe he'd drowned them in all those gallons of whiskey he must have got through after she left. At least he found he could wake up and get himself off to work now without the memory of it all leaping instantly into his head the second he opened his eyes. Sometimes it would still hit him, though, at unexpected moments during his day. Knowing that his babies were lost, Laura gone, his life changed for ever. But he also knew now that there was nothing he could do about it. Nothing but let life roll along and take him with it, see where it took him. The answer to it all, if there was one, was certainly not going to leap up at him from the bottom of a bottle.

The crosses meant nothing really. It wasn't as if he had any religious leanings, beyond a vague belief in a God who, when he thought about it now, can't have been quite the all-knowing, all-giving, all-loving being He was meant to be. If He was, then he would have seen more evidence of that benevolence in his own life by now. No, the crosses were just little pieces of wood, tacked to the wall above the bed. At the time he had made the first one, he had been pouring out his pain into something solid, something he felt was needed as a memorial, to ensure his baby, small and unformed as it had been, was never forgotten. And, having done it once, there was no option but to do the same for the others. But he knew now that they never would be forgotten. They were in his heart, not in three lumps of wood pinned to the wall. Perhaps Laura needed the crosses more than he did. He would have suggested she take them with her if he'd known she was about to leave. But he hadn't known. Hadn't had even an inkling, until it was too late.

He pulled himself up and knelt on the quilt. Time he took that off and washed it. There was no need to let himself turn into some sort of useless male who couldn't look after his own flat properly, let alone himself. Then slowly, one by one, he lifted the crosses down, blew away a thin film of dust and put them on the bed. Three crosses, one for each miscarriage, all so early it had been impossible to tell if they were going to be boys or girls. *Probably something wrong with them. Best lost early. Nature's way. More common than you think. It will be okay next time.* It's what people said. All well-meaning. And so horribly wrong.

He put the crosses away in a drawer. How could they help him to remember his babies when he'd never seen them, couldn't picture their faces, never even given them names? They weren't like Rosie. Rosie had been real. Although he had no memory of her, they'd shared a womb. For all those weeks she'd been his sister, and she'd come out into the world alongside the rest of them, with arms and legs and a face, and his parents had named her, and held her, and loved her, even though she never took a single breath. If they could cope with that, then it was time he manned up and stopped feeling sorry for himself.

He wished he knew where Laura was, so he could just hug her and tell her it wasn't her fault, that he would never have given up on her, that he would have loved her for ever, with or without children. But it was too late. She was gone. She didn't want him. Or the pain and grief that came from being with him. Because it could have been down to him, couldn't it? Something in the genes, something that stopped his babies from growing? Perhaps, in time, with somebody else, Laura might yet have the babies she wanted so badly. Living, healthy babies.

He looked at the clock. It was almost ten and he was hungry again. The steak pie and chips he'd enjoyed earlier were long gone, but the chicken leg was still in the fridge. As he chucked it into the oven, sprinkled with oil and turned up high, he wondered how Beth was getting on with Sean, if they were still there in the pub. He may have made a cock-up of his own love life so far, but there was still hope for his sister, and maybe even for himself. Plenty of time for both of them to start again. God, they were only twenty-nine. And not bad looking, either of them.

For some reason, probably because he was thinking of Beth, the nativity play popped back into his head and an involuntary smile crept up on him. On Friday, if the donkey costume was ready, they were going to have a full dress rehearsal, so he could see how the whole thing was going to look. Just a month ago, he would never have believed how happy and hopeful something that had previously been so utterly alien to him could make him feel. Maybe life was looking up at last.

Chapter 29

Kate, 1988

Dan rolled off and lay flat on his back beside me. I could feel a thin trickle of sweat – his, not mine – cooling as it slid down between my exposed breasts, and quickly pulled the quilt up to cover myself.

'Can't you at least pretend you enjoyed it? For fuck's sake, Kate, I'm not sure you even moved at all. Not once.'

'Sorry. I'm so tired, and if we make too much noise I'm worried one of them will wake up again. And is there really any need to swear about it? I'm doing my best, but it's not easy ...'

He didn't answer, just reached out and switched on his bedside lamp. I blinked in the sudden light and turned away, burying my face in the pillow.

'I'm going to make a cup of tea. Want one?'

'Dan, it's late. I just want to go to sleep. What do you want tea for?'

'Oh, sorry. I didn't realise I needed permission to be thirsty these days. Just go back to sleep. If you were even awake in the first place.' He climbed out of bed and grabbed his robe from the back of the door, then bent down and clicked the light off again, plunging me back into darkness. I tried hard to sink back into it, but suddenly sleep seemed to elude me and I just lay there, listening to him moving about downstairs. I fumbled about for the tissue box next to the bed and gave myself a half-hearted wipe between the legs. It had been, I think, the third time we'd had sex since I'd given birth, and I couldn't honestly say I had felt anything beyond a desire to get it over with as quickly as possible. Was this it now? What our marriage had become? After all the years of loving this man, all the times when we could hardly get enough of each other, suddenly even a quick bonk was more than enough.

We ought to do something about contraception. For so long, we hadn't had to think about it, with infertility hanging over us and all our efforts to conceive naturally falling flat on their faces. But wouldn't it be just our bad luck now to make another baby, without even meaning to, and when we already had more of them than we'd ever thought possible? The mood Dan was in, I wasn't sure I wanted to talk about sex at all, opening the door to discussions or complaints I really didn't want to hear, but maybe I should get him to buy some

Durex, or buy some myself, just in case. Or get a prescription for the pill. My chosen option at that moment would have been just to stop having sex altogether, but somehow I couldn't see Dan agreeing to that. For him it seemed that even bad sex was still (marginally) better than no sex at all.

I must have slept. When the first of the babies woke me at four in the morning I had no recollection of Dan coming back to bed, yet there he was, snoring quietly beside me, utterly oblivious to the hungry wailing coming from the other side of the wall.

***

I'm not sure why we had them christened. It wasn't as if I was religiously inclined in any formal sense, although I have always believed there must be something beyond the life we have here, but to Dan it seemed important.

'We got married in church, Kate. You didn't raise any objections then,' he said, and he was right, of course. The babies deserved their day, just as I had had mine, even if mine had ended up with me in a hospital bed, covered in my own blood, and was nothing at all like the wonderful white wedding I had wanted it to be. Sometimes I wondered if that day had been some kind of omen, warning me of what the future was going to bring. Disappointments, a constant seesaw of ups and downs – with the downs winning. I was just telling myself not to be so melodramatic, that none of it was anyone's fault, especially Dan's, when he added, 'And it's a great way to get presents. Everyone brings something to a christening, don't they? We might even get some cash ...'

Just what sort of a callous money-grabber had I married? Even when he was in full-on accountant mode, Dan had never been quite so money-obsessed before.

'*We?* Surely if anyone brings cash it's meant for the children, to go into some sort of savings account for their future? It's not for us.'

'Well, their future depends on us at the moment, and they're not going to get much of one if we can't find some money from somewhere, Kate. And pretty damn soon.'

'It would feel like robbing from our own children. Who does that? And when did you get to be so mercenary?'

'Not mercenary. Just practical. Realistic. The world turns on money these days, and we don't have enough of it. What are we going to do when they get bigger, eh? Feed them on stale bread and margarine and shove them all together in one big bed with a hot water bottle because we can't afford the heating?'

'Dan, you're being ridiculous. I'll go back to work if I have to. We'll manage somehow.'

'And who will look after the kids?'

'When they start school ...'

'That could be four years away. We could starve to death by then.'

'Now you really are being ridiculous.'

I turned away and went back to sorting out the clothes the babies had already outgrown. Despite their rocky start, they were growing well, and there were still a few things people had given them when they were born, made for the usual seven- or eight-pounders that Mr and Mrs Average laughingly called new-born size, and that just about still fitted them more than five months later. The upside of being born so tiny. It didn't feel like the right time to mention that within another week or two we would definitely need to buy more. At least Molly had come good with the christening robe, the one both Dan and his sister had worn at their own ceremonies, and which had arrived, all neatly packaged up in tissue, in the post. Mum had dug mine out from her loft, a bit yellowed but it's a wonder what a good overnight soak in a bowl of soap flakes can do, and we'd been really lucky to find a third in the charity shop that had only needed a bit of almost-invisible mending to a tear in the seam to bring it up to scratch. So, the three of them didn't match, and the gowns were all way too big, but that didn't matter.

'It's going to be fun tomorrow, Dan. All our family

and friends together. Even Linda's going to try and make it. So, let's not spoil it, eh?'

'I'd be a lot happier about it if feeding the five thousand wasn't going to cost us an arm and a leg,' he muttered. 'If only those damn Goo Goo people hadn't ruined it all and reneged on our deal.'

***

I still remember those words and how much they stung. Ruined? There I was, feeling happy, looking forward to something good for a change, sorting out what everyone would wear, hoping for fine weather. And there was Dan, thinking about money. Oh, I knew it was important, that we had to find a way to get by, but right then? Couldn't we put all that aside for a while and enjoy the moment? Accept that the christening was a special occasion, something to help us escape the everyday struggle for a while, that it was meant to be about looking ahead, celebrating what we had, sharing our joy in our children with family and friends. And for those who believed in that sort of thing, maybe even with God.

It wasn't ruined because we couldn't produce a five-star buffet, was it? It wasn't ruined because some big impersonal company had turned their back on us. No. But Dan saw things differently. He always did. And, although he didn't say it, I knew what he really meant. 'If only we'd had all four, we'd be rich. If only Rosie hadn't ruined it all by dying ...'

***

I loved Molly and Sam. I really did. What with the distance between us, the problems of us even contemplating travelling with three tiny babies, and their workload at the farm, we rarely saw them these days, but they had arranged at the last minute for someone to step in for a few days and had driven up to surprise us, laden with eggs and potatoes, and big solid frozen lumps of meat wrapped in layers of newspaper that I had to cram into our small freezer as soon as they arrived.

'Kate, my love ...' Molly threw her wobbly arms around me and enveloped me in the biggest hug. She smelt of a mixture of fresh air and lavender, with just a hint of sweat. 'You're looking so well, considering. I half expected to find you a worn-out wreck. Believe me, I know what new babies can be like, but at least I never had to cope with three at once. Although our Dan was as much trouble as three sometimes, the little sod! Not that I'd say that to his face, of course. Now, where are they? My beautiful grandchildren. Let me at 'em, and you can go and get your head down for a snooze. I bet that's what you need, more than any presents!'

'I'd love that, but let me make you a cup of tea at least. You've come all this way. I can't just disappear upstairs as soon as you arrive!'

'Oh, yes, you can, my love. And you will. And, if you want to stay there until the christening tomorrow, that'll be just fine with me. I've come to help, not to be waited on like a guest. We're family and that's what family do. Help. So, whatever you need while we're here, you just say. Sam here may be about as useful when it comes to babies as a bag of blind one-legged frogs, but you know you can count on me.'

She had all three babies settled in a row on the sofa with Sam on guard at one end to make sure they didn't fall off, and was rolling her sleeves up and making a start on the pile of washing up as I headed for the stairs.

As far as I was concerned, our money worries could wait. Sleep was all the currency I needed right then and Molly gave that to me. I nodded off to the sound of silence, in the middle of the afternoon, and didn't wake up again until nearly nine o'clock. When I put the light on and peered at the clock, I could hardly believe the time.

Downstairs, Dan was home from work and drinking a beer with his dad, the dinner had been cooked and eaten, the plates washed and put away, and a huge pile of food had been put aside for me and was quickly popped into the oven to warm up.

'You should have woken me ...'

'Nonsense. Whatever for? Everything's fine here. Babies fed and changed and tucked up in their baskets. I would have run the hoover round but I was worried the noise might wake you. Or them. Now, come and sit here next to me and we'll have a good old girly catch-up.'

'I'd like that. Other than my mum – and Trevor, of course, who's part of the package these days – I don't get a lot of adult company.'

'Oh, charming. What am I then?' Dan chipped in, and I wasn't entirely sure he was joking.

Molly leant across and clipped him around the ear with a magazine. 'Enough of that,' she said. 'It's a big day tomorrow, for all of us, and I don't want to hear any bickering. Now, how many are coming, and what can I do, sandwich-wise?'

For the first time in months, I felt relaxed and stress-free, and supported. It was half-past nine, the house was no longer a mess, and my eyes were actually open!

Now, all Dan had to do was shut up about bloody money all the time and we just might have a very enjoyable christening.

***

We came out of the church into warm autumn sunshine and the occasional flashing of Trevor's old camera. They had all whimpered a bit when the vicar poured water over their heads, not a full-on cry, and then only for a minute or two, but generally they had been good as gold.

Beth was fast asleep in Mum's arms, with a trickle of milky dribble down the front of her gown, and Ollie was wide-eyed awake and making gurgling sounds at Molly that I was trying hard not to panic about, the ever-present threat of another chest infection playing on my mind. Dan was cuddling Natalie, who I was beginning to realise was already his favourite, and trying to line everyone up for a group photo without shouting out instructions in case he made any of the babies cry.

We'd struggled over our choice of godparents, deciding in the end that letting all the babies share the same three would make life a lot less complicated. Not that we could have come up with nine suitable candidates if we'd gone for three each anyway. So, having dismissed Linda as having been a bit too long out of our lives, we'd settled on Dan's sister, Jane, and her husband, Alan, and good old dependable best man Rich.

We didn't see so much of Rich these days, but we were both still very fond of him. I did think that perhaps babies were a bit alien to him and the whole domesticity thing had scared him off. He was still resolutely single and still, amazingly, living in the same flat, although he no longer seemed to need a flatmate to share the rent and had spread himself out, using our old bedroom as some sort of home cinema, with piles of video tapes on every shelf, big black curtains to shut out the light, and the biggest telly of anyone we knew. I'd half expected him to say no when we'd asked him, but he'd actually jumped at the chance.

'Oh, wow! Godfather, eh? I've never been one of those before. Makes me feel like Marlon Brando!' He'd said that last bit in a weirdly exaggerated Italian accent that had sent me into a fit of giggles and reminded me what a good sort he was and always had been. I think we made the right choice.

Chapter 30

Beth, 2017

Beth peered at the illuminated alarm clock by the bed. Pleased to see she still had at least ten minutes before she had to get up, she snuggled back down under her quilt and thought about Sean Harper. She couldn't remember enjoying an evening as much as last night in ages, and they'd only had a pie and a couple of drinks in the local pub.

She knew what Ollie was trying to do, of course, going home early and leaving them together like that. And, to a certain extent, it had worked. They'd got on like a house on fire, sharing the same sense of humour and spluttering into their beer over silly jokes that sent them both into fits of laughter. He'd even given her a rather nice, and just a little more than brotherly, kiss when they'd parted outside, but that was it. Sean was an Australian. His home was on the other side of the world and pretty soon he would be heading back out there, no doubt for good. Clearly he was loving his time in England, and she was loving his company, but it was a temporary thing. It had to be. The last thing Beth needed right now was to lose her heart to someone who, before they even got started, was destined to dump her. But that wasn't to say they couldn't have a bit of harmless fun while he was still here.

The plans for the show were going fantastically well. The kids had thrown themselves into it wholeheartedly and little Victoria's performance, for a child of only ten, was a revelation. There was a star in the making there, and Beth wouldn't have been surprised to see her pop up on *Britain's Got Talent* in a few years' time, if Ollie hadn't got her name down for the British athletics team first.

They hadn't gone for anything too different, in the end. The nativity story wasn't one you could really mess around with, after all, and the new costumes and scenery alone were enough to lift the whole thing to a new level, replacing the old rather drab tea towels and lumps of wobbly cardboard the school had apparently been using for years. She and Ollie had had great fun sorting through three tatty old brown boxes marked 'Nativity' and emptying a good ninety per cent of their contents into the bin.

She knew that you couldn't just use songs plucked

from the charts, or pinch someone else's script, either. There were copyright and plagiarism claims to think about, or a whole lot of fees to pay to get proper permission. So, it had just seemed to make more sense to write their own script and use the good old Christmas carols that everybody was familiar with. With the show only a matter of weeks away, there were still a lot of loose ends to sort out and tie together, but she felt really proud of how it was going. It was working wonders on Ollie too. His drinking was almost non-existent now, and he had the light back in his eyes. She ached to tell him about Laura and the baby-to-be, but while he remained oblivious and sober, and thankfully much too busy to meet any other women, she forced herself to stick to her promise. Tell all now and Laura really might do as she'd threatened and disappear for good.

Beth dragged herself up and got ready for work. Jenny's door was open, across the landing, revealing an unmade heap of a bed but no sign of her sister, who would have gone off to get some of her elderly clients up out of their own beds long ago. When she went downstairs, her mum was flopping about in the kitchen, still in pyjamas and slippers, stirring a pan of scrambled eggs with mysterious green bits dotted amongst the yellow, and Natalie was sitting quietly at the table, sipping a coffee, her head buried in yet another bridal magazine.

'Want eggs?' Mum asked, not looking up.

'No, thanks. Cereal will do me. What are you looking at now, Nat? It's a bit late to be drooling over dresses when yours is already bought and hanging in your wardrobe!'

Natalie grinned. 'No, not dresses. Just thinking about what to do with my hair, that's all.'

'But I thought you'd be letting me worry about that. Hair's what I do.'

'Of course you'll be actually doing it, Beth, but there's no harm in getting ideas, is there? Something for you to work with. You know, inspiration ...'

'Right.' Beth poured herself a bowl of Coco Pops and sat down, adding milk from the open bottle on the table.

'Oh, don't be like that. You'll do a lovely job, I know you will, but ...'

'But what?'

'Could we have a trial run, do you think? Give me a make-over. You know, hair up or hair down? Maybe something with flowers woven in or a tiara on top. Make-up too, to see what I like. What suits me.'

Beth put her spoon down. 'Of course. That's what I would do for any bride. What made you think I wouldn't for you? We'll make a start at the weekend if you like.'

'Thanks. It's just that you've been so pre-occupied with Ollie and his school show that I wasn't sure if ... well, you know.'

Beth shook her head. 'You do get some funny ideas in your head sometimes. You're my sister, for heaven's sake. I'll always have time for you. And it will be my number one mission to make you the most beautiful bride this side of the Hollywood Hills. Well, the one with the most beautiful hair anyway. There's not a lot I can do about the rest of you!'

'Charming!' Natalie reached over and batted her on the wrist.

'Only joking, Nat. Honest! Now, shut up and let me eat my brekkie or I'll be late for work, and ...' She looked at her watch. 'As it's almost a quarter to nine, so will you, if you don't get a move on.'

'What? It's not, is it?'

She watched Natalie go into sudden panic mode, gulp down the last dregs of her coffee and wheel herself to the door.

'See you later.'

Natalie nodded and disappeared into the hall.

'You sure I can't tempt you?' Mum said, piling a dollop of egg onto a plate. 'There's lots of spinach in it. Good for building up your strength.'

'I think I'll pass, thanks all the same. Spinach and me don't get on too well. And I'm not sure I need building up. If I wanted Popeye muscles I'd go to the gym.'

'Oh, yeah? When was the last time you went to a

gym?' Mum laughed and started forking her eggs into her mouth. 'The same day I spotted Elvis Presley in Tesco's.'

'Very funny.' Beth stifled a giggle because, actually, it was quite funny. 'What are you up today, anyway?' Since her mum had retired from her job at the bank the year before, Beth wasn't at all sure how she spent her days. There had been no discernible increase in housework, if the dusty windowsills and occasional hanging cobweb were anything to go by, and she'd never been one for watching a lot of TV.

'Oh, this and that. I thought I might go and see your father, actually.'

'Really? Why?'

'No reason. Just that I've been a bit worried about him, that's all. Especially now he's upset Natalie over this wedding business. There's no excuse for it that I can see, and I intend to tell him so.'

'But, what about Fanny, or Franny, or whatever her name is?'

'Oh, I don't think she'll be there. That little dalliance is long over. Well, it was never going to last, was it? She must have been a good ten years younger than him, and, let's be honest, he's no catch these days, is he?'

'Mum!'

'Well, he's not. He's let himself go to seed these last few years. All that grey hair, and the paunch. I wouldn't be surprised if he hasn't even been cutting his toenails. They're probably making holes in his socks by now.'

Beth laughed. 'Why on earth would you think that?'

'Because, in all the years we were together, I never saw him do it once. Said he found it hard to reach, so it was always my job.'

'Cutting his nails? Yuk. How could you?'

'Love, I suppose,' she said, wistfully, taking her empty plate to the sink. 'Shame it didn't last. But then, what relationship does these days? Take you and Jake ...'

'I'd rather not, thank you. That particular ship has well and truly sailed. And, besides, I've met someone else.'

'You have? And I'm the last to know about it, as usual?'

Beth bit her lip. What had she gone and said that for? Sean had been an interesting distraction, that was all, and she was looking forward to seeing more of him as they worked together on the play, but as she'd told herself only this morning, there was no future in it.

'Nothing to know, really. Just forget I said it. And give Dad my love, won't you? But only if he agrees to come to the wedding and give Natalie away. If he doesn't, he can whistle for it!'

***

Weekends were always super busy, and Beth didn't usually cut men's hair. She was more of a curly perm and foils specialist, leaving the more basic washes and trims to Ellie, the salon junior, but this morning Ellie had interrupted her much-needed morning break in the tiny staff room at the back and was insistent that a new male client had asked for Beth specially.

Putting down her magazine and finishing her tea, Beth popped her head around the half-open door, purely out of curiosity and all prepared to say no, but was pleasantly surprised to see Sean Harper standing there at the reception desk. There was a trickle of rain water running slowly down his neck and into his collar, and his brown eyes seemed to sparkle as he turned his face towards her.

'Beth! I hope you don't mind, but you did say you worked here, and I thought you might be up for a coffee or something?'

'You don't really want a haircut then?'

'Afraid not. That was just a ruse! So, coffee? What do you say?'

'I'd love to, but I've only just had a break and my next client is due any minute.'

'Sorry. Silly of me, to think you could just walk out any time you like. And on a Saturday too, when you must be run off your feet. But it's tipping down out there and ...'

'Look, come through to the back and I'll make you a coffee here. Only the instant stuff, but it will keep you off the streets. At least until the rain stops. And I can pop through and join you while I'm waiting for the perm to take.'

'Take?'

'Oh, you don't want to know, believe me. It's a chemical thing.'

'Beth, I'm a teacher. I may be teaching a bit of everything while I'm over here, but I actually specialise in science. I do know a bit about chemical things.' He grinned. 'And a fair bit about biological things too.'

For some reason, although she knew he was only teasing, she felt herself starting to blush and quickly led him through to the staff room. 'Milk?' she asked, flipping the switch on the kettle and hunting for a clean mug that didn't smell of damp towels. 'Sugar?'

She half expected him to say the old 'I'm sweet enough already' line, but perhaps that was just an English thing. Who knew what quips Australians might come out with? Not that she wouldn't love him to stick around long enough to find out.

'Beth,' Ellie called from behind the door. 'Your lady's here.'

'You go.' Sean had settled himself in one of the two tatty armchairs crammed side by side in the small room and had picked up the same magazine article Beth had been reading just minutes before. 'How to bed any man in the zodiac.'

'I can sort out my own coffee,' he called after her. 'Oh, and I'm Aquarius by the way. Just in case you were wondering.'

***

Natalie's hair looked a picture. They had tried piling it high in a mass of curls and had used all manner of clips and nets, but nothing had looked quite right. In the end, Beth had given her sister the lightest of cuts, shaping the hair so it flicked under at chin level at the front and fell smoothly to her shoulders at the back. With a row of tiny white satin flowers pinned in here and there, and a good spray of lacquer to hold everything in place, both girls were finally happy with the result.

'Oh, Beth, I wasn't sure about not wearing a veil, but now I know I made the right decision. The hair's just perfect without, and now it's done I don't want it undone! It looks so lovely.' Natalie was waving a hand mirror about so she could admire herself from all angles. 'I think I'll sleep with it just the way it is!'

'You do and it will be an absolute mess by morning. Not to mention how squashed all the flowers will be. We'll take some photos, but it will have to come out. Oh, don't worry, we'll leave it in for a while, while we have a go at the make-up, okay? See the whole picture ...'

Natalie nodded, then nodded a bit harder until her head was bobbing up and down like a jack-in-a-box.

'Nat! What are you doing?'

'Just testing. Making sure it will stay in place, no matter what happens on the day.'

'Well, failing a force-ten gale or you two having the sort of wedding-night sex I've only ever seen in porn films, I don't think that hair's going anywhere, do you? Now what colour eye shadow do you fancy?'

'Let's start with something pale, shall we? Pink, even. To match the bridesmaids' dresses and the flowers. I don't fancy going all dark and broody. The Goth look's not really me, is it?'

'Right. And maybe a bit of glitter. Oh, don't look so worried. I'm not talking about Christmas-tree shiny, just something subtle. And, if it doesn't work, we'll just scrub it all off and try something else. That's what a trial run's all about.'

'Great. I'm in your capable hands. Oh, it is nice to have a sister in the beauty business. Some of these firms you see advertising on the internet charge the earth.'

'And what makes you think I don't? I don't remember saying anything about this being a freebie.'

'Oh ...' Natalie's face in the mirror had gone decidedly white.

'I'm only kidding, you numpty! Of course it's free.' She picked up a tiny brush and rootled it around in a tub of powder shadow. 'Now, pink, you say?'

'Beth?' Natalie said, after a few moments' silence during which Beth had been concentrating on her task and Natalie had been desperately trying to keep still.

'Mmmm?'

'What you said about porn films. Have you actually watched one?'

'Where did that question come from?' Beth stopped what she was doing, a mascara brush held aloft.

'Only, it's just that ... well, I think I've probably led a bit of a sheltered life. You know, what with the chair and everything, and Phil being my first – my only – boyfriend. I do worry sometimes that I'm not, well, you know, worldly-wise. Not exciting enough ...'

'In bed, you mean? Nat, I don't think your Phil would be marrying you if he wasn't happy with ... well, the way things are.'

'But in these films – not that I've ever seen one, but you read stuff, don't you? In these films, girls do things that I probably couldn't do, even if I wanted to. Or if Phil wanted me to. Get into positions I just wouldn't be able to attempt.'

'Because you're disabled, you mean? God, Nat, I may have legs that work but that doesn't mean I'd want to start twisting them in knots to copy some porn film.

They're not real life, you know. They're just fantasy, really, aren't they? What men might like to watch or think about sometimes but probably wouldn't dream of actually doing. Ever. Most of them are quite happy with very normal cuddly everyday sex, with the woman they love, in their own beds, after watching *Match of the Day*.'

'You think?'

'Yes, I think. Oh, Nat, I have no idea what's put all this nonsense into your head, but if it worries you, then talk to Phil about it. It's him you're marrying, not me. Now shut your eyes and let me get at those lashes. You blink in the next two minutes and I'll throttle you.'

Chapter 31

Kate, 1989

It had been one of those days. Ollie had been sick several times and was wheezing enough for me to take him to the doctor, who'd diagnosed yet another chest infection and wanted to send the poor little mite straight back to the hospital.

'It can happen, Mrs Campbell,' he'd said. 'Not unusual when babies are born so early. In fact, you should count yourself lucky it's just the one. Imagine if all three were poorly. And it's nothing too terrible. I'm only doing this as a precaution, really, because he's still so young. Nothing to fret about.' He patted my hand, the little bow tie he always wore wobbling at his throat, and let me sit in the waiting room, the cumbersome triple pushchair we'd bought to replace the two doubles almost completely blocking the door, while I rang Dan and asked him to come and get us.

And then, when we'd reluctantly left Ollie in the children's ward, with at least three nurses fussing and cooing over him, and Dan had gone back to the office to finish off some paperwork, and I had the others tucked up asleep at home, the phone rang.

'It's Trevor,' Mum said, before I'd even said hello, her voice so small and breathless I hardly recognised who was speaking. 'He's had a heart attack.'

'Oh, no. How bad is it? Is he alive?' I may not have been over-fond of Trevor but that didn't mean I'd wish him gone.

'Alive, yes, but it's quite bad, I think. We're at the hospital now. A&E. They're examining him. He's as white as a sheet, Kate. More grey, actually. And he was in such pain, doubled over, almost passing out with it. I didn't know what to do. I just sat and held his hand while I waited for the ambulance. I felt so helpless. Can you come, Kate? Please? I'm so scared I didn't do enough and he might die. What will happen then? How will I carry on without him? I don't think I can face this on my own.'

I didn't dare drag Dan out of work again, and he had the car. I couldn't think of a single person I could call at such short notice to watch the girls, so I bundled them both up warm, strapped them into their pushchair and did something I had never tried before. I took them on the bus. I can't say it was easy, what with hordes of schoolchildren chattering nineteen to the dozen and scrabbling for seats and me not even sure I was on the right bus. Plenty of people had barged past me at the bus stop before one kind man had stopped to help lift the pushchair up onto the platform, but just five stops later we got off outside the hospital and found our way to A&E. I just hoped we weren't too late.

'Ah, yes. Mr Brookfield ...' The receptionist studied a piece of paper on the desk in front of her before going on, 'was transferred up to Dixon Ward just half an hour ago. Fourth floor, but it's past visiting hours now, so they may not let you in until the evening.'

I looked at my watch. It was ten past four.

As we waited for the lift, I couldn't help wondering how Ollie was doing. I was planning on coming back later anyway, once Dan was home, but deep down I knew I shouldn't have left him at all, not even for a few hours, and if it wasn't for keeping the others out of infection's way, I wouldn't have done. Still, knowing he was here, just a couple of floors above me, all I really wanted to do was run back to him. But I owed it to Mum to be at her side now. If Trevor was out of A&E and onto a ward, that must surely mean he was on the mend, so I might not need to stay with her for long, and Trevor, assuming he was awake, probably wouldn't want me there any more than I wanted to be there myself. I pressed button four for Dixon Ward and tried, just for now, to push Ollie out of my thoughts.

They did let me in, on the understanding it was just for a few minutes and that the babies were quiet. 'There are very sick people in here,' the nurse at the desk reiterated. As if I couldn't guess that, what with it being the cardiac ward. Luckily, both girls drifted off to sleep after the excitement of the bus ride and the only noise they were making was a gentle snuffle.

They told me Trevor was in the bed at the far end, near the window. The curtains were closed around it, with just Mum's old favourite brown handbag, where she'd dumped it on the floor, showing underneath, so I knew I had found the right bed. There wasn't room for the pushchair so I left it just outside the curtain and slipped in. Mum stood up, shakily, a balled-up soggy tissue in her hand, and hugged me. 'Oh, I'm so glad you're here,' she said.

'How's he doing?' I didn't really want to look at him, but I couldn't help it. In such a small space, his proximity was unavoidable, and Mum was right. He was an awful washed-out grey colour. He lay flat, the blankets half back, wires attached to his naked chest, his name and that of his doctor chalked up on a board above his head.

'They say if I hadn't called the ambulance as quickly as I did, he might have died. But he's still here, and where there's hope ...' She stopped mid-sentence and just stared at him. 'I do love him, you know,' she said, as if there was any doubt. 'He's a good man, a lovely man, and I sometimes wonder what I did to deserve him.'

'Mum ...'

'Oh, I know you don't really like him, Kate. You've made that obvious over the years, but to me he's everything. He can't die. He just can't. I've lost one husband and ... well, I'm not ready to let this one go yet. Not ever.'

A nurse came in then and touched me on the shoulder. 'I'm sorry, but ...'

'Yes, I know. I shouldn't be here. I promised I'd only be a minute or two. Don't worry, I'm going.' I turned to Mum. 'I won't be far away, Mum. Just downstairs. Ollie's in again.'

Her hand went to her mouth. 'Oh, no!'

'It's okay. Another infection but we got it early. He'll be fine. Look, I'm going down to sit with him, so I'm right here in the hospital if you need me. If there's any change, come and get me. And I'll come back up during evening visiting hours to check on you before I go home, okay?'

I wheeled the babies back down the ward, as quietly as I could. 'Aaah! Twins?' a young nurse asked, stopping to look at them.

'No.' I was pushing a triple pushchair with only two babies in it, and the empty space seemed to speak volumes. Well, it did to me. There was obviously a baby missing. Couldn't she see that? In fact, there were two babies missing, but that was something nobody could see, would ever see ...

Suddenly, all I wanted was to get to Ollie, and to make sure he was all right.

***

Ollie soon recovered and so did Trevor, in time. They'd kept him in for a while, inserted a stent into an artery and passed him fit to go, but I could tell Mum was still worried sick about him. 'I don't want him doing too much,' she said, insisting that she take over the gardening and humping great bags of supermarket shopping in from the car while he sat indoors watching TV or working out chess moves on a board placed next to his armchair.

'You fuss too much, love,' he told her, but she wasn't one for listening when she didn't want to, and over the weeks that followed I could see him starting to put on a bit of weight around the middle. If he'd smoked the occasional cigarette before, I certainly never saw him with one again. I think she'd thrown the last open packet in the bin.

'Gentle exercise, that's what I'm meant to have,' he protested. 'You don't have to worry I'm about to keel over just because I walk up a few stairs.'

And so they took to going out, arm in arm, every evening straight after dinner, for a stroll. Never to the pub, though. It seemed that the new, post-heart attack Trevor had given up booze as well as tobacco, or that Mum had given them up for him.

***

'It's quite sweet really, isn't it?' Dan said, one Sunday morning, as we quickly wolfed down a plate of scrambled eggs before one or more of the babies woke up and had us dashing about like mad things again. 'Your mum, and the way she looks after Trev. Sort of romantic, for a couple their age.'

'Do you think we'll be like that? When we're older and the kids have left home. Still holding hands and worrying about each other the way they do?'

'We don't even do it now, Kate, so I think it's pretty unlikely we'll suddenly start when we're old, don't you?'

Beth started screaming then, so I didn't have the chance to say anything.

'Oh, here we go again. Which one's that?' Dan forked the last mouthful in and got up from the table.

'Beth. Can't you tell?'

'Babies all sound the same to me. And you spend more time with them, so you're bound to get to know them better.'

'You make it sound like an accusation. I'd love you to spend more time with them. And with me ...'

'Chance'd be a fine thing.'

I listened to his feet pounding up the stairs and just sat for a while, glad of the short break that Sundays were able to give me. Dan might moan about the hours he was having to put in at work, but there were times when I would have dearly loved to swap places, to get out of the house, unfettered by push-chairs and nappy bags and bottles, and spend time with adults whose only connection wasn't belonging to the same baby group and whose conversation didn't revolve around poo and puke and how to purée a banana.

I never expected to feel that way, so keen to get away from my own children, but I was missing work and, now they were getting bigger and stronger, I did wonder, just briefly, if I might be able to talk the bank into letting me go in for just a few hours, so I could keep my hand in and have some chance of holding on to my sanity. The busy Saturday morning shift, maybe, or a couple of lunchtimes during the week. I couldn't afford childcare, and going out to earn a few pounds just to have to hand it over to someone else defeated the object, but I felt sure Mum would help out, if she could be persuaded to leave Trevor's side for long enough.

'Here she is.' Dan came back in, cradling Beth in his arms, and plonked her down on my lap, screwing his face up in disgust. 'Needs a nappy change, I think.'

'And you couldn't deal with that?'

'Well, I could, normally, but I'm going out. Didn't I say?'

'No, you didn't.'

'I'm going over to see Rich. There's something he wants to talk to me about, but he couldn't do it over the phone, apparently. Or wouldn't. I shouldn't be too long.'

'But ...' Ollie had started wailing now, which meant Natalie wouldn't be far behind.

'Sorry, Kate. It sounded important. Why don't you go over and visit your mum? She loves to see the kids. I'll leave you the car. You might even bag yourself a Sunday roast, save you cooking.'

'And how about you? Don't you want to eat?'

'Probably grab something with Rich.'

'In some pub, you mean?'

'Well, you know Rich. Whatever it is he wants to talk about, there's bound to be beer involved! Another reason for me not to drive.'

'But, Dan ...'

Five Unforgivable Things

He bent to kiss me on the cheek, then did the same to Beth. 'God, how does such a tiny baby make such a huge smell?' he laughed, and was gone before I could think up any sort of reply.

Chapter 32

Jenny, 2017

Jenny stood on the pavement outside the small block of flats where her father lived and peered at his window on the ground floor. The curtains were closed, but there were no lights shining through, and no obvious signs of life. Although he was in his early sixties now, he was still out most of the day, with little sign of slowing down, still working at the same firm of accountants he'd been with since school, but – she peered at her watch under the glow of the streetlight – however busy he might be, she knew he would normally be home by now.

Without much hope of getting a reply, she pushed the bell with *D. Campbell* written on a scrap of weather-worn paper on the panel beside it. She should have phoned first. It would have made more sense to make sure he was going to be in before trekking over here, but if he'd been forewarned he just might have tried to avoid her. This way, if he was here, she would catch him out and make him talk to her. After the way he'd treated Nat, someone had to get to the bottom of things, and she probably had more hope of getting answers than anyone else did.

She took a step back. Was that a twitch of the curtain? She was fairly sure it was. Determinedly, she rang again, this time keeping her finger on the bell for so long that an old lady who lived in one of the other flats came tut-tutting out into the hall to see what was going on and opened the front door. Mumbling apologies, Jenny slipped past her, turned into the corridor to the right and ran straight to her dad's door.

Her fist was already raised to thump on his door when it opened. 'Okay, okay,' he said, so quietly she hardly heard him as he turned away and went back inside. 'No need to ring quite so violently, or to break the door down. I was just about to let you in ...'

'Really?' Jenny stepped past him. 'And what were you doing sitting here in the dark anyway? Forgotten to pay the electricity bill?' She flicked the switch just inside the door and flooded the small room with light. 'Ah, apparently not.'

'Jen, what do you want? I was just going to ...'

'Just going to what? Cook dinner? Go out? Get into bed? It's half-past eight. A bit late for the first two, and far too early for the third.'

'Oh, for goodness sake, get off your high horse and sit down.' He pulled out a crumpled hankie he had stuffed up his sleeve, coughed into it, and guided her towards the sofa. 'Let me get you some coffee or something.'

'Fine. Two sugars.'

'I think I know that by now. I am your father. I lived with you long enough ...'

Not long enough, she was tempted to say but she held her tongue. From her position on the sofa, with piles of books and DVDs teetering at both ends and a layer of crumbs scattered across the carpet at her feet, she took a good look around the flat. Since when had her dad become so messy?

'So, what brings you here? Your mother been telling tales, has she?' He handed her a mug of coffee, which she had to turn and move to her left hand to avoid drinking from the jagged-looking chip in one side. 'I knew she wouldn't be able to keep her mouth shut.'

'Dad, I have no idea what you're talking about.' She looked at him quizzically. 'Have you had a cold or a sore throat or something? Your voice is so hoarse. I might have a Strepsil in my bag if it helps.'

'No, it's fine. Honestly. Just a bit croaky today. The coffee will sort me out.'

'If you say so. And what did you mean about telling tales?'

He sat in the one armchair, its wide arms shiny with wear, and gazed straight at her. 'Nothing,' he mumbled. 'Sorry. Take no notice. Crossed wires. Now, how are you? How's the job?'

'Fine. Although I've decided to leave. I want to train for something. You know, a proper job. A career. Just not sure what it is yet.'

'You could always try accountancy. It's stood me in good stead all these years. People will always have money to move about, tax problems, invoices they can't make head or tail of. I could put out a few feelers for you, get you in somewhere.'

'No, Dad. Thanks, but no.' She'd visited his office often enough as a child, listened to all the boring talk and seen the piles of paper stacked up on the dining table at home, and knew instinctively, without having to think about it, that it was nothing like the life she wanted for herself. 'I know you mean well, but it's not for me.'

She took a sip of her drink, which was still too hot and, in the absence of a coffee table, leant down to balance the mug on the floor by her feet. It was only as she straightened back up that she noticed, for the first time, just how thin he was. His feet, without socks, sat loosely in a pair of tatty backless slippers, blue veins running in lines and bulging through the thin pale skin, and his lower legs disappeared, like bamboo canes, up into trousers that she now realised were way too baggy at the waist.

She'd come to challenge him about Nat, and why he had backed out of coming to the wedding and he'd instantly thought she was here because of something else. Something she might have been told, or overheard. And now, suddenly, she had a terrible thought that, if she was right, would make perfect sense of everything. Oh, God, no. Please, she thought, please let me be wrong.

'What exactly is it that you thought I knew?' she said, leaning towards him and studying the long deep furrows that seemed to have sunk themselves into his face since she'd seen him last.

He looked away. 'Nothing,' he muttered, but it was a look that spoke volumes.

'Dad. Dad, look at me. Are you ill? Is that what this is?'

'Look, Jen, I didn't want to say anything. Not to any of you. I didn't want to worry you.'

'You're our dad. Whatever it is, we should know. It's up to us to decide whether to worry or not. Not you.'

'Look, I only told your mother because ... well, because she came round here yesterday, demanding answers, and because I knew I had to put someone down as next of kin, and it didn't seem right to lumber any of it onto your Aunt Jane. She's had enough to deal with, since losing Alan, and looking after your gran now she's in the home. And she's miles away, so it's not as if she can come running at the drop of a hat. So ...'

'Next of kin? You have four children, Dad. Now you and Mum are separated, surely we should be your next of kin?'

'Technically, I suppose you are, but you're kids. I didn't want to burden you ...'

'We're not kids, Dad.'

'You are to me. And, anyway, it's just a routine thing, you know, for their records, just in case ...'

'In case of what? Just what exactly is happening here, Dad?' She could feel her throat tightening, a slow fear creeping over her, as she watched his mug shake a little in his hands.

'Jenny, love. Don't make a fuss now, but it seems I have cancer.'

***

She walked home slowly in the dark, letting two buses pass her, sure that the cold of the air and the sheer plod-plod of putting one foot in front of the other would help her to clear her head. When she reached home, her hands felt frozen and her legs ached, but her head was just as packed with thoughts as it had been when she'd stood and hugged him goodbye, so hard and for so long, at his door. Cancer! It was one of those words people didn't like to say, one of those illnesses people spoke about only in whispers, as if those terrible mutated cells could hear what was being said about them and might start growing and multiplying, simply out of spite.

Although work had never left him a lot of time for exercise, all in all, she'd always thought of her dad as fit and well. All those silly made-up ball games they'd played together in the park, the bouncy castles he'd insisted on jumping on at their many birthday parties, the years of eating Mum's dodgy but undoubtedly healthy attempts at cheap vegetarian meals ...

And yet, it was there, in his neck, lurking in his thyroid gland, and may have been for some time. And from there, until they tried to remove it, who knew where else it might travel? Thank God they were going to operate so soon. Okay, so he'd still be in the hospital on Natalie's wedding day, but these things couldn't wait. The sooner it was out the better, and it made sense to do as the doctors advised. Missing the wedding had to be preferable to option two, which was risking letting things get so much worse and maybe not being around at all.

The house was quiet. It looked like everyone else had already gone to bed. What should she do? Tell Beth and Nat, call Ollie, talk it all through with Mum?

Whatever she decided, it would have to wait until morning, which was probably a good thing, giving her more time to think. Would Nat really want her wedding preparations, and the big day itself, spoilt by the air of doom and gloom and misery that cancer, and its uncertain outcome, was likely to drop over everything like a shroud? It wasn't as if knowing would achieve anything, or change anything. And Dad was just trying, in his own inexpert way, to protect her, and all of them, from a truth that could only cause them pain. But sometimes knowing something, no matter how bad, is better than not knowing at all. Could she really leave Nat wondering why her own father couldn't come to her wedding, not understanding why he couldn't, or wouldn't, give her away? Blaming it all on some imaginary evil girlfriend who didn't even exist? Both options seemed equally cruel.

Sometimes secrets have to be kept, of course. To honour a promise, to protect those who don't yet need to know. After all, wasn't she doing exactly that for Laura? Keeping from Ollie the one truth that could turn his whole world upside down? But it wasn't the same, was it?

Jenny made herself a hot water bottle to warm her hands and took it up to bed. With her mind racing, she climbed under the duvet and hugged the bottle tightly to her chest. She would have to confront her mum tomorrow, find out exactly what she knew, how bad things really were, if there was anything her dad had deliberately omitted to say, so they could decide together what to do next.

But Laura's secret was different. Laura's secret had to stay exactly that. Just for a little longer, until the baby was born. Because she had promised, and because sometimes not knowing really was the kindest way. And because, if she told Ollie, got him all excited, and then anything was to go wrong, she knew without any doubt that it would break her brother's heart.

***

Jenny sat on the edge of her mum's double bed. It wasn't even light yet, but she knew it couldn't wait. Just thinking about it all had kept her awake for most of the night.

'They caught it quite early,' Mum said, resting a hand over Jenny's. 'The prognosis is actually quite good, considering.'

'Considering what? That he has cancer.'

'Keep your voce down, love. We don't want to wake anybody else, do we?'

'But your own dad died of cancer, didn't he? And he was a lot younger than Dad. To me that sounds bad. Really bad. There are so many questions I want to ask, so many things I don't understand. I mean, it's not as if he even smokes.'

'It's not in his lungs, Jenny. It's not the same.'

'But any kind of cancer is still cancer, isn't it? Still an awful frightening thing we can't control, and no knowing where it came from or why. And he's so thin, so pale.'

'He's feeling ill, love. He's had a lump in his neck he's been trying to ignore. It's what men do. Bury their heads, you know. And I don't suppose he's been eating properly. It will get better once he's had the op and the radio-therapy.'

'But it's nearly Christmas and he's going to be on his own.'

'I know, love.' Her mum closed her eyes for a moment and took a deep breath. 'We'll visit, make sure he's got all he needs, try to keep his spirits up. I do still care about him, you know.'

'Do you?'

Her voice dropped almost to a whisper. 'Everything was great at first. It was only later, when the problems set in and things got tough for us that it all fell apart. But he has no one else now. I do realise that. And, in many ways, neither do I.'

'But you've got us, and Gran ...'

'It's not the same, Jenny. Since your dad left ... well, I've missed him.'

'And now?'

'Well, just for once, after all these years, it isn't me who needs him, is it? It's the other way round. Now he needs me. Needs all of us. A lot of water's passed under the bridge, Jen, but I think maybe it's time I put the past behind me and thought about the future ... and your dad's future. Doing what I can to make sure he still has one. I think I owe him that much, after all.'

Chapter 33

Kate, 1989

So, Rich's big secret. The secret he had to drag my husband out on a Sunday for, and keep him out for most of the day, leaving me looking after three tetchy babies and eating my share of a low-fat heart-healthy chicken casserole that it was obvious, despite my mother's protestations, was only big enough for two. The secret Rich couldn't possibly discuss on the phone. The secret Dan tried to keep to himself, even after he rolled home the worse for wear after four pints of beer, roast beef and a pile of crispy pub potatoes I would have happily snatched from him and gobbled in seconds, given half a chance. The secret that dared not speak its name ...

Rich had a rash.

That was it. Nothing deadly serious. He hadn't got some girl pregnant. He didn't have heart trouble, or a

313

liver so addled it needed replacing, or some incurable disease none of us had ever heard of. He hadn't lost his job. Or his money. He just had a rash.

'Where exactly is this rash?' I asked, when Dan finally spilled the beans.

I watched his face screw up into a sort of painful squirm and his hands involuntarily lower themselves to below the belt.

'Oh, I see. There!'

'He was worried, okay? And not much liking the idea of showing it to a doctor. Especially as his doc is a woman.'

'So he thought he'd show it to you?'

'Well, no. I don't want to look at his bits. Not that I haven't seen them before, what with sharing a flat and everything, but ... Oh, I wouldn't expect you to understand. It's a man thing.'

'So, why exactly did he need you there at all?'

'Oh, you know, just someone to talk to. A bit of reassurance ...'

'But you could have stayed and talked to me, offered me some reassurance.'

'What do you need reassurance about?' He gave me a sloppy kiss that almost missed my cheek as I turned my head away. 'You're a fantastic mum. You're doing a wonderful job, and I'm so proud of you.'

It was no good. Why didn't he understand what it

felt like to be suddenly responsible for these three tiny creatures, left alone to deal with everything day in and day out, desperate for a few hours to myself, if only to sleep? Since when had discussing a mate's spotty crotch become more important than spending the day with his own family? It wouldn't do. It really wouldn't.

'It's just hard work, Dan. Hard, hard work and sometimes, just sometimes. it would be nice to think I had you here sharing the load.'

'And you don't think that what I do is hard work? Slogging away at the office from nine to five, or more often than not to seven or eight, every day, just to earn enough to keep our heads above water? Don't you think I deserve a day off, a few hours in the pub, every now and again, to help me unwind? And, besides, you weren't on your own today, were you? You went to your mum's. Didn't she share the load, as you call it?'

'Of course she did. But it's not the same, is it?'

'Why? Why is it not the same? I don't think any of them care who changes their nappies or shoves food down their throats, do you? Look at them fast asleep without a care in the world. It's you who seems to need the attention, not them.'

'Dan!'

I couldn't believe it when he stormed off up the stairs and started running the shower. He'd use all the hot water and I'd have none left for the babies' baths. Or

I'd have to put the immersion heater on to heat up more and have Dan moaning about the bills again. It was no good. We just didn't seem to understand each other at all any more. And, no matter what I did or what I said, I had a horrible feeling I couldn't win. I just couldn't win.

***

I would so like to say that things got better, but if anything, over the next few months, they got slowly but surely worse. I watched it happening, felt life as we had known it slipping away, but I did nothing to stop it. Well, what could I do?

Oh, Dan didn't go off drinking all day with Rich again. No need, apparently, as the rash turned out to be some sort of allergic reaction to a new washing powder and not a sexual disease or the beginnings of leprosy.

He didn't beat me or shout at me. Or see other women. Or not as far as I knew. Not back then, anyway.

But I'd look at him sometimes, when he was eating or staring at the TV, or when he was asleep and, through the strained line of his jaw and the beginnings of grey dotting at his temples I'd try to catch a glimpse of that young mousey-haired not-quite-handsome man I'd first seen dripping raindrops in the hallway and wonder where he had gone. And where I had gone.

Becoming parents wasn't what I had expected it to be. Yes, there were moments. Moments of sheer joy and wonder, as we watched them start to crawl, held their tiny bare feet in our hands and sang round after round of 'This little piggy went to Market'. Moments when I looked at Dan, my lovely, cosy, dependable husband, and felt so pleased to have him there, looking after us all.

And I loved my children. My gorgeous, cuddly, beautiful little children. Without any doubt. Loved them to distraction. Each and every one of them. And so did Dan.

But most of the time it was a slog, and one that I felt bearing down on me, day and night, until I could hardly breathe. Do all parents feel that way? Or was it just me, suffering in silence, too proud to admit I might have a problem? That looking after my own children was dragging me down into depths I hadn't known existed? But then, all parents don't find themselves coping with three at once, do they? Or mourning the loss of another who, had she lived, would probably have made the whole hard work thing even harder. Oh, I'm sorry. I'm so, so sorry. How could I even think something like that?

It's just that I had so wanted us to be the perfect family, Dan and me, strolling through the park on sunny Sundays, gazing lovingly into a pram or holding the little sticky hands of a bouncy blue-eyed toddler swinging herself happily between us. But that had been the dream. Not the reality.

Reality was more like a juggling act, an exercise in logistics, not being able to leave the house without thinking about where we would feed them or change them, getting them all in and out of the car and the pushchair, dealing with ear-splitting screams and random tears, not to mention packing bags of supplies so huge it looked like we'd just done a raid at Boots. But I don't even know why I keep saying 'we' because most of the time it was me, just me, doing it all on my own.

Becoming parents wasn't a new and exciting phase in our lives, strengthening our marriage, bringing us ever closer together. It was slowly but unstoppably tearing us apart.

***

'We shouldn't have done it,' Dan said, at two o'clock one morning, when Natalie was squeezed in the bed and fast asleep between us and I'd had to pull Ollie from his cot because he'd been fretful for forty minutes and was refusing to go back to sleep at all.

'Done what?' I switched on the bedside light and sat on the edge of the bed, finally conceding that I was not going to be able to climb in and go back to sleep any time soon.

'Had them all put in. All those embryos. We were crazy, Kate. The risk we took. Just imagine if we'd had all six. Three's bad enough. It's like a bloody nightmare sometimes.'

'Is it?'

'Oh, come on. Be honest. I don't know if I'm coming or going half the time, I'm so bloody tired. If we'd just had just the one we could have taken turns at night, paid for some childcare so you could go back to work, maybe gone on holiday ...'

'We *can* go on holiday.'

'No, we can't, Kate. It's too much. All just too much. I should never have let you talk me into it. Any of it.'

I could feel the tears welling up. 'I didn't know I'd had to talk you into it. Wasn't it what we both wanted?'

'A baby, yes. But babies, in the plural? I'm not sure that was ever the plan. Not all at once, anyway. I sometimes think we should never have gone in for the IVF. Or certainly never agreed to having more than one or two put in ...'

I felt a stab of guilt, knowing I'd thought the very same thing myself, often, but only for a few seconds at a time. 'Look at them. Look at them, Dan.' I angled my head towards Natalie, while rocking Ollie backwards and forwards in my arms. 'Our beautiful, perfect babies.'

'Yes, and look at what they're doing to us. No sleep, no money, no time for ourselves. No sex life ...'

'Things will get better.'

'Will they?'

'Of course. When they're a bit bigger, less demanding. This is the worst bit, but it won't last for ever.' For once it was me being the positive one, me trying to pretend everything was okay. But I had to. What choice did I have? Someone had to defend what we had done, defend the children who had had no say in their own making. *We* had done this. The two of us, together. And it couldn't be undone now. 'Oh, Dan, can you honestly say you wish we didn't have them? That it would be better if they'd never been born?'

'I don't know. If we'd never had them, we'd be none the wiser, so we wouldn't miss them, would we?'

'But we *did* have them. And we love them.' I pulled Ollie close to my chest, trying to calm him as he whimpered, both of us on the verge of tears.

'Yes ...' Dan lifted the sleeping Natalie and carried her back to her cot in the room next door, me a pace or two behind, still holding Ollie. He stood for a while, just looking down at Nat, the light from the landing falling across her little face. 'Of course we do. And nothing in the world would tear me apart from them now. I'm sorry, Kate, but it's late and I'm knackered, and I'm not thinking straight.' He bent over the cot and kissed Natalie, very gently, on the tip of her tiny nose. 'Take no notice of me. It's just the lack of sleep talking. Here, give Ollie to me and I'll sort him out. You get your head down. No point both of us staying awake.'

But I did stay awake. Of course I did. Long after Ollie had fallen asleep and Dan was back sleeping beside me, I lay awake, wild thoughts running through my mind. This wasn't how I wanted things to be. Not what I'd expected at all. I wasn't happy. Dan wasn't happy. And, for the first time, ever, I wondered if we were over. If the Dan and Kate who had laughed and talked and kissed and made such passionate love so often and for so long, really were gone for ever.

Chapter 34

Natalie, 2017

The wedding was just two weeks away and the nerves were kicking in. Natalie sat at the kitchen table and stared at the clock. It was only half-past six but she was already up, an uneaten bowl of cereal in front of her, going slowly soggy in its milk.

There was something going on, but she didn't know what it was. Twice in the last few days she'd caught her mum and Jenny in whispered conversation and been only too aware how quickly they stopped talking as soon as she came into the room. Was it something about the wedding? Something they were keeping from her? She would like to think they were planning some kind of surprise, but their faces said otherwise.

She'd tried to talk to Phil about it but he'd said she was just being paranoid, stressing about nothing, and if she was really that curious about what they were keeping from her – if anything – then she should just ask them. Maybe he was right.

She pulled her big notebook out from her bag and opened it to the guest list page again. Of the sixty people they'd invited, fifty-six had replied, with only two of them (including her own father) giving apologies, but there were still four who had not let her know one way or the other. How could people do that? Didn't they realise the amount of planning needed to make a wedding work? That they'd have to pay for sixty meals even if only fifty-six turned up? That who would be sitting next to who had kept her juggling bits of paper around for hours on end, day after day, until she'd got it right?

She put the notebook down and forced herself to eat. Looking at the list over and over again was not going to change anything. And, if she was honest about it, she knew that it wasn't the missing four who really mattered. It wasn't their thoughtlessness that was keeping her awake at night. It was the absence of her dad.

'Oh, what are you doing up so early?' Jenny came stumbling into the kitchen, rubbing her eyes. 'I thought it was only me that had to get up at the crack of dawn.'

'Couldn't sleep.'

'Wedding jitters, eh? Don't worry, it'll soon be over.'

'You make it sound like some kind of horrible ordeal!'

'Well, it is, in a way, isn't it? All that worry and anguish, and all that scary expense, going on and on for months on end. Years, even. And for what? One day. It's just one day out of a whole lifetime.'

'But the most important day, don't you think? And there are still some guests who haven't even bothered to tell us if they're coming. Don't they realise how important this is to me?'

'But it's just one day, Nat, and what will be will be. If people don't come, they don't come. A few empty seats? In the grand scheme of things, they don't matter. What matters is you and Phil, making your vows and starting your life together. Right? And who knows who might wake up that day with flu, even if they have already said they'll be there, or have their car break down on the way to the church? If it rains, there's nothing you can do to stop it. If Great Aunt Maud wears a hideous hat and ruins the photos, you can snigger behind your hand or fume about it in secret, but you can't make her take it off. Not without causing a whole load of aggro ...'

'Jen,' Natalie laughed, 'we don't have a Great Aunt Maud.'

'I know, but I'm just making a point. Chill, Nat. It's just a day, and whatever minor things may go wrong, it will all be okay. Really it will.'

'Even without Dad there?'

Was she imagining it, or did a guilty look flicker across her sister's face?

'Well, there's not a lot we can do about that either, is there?'

'Isn't there? Jen, tell me, do you know something I don't?'

Jenny turned away and made a great fuss over opening a fresh box of teabags. 'I don't know what you mean. Know what?'

'Well, if I knew that, I wouldn't be asking, would I? Jen, please, do you know why Dad isn't coming? Why he won't give me away?'

Jenny poured hot water into her mug, slowly swishing a spoon about so it made a chinking noise against the side. 'Do you want one? A tea?'

'Jen, stop it. You're just changing the subject. And, no, I don't want tea. I want answers.'

'Do you? Really?'

'Look, if you know something please tell me. Whatever it is, I can take it. It's killing me, worrying about it, trying to work it all out. And whatever it is, it can't be worse than some of the things I'm imagining.'

'You sure?'

'I knew it! You *do* know something, don't you?'

'Okay, yes, I do. You're right, it's not fair to keep you in the dark. But it's not what you're going to want to hear. Look, Nat, this is something everyone should know, okay? And talk about. All of us together. So I'm going to haul Mum out of bed now, and Beth. And I'll call Ollie, get him to come round before school. All for one and one for all, remember? Just hang on half an hour and I'll tell you everything.'

***

She may not have had the most exciting of jobs, but Natalie did have the most amazing bunch of workmates, and the greeting she got that morning was just what she needed to lift her mood. She was late getting in, but then it wasn't every day that you found out your dad had cancer and her brain still hadn't quite processed the information enough to make sense of it, let alone know what to do.

'Surprise!' they all chorused as the lift doors opened and she rolled into an office that was normally a standard beige box but was now decorated like a magic grotto from floor to ceiling. But, even though Christmas was just around the corner, these were not the usual gaudy red and green baubles dragged out of their cardboard box at the back of the stationery cupboard. Strings of white paper doves dangled from corner to corner above her head, silver bells tinkled over every desk, and a brand new white glittery tree stood by the window, adorned with cupids and horseshoes and lines of silver tinsel. And there were flowers everywhere.

'What ...?'

'For you, Nat.' Her friend Josie stepped forward. 'We do Christmas every year, but this year is different. We thought your wedding was more important.'

'More important than Christmas?'

'Christmas is everywhere. Every shop window, every street, every house. Even the funeral place has a wonky fir tree propped up outside. We can all get our Christmas fix from a thousand other places, so for the next week this office is all about you. And Phil, of course.'

'I don't know what to say.' Natalie brushed a sudden tear away and wheeled herself over to her own desk, picking up a pink heart-shaped pad of post-it notes that had certainly never been there before. 'It's wonderful. Whenever did you do all this?'

'The moment you went home last night. Oh, don't worry, it didn't take us long, and it was fun. And we may have had a bottle or two to keep us company.'

'Well, you could have kept some for me!' A good strong drink was exactly what she could have done with after Jenny had dropped her bombshell only two hours before. And to think her mum had known too, and neither of them had said a thing.

'What makes you think we didn't?' Josie slid open the bottom drawer of Natalie's desk and pulled out an unopened bottle of red. There were at least another two lurking underneath. 'White would have needed to be kept cold and we thought that lot from Accounts might steal it if we put it in the fridge. So, we'll have a little drink at lunchtime, okay? To celebrate your impendings.'

'Boozing at work?' Natalie said, not having the heart to tell them what she was really feeling right then. 'Whatever would Mr Baxter say?'

'It was Mr Baxter's idea!' boomed a voice from behind her, and her boss stepped forward and bent down to kiss her on the cheek. 'I know there's still another week until you go on leave, Nat, but we wanted to make it a week to remember. Oh, I still need the work to get done, so no slacking, all of you, but let's enjoy it for a change, shall we?'

'Hooray to that!' one of the girls shouted and everybody laughed.

'Thank you. Thank you everyone. I really wasn't expecting ...'

'What? That anyone would make a fuss, want to make this a special time for you?' Josie said, laying a hand across her shoulders. 'Nat, we haven't had an office wedding for years. We're almost as excited as you are!'

'Come on, now, you lot,' Mr Baxter yelled, clapping his hands together. 'Work to be done.' But he gave Natalie a cheeky wink as he walked away.

'I wish Phil could see all this,' Natalie said, switching

on her computer and sliding the desk drawer closed. She could really do with seeing him too.

'Bring him in. This celebration is as much for the groom as it is for the bride. Invite him over for lunch. The wine's on us, but tell him to bring chips. Plenty of them. I'm not sure my cheese and pickle sandwiches will be enough to soak up the booze if I want to stay sober enough to work this afternoon!'

'Thanks, Josie, I will.' She forced herself to smile. She couldn't tell them, couldn't burst the happy little bubble they had created just for her. Happy face. Happy face. Keep it jolly. But she did want to see Phil and tell him everything. So badly. 'I'll get him to bring some salt and a big bottle of vinegar too. The chip shop never put enough on.'

'Oh, don't bother. You haven't tasted the wine yet. Let's just say it was quite cheap. Vinegar has nothing on this stuff!'

Natalie's phone rang then and, as she answered it, she quickly switched into work mode, immersing herself in a world of irate customers and insurance claims and direct debit queries, but the strange and unexpected mixture of warm glow and terrible fear stayed with her all day as her thoughts swung wildly backwards and forwards between the good and the bad.

She was getting married in a few days' time. But her dad wouldn't be there. *Her dad had cancer.* She was going away on a wonderful honeymoon with the man she loved. But the other man she loved, almost as much, would be in hospital and missing it all. *Because her dad had cancer.*

She couldn't cancel it all now, could she? Not after all the planning and the flowers and the cost, and Phil having booked the airline tickets. *But her dad had cancer.*

She could hardly wait for seven o'clock, when they had decided they were all going round to see him, together.

But Natalie knew that seeing him was going to make it all feel very real. And it was going to do one of two things. It was either going to reassure her, that he was okay really, that this was just a blip that the doctors were going to put right. Or it was going to frighten the life out of her. And, as she gulped back the tears, the worst possible thought flooded in and wouldn't go away. Her wedding was going to be ruined because her dad wouldn't be walking her down the aisle. And he wouldn't be walking her down the aisle because he had cancer. And he just might die.

Chapter 35

Kate, 1991

It was the day that everything changed. Everything. One moment, life was as it always was. Chaotic, tiring, busy, but, at the same time, increasingly rewarding, fun, exciting. Bringing up three children at once was an experience that brought new challenges and new wonders, every day, and now that I was back at work, even if only on Saturdays, it felt like things were finally getting back to a manageable but slightly new version of normal.

But then the whole thing flipped over, like a train running out of control, hurtling at blinding speed until it left the track. My world shuddered and rocked and tumbled, tipping everything out, battered and broken and never to be the same again.

'Kate.' The bank manager's hand rested on my shoulder as he knelt down beside me and spoke quietly into my ear. 'Phone call for you.'

I didn't see it coming. I looked up from my counter, a pile of cash in my hand, a queue of customers still awaiting my attention. 'Can you ask them to wait? Or take a number and I'll call back when I have my break?'

'No, Kate.' There was something about his face, the look in his eyes. 'Go and take the call. Use my office. I'll take over here.'

I didn't argue, just stood up and went out to the back room, closing the door behind me.

'Hello? Kate Campbell speaking.'

There was a silence and then there was Dan, not really sounding like Dan at all. 'Kate?' His voice was shaking, racked by sobs as he finally managed to get the words out. 'You have to come, Kate. It's Natalie. She's been hurt.'

'Hurt? What do you mean hurt? How badly hurt? Where are you? Where is she?'

'We're at the hospital. All of us. We came in an ambulance. Nat ... she got hit ... by a car. She's ...'

'*What?* You were meant to be looking after her!' I was screaming at him now, sinking into my boss's leather chair, my knees suddenly unable to hold me up for a moment longer. 'What was she doing anywhere near a car?'

'I'll explain when you get here, Kate, but let's not get into all that now. Just get here, okay? Quick as you can. She's alive, but she's unconscious. And it looks bad. Really bad.'

I didn't stop to explain, to close my till, to find my coat. I just grabbed my bag and ran. I didn't have the car. Dan had kept it at home in case he needed to take the kids anywhere. Not that he ever did, not on his own. The hospital was only a few stops away on the bus but I couldn't stand there on the pavement, waiting and watching, not knowing when it might come, whether it was on time, how crowded it might be. There wasn't time for any of that, not when my little girl was lying on some bed somewhere, hurt, in pain, needing me to be there.

I ran and ran, my bag bouncing against my hip, not caring that my shoe was rubbing my heel, that there were tears streaking down my face, that I could hardly breathe with fear. And then I saw a taxi. It was going the wrong way, but it was empty, its 'For Hire' sign on display, so I flung my arm out to hail it and stopped running, panting hard, clinging to a lamppost and trying to get my breath back as the driver did a U-turn and pulled up beside me at the kerb.

'Hospital, please,' I spluttered, climbing in the back.

'You all right, love?' the driver said, peering anxiously at me in his mirror. 'Is it A&E you need?'

'A&E, yes.'

'You're not ill, are you? Only, I don't want anyone passing out in my cab. Or being sick or anything. We're not medically trained, you know. Cab drivers.'

'It's okay. It's not me. It's my baby. She's been in an accident. She's only three years old. Please, just get me to her. Please ...'

'Right you are, love,' he said, suddenly bursting into action and revving the engine as if we were at the starting line of a Grand Prix. 'Leave it to me. Three minutes, okay? Guaranteed. Or you can have the ride for free.'

***

Dan was pacing up and down by the reception desk when I got there, waiting for me, his face pale, biting his nails. 'Oh, Kate. Thank God.' He almost threw himself at me, and I could feel his hand shaking as he grabbed me and led me through a pair of glass doors marked 'No entry' and into the emergency room.

Natalie looked so small, lying on a narrow bed, all covered in wires and tubes, one of those big collar things around her tiny neck, her eyes closed as if she was fast asleep. She was surrounded by doctors and nurses, some rushing about, others standing to each side of her, touching her, talking to each other about things I didn't understand.

'This is my wife Kate. Natalie's mum ...' Dan spoke quietly, as if he didn't want to interrupt.

One of the nurses left the bed and came towards me.

'Kate. Hello, I'm Lucy. Please, try not to panic. I know it looks frightening, but a lot of this is routine. Tests. Precautions, while we establish what's going on.'

'Oh, my God. What happened to her?'

I shouldn't have left her. Not with Dan. Not with anyone. She was my responsibility, my baby. As I gazed down at her, not knowing if she was going to live or die, all I wanted to do was scoop her up and hug her, make everything all right. It was what mums were supposed to do.

'It seems she was hit, pretty hard, by a car. There were eye witnesses and the police will tell you more, as soon as you're up to it. But, for now, your daughter has injuries to both legs, a lot of cuts and bruises, a bump to the head, which means she's still very groggy. But our main concern right now is her spine, finding out what damage there is, if any ...'

'Her spine? Dan? What do they mean? What's happened to her spine?'

'I don't know, Kate.' He was grasping for my hand again, but I already knew it was for his benefit, not mine. He wanted reassurance, forgiveness. He had allowed this to happen to our daughter and he wanted me to say it was all right, that it wasn't his fault. But it was his fault, wasn't it? Three-year-olds don't just find themselves out in the street, going under the wheels of speeding cars. Three-year-olds don't understand danger.

Three-year-olds are meant to be looked after, watched over, kept safe. Especially by their own fathers.

I couldn't look at him. I pulled my hand out of his and shook him away.

'How? How did this happen?'

'She just slipped out. I don't know how. There was a parcel delivery. Something from one of your catalogues, I think. And the front door was open. I was signing some slip or other and I didn't even see her go. He must have left the gate open as he came in. The delivery man. The next thing I knew was the squeal of brakes, the scream ...'

I could see it happening. In my head. In horribly graphic detail. My child, running out onto the pavement, spotting something across the road, maybe a dog or another child, laughing to herself, wanting to go and investigate, the way she always did, stepping off the kerb ... I closed my eyes but I could still see her, bouncing off the bonnet, flying through the air like a rag doll.

I could hear the car screech to a halt, hear her scream, hear the awful deathly silence that followed. And I was there, seeing it all. Right there. Only I wasn't. I was at work, totally oblivious to my child's pain, and it was Dan who was there. Dan ...

Where was Dan? Where was he when my child was being hit? Being hurt? And where were the others? Then? Now? I felt a sudden panic wash over me.

'My other children. Where are they? Beth and Ollie?'

'They're safe, Kate.' Lucy, the nurse, pointed through the glass doors. 'You can see them whenever you like. We're looking after them, in the relatives' room.'

Safe? How could I believe my children were safe, ever again? Natalie was meant to be safe, but she wasn't, was she? She was lying there in front of me, looking anything but safe, and this was down to Dan. All down to Dan.

Before I even knew what I was doing, I turned round and slapped him, as hard as I could, across his face, my hand stinging with the force of it. I saw the shock on his face, his eyes widening, his mouth forming a startled O. See how it feels, Dan, I thought. Pain, that terrible unexpected pain, and from someone who's supposed to love you.

One of the nurses came at me, her arms stretched out, trying to make sure I didn't do it again, and I heard someone call for Security, but I didn't have the strength to hit him again. Or the will.. I just grabbed for the end of the bed to steady myself and let the tears fall. I couldn't have stopped them if I'd tried.

***

How do you tell a three-year-old that she may never walk again? Never run, like her brother and sister, never jump

337

or hop or dance the way other children do? That her whole future was now on a new path, and that none of us knew where it led. Career? Boyfriends? Marriage? Children of her own? They told me they were possible, probable even, but there would be barriers, difficulties, obstacles at every turn. There were bound to be.

They told me I shouldn't try too hard to think that far ahead, that I should concentrate on the here and now, that there was so much that disabled children were capable of. Swimming, riding horses. But not ballet, I thought, not twirling in a fairy dress or winning the hundred metres or showing me her somersaults. They said there were lots of schools who were adapting their classrooms and their playgrounds to accept children in wheelchairs, so she needn't be separated from her siblings, needn't feel different. That she could still lead a happy, well-balanced life. Read, learn, think. It could have been so much worse. But she wouldn't walk. That was what kept banging away inside my head. She would not walk. Could not walk. And, barring some future miracle of medical science, she probably never would.

The house would need work too. Natalie would never make it up the stairs without someone to carry her, and we couldn't do that for ever. She would grow, she would need her independence, her privacy, space to manoeuvre her chair.

I couldn't get it out of my head. Any of it. The accident, or my imagined version of it, and the fact I had not been there. It was driving me mad, haunting me, night and day, until I could hardly function. The vision of a changed future I could never have imagined, even in my wildest nightmares. I lay there for weeks afterwards, night after night, finding sleep impossible, all the uncertainties flying around in my head, buzzing in my ears like persistent angry wasps.

And then she was coming home, to a very different life from the one she had left behind, and I couldn't do anything to change it. No amount of widened doorways or wheelchair ramps or welcome-home toys were going to make up for what she had lost. Or for what Dan had done. And for that I didn't think I could ever forgive him.

***

'We can try for compensation,' Dan said, slowly, carefully, into the darkness. I tried to breathe evenly, but my heart was going into overdrive. What? He couldn't mean it, surely? But, of course, he did. I knew then that he was missing the point as usual, missing what really mattered. That nothing, no amount of cash, would ever be enough to compensate, and that Dan would never change. 'Or something from the insurance. We should make someone pay.'

'Who?' I lay, flat on my back, aware of him next to

me, on his half of the bed, not touching, the gulf between us widening by the day. 'That poor woman driving the car? She didn't have any chance of stopping in time, Dan. It wasn't her fault. The police told us that.'

'I know whose fault it was, Kate. You don't have to keep reminding me. Don't you think I feel bad enough already?'

I turned my back and stared into the blackness. Bad? Did I care how bad he felt? He deserved to feel bad.

I felt his hand on my shoulder, his body inch closer, the warmth of a bare leg pressing against mine. 'Kate?'

I tried to ignore him, pretend I was asleep, but he knew I wasn't.

'No, Dan.'

'Just a hug. Nothing more. Please, Kate, just a hug.'

But I couldn't. I kept my back to him, shook his hand away, and buried myself in the torment of my own thoughts until, what felt like hours later, I finally fell asleep.

NUMBER FOUR

Chapter 36

Ollie, 2017

They all sat around Dad's small living room and drunk mugs of tea that none of them had the stomach for.

Ollie had watched the girls all take their turn to hug him as they arrived, and had extended his hand to shake before realising that he needed a hug just as much as his sisters did, and pulling Dad in towards him. How thin he was!

And now they sat around under an invisible grey cloud they all knew was there, and struggled to work out what to say.

'So, it's all booked, then?' Ollie said, draining his mug and searching for somewhere to put it down. 'The op, and everything?'

'Yes, so I don't want any of you worrying. This thing has been caught early enough and I will beat it. I promise you I will. You don't get rid of me that easily! So, I don't want any negativity, okay? And ...' He was looking straight at Natalie. 'No tears! Ollie will do a fine job of giving you away. In fact, there's nobody I'd rather hand the responsibility to than you, son.'

Ollie gulped back his emotions and nodded.

'I'm signed off work for a while, and I've still got a day or two before they take me in, so you're all welcome to pop round again any time. It's always good to see you. Well, you know that. I can't remember the last time I saw you all together. A rare treat! And please come in and visit me in my sick bed once it's done. Not you, Nat, obviously. You'll be sunning yourself somewhere exotic. Bridlington, I think Phil said it was! Bring me in a bunch of grapes if you like. Do you remember, Kate, when Rich did that? Ate most of them himself by the time he'd gone, and left us the pips! Or sneak me in a bottle of wine if you like. And I'll want to hear all about the wedding, and see pictures ...'

'Now, come on, you lot. Your dad looks tired. Time we left him in peace.' Mum was shepherding everyone, just as she always had, ever since the days when it had been all about collecting up coats and toys, trying to stop the squabbles and squeezing everyone into the car. She hovered for a moment, as if unsure, as she watched them all hug their dad goodbye, whether she should, or could, hug him too.

'Good luck, Dad.' Ollie made sure he was the last out of the door.

'You too. With the show, as well as the wedding.'

'Oh, that! It's running like a well-oiled machine. Couldn't have done it without Beth's help, of course.'

'Ha, don't let her hear you say that. It'll go right to her head. Still, it's good, seeing you all helping each other out. You're good kids, all of you. We didn't do such a bad job, did we, your mum and me ...'

***

The donkey costume was hilarious. The mum who had made it had used an old pair of curtains which, although admittedly were just about the right shade of grey, had little pink triangles dotted all over them. As the Higgins boys clambered excitedly into it, a couple of plastic curtain hooks fell out of the head end, sending everyone into uncontrollable giggles.

The tail looked like it had been made from an old dressing gown cord with the end frayed, and it was slightly too long, so it almost touched the floor. The ears were not quite equal in size and at the mouth someone had attached a pair of toy false teeth, which gave the donkey a permanent but rather manic-looking smile.

'Perfect!' Sean said, smiling to himself as he watched

from the sidelines, although Ollie was fairly sure his mate's eyes had wandered in Beth's direction as he'd said it. 'The audience will love it. Comedy always goes down well.'

'I'm not sure the nativity story is meant to be a comedy,' Ollie said, absentmindedly patting the donkey on the head as if it was real and causing one of the boys inside to squeal.

'A bit late to say that now! It's definitely more panto than bible this year, that's for sure. And, anyway, it can be anything you want it to be. Your show, your rules,' Beth chimed in. 'And you did say the headmaster wanted something different this year.'

'Well, he's going to get that all right! Okay, boys, out you come. We don't want you suffocating in there. Now, where's Victoria? Time for a complete run through, I think. Everyone in their places, please.'

***

'Have you got your suit sorted out for the wedding?' It was Sunday lunchtime and Natalie had her notebook out on the pub table, before their plates had even been cleared away.

'Sorted out? What does that mean exactly?' Ollie swallowed his last forkful of roast potato and reached for his pint of orange juice and lemonade. He had vowed to cut down his alcohol consumption and, with Beth watching him like a hawk, was doing his best to stick to it.

'Well, you know ... out of the wardrobe, tried on, sent to the dry cleaners. That sort of thing.'

'It'll be okay on the day. Don't panic. I do have rather a lot of other stuff on my plate at the moment.'

Beth picked up Ollie's empty plate and peered at it. 'Really? I'm sorry but I must disagree. There's not a scrap left on it.'

Ollie groaned. 'Oh, ha, ha.'

'In fact, it looks like you've licked it clean, gravy and all. I must say, what with that huge bowl of soup and two bread rolls you demolished as well, you're eating like a horse today.'

'Or a donkey!'

He and Beth burst into laughter, leaving Natalie looking utterly bemused.

'I wish you two would take this more seriously,' she said. 'Not as if I have any idea what's so funny anyway. This is my wedding, remember, and I want to make sure everything goes smoothly. Or as smoothly as it can without Dad.'

'Of course.' Ollie struggled to put on his serious face and reached over to pat her hand. 'Your wish is our command.'

'Good. I should bloody well hope so. So?'

'So, yes, my suit is ready. As ready as it will ever be. It's not as if I ever wear it, so it's probably still got the tags on it from whenever it was cleaned last time. And, yes, it will still fit. One advantage of being a PE teacher is that I rarely put on any weight. Even when I do eat like a horse.'

'Good. Just checking. If you're going to be giving me away, you'll be doing the aisle walk and standing up the front with everyone watching, so I do want you to look your best.'

'Not show you up, you mean?'

Natalie shrugged, but he knew that was exactly what she meant. Perhaps it was time to try a bit harder to please her? She was the first of them to be getting married, and he did genuinely want it to be a special day for her.

'Anyone having pud?' Beth was studying the menu, with a hopeful look on her face. 'Only, I don't want to be the only one and look like some sort of glutton.'

'Well, in that case, give it here and let's have a look. I'm sure I could force something down to keep you company.' Ollie took the menu from her hands. 'Mmm, you could put on a few pounds just reading about this lot! Better not let Nat anywhere near or she'll never squeeze into her dress.'

'I'm sure an ice cream wouldn't do any harm,' Natalie said, raising her hand to call the waitress over. 'And, look, they have honeycomb flavour. Got to give that a try.'

They finished their meal and helped Natalie to tick off a few more of the bullet points in her book, so by the time they pulled their coats on and prepared to leave, she was looking a lot calmer. Outside, although it was only half-past three, the light was already fading, the December sky turning a dull and depressing grey. A bit like the donkey costume but without the little pink triangles, Ollie thought, smiling to himself.

He wasn't keen on winter, especially as a good part of his working day was spent outdoors, wrapped up in fleecy tracksuits with his hands turning blue. With less than two weeks now until the wedding, he hoped the weather would hold. A light flurry of snow might be quite nice in its way, bringing a bit of added magic to the occasion, but the full-on snow drifts and icy roads stuff could make it hard for guests travelling any distance, like Aunt Jane driving up from Somerset with Granny Molly in tow.

It was only a short walk back to the house and for once Natalie allowed him to push her wheelchair, the combination of two glasses of wine and a belly full of food making her a lot less stubbornly independent than usual.

'You coming in?' Beth said when they got to the front door. 'Mum's out. In fact, I think she was planning on visiting Dad again, taking him some of her magic soup!

But Jenny will probably be back by now from wherever it was she went.'

'You know, she's being so mysterious lately,' Natalie said. 'I'm convinced she's got a secret boyfriend. I just hope he's not married or something.'

'What makes you think he might be?' Ollie followed his sisters into the house.

Natalie called a loud 'Hello, anyone home?' up the stairs, and only when there was no reply, did she answer Ollie's question. 'Oh, I don't know. Sneaky phone calls … I just get the feeling she's hiding something, that's all.'

'She wouldn't. Not Jen. Little Miss Goody-goody Peacemaker couldn't bear the thought of hurting someone, even if it was some shady wife she'd never met. No, it'll be something else. If it's anything at all. Let's give her the benefit of the doubt, eh?'

'Or just ask her,' Natalie said.

'I suppose we could,' Beth said, looking far from certain about it.

'But let's not, eh? She's an adult, you know. She's entitled to her privacy.' Ollie filled the kettle and flicked the switch. 'If there is anything she wants us to know, I'm sure she'll tell us, in her own good time. Now, who wants coffee?' He opened the cupboard next to the sink and grabbed a jar of instant. 'I wonder if Mum's got any cake stashed away?'

'Cake?' both girls chorused. 'After that huge lunch?'

'Well, I do eat like a horse, remember? And, seeing as there isn't any hay ...'

***

There was something about the run-up to Christmas that always seemed to change the atmosphere in the school. The kids were happier, more excited, burying themselves in craft projects involving lots of cotton wool and glitter, and spending chilly break times in huddles, poring over toy catalogues and planning their present lists. Most of the teachers walked with a spring in their step too, as the end of term approached and lessons and homework, and therefore marking, started to tail off in favour of carol singing, board games and, of course, the upcoming nativity play.

Ollie had it all under control now. The show had been rehearsed to within an inch of its life, all the costumes were ready, and Sean had done wonders with the scenery. 'We're way ahead of schedule here, you know, mate,' Sean said, putting the finishing touches to the stable door at the side of the hall during an afternoon when neither of them had a class to teach. 'A week to show-time and there's nothing left to do.'

'That's good, isn't it? No last-minute panics, no unexpected disasters.'

'Oh, steady on there. Don't go speaking too soon and putting the jinx on it. It only needs your leading lady to go sick or one of the donkey boys to break a leg or something and you'll be panicking all right!'

'Point taken. But we do have a couple of understudies lined up who could probably just about step into any role if needed.' Ollie crossed his fingers. 'With a lot of prompting. But it's not gonna happen, okay?'

'If you say so. You're the boss!'

'And don't you forget it!' Ollie laughed, throwing the box of costumes back into a cupboard. 'So, what are your plans for the Christmas holidays, then? I don't suppose you're heading back to Oz, are you?'

'No, mate. I wish I was, but it's a long old flight and it doesn't come cheap. The only way I'll be seeing my family this Christmas will be on my computer screen. Whatever would we do without Skype, eh?'

'I've never used it, actually. The beauty of having all my nearest and dearest close by, I suppose.' His mind threw up a brief image of Laura's face and he blinked hard to push it away. 'Well, almost all of them, anyway.'

'It's not just you and Beth, then? Both parents still alive?'

'Yep. And two more sisters. One of them – Natalie – is getting married on Saturday, actually. The usual church affair. Bells and posh cars and wedding cake, the works. It'll be a big family get-together. In fact, this one'll probably put Christmas in the shade for once. And I'm doing the giving-the-bride-away bit.'

'Really? I thought you said your dad was still around. Wouldn't he normally ...?'

'Long story. He should be there, but he's a bit poorly so he's not going to be. Not unless there's some miracle between now and Saturday anyway.'

'Right. Sorry to hear that.'

'It'll be okay. I bloody well hope so, anyway. So, where will you be spending Christmas? You didn't say.'

'Don't rightly know, mate. Get a turkey ready-meal in and watch TV at the bedsit, I expect. I guess there'll be something on worth watching, won't there? We usually have a barbie on the beach where I come from, but I'm guessing that's not what happens around here. Too darn cold! Still, when you think about it, it's just another day, isn't it?'

'Is it?'

'Well, it'll have to be. I can't magic up my family from thousands of miles away, can I?'

'You could always come to us.'

'Don't be daft, mate. Your parents aren't gonna want a stranger hanging about. No, you're all right ...'

'Just Mum. Dad might still be in hospital, but he doesn't live at home these days anyway. And Nat will be off honeymooning, God knows where, because her fiancé isn't saying. So it will just be us, my little sister

Vivien Brown

Jenny, and maybe my gran. And Beth, of course. I know she'd like to see you.'

'I wouldn't mind seeing her either, but ...'

'No buts. You're invited, okay? No barbie, I'm afraid, and Mum's not the greatest of cooks so I can't promise cordon bleu or anything, but it has to beat a ready-meal for one.'

Chapter 37

Kate, 1992

If it wasn't for the lack of space, one of us would have moved into a separate bed, a separate room, even a separate house if it was up to me. Since Natalie's accident I had found it hard to be civil to Dan, even to look at him without wanting to scream at him or pound my fists against his chest until there was no breath left inside it. How could he have done this to her? To us?

We tried to hide things from the kids and I think, all in all, we managed that pretty well. Daddy waved goodbye after breakfast and went to work, Mummy fed them and took them to the nursery in the afternoons and fed them again before chucking them all in the bath, usually together, and Daddy was sometimes, but not always, back again in time to say goodnight, read stories and tuck them in. There were trips to the hospital with Natalie, and to the physio, to see how she was doing, but we all knew nothing was ever going to be quite the same again. Life chugged along like a clockwork toy that never stopped but every now and then ran quite frighteningly low on batteries, and it was on those days that I just wanted to scream as loud as I could and hide my head under the duvet and never come out.

Hiding things from Mum wasn't quite so easy.

'I do know how you feel, Kate' she said, one afternoon, right out of the blue, even though I hadn't said a thing. I was bashing a spoon hard and fast against the bowl, trying to let some of my fury out, as we made the cakes – three of them – for the kids' birthday. They were almost four already! Where had the years gone? 'Managing three kids twenty-four hours a day can't be easy ...'

I stopped stirring for a moment, to give my wrist a rest. 'It's not the kids that are the problem. Yes, I get tired and a bit ratty. Who wouldn't? But they're worth it.'

'Of course they are. But I do remember what it's like, even though I only had the one of you, not three.'

'I had four, Mum. *Four* babies, not three.'

'I know, love, and little Rosie will never be forgotten, but it's the here and now we have to focus on. The three you have now, the three who still need you. It's overwhelming, I know that. You're bound to be tired, or exhausted more like, but you're doing a great job, you know. Considering ...'

'Considering what? That one of them can't walk?'

Mum gave me one of her looks and shook her head.

'One dead and one disabled, before they're even four, and you say I'm doing a great job!'

'Kate!'

'Or did you mean considering that I'm married to a cold unfeeling bastard who spends as little time with any of us as possible?'

'Oh, Kate, no! Unfeeling? I'm not sure you're being entirely fair to Dan. He does his best, and I can only imagine how the poor man must be feeling since the accident, but isn't it time you forgave him? Gave him a bit of a break? I do believe he's genuinely sorry.'

'Poor man? Oh, Mum, come on! And he can be as sorry as he likes but it won't make her better, will it?'

'Of course not, but you should be helping each other, comforting each other. What good is it going to do harbouring all this anger and blame and animosity?'

'But he let her run out, Mum. He didn't even notice she'd gone. If she'd been with me ... If I hadn't insisted on going back to work ... If I hadn't ordered that dress from the catalogue and the delivery hadn't come while I was out ...'

'Ah, I see. All these ifs. If only this. If only that. It's not actually Dan you're blaming now, is it? You're blaming yourself.' She scraped her wooden spoon on the edge of the bowl and laid it down, then put her arms around me as I slumped forward, resting my forehead against her hair and breathing in the familiar smell of hairspray and eau de cologne. 'Look, love, what's done is done. Sometimes in life we just have to get on with things, make the best of what we have left.'

'I know, but it's so hard. You and Dad never had all this, did you? You were so lucky. I just wish I could have had what you had.'

'*Lucky?* He did die of lung cancer, remember. And long before his natural time.'

'Yes, I know. But before that, you were so ...'

'Oh, Kate,' she butted in before I could finish. 'Don't wish for things you don't understand, love.' She pulled back, holding me at arm's length. 'Marriages are not always entirely as they seem, even the apparently happy ones. They're a bit like icebergs, you know, with only the shiny tip on show. There are always parts hidden away underneath, the dark parts we don't want others to see.' She sighed and eased me away so she could look into my eyes. 'Even with Trevor. I love him to bits, but we do have our moments. Little arguments, you know. The odd bit of name-calling. I threw a rolling pin at his head last week but it missed, I'm glad to say. I'd have been happy for it to hit him at the time, though, believe me. And there are some nights when we sleep back to back, neither one of us wanting to make that first move and say sorry. Stubborn old goats, the pair of us. But ...'

'But it wasn't like that with you and dad, was it?'

'Of course it was. Look, Kate, I know you've always put him on a pedestal, and it's probably a good thing that you remember him that way, especially now he's gone, but there's something I've never told you before and I think now I probably should. About your father.'

She lowered herself into a chair and gestured for me to do the same, gently wiping a smudge of flour from my cheek. 'He had his ... problems, shall we say? With money. Oh, I know money isn't supposed to matter, not when you love someone, but it does. Especially when there isn't any.'

'So Dan is always saying. But you only had one child and Dad had a good job. A well-paid job.'

'He did. But that's not much good when someone is incapable of keeping their money where it belongs. In their pocket, in their wallet, in the bank. I'm afraid with your father that rarely happened. Come pay day, there would always be some dead cert running at Haydock, or a man down at the pub offering odds on the football. One way or another, there was never anything left. Sometimes it was just about all gone before he even made it home on a Friday night, and me trying to feed us all on last week's shrivelled potatoes and a few tins of cheap beans.'

'I don't remember that. And I loved beans!'

'Good job you did as you had so many of them! Thank God for your Gran and Granddad though, because I never could have managed without the few bits they'd bring with them every time they dropped by. A cake she'd baked, a bag of apples from their tree, a nice bit of shepherd's pie when they'd had some left over. They were just bringing treats, but they didn't know the half of it. Mainly because, like you, I didn't tell them. Or anyone. But your dad ... well, even when he won, he'd convince himself he was on a winning streak and put all his winnings on something else. Oh, I might get a bunch of flowers or a box of Milk Tray out of it, but they don't pay the electric bill, do they?'

'But Mum, you always seemed so close. Like you were glued together sometimes ...'

'Had to be, love. It was the only way to keep an eye on him, by meeting him from work and walking home together, going with him to the pub ... It's not that I didn't love him, because I did. I really did. But it's like trying to stop an alcoholic from drinking. When nothing else works, you just have to watch them like a hawk, throw every drop down the sink, try to take temptation out of the equation. And the person has to want to stop, of course.'

'And did he? Stop gambling? Or want to?'

'I'm afraid the cancer did the stopping for him in the end, love. He just got too ill to carry on, too ill to care. He left quite a lot of unpaid bills that I had no idea how I would deal with, but the life insurance money just about put things back on track for me after he'd gone. I was worried for a while that amongst all the debts we might have let the premiums slip but they were up to date, thank heavens. Oh, it wasn't much, but I don't know what might have happened without that to fall back on.'

I didn't know what to say. My dad? Some sort of compulsive gambler, squandering the money away? How on earth had they hidden that from me?

'So, you see, Kate, I do know what it's like to have problems, secrets, and how much you might want to protect your children from the worst of it, but if you want my honest opinion ...'

'Which you are going to give me anyway!'

'Of course. Well, it's that these things have to be faced head-on and dealt with. Have it out with Dan. Tell him how you feel. Listen to how he feels. Try to put it behind you and move on. Together or apart, but don't let it fester. It's not good for any of you, the children especially.'

'Okay. You're probably right. And I will, I promise. When the time is right. But, for now, I don't think I could talk about it without killing him. So it's easier for now just to do nothing. Say nothing.'

I gazed out of the window, at the thick, thorny stems of the rose bush, clogged with weeds, as it twined its way haphazardly and flowerlessly over the fence. In memory of Rosie, we'd said, choosing it to match the flowers we'd carried the day she was cremated, but when had we had the time lately to even go outside and look at it, let alone look after it?

'Well, I can't make you do anything you don't want to,' Mum was saying as I dragged my thoughts back from the past. 'But remember that iceberg. Only ten per cent is looking up into the light. That's your little ray of hope. But the murky ninety per cent could very easily drag you down, if you're not careful. Right down into the depths of darkness and despair. And then where will you be?'

Chapter 38

Beth, 2017

Sean Harper was coming for Christmas lunch! Beth looked at herself in the full-length mirror in her bedroom, turned from side to side and decided she was very much in need of a new dress. They didn't usually bother dressing up on Christmas Day, not when it was just family slumming it in front of the TV. Thinking back, she couldn't even remember what she had worn last year, although Jake turning up after tea, wearing jeans so old they had gaping holes in both knees, seemed to have left a lasting impression on her memory. And they weren't the intentional designer kind of holes either!

But Sean wasn't Jake. Sean was one of those people she knew instinctively she could trust, and he was fast becoming a close friend. A very handsome and charming friend, she had to admit, but she also had to keep reminding herself that he would not be staying around for ever, and that any thoughts of things turning into a proper romance needed to be utterly squashed every time it raised their insistent little heads. Still, he was just what she needed to brighten the festivities, and definitely worth trying to impress.

Everyone had taken a few days off work to see Dad settled into the hospital and to get themselves ready for Natalie's wedding, which was now only three days away. Everyone except Ollie, who wasn't really allowed days off in termtime and was in any case oblivious to the need to prepare at all, beyond finally giving in to Natalie's demand that he check his suit was actually clean and being persuaded to buy a new shirt for the occasion. And now Jenny was in the kitchen with her laptop, Nat had gone to meet Phil for a last-minute-check-list lunch, Mum had a headache, probably stress-induced, and was in her room having a nap, and everything was, temporarily at least, quiet again.

The house was awash with bags and boxes and bundles and, with so many women living together and all of them in a state of high excitement, the place was starting to feel like some kind of noisy and shockingly colourful Eastern harem. New underwear and sparkly jewellery, pairs of pink satin shoes, overflowing make-up bags, charging cameras, assorted hair curlers and straighteners (none of them being entirely satisfied with the hair nature had given them) and, of course, Natalie's already packed holiday suitcases, were scattered at every turn, and everyone kept bumping into things that they were sure hadn't been there the last time they passed along the hall or tried to find space at the table to sit down and eat.

Beth picked her way through and grabbed her handbag from the hall table. It was time to get out of the madhouse for a few hours and, despite the inevitable pre-Christmas crowds, hit the shops.

Outside, along the edges where the morning sun had failed to reach, the pavements were still frosted with white. Most of the trees lining the street were bare, their branches hanging overhead like skeleton arms, but the lawns were holding on, still providing little square pockets of faded green in the few front gardens that had not yet been concreted over to make extra parking spaces.

It was only a short walk to the high street. That was one of the better things about living where they did. The easy access to shops, offices, doctors, and all without having to take the bus. Within minutes she was passing the insurance building where Natalie worked, and then the hairdressing salon. She knew the place was short-staffed today, with two girls off sick with the flu, and right up to the previous afternoon it had been touch and go whether her boss would honour her request for leave, so she kept her head down and quickened her pace for fear of someone spotting her and calling her in to do a quick cut and blow dry.

There were only three or four shops likely to have anything to her liking, and she made straight for the first of them. Now, how should she play this? Casual and comfortable? That was probably the Ozzie way, what with them spending so much of their lives on the beach. But this wasn't Australia. This was England, and here Christmas party clothes always involved at least a little bit of sparkle. Not that she was looking for something to wear to an actual party, but even so …

She picked a black dress off the rail and walked over to the nearest mirror, holding it up in front of her. Okay for a funeral maybe, if you ignored the silver glittery collar and the fact that it was quite shockingly short. Deciding she didn't have the legs for it anyway, she quickly put it back. Red was very Christmassy, of course, but as the store's Father Christmas strode past on his way to his grotto she couldn't help remembering why they had so rapidly discounted it as a possible colour for the bridesmaids' dresses. Maybe something silvery and shimmery, then? Or with a touch of gold?

She found a dress she was eighty per cent happy with in the last shop she tried. If she'd carried on looking for perfection she knew full well she was never going to find it and, besides, her legs were aching and she needed to sit down somewhere and treat herself to a coffee and a big fat chunk of cake.

The coffee shop was warm and crowded, but it smelt delicious. She found a space at a table in the window but had to share with a couple of older women who glared at her for a few seconds but then reluctantly moved their shopping from the empty chair to make room. They were talking non-stop about some friend called Alice who had run off and left her husband for a bloke half her age who she'd only known five minutes. The way they were slagging her off, it was hard to believe this poor Alice woman was actually a friend at all, and as they spoke about the man in question, all body and very little by way of brains, Beth was pretty sure she could detect more than a hint of jealousy.

She sipped at her coffee, which, as usual, was much too hot, tore big mouth-sized pieces off her chocolate fudge cake with a fork, and watched the world go by.

It would seem strange at home when Natalie was gone. More changes to get used to. When they were all about eight or nine, Mum and Dad, with a lot of help from Granddad Trevor, had converted the garage into a bedroom for Natalie, with its own small en-suite shower and loo, so she no longer had to worry about using the stairs. It had given her so much more independence and had made more room upstairs for the rest of them too. When Ollie left a couple of years back, the girls had all finally had a room each for the first time, but Beth couldn't help feeling that something had been lost because of it.

She gazed out at the crowds bustling up and down the high street, bulging shopping bags bumping into each other, scarves wrapped around necks and coat collars turned up against the chill wind, and wished, just for a few moments, that time could go backwards, that they could all be together again, small and happy and untroubled by all the bad stuff in the world. Back to before Natalie's accident, before it had all started to go wrong ...

But change had to happen, didn't it? And not all of it was bad. By Saturday, Natalie would be glowing with happiness, married, and soon to be setting off for her surprise honeymoon destination. Mum would be weeping with joy as only mothers of the bride knew how, Ollie would probably be drunk, and she and Jenny would be sitting at the side of the reception hall like a pair of old maids – unless the mysterious James turned up – bemoaning the lack of boyfriends and knocking back the wine and handfuls of crisps like there was no tomorrow. It was what happened at weddings, so why should this one be any different?

The only person not featuring in her imagined scenario was her dad. Because he wouldn't be there. He'd be in his hospital bed, hopefully the operation behind him, and on the way to recovery. And maybe, once the ceremony was over and the meal eaten, they might be able to go down there, even if it was late, with phones full of photos and a piece of snaffled wedding cake, and the nurses would let them sneak in to see him before he went to sleep.

She hadn't spent nearly enough time with her dad as she should recently. Well, what with work and everything else, it wasn't always easy to find the time, or make the effort. But she would change that from now on. Much as they had all let the ties between them and their dad loosen and drift further apart in the years since he'd left home, it was time to tighten them again. They were still a family, and who knew how long they might have left?

She finished her coffee and wiped the crumbs of cake from her mouth. The dress she had bought was blue, with a narrow band of sequins around the neck. Now all she needed were shoes to match. At home she usually just walked about barefoot or, if it was especially cold, wore the old tartan slippers she had had for years. But Sean was coming and somehow that made everything different. There was no point in thinking too hard about her dad, worrying about things she couldn't change. They were all going to have a fantastic wedding, the school nativity play would be a roaring success, and then ...

Then it would be Christmas.

Chapter 39

Kate, 1993

I *always find it hard to believe those women who discover their husbands have been playing away yet say they knew nothing about it, didn't have a clue. Really? What about when he came home late, smelling of a perfume you didn't recognise? What about the whispered phone calls that ended abruptly when you came into the room? The lipstick on the collar, or the restaurant and hotel bills that turned up in pockets when you were taking his jacket to the cleaners? That's what always seemed to happen in books and in films. The clues, the give-aways, the sneaky suspicions that creep into the back of a woman's mind and lurk there, until they turn into cold hard truths she'd rather not have to face. But real life isn't quite like that.*

In real life, the clues slip by unnoticed as you battle with kids and work and tiredness, and an almost don't-want-to-know kind of apathy. The changes happen slowly.

So slowly you hardly notice them. The brand-new underwear that appears in the wash, the aftershave he's taken to wearing every morning, the important business meetings after work that bring him home later and later, the creeping up the stairs without his shoes on, hoping you will be already asleep and will stay that way, and the late-night shower that follows.

A slow withdrawal, a sullen unwillingness to take part in family life. Or a renewed energy and eagerness that comes out of nowhere, as he tries to overcompensate for the guilt. Maybe even, in a moment of thoughtlessness, being called by someone else's name.

For me, it was none of those things.

***

Dan was home from work on time for a change, and on a day he knew the kids were having their tea at my mum's, so it was just us. He came in, took a deep breath and sat me down on the sofa.

'Kate, I've been seeing someone,' he said. Just like that. He hadn't even taken off his coat.

'Seeing?' I didn't want it to be true but I knew instinctively that it was. All the clues I'd been carefully ignoring came crashing down around me in one great big blindingly obvious heap. 'You mean, seeing as in ...'

'Sleeping with. Yes.'

My God, why did he have to be so blunt? So matter of fact about it? And why did what he was saying, confessing, leave me feeling so utterly cold? It should have hurt. Like a knife to the gut. I should have cried, shouted, screamed. But I didn't.

'Who is it? Is it anyone I know?' Stupid questions. As if it mattered. But it's the first thing you ask, isn't it? Closely followed by 'How long, how often, when, where? Not in our bed? Please not in our bed.' And the inevitable gut-wrenching 'Do you love her?'

Dan stayed remarkably calm. And so did I, despite the rushing noises in my head and the hard knot that had formed somewhere deep in my chest and was making it almost impossible to breathe.

'I'm sorry, Kate. But things have been … well, difficult, for a long time. You know that. We don't talk. We don't share things any more. Not the way we used to.'

'And whose fault is that?' I didn't wait for a reply. 'And we don't have much in the way of sex, of course. Don't forget that one, will you?'

'That's true, but it isn't the reason. Well, not the only one.'

I stared at him, finding it hard to take it all in. Dan and some faceless woman, humping away like rabbits. A woman who was, quite possibly, about to steal my husband. I didn't really want to know, but I had to ask. 'Better than me, is she? In bed?'

'Kate ...'

'Prettier? Takes better care of herself? And of you? Ah, but then, I don't suppose she has three kids to contend with, does she? Oh, for God's sake, Dan, I trusted you. I may not have been the perfect wife lately. I hold my hands up to that, and you're not exactly the perfect husband either, but we have children together. I thought we owed each other at least some loyalty.'

'You're right. Of course you're right. And being parents means more than anything, but ...'

'But she flashed a bit of cleavage and dropped her knickers, and you just couldn't say no?' I knew I was shouting now, at last, but this wasn't a conversation I could contemplate having quietly. 'So, what happens now? You want to split up? Leave? Get a divorce? Do you know what that will cost? We hardly have enough money to keep one household, let alone two. And the kids, and me ... I'm telling you now, we're not going anywhere. This is our home and I'll happily bleed you dry rather than be forced to leave it.'

He reached across and took hold of my hand. 'No, Kate. I don't want a divorce. I don't want to leave. I love the kids. I love you. Oh, don't give me that look. I have a funny way of showing it, I know. Look, I don't even know what it is I do want. I just thought it was time to stop sneaking around behind your back. To try to talk things through. To be honest ...'

'Honest? God, Dan, how many times have I tried to be honest with you? About my feelings, about the state of our so-called marriage? But what did you do? Did you listen? No, you did not. You just turned your back, buried yourself in bloody work, spent longer and longer away from the house. Well, I know why now, don't I? Some bitch had got her claws into you and you were loving it. Made you feel the big man, did it? Juggling two women at once. Climbing out of her bed and back into ours.' I glared at him, pulled my hand out of his grasp and swiped it across his face, my knuckles connecting with the side of his nose. It was the second time, ever, that I had done that, but there are some things ...

'And you still haven't told me her name, by the way. I think I'd like to know that much at least.'

He didn't hit me back, just sat there in silence. I watched the thin trickle of blood run down his cheek where my rings had nicked his skin. He closed his eyes and took a long slow breath. 'Fiona. Her name's Fiona. She's a secretary at the office.' He stopped and took a deep breath.

'So, why have you suddenly decided to tell me? When, fool that I am, until five minutes ago I actually didn't have a clue she even existed, had no suspicions about any of this.'

'I thought it best I tell you, before you found out

some other way. Before you heard it from someone else. Office gossip ...'

'So, I'm the last to know, am I?'

'I'm sorry about that. But people notice things ...'

'I didn't.'

'Look, it's over, Kate. Between me and her. I was an idiot. I can't even explain why I did it, but I won't be seeing her again.'

'She's left then, has she? Left the office?'

'Well, no. I'll still see her at work, obviously. But I'll keep out of her way. Nothing more than colleagues. I promise.'

I couldn't look at him. Did he really think that was okay? That an arrangement like that could ever work?

'I suppose all I need to know right now is where this leaves us, Kate? I can see that you'll need time, to think about it all, work out how you feel, but what shall I do? Do you want me to stay? Go? Sleep down here on the sofa?'

'Oh, so what I want matters all of a sudden, does it?'

'Of course it does. I'm talking about all this so we can decide what to do about it. Together. I want a second chance, Kate. Somehow ... For the kids and for us. I want to put this right. I *need* to put it right. I don't love her. I never did. I love you. I've always loved you.'

'Maybe you should have thought of that a bit sooner, don't you think? Horses and stable doors come to mind.

And oats. Wild ones that you really shouldn't have sowed.'

'Okay. I know. If I could go back and change things, don't you think I would? We'll make it work from now on, I promise you. Whatever it takes.'

'That's two promises in as many minutes.'

'I know. And I'm sorry.'

'So, did you think about me, or the kids, while you were at it with this Fiona woman? Or your mum and dad? All the people you could hurt. And let's not forget my mum and Trevor. They'll notice too, you know. That things aren't right. What are we supposed to tell them?'

'Nothing. Let's tell them nothing. Not yet anyway. Not until we know how we're going to deal with all of this ourselves.'

'*We?* There is still a *we* then, is there?'

'Of course there is. I hope so, anyway. We are still a team, Kate ... aren't we?'

***

Right then I didn't feel part of any team. All I could see was a husband sitting in front of me who I'd thought I knew so well, but now would probably never trust again. But, looking back, that was the turning point, I suppose. That pivotal moment, when what I chose to do would shape all of our futures. Should I ask him to go, make him suffer, punish him? But that would surely have punished us all, separated my children from the father they so clearly loved. Or forgive and forget? Strangely enough, when I thought hard about it, I knew this wasn't the worst thing that could happen. Well, it wasn't, was it? We'd already been there, done those things …

And yet, we were still here. Still, just about, together. We had lived through it all somehow. Miscarriage, still-birth, Natalie's accident. And we would live through this too. Why should I let some other woman creep in under the radar and take my husband? Take away my children's father and jeopardise their future? Why should I be the one to roll over and give in?

It took a while, and I didn't make it easy for him, but this wasn't one of those unforgivable things. Perhaps it was my fault, almost as much as his. But, if it was true what he'd told me, that it was over between them, that he was sorry, then maybe we could get past it, learn from it, use it as the starting point for trying harder, holding on tighter, mending what we had left.

And we did. You know we did.

Until we were hit by the aftermath neither of us had seen coming …

Chapter 40

Jenny, 2017

Jenny looked up from the screen of her laptop and smiled. She had been researching courses and careers for a couple of weeks now and, finally, she had found what she had been looking for. It was a general counselling course, which would give her a proper recognised qualification, and from there she could start to specialise and move into working as a pregnancy counsellor. Helping frightened women, finding out they were pregnant when they hadn't expected, or wanted, to be, and those not pregnant who had desperately hoped to be. Encouraging them to talk, taking away some of the anxiety she knew must have beset both of her own parents, and seen at first hand when she'd met up with Laura.

She'd worked out how to get to the college, which shouldn't take more than an hour or so on the underground, with a quick bus ride at the other end, and it looked as if there were still places available, so she was going to apply today. Maybe, if she was lucky, they could take her in January. She could hardly wait. Of course, it would take a while to qualify, particularly if she was going to have to find the fees herself, but the course was a part-time one, which meant a lot of work online and only actually going into the college twice a week, so, with a bit of shift juggling, she was fairly sure she could fit it in around her current job. Okay, she might have to spend another three years helping people to wash and dress, and making yet more morning porridge, but she still had to earn and it would all be worth it in the end. It was time she stopped drifting through life and took control.

Jenny scrolled down the completed application form on the screen, checking for errors. She'd always been pretty good at English. Spelling and grammar seemed to come as second nature, so it was no surprise to see that what she had written made perfect sense and was typo-free. It was whether what she'd written actually said the right things that worried her now. At school she had followed the history, English and art route, not that she was especially interested in the wars with France or the Industrial Revolution, or been all that good at drawing, really, but they were the subjects she had always done best in. Picking them had helped her to a set of slightly better than average grades at GCSE and kept her away from the dreaded sciences she had loathed with a vengeance ever since she'd been introduced to her first Bunsen burner. And, while going off to uni had never appealed, she knew that a long-term job as a carer was no longer an option either.

Maybe her school subjects weren't exactly relevant. She hadn't studied sociology or psychology or anything like that, but the course information had made it clear that academic excellence wasn't what was needed. Counselling required empathy, an interest in people, an ability to listen to others and help them to explore their feelings, letting them make their own choices and choose their own path without taking over and giving advice. It was all about trust and confidentiality and caring. It was a career with her name written all over it.

She thought about Laura, about her dad, about the clients she was working with every day when she made them their breakfast and listened to their chat. Sometimes she was the only living soul they would speak to all day. Yes, she could do this. In a way, she was doing it already. Earning trust and keeping secrets. She quickly crossed her fingers, then released them again and pressed *Send*.

As she got up from her chair and stretched, she heard her mobile ring from somewhere upstairs. She must have left it on her bed. For a moment she was tempted to let it ring. It could be her boss trying to persuade her to take on an extra shift when she had already made it clear she needed time off for her sister's wedding. But, then again, it could be something important. Oh, God, what if it was something to do with her dad? What if he'd taken a turn for the worse?

He was having the operation tomorrow. By Saturday, as she stood there in church with Beth, in their pink dresses, and walked up the aisle behind Natalie and Ollie, he would be through it and on the way to recovery and she could concentrate on enjoying the day and not worrying herself sick any more. But if things were to go wrong, if the cancer had spread, if they couldn't remove it, if he was to die on the table ... It didn't bear thinking about. Any of it.

She bolted up the stairs two at a time and got there just as the final ring faded away into silence. Flicking the screen to view her missed calls, she was surprised to see it wasn't her boss's name, her dad's or the hospital's that was listed. It was Laura's Aunt Clara.

Oh, no. In all the worry over her dad in the last few days, she had forgotten to worry about Laura. Oh, please, don't let anything be wrong, she begged, to some vague god she had no real belief in and couldn't even picture. Not again.

She dialled Clara's number and sat down on the

unmade bed, pushing Mr Flops, her old childhood toy, aside, her heart racing with fear.

'Hi, it's Jenny. You called me. Is everything all right? With Laura? The baby?'

The voice that croaked back down the line sounded old and tired but at the same time bursting with joy. 'It's a girl,' Clara said. 'The baby. Born at ten to three this morning, a strong and healthy eight pounds and screaming like her little lungs were fit to bust. Laura wanted me to let you know.'

'Oh. Oh, wow!'

'She's going to call her Evie. It's a name she and Ollie had talked about and chosen before, apparently. And Rose for a middle name. Evie Rose.'

'Oh, that's fantastic news. I can't believe it. And Rose ... for poor little lost Rosie. Ollie will love that ... and such a good weight, seeing as she was early too! What does she look like? I bet she's beautiful. When can I come and see her? And what about Ollie? Is she going to tell him now?' For once, with everybody out of the house, Jenny didn't have to go for the usual cloak-and-dagger whispering in corners, which was just as well, as she couldn't have kept her voice down if she'd tried.

Clara laughed. 'So many questions! Yes, of course she's a beautiful baby. Gorgeous. But please, don't say anything yet, Jenny. To Oliver, or anybody. Laura wants to do this in her own way. She's a determined young woman and fit as a flea. I don't think she'll be kept in the hospital more than a few more hours. And after that ... well, all I can say, dear, is that I don't think you'll have to wait very long to meet your new niece.'

Chapter 41

Kate, 1993 – 1996

I felt so proud of our little Natalie as she bounced back into health and happiness. Perhaps adapting to something so life-changing comes more easily to children, when there aren't years of memories and milestones stacked up behind them and about to be knocked over like a sledgehammer hitting a pile of Lego bricks, when there isn't all that learning suddenly undone and having to be re-learnt. She had to do things differently now, give up some of her so newly found independence and allow herself to be helped more but, part from a few frustrated tantrums, which all kids seem to go through anyway, she took it all in her stride. Although that's probably not the most suitable of expressions as she was unlikely ever to be able to stride again.

Ollie and Beth treated her just as they always had.

They made no allowance for what she couldn't do. In fact they played upon it sometimes, in what might to others seem a cruel way, playing hide and seek in places she had no chance of accessing, running up and down stairs in front of her, knowing full well she couldn't follow. But it wasn't cruel. It was just kids taking her for what she was, offering her no special treatment. I loved them for it. And so did she.

So, the walls and the door frames took a battering as she learned to manoeuvre her chair, but none of us cared. It was only wood and paint, and all of that was replaceable. Natalie wasn't. She was alive, when she could so easily not have been, and that was all that mattered.

I had worried about her when she'd started school. Well, I worried about them all, just as any mother does, but Natalie the most. They hadn't had a kid in a wheelchair in the school before, and I'm sure most of the other children had no idea what it meant, but the staff had assured me that the three of them would be kept together, their classroom was on the ground floor, the doorways and toilets would accommodate her and the chair with ease, and everything would be fine. I remember standing at the gates that first afternoon, waiting for them to come out, seeing Ollie and Beth bouncing along, laughing, lunch boxes and book bags in hands, and wondering, with a lurch to the stomach, why she wasn't with them.

'I was waiting for Phil,' she said, when she finally appeared, a small skinny boy trailing along behind her, with a lop-sided cheeky grin and a layer of ingrained dirt on his knees. 'He's my new friend.'

I smiled at the only other mother still left standing. 'Yours?' I asked.

She nodded and we both laughed.

'Caroline King,' she said, holding out a hand.

'Kate Campbell.'

With Ollie and Beth holding hands by my side, we followed Natalie and Phil through the gate and along the pavement, watching as they chattered and giggled, the little boy pushing her chair as if he'd done it all his life, all the way to the corner of the next street, where, their homes being in different directions, they were forced to part company.

'I'm going to get married to Phil,' Natalie said that evening as they all tucked into fish fingers and beans, watching *Sooty and Sweep* on the TV, their uniform jumpers discarded on the nearest chair in favour of their favourite sweatshirts, the new book bags open on the carpet around them, and a new grown-upness about them I wasn't sure I was ready for.

'Are you?'

'Yes, and Beth will be my bridesmaid, and Ollie can drive the carriage.'

'What carriage?' Ollie looked up, startled, and spoke through a mouthful of beans.

'One with horses, silly. A glass one, like Cinderella had.'

'I thought you always said you were going to marry your daddy?' I tried not to laugh at her earnest little face as she looked up at me.

'Mummy, that's silly. Girls aren't allowed to marry their daddies. Don't you know that?'

'Oh, yes, I forgot. And he's already married to me, isn't he? So, when is this wedding?'

'When we're bigger. Like twelve or thirteen or something.'

'And how do you know this Phil wants to marry you?'

'Because he asked me, of course. When I gave him a ride on my lap in the playground. He's nice, but he is a bit heavy. I think he might have to get a chair of his own if he's going to be my boyfriend.'

Ollie sniggered and Beth, who didn't seem to be listening at all, told them both to shush as she couldn't hear the telly. I knew then that I needn't have worried about Natalie. She still had her dreams of a normal happy future and, despite what had happened to her and all the inevitable obstacles she would still have to face, the others were keeping her grounded, treating her just the same way they always had. She was still our brave, feisty little Natalie and I knew then that she was going to cope. No, she was going to do more than just cope. She was going to thrive.

***

It was raining heavily the evening life changed so drastically for us all. Dan hadn't come home from work, and he hadn't phoned to say why. A shiver of dread ran through me as his plate of shepherd's pie slowly congealed in the oven. Was he doing it again? Keeping secrets? Meeting someone else? I shook my head. Things were so much better between us now. We were talking more, sharing more, making up for lost time. Work was still busy but we were making time for us too. Family time. Sundays in the park, pushing the kids on swings, taking them for swimming lessons and to story sessions at the library, sometimes holding hands, not just with them but with each other. Getting soaked to the skin when the girls sat end to end in the bath, with Ollie in the middle, laughing like bubbly drains as they created mini tsunamis that splashed all over the walls and the toilet seat if we'd forgotten to shut the lid, and us.

No, I had to trust him. I'd promised myself I would.

A flash of lightning shot across the curtains, followed by a huge crack of thunder that echoed around the room. I held my breath for a second or two and listened, worried that the sound was going to wake the kids at any moment and stop me from doing a huge pile of ironing I had been putting off for days. Ollie would be all right. He'd just tell himself some tale about dragons breathing fire or spacemen battling across the skies like something out of *Star Wars* but, even at eight years old, the girls were still scared of storms. Everything upstairs stayed quiet and still. I let myself breathe out, reached for the iron and plugged it in.

Mum and Trevor had come round after school, bringing cream cakes and a pile of comics, and some home-grown roses for me. I laughed to myself remembering that old advert from the TV that said *Roses grow on you,* because Trevor, even when he wasn't carrying an armful of blooms, had certainly grown on me over the last few years. I couldn't help but notice the warm glow in Mum's eyes when she looked at him, and struggled to picture anything similar in the years she was with my dad. Of course, I knew why now, knew about the gambling and the debts, and although it didn't change the love I felt for my dad at all, I had acquired a new respect for Trevor. He had definitely changed Mum's life for the better. And mine, although I still wasn't supposed to mention his generous gift.

But the best thing about Trevor was what he had done for Ollie. Ollie had been in and out of hospital quite a few times over the years, usually only for a day or two at a time, sometimes only for a few hours, when one of his asthma attacks was particularly bad and refused to give in to the inhaler. There were days when we were torn between Natalie and getting her to her physio appointments and Ollie, feeling breathless and unwell, and, unfair though I know it was, Natalie, whose problems seemed so much worse, always came first. Days when Ollie had to miss school, sit around quietly, avoid running around with the others. Days when he was bored. And those were the days when Trevor always appeared out of nowhere, a chessboard tucked under his arm and a carved wooden box of chessmen clutched in his hand, and over several hours of deep concentration, near silence and an air of competitive spirit so strong you could feel it, transported Ollie out of the gloom and into a world the rest of us just didn't know how to inhabit.

'Checkmate!' Ollie had screamed excitedly earlier that evening as he had beaten Trevor, fair and square, for the first time ever, and I don't think I had ever seen my son look so happy.

I bent to pick up one of the pieces, a pawn, that must have slipped down when Trevor was tidying the game away, and laid it carefully on the windowsill ready for the next game, as I reached for the first shirt from the top of the ironing pile. Maybe that was what I needed. Not chess, but an interest of my own, a hobby, something to get me away from all the domestic stuff once in a while. Something that could make me feel the way Ollie felt in that moment of triumph. I was just toying with the idea of taking up badminton and wondering if Caroline King might consider being my doubles partner when I heard the key in the front door and the sound of footsteps in the hall.

'Dan? Where have you been? Your dinner's ...'

But I didn't get to finish the sentence. My mouth had stopped moving and fallen open like it was hanging on a loose hinge.

Dan was standing very still in the open doorway, holding the hand of a small girl in crumpled pink pyjamas. She stared up at me through wet, sleepy eyes, her tiny hands hanging on so tightly to a tatty floppy-eared rabbit that it looked like her life might depend on it.

Dan's face was deathly pale. His voice, when it came, wavered and almost broke. 'Kate,' he said, holding my gaze with his own, as he bent down to wrap his arm tightly around the child's shoulders. 'This is Jenny ...'

Chapter 42

Natalie, 2017

Natalie shivered as she sat up in bed, rubbed her eyes and tried to focus on the glass of buck's fizz Beth was holding out to her. She loved having her own little annexe here at the side of the house, but like any ex-garage, no matter how well carpeted and how many radiators were installed, it was still not the warmest of rooms at this time of year. She pulled the duvet tightly around her shoulders and peered at the clock. Not quite eight, and a bit early for booze.

'Happy wedding day!' Jenny shouted, bouncing in with a tray of warm croissants fresh from the microwave and a pile of cards she'd been picking up off the doormat for days and hiding until today.

Natalie sidled across the bed to make room for her sisters to sit, the tray immediately occupying the centre of the space she had left. 'Thank you,' she said, taking a sip of the cold drink and giggling as the bubbles hit the back of her throat. 'Although a trip to the loo wouldn't go amiss before I get too into the celebrations. And I need to brush my teeth.'

'Never too early to get started on the bubbly,' Beth said, taking the glass back temporarily while Natalie eased herself into her chair and wheeled away into the en-suite.

'If you say so. But I'm taking it slowly. I refuse to get drunk,' Natalie called through the partially open door, her mouth full of toothpaste, before eventually rolling back into her bedroom, still drying her hands on a towel. 'At least until after the ceremony.'

'Spoilsport!'

'Look, this is my day. You two just remember that. And what I want, I get. It's the law!'

'Yes, Ma'am.' Beth pushed the glass back into Natalie's hand. 'And what you want now is a drink, right?'

Natalie took another sip and gave in. 'So long as I get at least two of those croissants to help soak up the alcohol.'

'Alcohol? There's hardly any in this stuff. It's nearly all orange juice. Nat, you are such a lightweight!'

'Well, I just hope Phil agrees with you when he has to carry me over the threshold.'

'No problem. He's an old hand at carrying you about. He could do it in his sleep, that one.' Jenny picked up a croissant and started dropping flaky crumbs all over the duvet as soon as she bit into it. 'Mmm, these are good. Come on, Nat, tuck in. You have a busy day ahead of you. Can't have you fainting from hunger, can we? So, what's first? Open your cards? Hair, make-up, flowers ...?'

'No cards until Phil and I can open them together. And the flowers aren't being delivered until ... oh, I can't remember. Let me just find my list.' Natalie reached for her bag and pulled out the trusty notebook that had hardly left her side for months.

'Nat! Can't you ever just be a teeny bit spontaneous?' Beth was already running Natalie's hair through her fingers and holding strands of it up towards the light. 'Sit back and relax and let us take over for once. It's the last time we'll all be here like this, living under the same roof. We want to pamper you.'

'But ...'

'No buts, Nat. Come on, eat up and get up, then let's get this special day started, shall we?'

***

'I knew we shouldn't have booked a two o'clock wedding!' Natalie looked at her new diamante watch and shook her head. 'My hair's done, the flowers are here, everything's checked and double checked and there's still two hours to go. What are we supposed to do now?'

'Well, we could have some early lunch. It'll be a while until the meal gets served up, what with the photos and everything, and I don't fancy having a rumbling tummy in church.'

'Beth, I can't possibly eat any lunch. I'm still full of croissants, and my tummy's so fluttery with about a thousand butterflies dancing around inside it that I can't even think about food.'

'Well, I bloody can! How about you, Jen? Toasted sandwich, extra cheese?'

'Sounds good to me.'

'You two go. Give me a few minutes on my own so I can have a bit of a rest. I need to conserve my energy for later.'

'Woo hoo! Nat's talking dirty,' Beth screeched. A couple of glasses of bucks fizz and she was already getting silly. 'Saving herself for the excesses of the wedding night!'

'Beth! You know that's not what I meant. Go on. Go and stuff your faces, but don't come moaning to me when you can't do the zips up on your bridesmaids' dresses! Try and get Mum to sit down and eat something too, will you? I expect she could do with calming down a bit. She was replacing the pins in the buttonhole flowers with safety pins from her sewing box last time

I looked, just in case someone pricked their finger. I think she's got this wedding confused with something out of Sleeping Beauty.'

'Will do!'

Natalie looked at her watch again. 'God, I do hate all this hanging around. I just want to get ready and get on with it now. As soon as Ollie arrives, we can all get dressed and get out of here. The bells will be ringing, and people will be milling about in their posh hats, and the sun's out for a change ... and I don't want to miss any of it. Not one single second. And my gorgeous groom, of course. I can't wait to see how he looks. I do love a man in a suit.'

'There should be a fair few of those around today, so mind you pick the right one! But, honestly, Nat, we'll go as soon as we can, once the cars turn up. I don't fancy walking to the church. Not in those new heels! And we can't get there *too* early, can we? Not before they've all gone inside and Phil's stewed for a bit, wondering if you're going to turn up. Brides are supposed to be late, not early. It's tradition. And they do say patience is a virtue.' Beth ran her hand over the back of her sister's hair and gave it another squirt of hairspray. 'And, anyway, I might just want to do a few final tweaks here before we go. I'm not totally happy with this curl ...'

'Go! Out! The pair of you. My hair looks fine. And

bring me a cup of tea when you come back, will you? I probably won't get another one all day.'

'Tea? When there's a bottle of champers on ice in the kitchen? The condemned woman drank a last cup of hot sweet tea before going off to meet her doom ...'

'Groom! Not doom! And mock as much as you like, but it's my day, and if tea makes me happy, tea I shall have.'

'Fine. All the more booze for us then! But don't you go lying down on your bed while we're gone. If you mess up your hair ...'

Natalie smiled. 'I wouldn't dare.'

It was blissfully quiet after they had left. Time to think, to breathe, to be herself for a little while before the ring was slipped onto her finger and she became someone else. A wife. A real grown-up. She rolled over to the mirror and took a good look at herself. Still in her dressing gown, but with full make-up on and her hair in the most fancy style she had ever had, she made for a strange looking figure, like two halves stuck badly together, one on top of the other, a mixture of her most glamorous and her most sloppy selves.

It was weird to think that this would be her last day living here in this house, her last day as Natalie Campbell. And to think that her dad wouldn't be there, as she'd always hoped – assumed – he would be. She choked back a big lump of sadness that rose up into her throat and lay her hand there. Dad. How was he doing, she wondered? She would have loved to phone him, but she knew that since the operation he was finding it a strain to talk. With the lump now gone and his throat swathed in bandages, he had insisted he just needed to concentrate on getting better now, and that they should leave him to do just that. Just as she, under his express orders, had to concentrate on having a wonderful wedding day, and on being happy.

Dad's life had taken a very unexpected turn, but her own was sailing along on the track it had felt destined to follow for as long as she could remember, and from tonight, when they left the reception as husband and wife, her whole life would be moving in a new and even more wonderful direction.

It was something she had always dreamed of, being married, having her own home, doing the things other girls did. Whoever would have thought that, of all her siblings, she would be the first? Little Natalie, who hated to be the centre of attention, but who, despite the wheelchair – no, *because* of the wheelchair – had never let life's challenges get her down. Her chair had never defined who she was because she had refused to let it. And today was the proof of that.

Phil loved her, chair and all, and probably had done, in his own special way, ever since he'd first hitched a ride on her lap in the playground all those years ago.

That they had stuck together, all through school and Phil's years away at uni, neither of them even looking at anyone else as their friendship turned to love, had to be the most amazingly wonderful thing in the world, and something she would never ever swap, not even if she was offered a brand new pair of legs – walking, running, super-dooper working legs – and all the opportunities that came with them.

She picked up the necklace he had bought her, especially for today, and held it up. Tiny sapphires gleamed in the light. 'Blue, to match your eyes,' he had told her when she'd opened the satin-lined box. She probably would have cried if he hadn't immediately followed with, 'and because Chelsea play in blue, obviously!' and sent her into a fit of giggles instead.

She fiddled with the clasp at the back of her neck and finally managed to get it to connect, pulling the heart-shaped pendant carefully into position at the front. Chelsea, indeed! Still, if a man was willing to get married on a Saturday afternoon and miss going to the match, it surely must be love!

The doorbell chimed its usual Edelweiss tune and within seconds Jenny burst back into the room. 'Ollie's here!' she said, excitedly, a dribble of fresh tomato pips sliding down the front of her dressing gown. 'So, we can get ready now, Nat. Properly ready, dresses and shoes and everything ....'

'Just one thing first, though. Where's my cup of tea?'

'Oh, yeah. Forgot about that. Coming right up, I promise.' And she was gone again, leaving the door wide open and the smell of warm cheese wafting in from the kitchen down the hall.

'Hiya, Nat.' Ollie put his head around the door. 'All right if I come in?'

She nodded. Her brother was wearing his suit already, immaculately pressed and with what was obviously a new white shirt, because she could still see the creases from where it had been folded in its packet. Maybe I could offer to iron that for him, she thought, before pushing the thought away again. He wouldn't want the fuss, and she could surely find better things to be doing on her own wedding day than her brother's ironing. She had to admit he looked great, even though his tie was a little crooked. All he needed now were his button-hole flowers, safety pin and all.

'No nerves? Second thoughts? Cold feet?'

'None at all.' She beckoned him over to sit on the end of the bed and grabbed his hand in hers. 'But thanks for asking!'

'Apparently it's what I have to do before I give you away. Make sure you really do want to be given away!'

'Well, consider it done. And, yes, please. Give away to your heart's content.'

'You sure you're happy about me doing it?'

'Well, I don't have much choice, do I?' She grinned at him. 'Ollie, you will do me proud. Really, I know you will. And you're looking so handsome, no one will be looking at me at all. You never know, you might even pull today, if you're lucky.'

Ollie laughed. 'Chance'd be a fine thing. And don't you think for a minute that no one will be looking at you, because brides are beautiful. All of them. Always.' He spotted her dress hanging from the wardrobe door, still in its stay-clean see-through wrapper. 'And if that's what you're wearing, believe me, you are going to look stunning. This is one occasion where you're going to have to put up with being stared at – in the nicest possible way – whether you like it or not.'

'If you say so. But I mean it, Ollie. Someone is going to come along and snap you up one of these days, and then it'll be you walking down that aisle for your own wedding. If you weren't my brother, I'd go for you myself! Well, except for the wonky tie, maybe. Here. Let me ... There! You'll do. Now, go and keep Mum busy somehow so I can get ready in peace. It's bad enough having Beth and Jen fussing around me in such a confined space. I don't think I could tolerate Mum as well.' She looked across at her dress and felt her heart do a little flip. 'Tell her to expect the grand unveiling in about twenty minutes.'

***

The music swelled to a final crescendo as they glided the last few yards and reached the front of the church, her wheels polished to a super-shine, and the soft folds of her dress falling forward and concealing her feet. Beside her, Ollie took a step away and, as she turned her head, there was Phil, grinning from ear to ear, his eyes shining, the huge pink rose pinned to his grey suit lapel drooping just very slightly to one side. Where was Mum with her pot of safety pins when you needed her? She felt his hand slip gently into hers and squeeze it as Beth and Jenny let go of the back of her chair and moved to stand where she could see them, at the side of the aisle.

In the front pew, Mum and Gran sat close together, clutching hankies. And there were Aunt Jane and Granny Molly, in their unfamiliar finery, feathery hats and all, tucked into the row behind, Jane fiddling with a camera and Granny shuffling through the pages of a hymn book she was not going to need as all the words were printed on the order of service sheet in front of her. On the other side, Phil's mum Caroline was gripping her husband's hand and grinning like a cat that's got the cream, while behind them rows and rows of smiling faces had merged blurrily together as Natalie had come slowly down the aisle and tried to pick each one out through the mist of tears. Theirs as well as her own.

She could hardly believe, after so many long months of planning, that the moment had actually come, but here she was, about to marry the love of her life. She looked up at Phil, who gave her a reassuring wink, and then the vicar came forward, smiling, holding out his arms to welcome the congregation and gesture that they should be seated, and the last notes from the old organ finally faded away into silence.

'Dearly beloved ...'

There was a loud creak from the back of the church and the vicar stopped in mid-sentence, almost before he had begun. The heavy wooden door opened on its ancient hinges, just enough to send a long dusty beam of light straight up the faded red carpet that had been laid along the aisle floor, and onto the back of Natalie's dress. There was a muttering from the guests and, as the silence was broken, someone took the opportunity to cough. Natalie turned just as the door closed again and the beam disappeared, throwing the interior of the church back into semi-gloom, but not too late to see the unmistakable shape of her father edging his way around the pews and into the side aisle, making his way slowly and as quietly as he could towards the front.

'Well, you cut that a bit fine,' she heard her mum whisper, as he sat down in the space beside her, almost as if she'd known he would be coming all along. Natalie saw the vicar make some sort of sign to Ollie, who tipped his head enquiringly towards the front row, but Dad shook his head and mouthed something she couldn't quite make out. Nevertheless, Ollie walked over and took Dad's hand in his, pulling him to his feet, and without saying anything more, the two men changed places.

She felt something like relief flood over her. He had come, just as she had always hoped he would. Not quite in time to walk beside her up the aisle, and it was too late to change that now, but he would be the one to give her away. She gazed at him for a moment, noticed the white flash of a dressing taped to his throat and sticking up over his collar, saw how pale he looked, how his hands shook as he clasped the order of service sheet between them, but there was no time to ask how he had got here, to wonder if he was okay, to worry if he should have come at all. Not now.

'Dearly beloved,' the vicar began again, as everyone stopped shuffling about, and the ceremony finally got underway.

Chapter 43

Kate, 1996

I didn't need to ask whose she was. While Beth, Ollie and Nat, with their dark hair and round faces, all looked so much like me, this child was the absolute image of Dan.

'I'm sorry, Kate,' Dan said. 'Really sorry. I didn't want you to find out like this. But I had no choice. Her mum ... Fiona ...' He lowered his voice, almost to a whisper. 'She's dead.'

'Dead? How can she be dead?'

'An accident. She was running to her car, after work. Not looking properly, or couldn't see because of the rain, I don't know. She got hit by a bus, Kate. Right outside the office. Some of the girls went out to have a nose as soon as they heard the crash and realised it was her, but there was nothing anyone could do. The ambulance came quickly but she didn't even make it as far as the hospital.'

'Oh, my God.' Instantly, my mind flashed back to that other accident, five years earlier. To Natalie, lying in the road, crushed and broken. To that mental image I had never quite managed to shift, even though it was entirely of my own making.

My heart was pounding so hard I swear I could hear it, even above the rain that was once again thumping against the windows. Oh, God, not again. But this time, this time ...

This child was alive. Not dead, like her mother. Not hurt, like Nat. But motherless and probably utterly unaware of what that meant. I didn't know her, didn't know anything about her, except that she was so clearly Dan's. But I couldn't stand by and do nothing to help her. She was so small and she looked so scared, and so lost. What if she had been Beth or Natalie? Or Rosie? If it had been me who had died, I would have wanted someone to help them.

I stepped forward and took hold of her tiny hand as the other gripped her toy even more tightly, and led her to the sofa, pulling a cushion underneath her head as she curled up, sleepily, into a ball.

I should have been thinking all kinds of things. How could he be doing this? Bringing his child here? His secret child? I should have been shouting at Dan. But how could I?

'She shouldn't be listening to any of this. Poor little mite.'

'No, she shouldn't. But I need to explain ...'

'Explain away! If you think you can. Because it's pretty obvious she's yours, Dan. And she's what? Three? Just forgot to mention her, did you, all this time?'

I looked across to where Jenny had already fallen asleep, her toy rabbit pressed against her cheek, as Dan sank into a chair and closed his eyes.

'Later, Kate, eh? Can we leave all that until later? It's been a terrible shock, seeing Fiona like that. Dead, right in front of my eyes, her bag open and everything chucked all over the road, one shoe off, her hair all covered in blood. It was horrible, gut-wrenching. Poor, poor Fiona ...'

I didn't know what to say, what to feel.

'I went straight to the childminder's. Well, someone had to, and it was better than the police going, which was what was being suggested. But now ... I haven't even had the courage to tell her what's happened yet, not that I have any idea how. Angels, stars in the sky, I don't know. And now I have to work out what to do with her ...'

'*Do* with her?'

'Yes. Make plans, decide what's going to happen to her. Tomorrow, the day after, and the day after that. For ever. Fiona's parents are long dead, and she had one brother who lives in Canada. The hospital is contacting him about ... well, her body, you know, but they weren't close and he's never even met Jenny. And I'm her daddy. Like it or not, I'm all she has, Kate, and I need to talk to the brother and then decide what happens now. To her life, her future ...'

'And?'

'I suppose it's going to be largely down to you. How you feel. Whether you think you might ...'

'What? Have her here, you mean? Your bastard child, living here? With us?'

'Don't call her that. None of this is her fault,'

'I know that. I think we both know whose fault it is, don't we? But a child! You had another child and you didn't think to tell me. So, where has she been all this time? Have you been visiting her? Taking her to the park, like the others? Buying birthday presents? Christmas? Paying maintenance? '

'Yes, sometimes. Some of those things. *All* of those things. When Fiona would let me, anyway, which wasn't often. She didn't want me to have much to do with her really. With either of them. Certainly didn't want to take my money, in case it gave me 'rights'. Thinking about it, I was probably just a convenient sperm supplier.'

'And it's not as if we don't know all about that, is it? At least this time it didn't involve a cubicle and a pile of mucky magazines.'

'No.'

'Honestly, Dan, do you really think I want to hear all

this stuff? Are you expecting me to actually feel sorry for you or something?'

'Of course not. I just feel as if maybe she planned to get pregnant and then cut me out all along. I was *used*, if you like ... But I am on the birth certificate. I insisted on that much. No child wants to grow up not knowing where they came from, do they? Believe me, Kate, I didn't lie. Not at first. I really had no idea Fiona was pregnant when I told you about the affair, or when she ended it.'

'Hang on a minute. *She* ended it? You let me believe it was your decision. You'd been a fool, you said. Only wanted me ...'

'Does it actually matter who ended what? It was over, and I *did* want you. She was pregnant, okay, and she didn't tell me. Not for months. And then, when she did ... You and me, we were getting back on track. You'd forgiven me, let me stay, life was better. Why would I want to ruin all that? '

'So you said nothing? What I didn't know couldn't hurt me, is that it?'

Dan nodded.

'Well, I know now, don't I?'

Dan seemed to crumple before my eyes, his face a deathly white and his eyes now gazing up at me, brimming with unshed tears. I didn't know if it was the weight of responsibility coming down so suddenly on his shoulders or if it was the shock, or grief even, of losing Fiona. He had cared about her once, after all. Perhaps loved her, a little. Enough to produce a child together. *This* child.

We both sat in silence for what felt like ages, just staring blankly at each other, but that wasn't going to make things happen, was it? I stood up. 'Tea. I'm going to make you some tea now. With a drop of brandy in it.' I reached down to the electric socket and switched off the iron that I had forgotten was still on, and went into the kitchen. Clutching the edge of the worktop as I waited for the kettle to boil, I jumped as another loud crack of thunder echoed around the house. Before it had rolled away into the distance, it was replaced by the chilling sound of Dan's wracking sobs growing ever louder and more desperate from the other side of the wall.

I didn't know what to do. How is a wife supposed to deal with the grief her husband feels at the death of another woman? Help him through the loss of someone she has never met and never wanted to meet? What is she supposed to feel for a child, a confused and innocent child, who she has only just met but wished had never been born?

I took Dan his tea. We didn't have any brandy but I found an inch or two of rum in the bottom of a bottle Trevor must have left behind at Christmas, and dowsed it with that. And then I held him as tightly as I could as he shook, and listened to the rain pounding at the windows, and stared at Jenny, curled up asleep on our sofa, unaware that she had a half-brother and two half-sisters sleeping upstairs, and tried not to think too much about what might happen in the morning.

***

The kids loved her from the start. Perhaps, at eight, they were too young to question too closely where she'd come from, how she had the same daddy as they did, where she had been until now. We didn't try to keep secrets from them. Whenever a conversation ran that way, we were as open as we could be. They all knew that Jenny's mummy had died and that she was here to stay. When she cried, they hugged her and shared their toys. Ollie ignored her and huffed to himself when she played with her dolls, treating her just the same way he did the others, and Beth would grab a brush and play with her hair, as if Jenny was a doll herself, and Nat gave her wheelchair rides. She was one of them, a sister, almost instantly, and I wasn't at all sure how I felt about that.

'Right!' Trevor said, one afternoon, when we'd struggled by for weeks, all three girls crammed into the one bedroom, with boxes of toys and clothes piled so high they could hardly see out of the window. 'This can't go on, can it? And you having to carry Natalie up and down the stairs every day. It's far from ideal. The girl's getting past all that. She needs her chair with her, not out of reach for eight hours of the day. And she needs space. They all need space.'

'Well, we can't magic up another room we don't have.' Dan ran his hands through his hair in exasperation and took a swig from a big mug of tea Mum had handed him ten minutes ago and that was already almost cold. 'And Ollie's room's hardly big enough to swing a cat.'

'I'm not talking about Ollie's room. That one's called a box room for a reason! But boys manage. They get by, don't they? I know I did when I was growing up. A few pairs of trousers, a handful of t-shirts and pants, and room to slide the train set under the bed. What more does a boy need? The lad spends most of his waking hours outside kicking a ball about anyway. No, it's the girls we have to think about.'

'I think about nothing else. What I've done to my family. I know it's all down to me, Trev. Bringing Jenny here, expecting to just fit her into our lives ...'

'What else could you have done, Dan? And the little mite is fitting in, isn't she? Remarkably well. Now, tell me to keep my nose out if you like, but I've been thinking about the bedroom dilemma, and to my mind there's only one solution. The garage.'

'What about it?'

'Convert it. It's plenty big enough to make another room, probably a bathroom too, or a small one anyway. And when did you last actually park the car in it?'

'Never. A car the size of ours won't fit.'

'Exactly. What's in there? Piles of old junk, I bet. Stuff you haven't looked at in years. A ladder you never climb. Garden tools that could just as easily fit into a shed. Come on, let's take a look, shall we?' Trevor stood up and beckoned for Dan to follow.

A squeal came from the direction of the back garden as the kids ran around playing some new chasing game Ollie had invented and which he always seemed to win.

'I know Trevor means well, but we can't afford it, Mum.' I went into the kitchen to make another pot of tea and to keep an eye on them through the window, and she came in behind me. 'I know it's probably a great idea, but it will cost thousands, won't it? Tens of thousands, I shouldn't wonder.'

'I don't think you have to worry about that, love. Trevor and I have been talking and ... well, you're his family now. It's not as if he has any children or grandchildren of his own, and he's grown very fond of you all. Ollie in particular, though he hasn't said as much, what with the chess and everything. He wants to help you, Kate. Whatever it costs, he's going to pay for it.'

'No! That's far too generous.'

'Maybe. Maybe not. But who else are we going to leave our money to, if not you and the kids? Better you have some of the benefit now and we see you enjoy it, than after we're gone.'

'Gone? Mum, you're still young. You've got years yet.'

'After Trevor's heart scare, who knows? Treat every day as if it could be your last ...'

'But you might need that money to travel, to have some fun of your own. And what if you get dry rot in the house or the roof falls in or something?'

'Ha! Insurance. That's what it's for. And we're certainly not keeping money aside for the what-ifs of life when there's a real problem very much in need of sorting out here and now.'

'I don't know what to say.' I reached for the biscuit tin and prised off the lid, automatically selecting a handful of non-chocolate-covered ones to take outside to the kids, then making up a jug of weak orange squash.

'Then don't say anything. Just thank you. That's all Trevor will want to hear.'

'But I was so mean to him, for so long. I didn't give him a chance, did I? I didn't like him, just because he wasn't Dad.'

'And now?'

'And now ... well, I feel a bit ashamed, to be honest. He's all right, isn't he? And Dad wasn't quite the saint

I wanted him to be, after all. That's the trouble with putting people on pedestals. Sometimes they topple off.'

***

Trevor. How could I have been so wrong about Trevor? And the way I treated him! It was as if I hadn't felt confident enough in my mother's judgment, in her right to make her own choices. In my head, only what I thought, felt, imagined, had ever mattered. But she loved this man, and I had to admit that, finally, I could see why.

All those years I tried to avoid him, ignore him, wish he would just up and go away. He wasn't my dad. That was the only reason. A selfish, stupid reason. He had given us the money to allow us to pursue our dream, and there he was doing it again.

Of all the bad things, the reckless decisions, the wrong turns that had shaped my life, this was the one I could put right. I could open the doors and let him in, the way Mum had, the way Ollie had. Let him be a proper part of the family, the stepdad and granddad he so clearly wanted to be, and deserved to be.

How was I to know I would never get the chance?

***

Mum patted my arm and sank into a chair. 'I loved him, Kate. Your dad, God rest his soul. Just as much as you did. More. But I love Trevor too. It is possible, you know, to love someone else, to let someone step into the shoes of the one who's died. If you let yourself ...'

'You're thinking about me and Jenny now, aren't you? She's never going to be my little Rosie, is she? Never going to take her place. Nobody can. And I'm not sure I can love her the way I love my own kids, but ....'

'I know. But I also know you'll try.'

'How's she going to see me, though? The stepmother, the interloper, the one who's trying to replace her real mum but never really can?'

'You may not be her biological mum, love, but you can be the next best thing. Give her a home and a loving family, the stability she needs. It won't be easy, but people do it all the time, take on stepchildren, merge families together. And she's still young enough to adapt. Maybe not to forget her own mum entirely, but you'll be the one who's there for her now, and in the years ahead.'

'I can be her Trevor, you mean?'

'Ha! If you like, but let's hope it doesn't take her quite so long to accept you as it took you to accept him, eh?'

'It's the other way around that worries me, Mum. I just hope, for her sake, that I can accept *her*. A child who is always going to remind me that my husband cheated on me. One who looks like another woman instead of me, but with Dan's hair, Dan's smile. It's not going to be easy, is it? Loving another woman's child. *That* woman's child ...'

Chapter 44

Ollie, 2017

Ollie watched from his newly acquired seat in the front pew as his sister made her vows. Beside him, his mum was weeping silently into a tissue, which she clutched in a screwed-up ball in one hand, her eyes never leaving his dad's face.

The final hymn over, the vicar gestured for everyone to sit. The organ music started up again and the vicar led the bride and groom, followed by the bridesmaids and best man, into a room at the side, to sign the register. His dad looked like he wasn't sure what to do next, which wasn't surprising, as he hadn't been at the rehearsal, but Mum stood up quickly, tottering on her new high heels, stepped forward and gripped his arm, and they went in together, closing the door behind them. Ollie wasn't sure who was supporting who.

By the time they all emerged into the last of the weak

December sun, Nat had slipped a fluffy stole around her shoulders and Phil was edging her chair down the bump from path to grass, dodging a gravestone as they went, ready to pose for the photos.

Fifteen minutes later, with the parents of the bride and the close family groups done, his mum struggling to pull one of her heels out from where it had stuck in the grass and both bridesmaids eyeing up one of Phil's extremely well-built mates, it took Ollie a while to realise that his dad was no longer there.

'Where's Dad?' He held on to his mum's arm and helped her steady herself as her shoe pulled free. 'Not gone already?'

'He couldn't miss seeing Natalie married, but you know he couldn't stay. He should never have left the ward, but you know your dad ...'

'You mean he just walked out? Without permission?' Ollie's voice had risen loud enough for several guests to turn around in alarm.

'Sssh. Not now, Ollie.' She gave him a stern look. 'No need for everyone to know our business. And we don't want to spoil your sister's big day.'

'Come on, Mum. Dad turning up like that has *made* her day, but what's it done to him? Will he be okay, do you think? Shouldn't one of us have gone back with him?'

'He had a taxi take him from the hospital to the flat

for his suit and bring him here, and he'd arranged for the same driver to come and collect him. He just needed to slip away and get back to his bed.'

The photographer was calling the whole group together for one last enormous photo, and Ollie was quickly pulled into his place in the line. His dad may have been missing from this one, but he had never seen Natalie looking more radiant, or more relieved.

***

Ollie came out of the gents and felt for the scraps of paper covered in scribble that were tucked inside his top pocket, making his way back to the top table to tell everyone who was prepared to listen just what a fantastic sister he had and what a lucky man Phil was to have finally taken her off their hands.

Everyone laughed in all the right places and cheered when he sat down. Ollie sighed. Job done! Now he could whip his tie off and get on with the fun part of the day, relaxing over a few drinks.

The waiting staff soon cleared the tables and moved them to the sides of the room, and a queue rapidly started to form at the bar.

'Do you fancy a dance?' Ollie asked Jenny, once they'd downed a beer each and the music was in full swing. 'I know it's probably not cool to be seen dancing with your big brother, but let's face it, we don't have anyone else to claim us, do we?'

'Not unless James turns up!'

'James? Who's James?'

'Oh, nobody you'd know.'

'Really? Boyfriend?'

Jenny blushed. 'I wish! No, there is no James. I've just been teasing the girls. Winding Beth up really. She can be so gullible! But, yes, a dance would be good. So long as they don't put a smoochy one on. You may be my favourite brother but ...'

'I'm your *only* brother!'

'And a great one you are too, but come on, let's dance. And then you can buy me another drink. It's thirsty work, all this bridesmaiding!'

It might be winter, but the room was buzzing with the heat of too many over-active bodies. Ollie shrugged off his jacket and slung it over a chair to claim it for later, and Jenny did the same with her bag. They picked their way through an assortment of flailing arms and legs to find a space large enough to join in with what just about passed as a twist, and spent the next twenty minutes or so putting their worries about their dad aside and just having fun.

'Ha, ha! Look at the state of Aunt Jane's hat. I think someone must have sat on it!' Ollie pointed across the room to where Jane was trying to stick a bunch of stray feathers back into its misshapen brim. 'Oh, Jen, we should have weddings more often. I'd forgotten what a laugh they can be.'

'Don't let Nat hear you say that. She was so deadly serious about everything, with her lists and all. Thank God everything went off okay.'

'Better than okay. She's enjoying herself now, though, isn't she? All seriousness gone. The lists in the bin hopefully, where they belong.' They looked across at their sister, being whirled around in ever-decreasing circles on the dance floor by Josie, her friend from the office, with a glass of bubbly slopping about precariously in her hand. 'She's having a whale of a time.'

'Of course she is. She's just married the love of her life.'

'Every girl's dream, eh?'

'Don't tell me men don't want the same thing! Now, where's that drink you promised me? I must have sweated out the equivalent of two gin and tonics at least.'

'Gin? That's an old woman's drink. You'll have another half of lager, and like it.'

'Oh, will I now? There are things about me you just don't know, Ollie Campbell, and my passion for a drop of gin is clearly one of them.'

'Okay, you win. Can't deny a girl her passions! Ice and lemon?'

'Yes, please.'

They returned to their table and Jenny sat down and kicked off her shoes. As Ollie headed towards the bar, he saw her reach for her mobile, its screen flashing with an incoming call. By the time he came back, with a drink in each hand and a bag of crisps tucked under his arm, she had gone.

He sat for a while, gulping down his pint and watching the others dance. His two grandmothers sat together at a table near the door, heads bent towards each other, trying to chat above the din, and Aunt Jane had obviously decided her hat was beyond saving and had allowed a little girl who couldn't be more than about five or six to wear it. With Natalie's stole wrapped around her tiny shoulders, with ample room to spare, and trying to balance in a pair of shiny blue stilettos someone must have discarded while they danced, the child paraded up and down along the edge of the room like a catwalk model, and made him laugh out loud. She reminded him of Jenny in a way, in the days when she would be engrossed in playing with her plastic tea set and her line of dolls and teddies, living in a little world of her own, happily amusing herself in a room where everyone else was older.

Where was Jenny anyway? Since she'd taken that call, she'd vanished into thin air. The mysterious James, maybe? He wasn't at all sure whether to believe her protestations that he didn't exist. Now that Natalie had tied the knot, and with Beth growing ever closer to Sean over the last few weeks, it would be good to complete the hat trick and find someone for Jenny too. If she hadn't already found him, that was. As for himself, well ... despite his one rather half-hearted attempt at speed dating, he wasn't really looking.

'Ollie?' Jenny had crept back up behind him, her hand now resting on his shoulder.

He turned around. 'I was wondering where you were. Come on, your gin's getting warm. It started out with ice, honest, but now ...'

'In a minute. First there's something I need you to do.'

'What? *Now?*'

'Yes. Now.'

'Well, I hope it involves raiding the buffet or carrying in another case of champagne, and you don't just need me to come and unblock a loo or something!'

'As if! No, really, I do need you to come with me. Outside.'

'What's the matter, Jen? This sounds serious.'

'It is.' She pulled him to his feet and through the door that led out into a small corridor, past the toilets and then out towards the car park. They passed the best man, coming out of the gents, still doing up his flies. 'All right, mate?' he slurred, clearly the worse for wear although it was barely seven o'clock, patting Ollie on the back and peering down the front of Jenny's dress.

'Fine,' Ollie replied, as Jenny pulled him away. '... I think.'

And then they were outside and approaching a car with its lights on, lurking in the shadow of the trees.

'Ollie, there is something I haven't told you. A secret ....' Jenny had stopped still on the gravel.

'Is it James?'

She looked mystified for a second or two. 'James? No! There is no James. No, it's something else. Something I swore not to tell you, and it's been really hard not to, I promise you, but now ... well, now I don't have to keep it a secret any more.'

Jenny pushed him gently towards the car, an interior light coming on as its back door swung open and she slipped away back into the darkness, leaving him staring, disbelievingly through the open door. At Laura.

She was sitting in the middle of the back seat, but as he moved nearer she leaned away from him and lifted something out of some kind of container on the seat beside her, something wrapped so tightly he couldn't see what it was.

He stepped towards her, feeling as if he was suddenly in a weird unbelievable dream. He hesitated with one foot on the sill, not sure what to do or why she was here. 'Laura? What are you ...?'

'Ollie,' she said, quietly. 'You're letting all the cold air in. Come on, get inside and shut the door. Please.'

He climbed in and closed the door. An elderly woman he thought he vaguely recognised turned around and smiled at him from the driver's seat as the light faded and went out, Aunt Clara? The familiar light perfumy smell of Laura's hair caught in his nostrils as she inched towards him and, although he could barely see her face, her arm brushed against his through his thin white shirt and he knew that all he wanted to do was hug this woman, who he still loved with all his heart, and never let her go.

'Ollie,' she said, before he could move, her voice wavering as she dipped her head towards the bundle now lying in her arms. 'I think it's time you met your daughter.'

Chapter 45

Kate, 1997

I wish I could have known. Wish I'd had the chance to tell Trevor how grateful I was, for everything he'd done for us, and how sorry I was for not giving him the chance he deserved. Natalie's room had taken a long time to complete but it only been finished for a month when the next heart attack struck. He'd worked so hard, never just sitting back and letting the builders get on with it. He'd been there every day, watching, supervising, helping to fit wardrobes, getting down on his back on the floor to fiddle with the plumbing, wielding a paintbrush as if he was about to create a work of art. He'd been in his element, seeing his generous gift come to fruition, but was it the physical effort of it all that had pushed him over the edge? I'll never know. None of us will.

'He's not going to make it this time,' Mum sobbed, sitting at his hospital bedside, just staring at the monitors. 'His heart is too weak. He hasn't opened his eyes, Kate. I'm not sure if he even knows I'm here.'

'Talk to him anyway. They say hearing's the last thing to go, don't they? Say all the things you want him to hear and maybe he'll hear them.'

'I will, love. I will.' She grasped for his hand on top of the blanket and gave it a squeeze. 'There's no need for you to stay. Nothing you can do. Get on home to the children.'

'Maybe you should go home too. Get some rest. Come back later.'

'No, Kate. I need to stay. And Trevor needs me to stay. I'd never forgive myself if something happened while I wasn't here. And, besides, like you said, there are things I need to tell him. By ourselves ...'

Reluctantly, I walked away. As I stopped at the end of the ward and looked back, I could see Mum leaning low over the bed, hear the low mumble of her voice speaking quietly into his ear. A woman in a pale-pink overall appeared with a tea trolley and started trundling it from bed to bed. That's what Mum needed. A good strong cup of tea. And for Trevor to open his eyes, of course. But he didn't.

I stepped into the lift and headed for home. I never saw Trevor alive again.

***

Jenny stared at the chessboard for a moment, picked up one of the pawns and dropped it carefully into her pink plastic shopping bag.

'Jenny! What did you do that for? I can't finish the game now.' Ollie stood up angrily and flung his arm out wildly across the board, knocking all the remaining pieces flying, and Jenny ran out of the room and up the stairs, probably worried he was going to do the same to her.

'Ollie, it's not her fault. She just wants to play.' I bent to retrieve a bishop that had rolled right up to my feet.

'Well, let her play with her own things. I don't grab her stupid dolls, do I?'

'She didn't mean any harm. She's just collecting bits for her pretend shop. You only had to ask nicely and I'm sure she would have given that piece back.'

'What's the point? There's nobody to play chess with now anyway.'

'I'm sure your dad will have a game with you, if you ask him.'

'He's not here though, is he? And when he is here, he's always too busy. I like playing with Granddad Trev. He doesn't get cross with me.'

'I know.' I gulped back a tear. 'Granddad Trev was a very patient man, and he had all the time in the world for you, but you can't play with him any more, Ollie. You do understand that, don't you?'

I watched Ollie run his sleeve over his face, then look down at his own feet.

'But it's not fair. I don't want him to be dead.'

'None of us do, but we can't change things, sweetheart. It's very sad, but we have to get used to not seeing him any more.'

Ollie slumped down onto the carpet and picked up the king, twirling it in and out through his small fingers.

'It doesn't stop us thinking about him, though, does it?'

He shook his head slowly.

'Now, why don't you tidy away all the pieces in their box? I'm sure Granny will want you to keep the chess set. It can be your special reminder, and every time you play a game with it you can think about Granddad Trevor and know he's watching over you.'

'Will he help me to win?'

'Oh, I think he's already done that, Ollie, just by teaching you to play so well.'

'He taught me lots of other things too.'

'Did he? Like what?'

I sat down on the sofa and felt my son sidle along the floor and snuggle against my legs.

'He showed me how to screw things with a screwdriver so they stick together, and how to get a paintbrush into all the corner bits and round the light switch, and how to cut up wood with a saw ...'

'Did he? That sounds a bit dangerous.'

'It's not dangerous if you do it properly, Mummy. Granddad showed me how to be safe. He said being safe is the most important thing.'

'He was right. It is. Being safe, and being loved. He was a really good granddad, wasn't he?'

'The best,' Ollie said, and then he threw himself onto my lap and burst into tears.

***

The house seemed so much bigger once Natalie had moved into her new room. She liked nothing better than wheeling her chair inside and closing the door to her own private space. She could leave her shampoo and toothbrush and towel wherever she liked in her small en-suite bathroom knowing the others were not going to push them aside or, worse still, use them themselves. The room gave her a level of independence she so badly needed just at a time when she was old enough to manage it and enjoy it. Her confidence grew before our eyes.

Upstairs, we no longer had the jam-packed sardine-tin existence we had been struggling with. Beth and Jenny learned to share a room quite amicably, as long as Jenny always remembered who was the older sister and therefore the boss, and Ollie just carried on being

Ollie, although the chess set came out less and less often now and he spent as much time as he could on some sports field or other, or pounding around a running track. I sometimes thought that all the physical exertion was his way of dealing with his grief but, if it was, it seemed to work, and I knew as well as anyone that we all had to find our own ways to grieve.

In our bedroom nothing much felt right.

'Not tonight, Dan. I'm too tired.'

'Yuk! Your breath smells of beer and curry. I don't know why you don't try cuddling up to Rich instead of me, you spend so much time with him lately. And I'm sure he probably smells exactly the same.'

'No, Dan. That hurts. Leave it for now, eh?'

***

If there wasn't a book of excuses out there somewhere, I could have written one. It wasn't that I hated him. Or that I still felt red-hot angry with him for what had happened to Nat, or for cheating on me. Well, not consciously. That had subsided, somehow, into something else. Something I couldn't quite name, but had learned to live with. But there was a new barrier now, a blockage, something lying there unseen and unspoken between us.

He swore that he had never loved Fiona, but I couldn't quite get the image of them together out of my head.

Naked and twisted together, sperm and egg uniting in a way, a natural way, that ours had struggled to do. My babies had been made in a dish, but hers had come out of something real. It didn't matter to me whether love had come into it or not. Dan had done something unforgivable, with this random woman, this now-dead random woman, something that he had never been able to do with me.

He had created a child, without any medical intervention, naturally and seemingly as easily as shelling peas, and then, knowing how that would make me feel, he'd hidden the fact, lied about it.

I couldn't help thinking that it was the lie that hurt the most.

NUMBER FIVE

Chapter 46

Beth, 2017

Beth hadn't seen Ollie for a while and was starting to worry about him. With all this available booze about, she couldn't help but worry he was outside somewhere knocking it back and that all his hard work of the last few weeks, trying to stay away from it, was about to disappear down the drain, but when he came back into the room he looked as if a huge weight had lifted from him. Beth didn't think she could ever remember him looking so happy and so sober both at the same time.

'Ollie? You okay? What's up?'

'Beth, Mum, I need you to come with me.' He pulled them both to their feet.

'What? What for?'

'It doesn't matter what for. Just come. And Nat. I want Nat with us too. Where is she? Can you go and grab her for me, Beth? Meet us over there ...'

'But she's dancing.'

'Please. She won't mind. Not when she sees who's here.'

Beth sighed. What was going on? He was rounding the family up like sheep and herding them towards the door. He'd be grabbing the grannies next, and Aunt Jane if he could catch her. It was only as she went to get Natalie that she spotted Jenny on the other side of the dance floor. She had the most enormous grin on her face and was signalling something, making silly little winks and pretending to rock something in her arms.

'What?' Beth mouthed silently, dodging Jane as she whirled past in the arms of a man she didn't recognise, giggling like a schoolgirl. And then it dawned on her, in a blinding flash. 'Laura?'

Jenny nodded and bounded across the room, grabbing one side of Nat's chair as Beth grabbed the other, and together they swished and swooped their way across the room and followed the others into the corridor.

'In here,' Ollie said, pushing open the door of the ladies.

'Ollie! You can't go in there.'

'No? You just watch me!'

'But ... Oh! Laura!' Beth squealed. 'Oh, my God, you've done it. You've only gone and done it!'

Laura was sitting in a small red velvet chair tucked away by the mirror in the corner, still wearing her coat, the baby clutched tightly to her chest and wrapped up in a big white blanket so only her tiny face peeped out at the top, an elderly woman who could only be Laura's Aunt Clara beaming with pride beside them.

'Yes, I have.'

Beth wanted to throw herself at Laura and scream with delight but she was aware of her mother standing beside her, very rigid and still, open-mouthed with shock.

'Laura ... is this ... is this what I think it is?'

Ollie stepped forward and rested his hand protectively on Laura's shoulders. 'Yes, Mum, it definitely is. Laura and me ... we have a daughter. You have a grand-daughter. At last. And her name is Evie. Evie Rose ...'

'Oh.' Kate's hand flew to her face. 'But how? When? Why?'

'*How?* Well, it might have had something to do with the birds and the bees, or was it a gooseberry bush and a stork? Mum, do you really want me to spell it out for you?' Ollie laughed. 'Look, it doesn't matter about any of that, does it? Laura's had a baby, with a lot of help and support from her aunt here. And, yes, I wish I'd known sooner, but I didn't, and there's nothing I can do about that now. But she's here. Our little Evie's here, and I couldn't be more proud. Or happy. I'm a daddy at last and nothing else really matters right now. We can talk about the details later. But for now ... well, here she is. Don't you want to give your new grand-daughter a cuddle?'

'Of course I do. Oh, Ollie, I can't believe it. Nat, come on in and look. It's like a miracle, and at your wedding too. I didn't think this day could get any better, but ...' Kate nodded a belated hello to Clara, lifted the baby from Laura's arms and looked into her sleepy scrunched-up face. 'Oh, she's adorable. She has your nose, Ollie, and Laura's hair, oh, Ollie, I wish your father was here to see her.'

'Do you?'

'Of course. This is his grandchild too, and she's just what he needs. Something to fight for. He'll get better now, I'm sure of it.' Was she crying? Beth felt sure that she was. 'He'll have to.'

'Now, can we all have a cuddle of this scrumptious new niece of ours?' Beth said, trying to lighten the mood before everyone ended up in tears, and pushing Nat's chair closer so she could see. 'Because we are aunties now, girls. Aunties! All of us. Can you believe it?'

'I bet *you* can,' Ollie said, turning his gaze on Beth. 'You weren't at all surprised. You knew, didn't you? Not only Jenny, but you too?'

'I ...'

'All the time we've spent together lately, getting ready for the show, and you didn't say a word.'

'Don't be too hard on her,' Laura said, taking the baby back from her doting grandmother and kissing the top of her head. 'I was so scared something would go wrong. After all the others, I'd more or less convinced myself it would. That there was something wrong with me, and I'd never be a mum. All that pain we went through before ... I couldn't put you through that again, so I asked them not to say anything and they didn't. You have two very loyal and loving sisters here.'

'Three!' Natalie added, sounding annoyed. 'Don't forget me. When it comes to secrets I'm always the last to know, but I know now ... and just think, I've not only become Mrs Natalie King today, I've become *Auntie* Natalie King! I like the sound of that.'

'You look lovely, Nat, by the way. And congratulations.' Laura smiled across at Natalie and passed the baby to her. 'This is your special day, and the last thing I wanted was to steal your thunder.'

'Thanks,' Natalie said, before burying her face in her niece's neck and breathing her in. 'But there's nothing for you to apologise for. I am so glad you came. Oh, wow. This is just so unbelievable!'

'Group hug!' Beth shouted suddenly, unable to contain her excitement any longer, and rushed to grab everyone at once just as two old ladies who had been about to come in to use the loo quickly backed off in alarm, legs crossed, and went away again.

***

The final dress rehearsal went like a dream. As Beth watched Victoria Bennett step onto the stage in her brand-new Mary costume, all roundly padded out with pregnancy-bump cushions, and launch effortlessly into her solo of 'Little Donkey', the emotion and excitement of the last few days almost sent her into floods of tears. The little girl's voice had something magical about it that matched Beth's mood and she was glad of the twins' entrance, in their donkey outfit, tripping over their own feet and knocking the door off the inn, to make her laugh out loud again.

'It's great, isn't it?' Sean walked up beside her in the wings and gave her a playful peck on the cheek.

'What was that for?' It was all she could do to stop herself blushing like a teenager.

'Don't need a reason, do I? Just happy to see you.'

'You too.' She beamed at him. 'And, yes, it is great. All of it. Even the wonky door.'

'Hmmm, not my finest work, was it? If one knock from a donkey's bum can pull it off!'

'I'm sure you can sort that out easily enough. I have every faith in you.'

'Do you?'

'Of course. You are this show's answer to Bob the Builder. Can he fix it? Yes, he can!'

'Well, I'll do my best. Now, tell me. How's the newest addition to the family?'

'Settling in very well, thanks. Laura and her aunt were booked into a hotel on the day of the wedding. Well, Laura couldn't be one hundred per cent sure Ollie would take her back. But I'm pleased to say he did. With open arms! So she's moving back in with him now and they spent what was left of the weekend frantically buying cots and clothes and buggies and God knows what else. And they've still got to drive back up to her aunt's to pick up what's left of Laura's things. I'm surprised Ollie's been able to drag himself in to work this week, to tell you the truth.'

'Only a couple more days and it'll be the Christmas holidays. He can be a full-time daddy for a while then, but for now he's still got to run a bunch of kids round a frosty field several times a day. And, more importantly, he's got a show to put on.'

'And he's loving it. If only he can stay awake long enough!'

'Baby keeping him up at nights, is she?'

'Only because he can't stop gazing at her! Talk about doting father ...'

'He deserves it, Beth. He's a good guy.'

'I know. And she is a beautiful baby. I can't wait to start buying her piles of presents. Her first Christmas! Not that she'll know that, or remember anything about it afterwards. And, of course, this does mean there'll be two more at home on Christmas Day. Laura's not going to want to cook.'

'You still want me to come? I won't be in the way? You know, intruding on a family occasion ...'

'Don't be daft. More the merrier, as my old Granny Molly always says. And I want you there.'

'Do you?'

Oh, God, she was starting to blush again. Still, he'd be gone soon enough, in a few more months, back to Australia. If she made a complete and utter fool of herself, the embarrassment wouldn't have to last long. There was nothing to lose really, was there?

'Yes. Very much.'

'Fancy a drink tonight? Maybe dinner? My treat?'

Ollie jumped up from his chair at the back of the hall as another song came to its close and the inn keeper trailed off stage, still muttering his two lines under his breath, over and over again, as if he was worried he might forget them.

'Okay, everyone,' Ollie shouted, clapping his hands together to get some attention. 'That was perfect. Well done. Now, places for the final scene, please.'

The donkey wobbled past, trying to replace its head, as hordes of excited children in assorted animal costumes bounded onto the stage.

Beth nodded at Sean. 'Yes, I'd like that. Thank you.'

'My pleasure.'

A feeling of warmth flooded through her. Just being with Sean was a pleasure. Having a drink, a chat, a laugh. It didn't matter what. She would probably have a fantastic time at the dentist if Sean was there to hold her hand! She had never met anyone quite like him. When she thought of all the years she had wasted on Jake ... but then, if she hadn't spent so long with the wrong man, she may never have recognised the right one when he came along.

As the children found their positions and gathered around the manger, each face gazing down at the plastic doll lying half-buried in its bundle of straw, their voices rose together, not all tunefully, but happily, in one big, joyful, overwhelmingly powerful swell. Beth let the sound wash over her and felt the tears she had been holding back well up again. And that was when she realised, without any sort of sudden jolt or thunderbolt moment, but calmly and naturally, as if she'd known it and felt it for ever, that she was in love.

***

'What's it like? Australia?' Beth put her cutlery down and turned to face Sean, sitting on the bench seat beside her in the window of The Golden Parrot.

'Hot.'

'Oh, come on, there must be more to it than that. Do they have pubs, for instance? Like this one? And fish and chip shops, and KFC, and Marks and Spencer?'

Sean laughed. 'It may be the other side of the world but it's not the back of beyond, y'know! Of course it has its wild areas, its deserts and bush fires, koalas in the trees instead of squirrels, but it's also a very civilised country. If you measure civilisation by chain stores and fast-food outlets, anyway!'

'I didn't mean ...'

'No, I know what you meant. It's hard to sum it up, really. It's a huge place and one end of it can be as different from the other as ... well, it's like trying to compare central London with the Isle of Skye, I suppose.'

'I've never been to the Isle of Skye.'

'No. Me neither! But Oz is different things to different people. Whether it's the big beautiful beaches, or the grand opera house, or kangaroos in the outback, or just an ordinary suburban street ...'

'Like in *Neighbours*, you mean?'

'I haven't watched that in years! But, yeah, I guess. Is Doc Kennedy still in it?'

'I don't know. Probably!'

'And did you know we even have penguins in Victoria, where I'm from? Cute little fellas they are too.'

'Really? But I thought you said it was hot?'

'It is.'

Beth laughed. 'I give up.'

'Don't do that, Beth.' He slipped his arm behind her and leant it across the high- cushioned back of the seat, a thigh brushing lightly against hers, but not so lightly that she wasn't acutely aware of it. 'You know, if you really want to see what Australia's like, you should come out there.'

'Oh, I don't know about that. It's such a long way, and I bet it costs thousands.'

'It's a long way, yes, but, let's face it, a trip up to the Isle of Skye would probably take you nearly as long, and you'd get there feeling knackered. At least on a plane you can sleep, and eat and drink, and watch movies. You're there before you know it! Think about it, Beth. I'll be going home in July, soon as the school year ends. Come with me. Take a holiday. You can stay with me. There's plenty of room. Mum and Dad won't mind. In fact, they'd love it. So it's not going to cost you anything except the flight ...'

'I'll think about it.'

'Of course, you could always chuck your job in and come for longer. I'm sure there's a need for good hairdressers in Oz.'

'Is there?' Beth could feel her heart starting to flutter.

'There's always work if you look hard enough. Take a chance, like I did when I came here. Work, play, have fun. You really can't see Australia in a couple of weeks, y'know. It's the sort of country you need to experience longer term. Sort of absorb it, if you know what I mean. And what's to keep you here? You're young, free ...'

447

'... and single.' Beth laughed, finishing his sentence for him, automatically, before thinking about what she was saying.

'Not if you don't want to be,' Sean said, taking hold of her hand. 'Because the real reason I want you to come with me is ... Well, I like you, Beth. I like you a lot, and I already know just how much I'd miss you if you weren't in my life. So, come with me. *With* me, as in us being boyfriend, girlfriend ... a couple.'

'Sean ...'

'Okay, I know it's all a bit sudden.'

'Sean ...'

'And you really don't have to make up your mind right now. I'm gonna be around for months yet, so let's just see how it goes, shall we? I'm not trying to rush you or anything.'

'Sean, will you shut up?' She lifted her hand to his chin and pulled his face towards her. 'And just kiss me.'

His lips found hers as he tilted his head, his eyes closed, his arms wrapping themselves tightly around her in a perfect fit. She could feel the warm strength of him pressing against her, the intoxicating mix of gentleness and raw need pulling her deeper and deeper into the kiss.

'Beth ...' He eased himself back, his face just inches from hers.

'It's okay. I don't need months to make up my mind.

I'd miss you too. In fact, I miss you already!' She snuggled her head under his chin and rested it against his chest, listening to his heart beating solidly, rhythmically, beautifully, in her ear. 'And the answer's yes. I will come with you to Australia.'

Chapter 47

Kate, 1997– 2001

Jenny was a little treasure. Despite all my reservations, I couldn't help but fall in love with her. I would watch her as she slept, all curled up in a ball, the same way she had on the night she'd arrived, and marvel at how resilient she was, how adaptable, and yet how vulnerable. She had lost a mother, just as I had lost a child. Together, we seemed to find what was missing, and it felt good. It seemed I had needed her as much as she needed me.

I couldn't give up my job so we kept sending her to the childminder she was used to. It helped to keep things normal for her, maintaining her routine. But in the evenings and at the weekends she was ours. Pretty, funny, a breath of fresh air. Separate from the others in age and looks, yet she melded in, so quickly.

She would ask about her mother, often at first. Where

she was, when she was coming back ... But her memories seemed to fade slowly away, as I suppose they do at so young an age, until one day I realised she was calling me Mum and the questions had stopped.

I couldn't have done it without the others, of course. Their happiness had to come first, as it always had. If they had shown any jealousy or resentment, how on earth would I have been able to have her there, expect them to absorb her into our family? It would not have been fair. This wasn't some new baby sister they had had nine months of a pregnancy to get used to, the way other siblings did. She had arrived, fully formed and with no warning whatsoever.

Maybe children just don't see things the way we do. They adored her. And so, amazingly, did I. It was just Dan I felt unsure of. Because I never lost sight of the fact that it was Dan's fault she existed, never hers.

***

Princess Diana died that summer. We sat at opposite ends of the sofa, Dan and I, with all four children between us, watching the TV in awe as the thousands upon thousands of bunches of flowers piled up in front of Kensington Palace. Outpourings of love for a woman the vast majority had never met, but loved just the same. My heart went out to her boys. I could hardly believe how brave they were. In the midst of all that grief, they were still able to hold things together, come out to greet the crowds, put on a dignified face for the world. If losing her mum had had to happen to Jenny, at least it had been while she was still so young, still unable to fully understand, or perhaps, in the years to come, to remember.

For a few short hours, as we wept disbelievingly with the rest of the nation, what was happening in our own small world at home paled into insignificance, and I sent up a silent prayer for Trevor, and for Mum, a sort of angry frustration building up inside me at death and the power it had to just turn up unannounced, deliver its cruel blow and crush those it left behind.

'Do you ever wonder ...' Dan said that night, lying beside me, staring up at the ceiling, talking into the dark, 'what life would have been like if the IVF had failed? If the embryos hadn't hung on? Any of them? If we had never had children at all?'

'I used to. Before. When we were still trying, when the money was running out and neither of us knew if we would ever get lucky. I would lie awake sometimes and imagine us getting older on our own, both of us still working, having money to spend, going on holidays, just carrying on doing what we had always done, but it always felt like something would be missing. That we were ready for a change and, if it hadn't come, then ...'

'Then what? We wouldn't have survived?'

'Maybe. But it did work, didn't it? So we'll never know what might have happened to us if it didn't. There's not a lot of point in trying to work out what-ifs. We have what we have. And all the ups and downs that have come with it. The good luck and the bad.'

'And have we survived, do you think? You and me? Because it doesn't always feel like it.'

'I don't know. We're still here, aren't we? Still married. Still together. Parents.'

'And is that it? We limp along, side by side, for the rest of our lives, just being parents?'

'Maybe. But what about you? Do you still love me, Dan? Or do you still think about *her*? Fiona? Who knows where we would be now if she was still here. You would have had to find a way to bring Jenny up together, wouldn't you? And to tell me about it, eventually. And now I can't even have it out with her, rant and scream at her, smack her in the face. I can't even be sure you wouldn't have left me for her in the end, can I? Because the bloody woman had your baby and then went and died, just like Princess Diana, and that makes her the saint and me ...' I stopped, not even really sure of the point I was trying to make, just aware of the sheer unfairness of it all.

'Comparing us to royalty now, are you? Charles and Di? It's hardly the same. They were already divorced, for a start ...'

'Exactly. And whose fault was that? He was carrying on, wasn't he? With someone else ...'

'Oh, Kate, how many times do I have to tell you ...?'

'I don't know. Until I believe it, I suppose.' I turned my back and curled my knees up, trying to stop my legs from shaking, pushing my face into the pillow, and tried to clear my head of that image. The same one that always crept in when I least expected it to. A face I didn't recognise but knew must be Fiona's. A face I wanted to smash to a pulp, but a face that slowly blurred and shrunk until it became Jenny's face. That sweet little face I was growing so fond of, day by day. And that's what I couldn't make any sense of. No sense at all.

***

Dan and me; me and Dan. Love and marriage; horse and carriage. What more can I say? We had made four beautiful children, lost one, gained one. And, whatever we did or felt, or wished we'd done or felt, we were together and we had to see it through. We were parents and, once the carefree fun stuff of our twenties and early thirties was behind us, being parents was what came next, what we had both wanted more than anything. And once we had that, there was no walking away.

Perhaps everyone loses it in time. The spark, the fire, the passion. It gets buried under piles of nappies, sleepless nights and endless bills, years of bickering and boredom and blame. It's easier to get into comfy pyjamas and curl up with a cup of cocoa and a book, even though you usually nod off before reaching the end of the chapter, than it is to make the sort of effort that good sex, and a good marriage, needs.

Looking back, I know that I still loved him, even then, despite everything, but I couldn't admit it, and more importantly, I couldn't say it. Not out loud. It would have felt like backing down, like I was forgiving him, letting him get away with all that he'd done.

It would have felt like a betrayal. Of all that was important to me. My dignity. My family. You …

***

On New Year's Eve, 1999, we all went up to the Mall, lapped up the atmosphere of the crowds, opened a bottle of champagne and let the children have a sip, watched the fireworks lighting up the London skyline, sang and danced our way back through the busy streets, and propped each other up on the tube on the way home as the heralding of a new millennium and the elation of the occasion sank back into tiredness and normality.

And normality it was. Nothing felt any different the next day or the day after.

Dan did well at work. They made him a partner, gave

him a pay rise, let him have time off when he needed it, for fatherly stuff like school sports days and those meet-the-teacher evenings when parents got to find out the truth about their kids' behaviour and their chances of making something of their lives.

Fiona had been well-liked in the office. I wondered sometimes if the way he was treated was more about compensating for her loss, making a better life for her child, than it was about anything he had done to deserve it, but what did I know? I never went there. It was her domain – theirs – and not somewhere I could ever feel I belonged.

When the older children were eleven, they moved up to the big school and, separated into different classes for the first time, they really began to blossom and grow as individuals with different interests, different friends.

Ollie threw himself into sport, joining the football team in winter, the athletics team in summer, swimming club after school, going off to camps. Anything but chess, the board and pieces pushed away under his bed, pretty much since the day Trevor had died. I did worry about his asthma, checking his bag and his pockets to make sure he had his inhaler with him at all times, but he rarely needed it any more.

Natalie's hospital appointments tailed off too, although she did upgrade from one wheelchair to another, each one bigger and better, as she grew. Her new room became her haven, a place she could hide away in when the others got to do things she couldn't join in with, no matter how much she might want to, or when life in general got too much for her. We all understood and left her to deal with it in her own way and, heart-breaking though it was, it was a method that usually seemed to work.

And Beth. I often thought Beth was me, all over again, but in a younger, smaller form. She made up her mind about things quickly. Too quickly sometimes, and it would take a ten-ton truck to shift her, even though she wasn't always right. She looked like me too, even more than the others did, her huge mane of wild near-black hair marking her out as the warrior she undoubtedly was. Beth was tough on the outside, but there was also a softness, a vulnerability about her that I always knew was there. And a naivety, a romantic, see-what-turns-up view of life that got in the way of any real career ambition or sensible longterm life plan, although she would never admit to it. I didn't have to worry about Beth, because I understood her.

Jenny was the real enigma of the family. She was smart, but she hid it, never wanting to overshadow the others in anything. We'd do spelling tests and I'd know for sure she deliberately got some wrong. She'd hang back in races too, fiddling a little too long with her sack or her spoon, just long enough to make sure someone else ran past her and got to the finishing line first. I sometimes thought she was doing it because she didn't feel she deserved to win. Other times I thought maybe it was just her kindness, wanting to see others succeed, not really caring that much about herself. But, in the end, I decided she was just so desperate to fit in, to be accepted, and giving others the glory removed any rivalry, any sense of threat. It made them love her.

***

Dan's dad was seventy-two when he decided to retire. Farm work was hard. Early mornings, back-breaking physical labour, constant worries about the weather, taking so few days off and virtually no holidays, yet still having the kind of brown and wrinkled skin that smacked of the outdoor life and far too much exposure to a cruel and gruelling sun. Sam had left it as long as he could, but the arthritis that was slowly bending his fingers into stiff misshapen stumps, and a small stroke, had finally made up his mind for him. It was time.

'What will happen to the farm? And the house?' Ollie had his worried face on. 'Will Gran and Granddad have to move out and go and live in a flat or something? Where will all the animals go?' He kicked off his boots, sending a shower of muddy clumps across the kitchen floor. 'And where will we stay if we go to visit? Can I put a tent up in their new garden? Or won't they have a garden?'

Dan shook his head. 'Slow down, Ollie. I don't know much about it all yet, but I'm sure you don't have to worry. The farm is actually worth quite a lot of money.'

I raised my eyebrows. Money again. It had always been the first thing Dan thought about. Whatever life threw at us, it was always the money side of it that came into his head before anything else. How about his parents? Their entire life was about to change. Didn't he care about that? About them?

'I think we should go down there. It's ages since we've been. And the school holidays are coming up, so we won't have to worry about rushing back.'

'Really?' I asked. 'How about work?' Dan never took more than a week off at a time, and then only if he could stay in touch on the phone. 'Won't they mind?'

'Work can wait. Family comes first.'

There was so much I wanted to say in response to that sweeping and very uncharacteristic statement, but I bit my tongue.

'Well, I suppose I could ask for some time off at the bank.'

'Of course you can. It's not as if filling your shoes is going to be hard, is it? There must be loads of students and housewives out there looking for an easy job behind that counter of yours.'

'Oh, thanks very much! Make me sound so indispensable, why don't you? And why should they need to fill my job anyway? You're making it sound like we won't be coming back.'

'Maybe we won't be.'

'What are you talking about?'

'I just thought that, what with Dad stepping down, he might be happier knowing the farm was staying in the family. You know, not having to sell to strangers ...'

'Staying in the family? Dan! You don't mean us?'

'Well, why not us? It makes sense, doesn't it? Going back to where I grew up, moving in, taking the pressure off Dad, running things, having all that space, all that country air, giving the kids the sort of childhood Jane and I had?'

'Childhood? Dan, they're teenagers. They have school, exams, friends. Their whole life is here. Not miles away in some tiny country village. It's too late for all that. Maybe it could have worked when they were small, but not now.'

'You haven't had a chance to think it through, Kate. I've sprung it on you, I know that, but there's so much going for it. The back-to-nature sort of a life. Escaping the rat race. It could be good for us. All of us.'

'You *are* joking? You must be.'

'Of course I'm not joking. Look, let's go down there, stay a couple of weeks, work out some figures, see what

Dad has to say. And Jane, of course. Half the place will be hers, after all.'

'When your parents die, yes. But at the moment they're very much alive.'

'But it's going to happen one day, Kate. Might as well make decisions now, decisions everyone's going to be happy with.'

'Jane and Alan might want to run the farm themselves. Have you thought about that? Or your mum and dad might want to sell up, have a clean break, use the money to buy a little bungalow or something?'

'Dad, in a bungalow? Pigs would fly first!'

'Well, it's not really your decision to make, is it? It's their farm, their money.'

'I know that. But there's no harm in exploring all the options, is there?'

'Well, I'm not going.' Ollie had been sitting so quietly I'd almost forgotten he was there. 'I like my school, and I want to stay there, with my friends, and do my exams there. Not be stuck in some stupid village school where all they learn about is milking cows and stuff. I want to go to uni and study sport. And Mr Braithwaite says I'll be good enough to be in the county athletics championships next summer. *This* county, not bloody Somerset ...'

'Oliver! Mind your language. And as for playing in some sports team, you can do that anywhere,' Dan said, dismissively. 'There are universities all over the country, so you'd be moving away from here when you get to that stage anyway. And I hardly think sport is a suitable course, do you? Sport as a hobby maybe, but not ...'

Ollie stood up. 'I thought you said it was important to make decisions we were happy with, Dad, and to explore all the options. Time you started practising what you preach, don't you think?' And, with that exceptionally adult remark, he left the room, slamming the door hard behind him.

'He has a point, Dan. Any move like that would have to be by agreement, not dictatorship. It's something we'd all have to want.'

'Might as well give up now, then. It's been so long since we've wanted the same things ... if we ever did.'

I took a deep breath. If Dan was hoping for an argument, I wasn't going to give him one. Let him go and play at farms, if that's what he really wanted. But I was staying put, with the kids, where I belonged.

If he went, he'd be back soon enough. I knew he would. Dan was an accountant. Always had been and always would be. He probably had the word written all the way through him, like a stick of seaside rock. I couldn't see him getting his hands mucky shifting mounds of silage and prodding cows. This was all pie in the sky.

'I suppose we could always get a manager in,' he said,

so quietly I thought perhaps he hadn't meant to say it out loud. 'Take over the business side ourselves, but get someone else to do the outside physical stuff.'

Now, that was the real Dan talking. Dan the money man, not Dan the milk man! As soon as he realised there was no money to be made, especially after having to pay a manager, he'd change his mind. I knew he would.

***

Dan's old bedroom hadn't changed in all the years we'd been married. The walls still had their old stripy paper and the curtains were still too thin, letting in the early morning sunlight as soon as it appeared and fluttering wildly whenever the window was left open, even by a crack. The bed was old and high, the mattress too soft and with a dip in the middle that we used to love because it would roll us towards each other in the middle of the night. Now it just felt uncomfortable and the effort of trying to stick to our own sides made proper sleep tricky, if not impossible.

Sam looked noticeably older. It was as if his decision to slow down and stop working had given his body permission to slow down and stop too. The kids loved him, though. And Molly too. Watching them together made me all too aware that they didn't see nearly enough of each other, and that the older they all got the fewer chances there might be.

'That looks lovely, dear,' Molly was saying as Beth held a small mirror up and her gran admired the new wavy hairstyle Beth had created for her. I had just come back into the kitchen from walking the dog. Poor old Micky was long gone, as was Honey, the collie who had followed. This was Petal, the newest addition to the family, a young springer spaniel whose future was clearly mapped out for her as a family pet, now that a working farm dog would no longer be needed. Sam held out a hand and the dog moved across to him and buried her nose in it, sniffing for the treat she knew she would find there. 'Good walk?' he said, heaving himself up and rubbing the dog's muddy paws with an old towel. 'I see she's been in the stream again!'

'I couldn't stop her,' I protested.

'That's okay, my lovely. Dogs and water are meant to go together. A bit of mud's no matter to me.'

'That's because you're not the one who has to wash the floor,' Molly chipped in, but there was a twinkle in her eyes that meant she didn't mind either. 'Now, go and find the others, Beth, and we'll have a nice pot of tea, shall we? And a scone and jam. Made fresh this morning, both of them!'

I sat down at the old oak table and pulled off my boots. A big clock ticked rhythmically on the wall behind me, but otherwise the room was quiet, with just the three of us and the dog.

'Is there anything wrong, Kate?' Molly laid a hand on my sleeve and peered into my face. 'Only, I can't help noticing that you and Dan are ... well, not saying much. To each other, or to us. Is there something we should know?' She left a moment's silence but I chose not to fill it. 'You're not splitting up, are you? I know I shouldn't ask, but it's a worry, and I think we'd rather know than be left guessing.'

What should I say? What could I? I didn't really know what was going on in my own marriage, let alone feel able to explain it to someone else.

'Things are ... well, not great, I suppose, but we're ticking along.'

'Ticking along? Clocks tick along, Kate, not people. Where's the fire gone? That get-up-and-go you used to be so full of? Dan can be a bit serious, a bit difficult sometimes, I do know that, but he means well. And he does love you, and the children. You've been together so long. It would be a great shame if ... What I mean is that whatever it is, it can be fixed. Can't it?'

'I'm not sure. Ever since Jenny arrived ...'

'Ah. Jenny. I see.'

'Don't get me wrong. None of this is her fault and I love her to bits, but she has changed things between us.'

'I don't think she has, Kate. A child can't do that. She wouldn't know how. No, it's you and Dan who have changed things. And only you and Dan who can change them back again ...'

'Oh, I don't want to go back. It's Dan who seems to want to do that. Come back here, relive his past, drag us all into some fool's paradise of a country dream.'

'And you don't want that?'

'No. I'm sorry. I'm nearly fifty, Molly. It's too late to contemplate that sort of a massive change. It's all too much. Don't get me wrong, I have every respect for you and for your way of life, but it's not mine. Not ours ...'

Sam shuffled in his chair, Petal curled up and snoring at his feet. 'That's why we've decided we're going to sell,' he said. 'Let someone else take the strain, move ourselves into town, close to the shops, the buses, the hospital ... all the things we're going to need in our old age. It's the only way. Fair to everyone. There'll be a good bit of cash left over, I shouldn't wonder, if we can get a reasonable price for this place, and the land. Some for you and Dan, some for our Jane and her Alan. It might help get young Ollie through university too when the time comes, as it seems to be what he's set his heart on. The others too, if they decide it's what they want. But we'd like to see the money being used now, enjoyed now, not after we're gone, you hear?

No arguments. That's why we're not going to burden any of you with running a farm none of you really wants. We're selling up, and that's that! I'll set Dan straight later, when he gets back from the pub. He'll thank me for it in the end. They say it's in the blood, the land, but our Dan's no farmer. Not that I'd say it to his face, but he's not.'

It was probably the longest speech I'd ever heard Sam make.

'Thank you,' I said. I didn't know what else I could say, and anyway, Beth was back, with Jenny and Natalie in tow.

'Ollie says he doesn't want tea. He's going down to the pub to join Dad.'

'Oh, is he now?' I said, indignantly.

'Oh, leave him be, Kate,' Sam chuckled. 'Boys will be boys, wanting to grow up and be like their fathers, take a sneaky sip of beer when nobody's looking, even if they're only thirteen! No real harm in it. It's a nice little pub, no trouble or anything, and it's the local chess league down there this afternoon. You never know, he just might rediscover his love of it. It was his favourite game for a while, wasn't it? And there's a fiver in prize money for the winner.'

***

'That's it, then,' Dan said on our last night, turning over in bed as he tried to get comfortable. 'Last time we'll see this place; the end of an era.'

'Everything has to end sometime, Dan. It was good while it lasted, but things change.' Was I talking about the farm, or about our marriage? Our life together? I really wasn't sure. 'No going back.'

'No,' he muttered into his pillow. 'No going back.'

I could hear the catch in his voice, the emotion bubbling up, and if he had allowed the dip in the bed to draw us closer together, if he had taken me in his arms and hugged me then, I would have let him, welcomed him, maybe even loved him again, just a little, but he didn't.

I lay awake for what felt like hours that night, listening to the deep, dark silence of the countryside all around us, the occasional bark of a fox, the sleepy dreaming whines of the dog in her basket downstairs, and Dan's slow breathing, his chest moving up and down as he slept, taking the quilt with it.

***

And so we went home, back to the way we were, and what we had been, before. We would never return. Not to that house in the country, that life, that bed. We weren't going to run a farm, weren't going to pretend that a new home would give us a new life or mend the old one.

Dan couldn't see it. What he had been trying to do. In his eyes, of course, I had worked my evil magic on his parents. I was getting my own way. I was a breaker of dreams.

But I didn't want to go backwards any more; only forwards. With Dan or without him. His choice.

Chapter 48

Jenny, 2017

Jenny stood in the queue outside the school, shivering in the cool of the early evening air and wishing she'd brought a proper coat with her. Ollie had said that the seats in the hall were meant to be for parents and that the families of staff were not really expected to come, but she'd taken no notice. After all the work her brother and sister had put into this show, there was no way she was going to miss it, even if she ended up having to stand at the back.

Somewhere inside, Ollie and Beth would already be busy with their last-minute preparations, and a few panics too, more than likely. And Beth's mystery man would be in there too, the one she was bringing to the house on Christmas Day. Jenny couldn't wait to get a look at him.

The queue edged forward, slowly snaking its way

through the open doors but never seeming to get any shorter as more families joined it at the back. There were going to be two shows this year, one tonight and one tomorrow, as Ollie said word had got round about the show being the best yet, and demand for seats had been high. There was certainly plenty of excitement and chatter going on around her, some mothers proudly boasting that they had helped to make costumes, one handing out crisp packets to her kids while moaning they'd not long had their tea, one so pleased that her child, who couldn't sing for toffee, had been given a part. One father was telling another that he was sick to death of hearing his son practise the same songs over and over again at home, but there was still an obvious hint of pride in his voice as he ruffled the boy's hair and sent him scampering backstage to join the rest of the cast.

'When will the fireworks be starting?' one small boy asked, pulling at his mother's coat as she eased a buggy through the doors and parked it in a corner of the lobby, bending to retrieve a sleeping baby bundled up in a bright-red ski suit. She shushed him with a tut-tut and a raise of her eyebrows. 'I don't know where he's got that idea from,' she muttered to the couple next to her. 'I don't remember any rockets in the nativity story, do you?'

'No. There is a very bright star in the sky, though,

isn't there? He's probably thinking of that. And there's gonna be a big musical number, like something from the West End, so I've heard. Tap dancing, and everything!'

Jenny smiled to herself. Ollie's show had a massive reputation to live up to, by the sound of it, and she hoped no one would be disappointed when so many of the rumours turned out not to be true. She made her way along the central aisle, looking for a seat somewhere near the front, but the place was already crammed full and she was about to turn back and settle for something much nearer the back when a hand reached out and tapped her arm.

'Jen! Here, I've saved you a place.' It was Laura, sitting at the end of a row, with a big pink bag beside her, hogging a seat of its own, and baby Evie asleep on her lap. 'You wouldn't believe the amount of stuff I have to carry about with me, just to keep this little one fed and clean.' She hoisted the bag onto the floor at her feet and Jenny squeezed past her and sat down.

'How did you know I'd be coming?'

'I can't imagine anything stopping you! And Ollie said you were keen.'

'Of course. Wouldn't miss it for the world.' Jenny ran her hand gently over the baby's soft head. 'Oh, Laura, she is such a sweetie, isn't she? And here to watch her daddy – if she wakes up in time! Where is he, anyway?'

'Oh, we won't see him for ages now. He saw us to a seat and left us to get on with it while he faffs about back there, checking everything and everyone. Making sure it all runs like clockwork. Which, of course, it will.'

'Sounds like Nat with her pre-wedding notebook and her interminable lists. Why check something once when you can check it a dozen times?'

'You can tell they share the same genes!'

Jenny smiled. 'Well, I have some of them myself, remember. But not those ones, thankfully.' There was a screeching, like the howl of a frightened cat, from a violin up at the front and the lights slowly dimmed. 'Ooh, I think it's about to start.'

The little orchestra, made up mostly of tinny recorders and over-enthusiastic tambourines, with one of the teachers carrying the tune on the big old school piano, did its best to quieten the audience with its just-about-recognisable version of 'There's No Business Like Show Business' and then three little girls dressed as sheep stepped cautiously onto the stage and took up their positions, huddled together in a corner. The audience hushed, although a few 'Aaahs' crept out as proud mums pointed and pulled tissues from their sleeves.

'Long, long ago,' the sheep began, baa-ing in unison. 'In a galaxy far, far away ...'

Everybody laughed as three shepherds bounded on,

carrying light sabres instead of crooks, and the show was under way.

***

'She must be hungry,' Laura whispered, shifting in her seat, trying to rock Evie and stop her from crying. From the row behind, somebody sighed loudly and muttered something under his breath. 'It's no good, I'm going to have to take her outside.'

Jenny turned round and glared at the man behind. They were all parents here. Surely they knew that babies cried sometimes, and there wasn't a lot anyone could do about it?

'No. You can't miss the show. Let me.' Jenny took the baby from Laura's arms. 'I'll take her out and feed her. Have you got a bottle?'

Laura rummaged about in the bag, dropping a couple of nappies in the dark, and pulled out a small bottle of lukewarm milk. 'Freshly squeezed,' she laughed, pointing to her breast and handing the bottle over. 'Just in case …'

Jenny eased herself past Laura and into the aisle. Already Evie had quietened down, probably because she was being bounced as Jenny hurried along, making her way to the back of the hall. Away from the mass of coated and booted bodies, the lobby was chilly and suddenly bright.

'Everything all right, love?' The school caretaker, who was having a crafty cigarette just outside the doors, popped his head in as he flicked a spray of ash out onto the grass.

'Is there somewhere I could sit and feed the baby? Somewhere warm?'

'Of course, love. Just follow the corridor there.' He pointed vaguely in the direction of a set of double doors. 'Staff room should be free.'

Jenny should have known the school like the back of her hand. It was the one she had attended from the age of four, until she'd followed the others up to the big school at the other end of town, but that all seemed so long ago, and everything felt smaller now and strangely unfamiliar. As she pushed the doors open, she found herself in a carpeted area she had never ventured into before. The staff corridor, where children had feared to tread, only ever finding themselves there if they'd been sent with a message or were in trouble for some misdemeanour and had been summoned to see the Head.

From somewhere behind a wall at the far end she could hear a jumble of sounds, like a humming, squawking, roaring mix of wild animals getting restless at the zoo or sensing an impending storm. It could only be the children from the show, letting off steam in some kind of makeshift dressing room or holding area. She looked down at Evie, who had magically nodded off back to sleep and, popping the bottle into the pocket of her jacket and walking past the entrance to the staff room on her left, moved curiously towards the noise.

The first person she saw was Ollie. He was lining children up by a door at the side of the room, ticking off names on a crumpled sheet of paper, his shirt open by a couple of buttons and a patch of sweat staining the back of it.

'Ready?' He pulled a headdress straight, retrieved a lost shoe and took an open can of lemonade out of someone's sticky hand just as it was about to spill down the back of the child in front, then ushered them all through towards Beth, who Jenny could just make out waiting in the semi-darkness beyond. 'And ssshh now, okay? We don't want anyone to hear you until you're on that stage.'

He turned and took a deep breath and was just running his finger down the list to work out who he needed to grab next when he spotted her.

'Jen! You're not supposed to be back here. And Evie ...' His face softened at the sight of his daughter. 'Why's she with you? Where's Laura? Is everything okay?'

'It's fine. Laura's watching the show. And enjoying every minute, by the way. Evie and I are just spending a bit of quality time together. You know, favourite auntie, cuddles, milk ...'

'Favourite auntie, eh? I wouldn't let the others hear you say that.'

'Well, Nat's miles away on honeymoon and Beth's hiding out in that corridor over there, so I know for a fact neither of them can.'

'Look, Jen, I need to get on. I know it's a bit hectic in here, but stay if you like. Sit over there, and if she needs a feed or a nappy change or anything ...'

'We'll be fine. You get on and do what you have to do, Mister Director, sir!' She clicked her heels together and saluted.

'Cheeky mare!'

Evie was stirring again, her tiny fists opening and closing almost in time with her mouth. Jenny sat on a pile of coats in the corner and slid the teat of the bottle between the baby's lips, watching transfixed as she started to suck, greedily and noisily. It was amazing to think that this little person, who hadn't existed until just a few days ago, had had such an impact already. And how different Laura was, all that anxiety lifted from her like the dispersal of a rain cloud, and the sun suddenly shining through. She'd even handed her baby over perfectly willingly, which gave Jenny a sudden sense of pride. It was lovely to know she was trusted.

Evie was soon full up and asleep again, snuggled against her. She gradually eased her onto the warm coats beside her, making sure her head was supported, and pulled her blanket around her. She wondered which of the many buggies lined up in the lobby was Evie's, and whether she should try to locate it and lay her in it, but the sheer joy of sitting so close to her, watching her eyelids flicker and her legs give occasional little kicks as she slept kept her rooted to the spot.

Cast members came and went, their faces heavily made up with thick black eyeliner and splashes of colour that could have been plastered on with a trowel. Every time the door opened snatches of music came from the direction of the stage and Beth would appear, ushering a group of children back in and summoning the next. Jenny didn't think she had even noticed her sitting there, or, if she had, then she was just too busy, too focused, to acknowledge her.

It was fun watching her big brother at work. At home he was just Ollie, sad Ollie who drank too much, Ollie who they had all worried about for months now, but here he was a teacher, in charge of things, respected, obeyed. With just the rising tone of his voice, he seemed able to bring order and silence to the chaos all around him. It warmed her heart to see him the way others saw him and to know that now Laura was back, he was so clearly happy again. And he would be happy for her too, when she told him, and all the family, that the counselling course she had chosen had places available and she had been accepted. From January, she would

finally be on her way to a proper future, doing something important, something that made a difference to
people's lives. Just like Ollie did.

'Donkey!' Ollie called now, and two boys hurriedly
climbed into their costume, arranging their limbs in
some sort of front and back order, and made for the
door, a large grey head in hand. 'Mary, Joseph, stand
by.'

One of the girls rushed forward, stuffing a cushion
inside her dress and tying a sash tightly around her
waist to keep it there.

'Great, Victoria. Ready for your song?'

The girl nodded and was joined by a boy who looked
like he might be sick at any moment, before both were
whisked away by Beth, and for a few moments the room
fell still and quiet as everyone strained to hear what
was going on out there, on the stage beyond.

'Inn keeper next.' Ollie ushered the right child into
position. 'And Star, get ready please.'

Jenny smiled to herself as a small boy waddled
forward, encased in an extremely shiny and heavily
padded five-pointed star, one point following the line
of each arm and hip, while the fifth hung down between
his legs in a way that looked highly comical and almost
obscene. She could tell it was making walking uncomfortable, but it was not going to stop him from having
his five minutes of fame.

'Lots of twinkling now, remember?' Ollie said, gently, and the boy pressed a button built into his costume that set a whole collection of tiny white lights flashing all over him, like a mini Christmas tree. 'Excellent. Turn them off now, though, Ben. Save the batteries for your big moment, okay?'

Twenty minutes and several big razzamatazz song-and-dance routines later, Ollie was calling everybody together for the finale. The thunderous applause from the audience after each number was already making the walls shake and Jenny wondered what on earth he could have lined up to end the show that could possibly top that.

'Oh, no. Where's the doll?' It was the first time she'd seen Ollie flustered as he dragged a wooden manger packed with straw across the floor and grabbed various props from their places on a shelf behind him, passing them quickly and efficiently into the correct hands as all the children moved away, chattering excitedly, towards the stage. 'Ssshh,' he called after them. 'Save the noise for after the show.'

He turned towards Jenny. 'The doll. It's meant to be the baby Jesus. I bet one of the girls has moved it, or taken it away to play with the damn thing. We've got about thirty seconds to find it, before the curtain goes up again.'

'*We?*' Jenny laughed. 'I don't know where it is.

Wouldn't even know where to look. Can't you get another one? Out of a toy box, or something?'

'No time, Jen. And I wouldn't know where to look either. Dolls aren't really my department. Ask me to locate a football or a beanbag and I'm your man, but dolls ... I'd probably end up with a Barbie or something that sings Disney songs. Hardly Jesus material!'

Outside, the orchestra was starting up again. 'Oh, no. They've started. I have to get a doll into that straw pretty damn quick or the curtain will go up on an empty manger. No son of God. No miracle. Not quite the magic of the Christmas story ...'

'There's only one thing for it then, isn't there?' Jenny looked towards the sleeping Evie and tilted her head. 'Give them a real baby. A real miracle. Because she is, isn't she?'

'*Evie?* Put her on stage, you mean?'

'She's fast asleep. She's not going to object.'

'Do you think we should?' He was halfway to picking her up, then hesitated. 'What will Laura say?'

'With her daughter the star of the show? She'll be the proudest mum in the room, I should think!'

He bent down and lifted the baby very carefully, adjusted the blanket around her, then started to walk towards the door.

'Well, hurry up,' Jenny said. 'Or she'll miss her cue!'

Vivien Brown

***

An enormous collective 'Aaaah' went round the hall as the cast of children, with Victoria Bennett at their centre, stood silently around the manger before delivering the most poignant version of 'Silent Night' Jenny had ever heard. She had found Beth in the corridor between dressing room and stage and they stood together now, out of sight, and watched the parents in the front rows reach for hankies and dab at their eyes. Further back in the hall they could only see a blur of faces, lost to the darkness and the moment, but Jenny knew Laura was out there somewhere and hoped that the last-minute decision to put little Evie on the stage had been the right one. And that Ollie would not find the doll pushed under the pile of coats, or figure out she had been the one to hide it there.

When the song ended, everyone leapt to their feet, clapping and cheering. Ollie slipped onto the stage and scooped Evie gently up in his arms, as if he couldn't bear to leave her there, unattended, a second longer, strands of straw slipping from the blanket and sprinkling at his feet as he carried her to the side and let the excited children take centre stage.

From the front row, the Head stood and walked up the three wooden steps to the stage.

'I'm sure ...' he began, his voice drowned out by the

482

cheering that seemed never to be going to stop. He smiled, nodded towards Ollie to come forward and stand beside him, then tried again. 'I'm sure you will all want to join me in thanking Mr Campbell for putting together the most original, accomplished and ... emotional show this school has ever seen. And for those who are not aware, I believe I am right in thinking that the youngest member of the cast is in fact his own baby daughter.'

More 'aaahs' broke out as Ollie snuggled Evie against his chest.

'And, of course, we have to thank all the children and parents, and indeed Mr Campbell's own sister, who gave up so much of their time and energies to take part, whether on the stage or off. A big round of applause again, please.'

All the children on stage bowed, huge smiles on their faces, as they clustered around Ollie, each peering out and trying to find the faces of their own families in the audience. Ollie stood still, looking embarrassed but extremely proud as he ruffled the hair of the children closest to him and kissed the top of Evie's head, but just as he was about to walk offstage, Jenny saw a sudden determination cross his face.

'If I could just say a few words,' he said, turning to face the audience, his voice faltering with emotion. The hall gradually fell silent and those who had started to get up and button their coats sat down again. All eyes were on him.

'This show has been a huge challenge for me, and a great joy. I've loved every minute I have spent putting it together and I just want to echo the words of the Head and thank everyone who helped me. Beth, Sean, too many parents to name, and all the children standing here. You are all superstars, every single one of you!' He leaned over to the little boy in the star costume and pushed the button to set all the lights flashing and everyone laughed. 'Without all of you, I couldn't have done it.'

Beside her, Jenny heard Beth gasp as a man crept up from behind them in the wings and flung his arms around her. So this must be the elusive Sean?

'But nothing,' Ollie continued, 'can beat the joy of welcoming my daughter Evie into the world ... and her mother back into my life. Laura, wherever you are ... In fact, could we have some lights, do you think?'

After a short delay, the hall lights came on and Sean looked out into the sea of parents and children who all seemed, despite blinking in the sudden brightness, to be looking straight back at him, and ran his gaze rapidly from row to row until he found her.

'Laura. I know this is all very public, and you might well feel as embarrassed as I do, but ... this just has to be done. Right here, and right now. While we're surrounded by all these wonderful children, and while we're celebrating the birth of a baby and the miracle of Christmas. And while I still have the courage. So ...' Holding Evie very carefully, he slowly lowered himself down onto one knee. 'Laura, will you marry me?'

Jenny's hands flew up to cover her face. She could feel the tears spring up in her eyes as she watched this unscripted and totally unexpected finale to the show, a real-life happy ending in the making. Beth and Sean sprang apart and, throughout the hall, all heads turned to pick Laura out from the crowd.

Laura just stood there, rooted to the spot, taking no notice of the people buzzing with anticipation all around her. She kept her gaze directed straight at Ollie and slowly nodded her head. 'Yes,' she said, her face lighting up with a smile bright enough to outshine even the biggest flashiest Christmas star. 'Yes, I will.'

Chapter 49

Kate, 2017

We stuck it out for another ten years, Dan and I, after we walked away from the farm for the last time. Because it was the right thing to do. Like the old clock that still hung on Molly's wall – I can't bear to think of it as Sam's any more, now he's gone – we hung on, ticked along, passed the time, got by. We had money at last, but it didn't seem to make us any happier. Not even Dan.

We went through the motions, side by side, like so many others probably do. Until Ollie went off to uni and came back again. Until the girls had jobs and boyfriends, and Jenny reached eighteen. Until they were all adults, with lives of their own, and none of them seemed to need us in quite the same way any more.

And then we finally let go. Stopped pretending, stopped trying and went our separate ways.

I have tried to fill the gap in my life with other things. Supporting good causes, a bit of half-hearted gardening (which has at least helped me to prune the rose bush back into shape), occasional yoga (which is meant to help still the mind but somehow never did) and badminton with Caroline (which I was terrible at, but we enjoyed the glass or two of wine in the bar after), trying to improve my cooking ... I even took up knitting for a while, but what a disaster that was! My little projects, the girls laughingly called them.

And Dan tried to fill the gap in his life with other women, none of whom stayed very long.

But things felt different now.

I watched the school show, by myself, on its second night, so I missed the big proposal. But I am so proud of what Ollie has become. I know Dan must be too. No longer that sickly asthmatic child I fretted over, but a sportsman, a teacher, a father, with a lifetime of good things ahead of him. And of Natalie too: independent, happy, utterly accepting of what life threw at her, and sharing her life with a man who has loved her almost as long as I have. And then there's Beth, our brave and adventurous Beth, making plans to cross the world, her eyes shining with what already looks suspiciously like love for a man I have yet to meet. But I trust her decisions, her judgement, because she is strong and because we made her that way.

And little Jenny, soon to set out on a course that has the potential to help so many frightened and grieving women in the years to come.

***

I could have done with a Jenny when I lost you, couldn't I? Someone warm and caring, and real, to listen and to understand. But I am so glad that I have her now. She was never a replacement for you, my baby girl. Nobody could ever be. She's Jenny, just Jenny, and I love her, just as I love all of you, as if she was my own.

But you ... In my mind, you will always be that tiny dot of a baby I lost too soon, and you will always need me. Or is it that I will always need you? My little Rosie, my confidante all these years. The keeper of my secrets and my sanity.

But now, suddenly, your dad needs me too. He is sick and he is lost. The fear of losing him, the way I lost you, to death and eternal darkness, is all I can think about. Just as our children have blossomed and bloomed, just as the next generation of Campbells is bursting into life, the roots of our family are being chopped away from under me and all I want is to scrabble at them with my bare hands, no matter how messy or how torn, and pull them back together again.

It's never too late, is it? Tell me it's not. Never too late to swallow my pride, throw all the past hurts aside, open my heart and find out if he wants to step back in? Because I know we can't go on like this, full of regret and recriminations. Or I can't, anyway. Life is too short, too precious. Evie is here now and she marks the beginning of our future, a future that should be full of joy and hope ... and love. It's what we all need, isn't it? Because there is joy out there, waiting to be had. I felt the first stirrings of it the first time I held her, so I know it's there, but we have to reach for it. Just as we have to hold out for hope, no matter how bad things might seem. And as for love ... I do still love him, Rosie, and I want him to live. More than anything in the world, I want him to live.

***

They say that time is a great healer, don't they? But who knows how much of it any of us has left? When Dan arrived on Christmas Eve, fresh from the hospital, he still looked terrible. Pale and thin, like an old man. But then, he was an old man, really, wasn't he? And I was an even older woman. We had somehow slipped into our sixties, an age my own father had never reached. Something about that scared me.

Ollie and Laura had been to collect him, proudly introducing him to his granddaughter for the first time. He was still smiling when they arrived. 'She looks a lot like you, Kate,' he said, his voice still hoarse and weak, touching my arm, pressing flowers into my hands. 'Beautiful.'

It had been a while since he'd spoken to me like that and it felt strange, almost embarrassing, though I couldn't think why it should. I turned away and hunted for a vase. Where had he found flowers? I'd thought Ollie and Laura had taken him straight back to the flat to pack his bag before driving him to me. Even when he was so ill, it seemed, he was still capable of surprises.

'Go and sit down, Dan. Make yourself at home.' It was a stupid thing to say. This was still his home, in a way. His name was still on the deeds and lots of his belongings were still crammed into boxes in the attic, just in case he should need them, although most of it hadn't been touched in years. It was where we had raised our children and where two of them still lived. It had just felt easier, in the end, to live our day-to-day lives separately, and what was left of our share of the farm money had helped to make that possible. But neither of us had ever said it was for ever.

I made everyone tea. 'Just the way I like it,' Dan said, sipping it slowly. 'Hot and strong. Some things you never forget ...'

The heat from the radiator was making one of the branches of the Christmas tree move slightly and, behind Dan's chair, a small paper angel Beth had made years ago looked like it was gently waving its wings. I lifted little Evie from the car seat they had used to carry her in and rocked her gently on my lap as the tree lights twinkled, turning her towards them so she could see.

'It's good of you to let me stay, Kate.' Dan turned and slid his cup back into its saucer on the table beside him, and I saw his hand tremble with the effort. 'I could have managed okay, you know, on my own. I have done for long enough.'

'Not when you're sick, though. And at Christmas too. I think we'll all feel better knowing you're not on your own, that you're being looked after properly.' I looked across to Ollie for reassurance. 'That you're eating, and you have people to talk to. Clean sheets, someone to go with you for the radiotherapy, that sort of thing ...'

'I'm not really up to the three-meals-a-day routine yet. Just a bed and a bit of company, and plenty of your tea, that sounds good enough to me.' Dan closed his eyes for a few moments. He looked so tired. 'Thank you, Kate. I do appreciate it, you know.'
'Well, we are still married, aren't we?'

He opened his eyes and gazed at me for a long time. 'Yes. Yes, we are. And I am so grateful for that.'

Once he had nodded off to sleep, I lay the baby back in her car seat and saw Ollie and Laura to the door.

'Will you be all right, Mum? Having him here, I mean.'

'Of course. He can have Nat's room. It'll save him the stairs. I'll hardly know he's here.' I bent and kissed Evie's head, breathing in the sweet talcy scent of her. 'And it's not for ever, is it? Only until he's better.'

'We'll see you tomorrow, then.'

I closed the front door after them and went back into the living room. The remains of Dan's tea had gone cold in the cup, and his head had tilted to one side, the dressing on his neck exposed and staring at me, stark and white. Just until he's better ...

I sat down and watched him, remembering the first time I'd seen him, dripping rain in that dingy hallway, his glasses all steamed up, the sound of that dreadful party reverberating through the walls. The mousey hair had been replaced by grey lately, and there was a lot less of it, but he still wore glasses. Contact lenses had never appealed to him. There were more wrinkles now too, more worry lines around his eyes, more wiry little hairs around the base of his ears. But this was Dan. Still Dan. Just an older, more careworn version.

I don't know quite what I felt in that moment, but I did know, above all else, that I didn't want him to die.

I looked at my watch. This wouldn't do. It was Christmas Eve. Time to bring the presents down while the girls were out and pile them around the tree, time to dig out the red festive tablecloth we'd used every year since we'd bought this house, time to peel the potatoes and pop them in a pan of water, ready for the morning. It would be so good to have everyone here together. Except Natalie, of course, but there was no need to worry about her any more. By the time I'd finished my preparations, the light was starting to fade. I swished the curtains closed, shutting out the cold, dull world outside, and Dan slowly opened his eyes.

'Oh, sorry. Did I nod off?'

'No need to apologise. You obviously needed it.'

'I suppose so. Do you mind if I go to bed for a while? It might help me be a bit more alert for the big day tomorrow if I get a decent sleep now.'

'Don't you want any dinner? I can do soup if solid stuff's too difficult.'

'Maybe later.'

He struggled with the holdall that lay at his feet, so I grabbed it for him and led the way. 'I thought Nat's room ...'

'Of course.'

As he sat down on the edge of the newly made bed, I reached over and pulled the curtains shut behind him.

'Do you remember the day Trevor came up with the idea of converting the garage?'

I nodded. 'He worked so hard on this room. And paid for most of it too. I sometimes wish ...'

'That you'd been a bit kinder to him?'

'Yes. I was awful to him. I don't know how he put up with me.'

'But he did. He loved your mum very much, so I think that was why. That's why he wanted to help with the costs of the IVF too, just to make her happy. But I think he came to love all of us, in the end. He was a fine man, and taken way too soon.'

'Oh, Dan. Don't.' Thoughts of death were in the room and the urge to throw my arms around him and sob my heart out was so strong, but I couldn't let him see how ashamed I felt, or how afraid. Not when I needed so badly to be strong.

He patted the bed beside him, and I sat down, my hand shaking as it brushed against his.

'We did a good job, didn't we? Despite our problems. The kids are all healthy, happy, doing what they want to do ...'

'They are.' I smiled at him. 'And now we have Evie. What a Christmas present, eh?'

'The best. Bit odd though, isn't it? Just having the one. We're really only used to dealing with babies three or four at a time.'

'That's true!'

'It should make babysitting a doddle, shouldn't it? Do you think we'll get to do much of that? Looking after Evie, by ourselves?'

'I bloody well hope so. It's what grandparents are for – and spoiling them rotten.'

'And giving them back when they start playing up?'

'Oh, yes, that too. I'm really looking forward to it, Dan. Being a granny.'

'Granny Kate. God, how did we get to be so old?'

'Don't think of us as being old. Just wiser, more experienced, and with more time on our hands. That makes us perfect babysitting candidates, I'd say.'

'Sure you'll have time for it, though? You don't have any frogs to protect, or trees to save, or any of your other hare-brained schemes?'

'The trees can wait. They've been around for centuries. Another eighteen years won't matter.'

'Eighteen?'

'Until Evie's grown up, of course.'

'There'll probably be others by then, Kate. This grandparenting lark could be a long-term occupation. I mean, Laura might want a second one. Nat's just married. And Beth ... well, Ollie tells me she's fallen for some Ozzie teacher, so who knows ...'

'You'd better make sure you stick around long enough to meet them then, hadn't you?'

He took my hand in his and squeezed it.

'I intend to, Kate. And, with you here to help me ...'

'I know.'

And I did. Suddenly I knew. That we were still a

couple, still a family, and that there was still hope. I could still save it, put it all back together. Save us. All Dan had to do now was live.

I lay my head against his shoulder, in the place it had always fitted so well, and let the years wash away with my tears. Just until he's better, I'd said, but what about if that never happened? Letting him face an uncertain future alone, not knowing what it might hold, would be unforgivable. Possibly the most unforgivable thing either of us had ever contemplated. And I knew I couldn't do it. Didn't want to do it. And that I never would.

Epilogue

Kate

August 2018

*D*an is still with me. He's stronger, happier, healthier than I think he's been for years. Giving up his flat and moving back into the house seemed a natural, inevitable step, as if it had always been supposed to happen. As if it had only ever been a matter of time.

Dan hardly mentions work any more, or money. It's as if that was all in another life, a life he no longer wants to remember, or to live. Since he decided to retire a year early, we find we have time to do all the things we could never do before. He has thrown himself back, headlong, into us. He has become a decorator, a gardener, a babysitter, a friend. Sometimes, although a lot less energetically than in our much younger days, a lover too.

We curl up together in front of the TV, squabbling over

the remote, we eat out at restaurants with flickering candles on the tables, and we stand side by side, in baggy pyjamas, to brush our teeth. I have bought him Donald Duck undies and he wears them on Sundays. He has bought me lacy red ones that I refuse to wear at all.

We once again sleep wrapped into each other like spoons. Maybe not the shiny new teaspoons we once were, but old well-used and rounded ladles that still fit together the way they always did. He even pushes the vacuum cleaner about sometimes, and waves a duster around, ineffectually, in the air, as something hot and steamy bubbles on the stove. His cooking always was better than mine.

The cancer has gone. It could come back, we know that, so he takes his drugs and goes for check-ups, but we are hopeful it's over. Hopeful about a lot of things …

Little Evie sat up in her buggy and giggled at the ducks this morning as we strolled in the park, her dark curls buried beneath a floppy white hat, her cheeks pink in the sun. I can't be sure but I think the 'Gug' sound she was making as she pointed at a fat green duck might have been an attempt at her very first word, not that I'm going to say anything to Laura as I'm sure she's hoping it will be 'Mummy' and that she will be the one to hear it for herself.

We will be doubling our grandparent duties soon, when Natalie's honeymoon baby arrives in a few weeks. And *who knows how many more might follow? It will be lovely to have the house filled again, with the joyful sounds of tiny feet and jingly toys and laughter.*

Jenny still lives with us. The only one left now. She has taken over Natalie's downstairs room, giving both her, and us, more privacy and space. Her training is going well, and with a bit of financial help from my mum (who at nearly ninety has been giving her money away like there's no tomorrow), she's given up the caring job, so she has more time to study. And she's met someone. His name is David and he's a doctor. Older than her, but that's not always a bad thing. I can see her confidence growing every day, and it probably won't be long until she wants to branch out too, fly the nest, find her own place in the world. With or without him, it's up to her. She has been talking about tracking down her uncle in Canada, trying to find out more about her birth mother, but that doesn't worry me. She is my daughter and has been for more than twenty years. Nothing is going to rock that now.

Beth left a month ago for her big Australian adventure. I don't think I have ever seen her so settled, so sure of anything. I miss her, but knowing she is happy helps with that, and she'll be back. Or says she will. Only time will tell.

It's what we want for our children, though, isn't it? For them to be happy. And healthy. I couldn't give you that. You were the one who got away, and for that I will always be sorry.

I opened your memory box today. I hadn't done that in such a long time. I looked at your photo, held those tiny impressions of your feet, and for once I didn't cry. Then I put the lid back on and pushed it all away, to the back of the wardrobe.

I failed you, I know that, and nothing I do will ever bring you back to me, but you will live on, always, I promise. Not in that stale old box that conjures up only images of a desperately silent hospital room and floods of unstoppable tears, but in the glorious pure-white roses that grow and flourish, ever more beautiful year on year, curling their way into all the little nooks and crannies of our old garden fence. And, of course, for ever in my heart.

I don't think I will need to talk to you quite so often now, sweetheart. So, I think it's time to let you go. It's time to concentrate on the here and now, and on what is yet to come. Time to put the past behind me, to forgive, and forget, and to start all over again. Time I concentrated on talking – properly talking – to your dad. While I still can.

Rest in peace now, beneath the roses, and be the baby you still are, and always will be. Sleep well, my precious Rosie, my little angel. Until we meet again.

THE END

Acknowledgements

As an IVF patient in the late eighties, having already undergone years of infertility investigations and a traumatic ectopic pregnancy, I came across a lot of would-be parents just like me, all struggling to cope with the disappointment, discomfort and despair as yet another painful and emotional treatment cycle ended in failure.

Sadly, with IVF success rates of only around 20% at best, and time ticking away, many of those patients – already well into their thirties or beyond, either too old for free NHS help or stuck in a long waiting list, and often with no choice but to pay for private treatment – were destined never to have the baby they so desperately wanted. Yet, just like Kate and Dan in this novel, they kept on trying, taking enormous risks and throwing every ounce of energy, emotion and willpower, and every last penny they had, into having 'just one more go', unprepared and unwilling to give up hope.

In the end, I was lucky. My own bumpy road through the IVF process – with a total of 43 eggs collected and 24 of those transferred as embryos into my womb over the course of five cycles (seven at once on one occasion) – led to the birth of twin girls, but it could have ended so differently and I can't help wondering what if...

I couldn't write a book like this without remembering those emotional and heart breaking times, or of taking the opportunity to thank the dedicated doctors, embryologists and nurses at the Humana Wellington Hospital's infertility clinic in St John's Wood who looked after me so well, and especially the pioneering Professor Ian Craft (responsible for Europe's first ever IVF twins and many other incredible breakthroughs) and his then deputy Dr Peter Brinsden, both so passionate about the incredible work they were doing. Without them I would be a very different person today. I would have no children and no grandchildren, and my life would inevitably have taken a much sadder and emptier path.

IVF research and practice have come a long way in the intervening years. New drugs and techniques have been developed, and far more restrictive limits placed on the number of embryos that can be used. National Health Service funding remains a contentious hit-and-miss issue, often governed by geography rather than need, and private clinics are far from cheap but, on the plus side, success rates have increased significantly and the days of unexpected multiple births and terrible 'selective reduction' choices are long gone.

So I'd like to give a very special mention to all those around the world who have bravely set out on the perilous IVF journey, and to the estimated 6.5 million children born as a result of IVF and its associated procedures since Lesley and John Brown and their baby Louise Joy paved the way in 1978. I also want to say 'Well done' to Erin and Louisa – young ladies who I have known and cared about for a long time. Having shared their infertility stories with me, I am so pleased that they have both since been blessed with beautiful IVF babies. And, yes, they only had one each! Welcome to the world, Nathaniel and Jemima.

And welcome too to my second granddaughter, Olivia, who arrived just as this book was going through its final editing stages, helping (along with her big sister Penny) to prove that the IVF babies born out of all that early experimentation, intrusion and risk can, and do, grow up to have healthy babies of their own, and that infertility is rarely in any way hereditary.

As ever, there are lots of people I need to thank for supporting and encouraging me in my writing life, and especially through the writing of this novel. My husband, Paul, of course, and my daughters, Laura and Vicky. My editor, Kate Bradley, who always knows the right things to say and manages to convince me that whatever I am writing is actually not half bad. Charlotte Ledger, and all at Harper Impulse, for producing such wonderful books and continuing to include me in their talented 'team' of authors. The members of Phrase Writers, my local writers' group in Hillingdon, real friends who are always there, offering endless enthusiasm, encouragement and cake. The SWWJ (the UK's oldest organisation for women writers), where, as a long-standing member, I have always found support and friendship, and have met so many amazing and inspirational people. The Romantic Novelists' Association, where I served my novel-writing apprenticeship, and in particular my little group of fellow author and short story writer pals, Elaine Everest, Elaine Roberts, Francesca Burgess, Natalie Kleinman and Sarah Stephenson, with whom I have shared so many meals, meetings, conferences, successes, secrets – and laughs – along the way. Onwards and upwards, girls!

I'd also like to say a big 'Hello' to Tiggy Hart, already an avid reader at the age of ten, who proudly tells everyone that her auntie (that's me!) is a real author, and a sad 'Goodbye' to my friend Becca Ousby who was always asking for updates about my books but died earlier this year, at the tragically young age of thirty, before she got the chance to read this one. But then, heaven couldn't possibly be heaven if it has no books, so you never know...

A special thank you also goes to author and tutor Simon Whaley who, in his article writing workshops, impresses upon his students the value of including a number in the title. Write about the 100 richest people in the world, the ten best English castles, or seven top tips for staying young and beautiful, and readers are instantly curious about who or what is included in the list. From the moment I told people the title of this novel they started trying to guess what the five unforgivable things might be! Anything that intrigues potential readers and makes them pick up a book and open the pages can only be a good thing.

And so to my readers... Half the joy of having written and published a novel is in knowing that someone, somewhere, is reading it. Oh, how I would love, totally out of the blue, to spot someone with a novel of mine on a beach or train, and see them smile, or maybe even cry, as they turn the pages. So, a great big thank you to all the fantastic readers and bloggers whose opinions, social media posts, reviews and recommendations helped to make my first novel, *Lily Alone*, a success. I do hope that you all enjoy this new one just as much.